Her Watchful Eye

Her Watchful Eye

Julie Corbin

MULHOLLAND
BOOKS
HODDER

First published in Great Britain in 2018 by Mulholland Books
An imprint of Hodder & Stoughton
An Hachette UK company

3

A CIP catalogue record for this title is available from the British Library

Paperback ISBN 978 1 473 66321 3
eBook ISBN 978 1 473 66322 0

Typeset in Plantin Light by Palimpsest Book Production Limited,
Falkirk, Stirlingshire

Printed and bound in Great Britain by Clays Ltd, Elcograf S.p.A.

Hodder & Stoughton policy is to use papers that are natural, renewable
and recyclable products and made from wood grown in sustainable forests.
The logging and manufacturing processes are expected to conform to the
environmental regulations of the country of origin.

Hodder & Stoughton Ltd
Carmelite House
50 Victoria Embankment
London EC4Y 0DZ

www.hodder.co.uk

For my daughters-in-law, Cristina and Antoniya,
with love and thanks

Prologue

Prison isn't as she imagines it. Nobody corners her in the shower or spits on her food. She's allowed to read, send emails, write letters. They have daily computer time when they surf the net to their hearts' content. And twice a week they are allowed visitors.

While she awaits trial she sleeps in the Vulnerable Prisoners Unit and that means she's kept apart from most of the other women, the ones who have sold drugs or sold themselves or burgled one time too many. At meal and recreation times, all the women are supervised together, including the violent offenders, but still they are mostly wary of her; some even give her a nod and she senses respect. As if she could harm a fly. As if she's ever so much as killed a spider. She used to scoop stray spiders onto card or paper, and ease them onto the garage floor, where she watched them scuttle off into the shadows to make themselves a home. She would open the window wider for wasps and shoo them outside. She once nursed a half-frozen hedgehog back to life with a pipette of warm milk and a hot-water bottle.

The prison officers aren't unkind to her, but they make their expectations clear. She needs to fall in with the routine because she has no power in prison. She's not special, she is nothing and no one, and her job is to conform. She's done more than her fair share of troublemaking, so while she's on the inside, she answers to whichever officer is on duty.

The first week passes in a blur of fear and favour. She doesn't have time to think too much because she's busy living moment by moment, learning how best to survive, who to please and who to stand up to.

It's the beginning of the second week when the feeling creeps up on her. At first, she barely registers the sound of the door locks sliding into place – bolt, screw and rock-hard metal, keeping her inside her cell. But on the eighth night, panic rises like a cold-water bath inside her chest. She clutches at her throat; she begins to shallow pant, and then to scream: high-pitched, the sound of the insane, the grief-stricken, the dying, and it's loud enough to draw the duty officer.

'It's a panic attack,' the officer tells her. 'Calm down. You'll be fine.'

No sympathy, no time in the health centre. Because prisoners having panic attacks – this is routine too. Run-of-the-mill anguish.

Her cellmate is called Tiffany. She has red-rimmed eyes and the keen expression of someone on the lookout for the next trick. She watches her fall to the floor and pass out but she doesn't move to help.

'There's no air in here,' she says to Tiffany when morning comes and she's lived through another night. 'There's no air,' she repeats. 'I can't breathe the way I used to. And it's not fair. It's all a mistake!' she rushes on. 'I should have known. I should have guessed and then I would have stopped her.' Her voice catches on a cry. 'If I'd known. If only I'd known.'

'Should have could have would have,' Tiffany says, running the words together. 'If only this if only that.' She speaks loudly as if conversing with the hard of hearing. 'You think too much.' She taps her forehead. 'You have to get your head in the game.'

She nods her thanks because this is what she needs to hear. She wants to – needs to – get a grip, to stop the slide into despair because this doesn't have to be her fate. She doesn't have to be in here. She could get out, couldn't she? The door would slide open and the guard would say, 'You're free to go.'

Free to go. The words alone give a lift to her heart. She just needs to tell the truth.

Chapter One

Her mobile rings as she's running across the road. 'Ruby, get me a coffee, will you?' Lennie asks. 'An Americano.'

'You've not gone and broken the machine again?'

'Not me. Not this time.'

'Who then?'

'No one's fessin' up. But it's fit for the knacker's yard anyway.'

'Okay.' She's late, breathless, feels fit for the knacker's yard herself. 'But I'm not sure I'll be able to—'

'You're twenty metres from Caroline's Coffee.'

She laughs and stares up, past the tops of traffic lights and lampposts, blinking as a drop of rain lands in her eye, before she focuses on the camera attached to the outermost edge of the tenement. She stretches her arm out above her head in the direction of the camera and aggressively raises her middle finger.

Lennie chuckles. 'Now, now. Keep it clean. And mind the old lady.'

She moves to the edge of the pavement to allow a woman on a disability scooter to hurtle by. 'Could you stop watching me now, please?'

'Keep walking.' He's urging her on. 'That's it. Push open the door.'

'You know I'm already late?'

'Aye. And not for the first time. But don't worry, I'll cover for you.'

'Has he arrived, then?'

'He's warming up his iPad as we speak,' Lennie says. 'See you in ten.'

'Two Americanos,' she says to the girl behind the counter. 'Both to take away.'

'Can I interest you in our reduced sandwiches and muffins?' She points them out at the front of the counter. 'Take a rest from cooking tonight.'

'I've been asleep all day,' Ruby says. 'I'm on my way to work.'

'Night shift? You a nurse, then?'

It's a fair assumption with a hospital close by and Ruby dressed in her comfy flats and navy trousers. But nevertheless – assumptions, Ruby thinks, make an ass out of you and me.

The girl starts to tell her about how her mum is also a nurse and has worked nights her whole life. 'Do you often work nights?'

'Almost always,' Ruby says. 'It's antisocial but it suits me.' It's not only hospitals that are open at night. She could be a shelf-stacker or a firefighter, an office cleaner or a lorry driver. Or she could still be a police officer.

She pays for the coffees, buys half a dozen muffins too – might mitigate her lateness – and walks the final few hundred metres to work. The entry door is made of a hard redwood, weathered into a dirty grey that blends in with the stonework, belying the fact that the door is reinforced with steel through its centre and only opens with the right sort of electronic persuasion – a thumb on the keypad followed by a six-digit code, a safeguard that was put in place two years ago when the CCTV centre moved premises.

Her hands full, she presses the entryphone with her elbow and shouts, 'Let me in somebody! I've got muffins!'

Within thirty seconds the door swings open and Lennie's standing there. She hands him his coffee. 'Has the meeting started?' she says.

'No, I told him you had a doctor's appointment.' Lennie walks behind her down the stairs into the bowels of the building. 'I whispered it to him so that he'd get the vibe it was private and wouldn't ask you for any details.'

'Cheers for tempting fate,' Ruby says, opening her locker. 'Couldn't you have said my boiler was broken or something?'

'I can't come up with a lie as quickly as you can.'

He's got a point. She tosses her bag inside the locker and runs a brush through her hair, four strokes and she's finished. 'Do we know why he's here?'

'He hasn't said, but when does management ever appear with good news?' He swigs a mouthful of coffee. 'Bugger me, that's hot!'

'It'll be more cutbacks.' Ruby uses her pinkie finger to rub Vaseline across her lips, then slams the locker door shut. 'I bet they're not replacing Jim.'

The whole team are gathered in the control room – all ten of them. There aren't enough seats so several are balanced on the edges of desks. Some of them half smile as Ruby comes into the room but most are too tense to acknowledge her. The lights are on, a rare occurrence as darkness makes it easier to watch the CCTV feeds. Dark but never silent, what with the constant buzz of machinery and the intermittent chatter of the police radio.

On the front wall, six huge, square screens are divided into grids with nine views to each screen. One of the screens has been hijacked by their boss Alan *'call me Al'* Magnusson and the words 'Moving Forward with

Spectra' shimmer on the screen in bold, red caps. There
are three fingers in the CCTV pie: police, council and
for the last two years Spectra, a management company
that has profitability at the heart of its decision-making.
The money is pooled and services rendered but as far
as Ruby is concerned most initiatives boil down to the
fact that nobody wants any of the costs coming out of
their budget.

'Sorry I'm late,' Ruby says. She hands the bag of
muffins to Fiona, a wide-eyed trainee. 'Help yourself
and pass them along.' Instantly Fiona presses the bag
into Freddie's hands, as if it's a game of pass the parcel
and she's terrified the music might stop.

'Good to see you, Ruby,' Al shouts across the room.

'And you, sir,' Ruby hears herself replying and immediately makes a where-did-that-come-from face at
Lennie. Sometimes she slips back in time, finds herself
in police mode. Once a copper …

'I know a visit from head office fills you all with dread
but' – Al pauses to smile – 'rest easy, the news is mostly
good. Let's start by reminding ourselves of our recent
successes.' He moves his finger across his iPad, and the
screen on the wall reacts at once. The red lettering slides
off to one side and a multicoloured productivity graph
appears. 'So … what have we done well this quarter?'
He glances around as if expecting an answer before
providing one himself. 'Three investigations are moving
forward on the strength of our CCTV evidence. That
makes it ten so far this year.'

'I thought it was more than that,' Freddie says. His
arms are folded and he's frowning. 'Nearer twenty.'

'These are accurate figures,' Al says. 'But we can talk
about it later, Freddie, if you like?'

Freddie stares down at his feet and shakes his head.

'Okay,' Al says. 'Let's move on.' He tells them about recent company plans for expansion, goes over health and safety concerns and then, just as the fidgeting starts, he raises his voice and says, 'Whenever we get together, it's a good time to remind ourselves of current legislation.' He takes a significant breath before reading from his iPad screen: 'Camera operators are obliged to obtain authorisation from senior managers under strict surveillance rules set out in the Regulation of Investigatory Powers Scotland Act 2000 before tracking individuals.'

Silence.

'As you know, there have been some issues in other parts of the UK, notably Greater Manchester, where an operator is being prosecuted for using CCTV to stalk his ex-wife.' This time there is a rumble of assent.

'Been on the news,' Lennie says.

'Following your children home from school, doing some window shopping, or worse' – not much imagination is required for what could be deemed as worse so he doesn't elaborate – 'is *directed* surveillance without due cause and as such is illegal.'

Several people are avoiding eye contact and Lennie whispers into Ruby's ear, 'No comment.'

'So ... Some of you might be wondering whether we're planning any redundancies over the next quarter? The answer is that we're not. We can all relax. I include myself in that.' He holds the palm of his hand against his chest. 'None of us are exempt.'

Everyone breathes easy and Lennie mouths at Ruby, 'Man of the people,' while Freddie mutters, 'He could have told us that from the get-go.'

'Productivity is up. Staff relations exemplary. Give yourselves a round of applause.'

Most people put their hands together for a few seconds

of half-hearted clapping, and when it ends Freddie says, 'We'll be getting a pay rise, then?'

'Not this quarter,' Al says. 'But it is management's intention to review all salaries next April.'

'Thought as much.' Freddie stares round at his colleagues to see whether anyone will follow him into battle. Nobody does. 'Keep the profits for the shareholders,' he says, resigned. 'Nothing changes.'

'Finally.' Al glances across at Ruby and Lennie. 'As I'm sure you've already guessed, we're not going to be replacing Jim. And as this only affects the night shift, if the rest of you want to head off before the rain gets any heavier, then feel free.'

He doesn't have to say it twice and Ruby gets out of the day shift's way while they gather their belongings. She goes into the toilet and sits on the loo with her eyes shut. The coffee's gone right through her, she's got her period and her head hurts. And then there's the business of why she was late. Why? *Why?* 'Torturing yourself has become a habit,' she says out loud. 'You need to get a handle on it, Ruby Romano. Soon. Now, in fact. *Now.* Now, Ruby. *Now, for fuck's sake.*' She passes the palm of her hand in front of the flush button and comes out of the loo. Fiona is standing there.

'I was just … I mean, I was …'

'Don't mind me, Fiona,' Ruby says. She makes a face at herself in the mirror and sighs. 'My advice, Fiona, for what it's worth, is live life to the full. *Carpe diem.* Because before you know it, you'll be thirty-nine, staring at your ageing face in the mirror and wondering what happened to your life.'

'That's what my mum says.'

'I rest my case.' Ruby smiles at her. 'Mums are never wrong.'

She leaves the bathroom and joins Lennie and Al, who are standing in the control room. They are in mid-conversation and Ruby can see that Lennie is already frustrated, his fingers tapping against the side of his thigh.

'I'm not convinced, Al,' Lennie is saying. 'Joints are beginning to creak.'

'Jim has been on sick leave for six months and it hasn't affected your productivity.'

'You can't say that.'

'I just have. And I'm right. You know why? Because on almost every occasion this year when the police have asked us for corroborating CCTV evidence, we have been able to give it to them.'

'Almost being the operative word,' Lennie says, and his fingers stop tapping as his hands fly up from his sides to help him do the talking. 'Because that's not the whole story, is it? Surely part of what we're here for is to observe patterns, and for that you need to watch certain areas' – he points towards the screens – 'not just have the camera recording in case you need it, but actually watch what's happening, *as it's happening.*' His hands move sharply downwards, emphasising the words.

'The criminals aren't daft,' Ruby says, adding her voice to Lennie's. 'They know how to outsmart us. And it stands to reason that three people can watch more feeds than two can.'

'But the cameras don't need to be *actively* watched, Ruby. That's the beauty of it, isn't it? As long as they're pointing in the direction that's most likely to yield results, those recordings can be called upon later. It's a win-win.'

'I'm talking about crime prevention,' Lennie says. 'Proactive not reactive.'

'I hear you, Lennie.' Al glances at his watch. 'It's the

wife's birthday so I'm going to have to get going.' Lennie tosses a dismissive hand in his direction and Al turns to Ruby. 'How are you holding up?'

Ruby's eyes widen. 'What?'

'Losing Grant. I know it's been four months now but I also know that four months is nothing.'

His tone is sympathetic but still his words are like a sudden slap in the face, the harsh hand of reality reminding her that beyond these four walls her life is sad and lonely and more than just a little bit desperate. Work is her saviour. Work is a Grant-free zone, somewhere she can shut out the memories because Grant never came to the CCTV centre and she never saw him on camera. He didn't work in town. Glasgow was his stomping ground when she first met him, and after they became a couple Glasgow remained his stomping ground. They only set up home in Edinburgh because she worked here.

Tears.

She feels them trickle down onto her cheeks and she's not happy about it. She turns away from Al and presses firm fingers against her eyelids before she looks back and says, 'Thanks, Al. I appreciate that.'

'Cancer, wasn't it?'

Her throat is a bottleneck. She tries to speak but no words come; her mouth opens and closes like an oxygen-starved fish.

'My mother had cancer,' Al is saying. 'There was nothing anyone could have done but we were still left with that terrible sense of loss.'

Ruby clears her throat with a sound that's a cross between a sob and a cough. 'You're ...' She tries to assemble her thoughts but they're ballooning away from her, fragments of sentences that she can barely catch hold of. '… being able to … It's just that … I miss … It's just …' – God help her – she's turned into Fiona. Serves her right for her smart-arse advice in the loo just now. As if she's qualified to give anyone advice, even a nervous trainee like Fiona.

'I was sorry I couldn't make it to the funeral.'

'That's … Grant's mother wanted …' She trails off, looks to Lennie for help.'

'The funeral was private,' Lennie says. 'Just close family.'

'I got the flowers,' Ruby adds. 'Thank you.'

Al's eyes are soft. 'I know you refused the option of compassionate leave, Ruby, but you can still change your mind.'

She forces in a huge breath and when she breathes out she manages to say, 'I'm better when I'm at work,' and follows it with a mock salute. 'Onwards and upwards.'

'Good for you.' Al pulls her in for a hug. 'But remember to let yourself grieve when you need to.'

Ruby leans into him. She can't help herself. It's not that she fancies him – his physicality is simply an invitation to be held. Ruby lives alone and days can go by without anyone touching her. She closes her eyes and rests her head against his chest, and when after a few seconds Al moves away, she catches Lennie's eye. Judging. Dubious. *What the …?* written across his face.

'Management doesn't take either of you for granted,' Al is saying. 'Ruby, Lennie – you're the stars of the show. Don't think we don't know that.' He packs his iPad into his suitcase. 'How's Fiona shaping up?'

'Scared of her own footprint on the ground,' Lennie says.

'Give her time,' Ruby says, suddenly sure that standing

up for Fiona is akin to standing up for herself. 'I think she'll improve.'

'You've changed your tune,' Lennie says.

'She just needs to build her confidence.' Ruby looks at Al. 'She's about to start on the night rotation, isn't she?'

'She is. She'll cover each of your nights off.' He walks along the corridor and up the stairs to the exit; Lennie and Ruby follow him. 'See whether she can tick off a couple more learning objectives from her training folder.'

'Will do,' Ruby says. She much prefers working with Lennie but as senior members of staff they work a rota and don't normally have the same nights off.

'And be sure to get in touch if you have any concerns.' He glances back at them before climbing into his car. 'You have my number.'

They watch him start the engine and listen to the low growl of excess horsepower as the car pulls away from the kerb. 'He's upgraded his car since he was last here,' Lennie says. 'While we' – he shuts the door with a loud slam – 'we are the victims of our own success.' He stares at Ruby and frowns. 'And could you have got any further up his arse?'

'What?'

'I know you're recently widowed, Ruby, but ...' He shakes his head at her, a disappointed dad. 'I was watching your face. Transparent as bloody cling film. And him a married man.'

'Actually, Lennie. *Actually* ...' She trails off. Why can't she just admit to needing a hug? Why was being honest so often beyond her? 'He was being kind! What was I supposed to do? Push him away?'

'It was the look on your face.'

'For a man of forty-five you sound like a granddad

sometimes.' She pushes his shoulder. 'He does have well-defined muscles, though, should you be interested.'

'Protein shakes,' he says. 'Bad for the kidneys, so I hear.'

Chapter Two

They come into the control room and turn off the lights. Edinburgh's darkening skies bear down on the city. Streetlamps light up pavements and roads, from nook to cranny, and all points in between. 'Any requests from the police?' Ruby asks.

'They want us to keep an eye on those lads who've been hanging around Cockburn Street,' Lennie says. 'I can do that.'

'Okay.'

A hush descends between them as they concentrate on work. Ruby settles into her seat, puts on her headset so that she can hear the police chatter, and stares up at the screens on the wall before deciding where to focus her attention. It's half past six on a Thursday evening. People are heading home, spilling out of shops and offices onto shiny wet pavements. The rain is heavier now and umbrellas are going up. Ruby sees what appears to be a disturbance taking place at the west end of George Street and with a few strokes of her keypad she brings two camera feeds down onto the spot screens in front of her. She uses the joystick to vary the camera angle, and zoom in on the three youths who are pushing each other. It quickly becomes apparent that they're not being aggressive, just testing their strength, laughing as they nudge one another off the pavement. No need for Ruby to be concerned.

Lennie catches her eye. 'Look.' He points to his screen. 'It's the old guy from a couple of weeks ago.'

Ruby swivels her chair around so that she can see Lennie's spot screen. An elderly man, barefoot and wearing pyjamas, is weaving his way along the street. Lennie briefly zooms in to catch the expression on his face – confusion battling with intense deliberation. 'Bless his heart,' Ruby says. 'He's getting soaked.' She picks up the phone. 'I remember the ward he was in. I'll give them a call.'

Lennie flicks the switch on his headset to talk to the community police and direct them to the man's whereabouts, while Ruby calls the ward. 'One of your patients,' she tells the nurse. 'He's about a hundred metres from the hospital entrance. Almost in front of the cinema. And he's barefoot.' The nurse thanks her and Ruby ends the call, watching the screen as the police arrive, closely followed by two nurses who are running along the pavement, holding on to the pockets of their uniforms as they run.

'Mission accomplished,' Lennie says, as the man is redirected into the back of the police car. 'I thought he was in one of the locked wards?'

'He must be finding ways around it.'

'Hats off.'

'The human spirit.'

'We've all got to go down fighting.'

'Do not go gentle into that good night …' Ruby says, trailing off.

'… Rage, rage against the dying of the light.' Lennie smiles across at her. 'Dylan Thomas. You'll have to try harder than that to catch me out.'

Ruby laughs and stretches her arms towards the ceiling. 'Coffee?' she asks.

'It'll have to be tea,' Lennie reminds her.

'I'll see if there are any muffins left.'

'Freddie went off with the bag!' Lennie shouts after her. 'You know what he's like for a freebie.'

'Greedy bugger!' Ruby says. She goes into the kitchen to find that the coffee machine really is broken. It's in half a dozen pieces on the work surface. Two of the pieces are bent out of shape as if someone tried to fix it and didn't know their own strength. Ruby makes two mugs of tea and takes them back to the control room.

'When they can get robots doing our job, they will,' Lennie says, taking a mug from Ruby's hand. 'But I don't believe robots will ever be programmed to react *before* the trouble breaks out.'

'*Minority Report*,' Ruby says. 'They have those three women in the water, seeing a possible future.'

'They're not robots. They're psychics, pre-cogs.'

'Same difference.'

Lennie has zoomed in on two blokes who are chest to chest at the top of the Mound. One of them is holding a beer bottle as if it's a weapon. Lennie talks into his headset and directs the police to the scene.

'Al just doesn't get it,' Lennie says, as they both watch the police car arriving next to the men. 'Low-level anti-social behaviour leads to mid-level criminality. Everyone knows it's a sliding scale. Everyone knows that the psychopath starts small, the petty burglar moves on to the job to end all jobs, the flasher becomes rapist becomes murderer.'

Maybe. Maybe not. Ruby listens but doesn't join in when Lennie falls into a rant. She doesn't mind. He works hard; he's entitled to complain about management. Complaining makes things better. You get everything off your chest. You've said your piece and now you've let it go. It's out there, floating in the ether, no longer weighing you down.

'Sometimes you don't know what the big stuff is until it happens,' he says, shaking his head. 'It's not rocket science, is it?'

'Not even close.'

They relax into a companionable silence again and Ruby checks through the police reports for the day to see whether there's anything that sparks her interest. CCTV operators tend towards a favourite type of monitoring. Freddie loves to catch fly tippers and will sit for hours watching one particular spot until he gets lucky and he can zoom in on a number plate. Lennie loves his 'wanted' criminals and in the last five years he's spotted three such men and contributed to their arrests, which is no mean feat.

Missing persons is Ruby's thing. Missing persons she loves. People who disappear. Willingly disappear. They've had enough of their bosses or their families, or the whole enormous machinery of modern life that demands jobs are done and bills paid and you just keep on keeping on, showing up every day for whatever shit might be lobbed your way. It's surprisingly common for people to simply opt out. Walk away and never look back. And it's an irony, isn't it? Most missing persons live in cities, hidden in plain sight, where you're just one more body in the moving crowd.

Lennie nudges Ruby's elbow. 'Look at these numpties.'

There are two couples in front of the Tron Kirk. Both the women are holding bags of chips. One of them is shouting, waving her arms, unsteady on her feet. She holds the chip-bag tight to her chest and swings her handbag at her partner. Ruby's seen this behaviour more times than she can count and the outcome is less dependent on the woman's character than it is on the man's. Some men will automatically calm a woman down, or throw up their arms and walk away. Others will argue back and that will often end up with a punch or a slap because, to put it crudely, there are men who are primed to end the evening with a fuck, and if that's not on offer, they'll rev up for a fight.

Lennie and Ruby watch as the man strokes her cheek. Lip-reading would be a valuable skill but Ruby has never mastered it and in most cases it's unnecessary because you can guess what's being said. The cheek-stroking is working; she is placated and they lean back against the church wall to embark on a hearty snog. Meanwhile the other couple light cigarettes and alternate puffs with chips. Their relationship is less intense. They are side by side, not talking, not even looking at each other, just idly marking time.

The first woman pulls back from the kissing and shouts to her friend, who totters over on four-inch heels to take the bag of chips from her.

'Hold my chips while I have a shag,' Lennie says under his breath.

'David Attenborough eat your heart out.' Ruby laughs.

Lennie swivels the camera away just as the woman's knickers drop. 'Did I tell you my latest idea for *Mastermind*?' he says.

Ruby shakes her head. On the spot screen in front of her, an elderly lady is inching her way home, one sore foot after the other.

'Einstein.'

Ruby raises her eyebrows. 'Complicated science.'

'It'll be his life story more than the science,' Lennie says. 'I'll only have to worry about the big issues science-wise, like the theory of relativity.'

'Sounds doable then,' Ruby says, her tone ironic. 'It's late for her to be out, isn't it?'

Lennie leans across to have a closer look at Ruby's screen. 'Auntie Angela,' he says. 'No dog with her tonight, though.'

She isn't their auntie and it's unlikely her name is Angela but this is one of the reasons Ruby likes working with Lennie – they give their regulars names. It becomes personal. And that means they care. The people they see week after week are as familiar to them as their own families. Okay, so Ruby doesn't know whether they like milk in their tea or their sex in the missionary position but she does know their habits. And because they don't know they're being watched, masks are lowered. They slump at bus stops, shed a quiet tear, steal.

Yes, they steal. Because for some people their day is set up if they can snaffle a free newspaper – every morning, at six o'clock, it's the same routine. Walter – so called because he has gravity-dragged cheeks like Walter Matthau – turns up just after the van has dropped the newspapers in Caffè Nero's doorway. Walter won't see this as stealing. He will justify it to himself by saying that he only steals from the multinationals – never from the small man working his bollocks off.

'What have you brought for midnight snack?' Lennie asks.

'A bag of Cheesy Wotsits and a Cup A Soup.'

'Not exactly singing nutrition, Rubes, is it?'

'What have you got?'

'You really want to know?'

'Hit me with it.'

'Assume the brace position.'

Ruby does as she's told, pulling her legs up and dipping her head down onto her knees.

'Grilled mackerel, beetroot pickle and cauliflower mash with a hint of horseradish.'

Ruby lifts her head and blows her hair out of her eyes, 'Why don't you just apply for *MasterChef* and be done with it?'

'Because I haven't given up on *Mastermind*.' He stands up. 'I'm happy to share?'

'Go on then.'

Lennie is one for making their midnight meal special and while he's in the kitchen fixing plates for them both, Ruby watches a girl come out of the restaurant on the Royal Mile. Ruby calls her Alice because, even from a distance, she has a wide-eyed quality about her that reminds Ruby of illustrations of *Alice in Wonderland*. She first noticed her a couple of months ago, then last week she was being aggressively harassed at the bus stop and Ruby was seconds away from alerting the police, but after a push from Alice the drunk fell back into the gutter and then staggered off. The incident seems to have spooked Alice a little, though, and she no longer stands in the bus shelter absorbed by her phone but glances behind her as if she thinks the drunk might reappear.

'Here we go.' Lennie lays the plate carefully in front of Ruby. 'The mackerel was caught yesterday and the beetroot is heritage.'

'I'm sure I'd be impressed if I knew what that meant.'

'Philistine.'

Ruby takes a mouthful and can't help but make an appreciative face. 'No wonder Trish married you.'

'I couldn't cook back then,' Lennie says, loading his fork with a little bit of everything. 'So anyway, why were you late this time?'

'I dropped in to see Celia and she left me to babysit,'

Ruby says, wincing against the lie as she shovels more food into her mouth. Lennie's watched her be economical with the truth with their boss but she knows he doesn't expect her to lie to him. They're mates. Why would she need to? 'Only for five minutes, she said, while she nipped out to buy Tom a present. But Celia's five minutes are everyone else's hour.'

Lennie nods, satisfied with this explanation, and then his fork gestures towards Ruby's plate of food. 'You know no one's going to take that from you, don't you?'

'I like eating fast. It doesn't mean I'm not savouring the flavours.' He isn't good at hiding his disappointment so she relents. 'Ok-*ay*,' she says. 'I'll eat slow-*ly*.'

They sit in silence, watching the screens as if they're watching television, every now and then pointing out something of interest to each other. The main course is followed by a palate-cleansing lemon sorbet. Ruby lingers over it for so long that Lennie takes the spoon out of her hand before she's completely finished. 'You've made your point,' he says.

'Leave the washing up for me.'

'Too right.' He walks partway to the kitchen before turning back. 'Would you mind just looking out for Shona? She'll be coming out the Venue around about one.'

'No bother,' Ruby says. 'I'll make sure she gets on the bus.'

'Cheers.'

Unless they're busy, Lennie always has a nap between one and two, and that's just fine with Ruby. He has four daughters and his wife Trish breeds West Highland Terriers, so his house is full of 'barking and bitching'. Ruby doesn't begrudge him the peace and quiet of a stolen night hour. She enjoys working with Lennie – the easy banter between them helps to pass the time – but being by herself feels special, exciting, powerful.

It feels powerful.

Watching.

The public are oblivious to the power of the modern camera, able to zoom in and magnify up to thirty times. Ruby can spot a rose in bloom in Princes Street Gardens, read a number plate, isolate a toddler's lost shoe.

The all-seeing, endlessly roving eye.

It's like sitting on top of a cloud. She's present but she's removed. She's wearing Harry Potter's invisibility cloak. She can fly. She can glide along a street, nip over a roof and land in the middle of a fight. She can get up close and personal without an iota of suspicion from the people she watches. She can read what they read, see what they see, feel what they feel.

She stands in front of the large screens and stares at each and every camera feed in turn. Mostly she sees nothing untoward but every so often she spots an anomaly. Most people would find it tedious; she knows this. After the novelty had worn off, they would be bored stiff. Their eyes would hurt and their necks would creak and they'd want to lie down on a sofa and fall asleep.

Not Ruby. Ruby loves being on high, looking down, seeing but not judging. Because she doesn't judge. She's the last person to judge, what with the mistakes she's made. She watches; she alerts the police ... or she doesn't.

It depends.

She bends the rules but she doesn't break them.

Is it hubris? Grant used to tell her it was. 'Playing God, Ruby. Sooner or later you'll be struck down for it.'

This would make her laugh and she'd pull him in

close, feel the strength of his heartbeat under the palm of her hand. They would be in bed when he said this because they were always in bed. All her memories begin and end with them in bed. Every last one.

Without thinking, she begins to dig around in her handbag, ignoring her inner voice.

Don't do it. Please, Ruby. Just don't do it. You'll only make yourself miserable.

She takes a photo out of her wallet. There they are, the two of them – Grant and Ruby. Ruby and Grant. Happy is as happy does. She's smiling a light-filled smile. They're in a hotel in New York. And they've just had blow-a-fuse sex.

Breakthrough sex, she called it.

With me, he said.

With you, she said.

You and me.

Together for ever.

Don't torture yourself.

Too late. She's tortured herself. Her stomach is knotted, her eyeballs ache with unshed tears. She wants to lie on the floor and roll herself into the smallest, tightest ball. She breathes her way through the minefield of lost love, what-ifs and buts, the pain of missing him, missing him, missing him.

The pain bleeds into anger that burns in her chest and asks the question, Why? *Why me?* What did I do to deserve it? She swallows down the bitter taste and tries to breathe through it. She's tired of feeling this way. It's an emotional merry-go-round – except that it isn't merry – and she needs to get off.

She slides the photo back inside her wallet and brings out a piece of paper that's fraying at the edges from frequent handling. After the pain of the happy couple photo comes the list. She reads aloud: 'Simple Things That Make Me Happy: blue sky, Joseph's laugh, delphiniums in a crystal vase, soft-boiled egg and soldiers, a gripping box set.' And so on ... Over fifty happy reminders to calm and comfort her.

When she's finished reading she moves her lips into the shape of a smile. She read somewhere that if you physically smile, you can literally fool yourself into happiness. The brain senses the physicality of a smile, releases endorphins and then you really do feel happy.

It does work. Maybe not all the time, but mostly it works.

It's Saturday, and Lennie has spent the earlier part of the evening quoting Einstein but now he's having his nap and Ruby's watching her sister Celia wobble her way out of a club in the West End. Ruby uses her mobile to call Celia's number, sees her sister fumble in her pocket and squint at the screen before answering.

'I'm watching you,' Ruby says.

Celia's laugh is a drunk, exaggerated cackle. She raises the bottle of wine she's carrying and does a twirl.

'Don't drink it all at once, will you?'

'I'm not even going to use a glass!' she shouts. Celia likes to imagine that she's living it large, going at life with a rebel's sensibilities. She's not. She's a mother of four children. She goes to church twice a week, confession every other. She teaches Sunday school, for heaven's sake.

'Are you listening?' she shouts in Ruby's ear.

'I'm a woman. I can do more than one thing at a time. Now you listen – Tom's car will round the bend in exactly ten seconds. Wave to the camera, then off you go.'

Celia does a pretend curtsey and then stares up at the camera, her smile illuminated by the streetlamp. When her husband's car stops at the kerb, she falls into the back seat, losing a shoe in the gutter so that he has to come round to retrieve it for her.

Ruby puts her feet up on the desk and settles back in her seat. She pulls camera thirty-one down onto her spot screen and sees the girl she named Alice come out of the restaurant, her shift over. This time she's with a young man wearing a leather jacket, his collar pulled up to his ears. Alice is animated and it makes Ruby smile. They are almost at the bus shelter when Alice laughs and glances up, her face caught and held by the light.

Time stops.

Something deep inside Ruby detonates. A chord struck on the piano, a pitch-perfect note that shatters glass. Her feet hit the floor and her hand shakes as she uses the joystick to zoom right in. She freezes the frame and leans in closer to the screen. She isn't breathing. She touches the screen with her fingers, traces the girl's smile, the tilt of her head. Then she stands up and paces around the room, almost skipping, her body light, air-expanded. The buzzing in her head is louder than the computer noise. *You're wrong, Ruby. You're wrong. It can't be her! Can it? Is it?*

She sits back down again; her feet drum on the floor. She finds the frame of her sister, freezes that too, lines Alice and Celia up side by side to compare them. The power of genetics, of resemblance, of shared characteristics that telegraph a relative – the shape of a smile, the angle of the head, the glitter in her eyes. But even without Celia for comparison, it's only five years since Ruby last saw her and although she's grown from a teenager into a woman there is no denying that it's her.

It's definitely her.

The door creaks and Ruby jumps. It's Lennie coming back from his nap. 'Your sister get home?'

Ruby quickly switches the camera to an innocuous view of the city bypass. She opens her mouth but words fall unspoken off her tongue.

'You okay?' He glances at the screen in front of her.

'Fine, yeah.' Her heart hammers denial. 'I don't know, I just – I must have been nodding off myself! It's been a snooze fest this evening.'

'Go for a lie down if you like,' Lennie says.

'I'll be fine,' Ruby replies, her smile over-bright. 'Thanks, though.'

Lennie puts on his headset and opens his book. 'Back to Einstein then.'

He begins to read aloud while Ruby's heartbeat slows and her breath steadies. This girl, she's not called Alice; she's called Hannah. Ruby knows this for a fact. Her fingers itch to call someone. But who should she call? Who would care apart from her?

She half hears Lennie's voice, catches the tail end of a sentence. 'What was that?' she asks.

'Something Einstein said,' Lennie tells her. 'Coincidence is God's way of remaining anonymous.'

Chapter Three

For the last four months, Ruby has had trouble sleeping. Her vast, Grant-less bed is an ocean of space that was once dominated by her husband's bulk. He had a rugby player's build, a prop forward, six foot two with shoulders twice as broad as hers. He radiated heat and she gravitated towards him, spooning into his back. The lack of him leaves her freezing cold, drifting around in the bed, sometimes on her own side, sometimes on his, often in the middle, betwixt and between, her head falling down into the gap left by the pillows.

But today she isn't thinking about everything she's lost. Memories of Grant are eclipsed by the girl.

Hannah.

Hannah Stewart.

The curtains in Ruby's bedroom are lined with blackout material but light seeps under the doorway from the hallway to form shadows on the ceiling and Ruby stares up at the shapes. She imagines Hannah is smiling at her. And Ruby smiles back, lights up the darkness around her with a spark of laughter. She says the girl's name out loud. 'Hannah?' She extends her right hand upwards into the empty air. 'Hi, Hannah. Good to meet you at last.' Or should she say 'again' instead of 'at last' because they have met before?

There are a thousand and one different ways for her to introduce herself: words, tone of voice, volume, intonation.

And should she hug her? Too much. A kiss on either cheek? That wouldn't feel natural to Ruby. Too English. Too ordinary.

She plays the scene over and over again until it's three o'clock in the afternoon and, knowing sleep will continue to elude her, she gets out of bed. She pads around in bare feet from bedroom to bathroom to kitchen, where she sits at the dining table. She doesn't feel tired because excitement is its own energiser and she has plans to make. The dining table is covered in paperwork – the important and the unimportant – and at some point she'll get round to reading and signing it or throwing it out, but for now she ignores the mess and rummages under piles of loose paper and empty envelopes until she finds a notepad and pen. The last thing she wrote on the pad was – Cat or dog? This was Celia's suggestion because Celia decided that Ruby needed a living, breathing creature to come home to, a presence in the house to stave off her loneliness. The garden was plenty big enough. She could well afford a pet. 'A furry body! Warmth! Company!' Celia squeezed her in a hug. 'Talk to Lennie's wife! She breeds dogs, doesn't she?'

'I lose my husband and you advise me to buy a puppy?' Ruby said as she ushered her sister out through the front door. 'Really, Celia? *Really?*'

Ruby rips out the page and writes HANNAH in large letters at the top of a fresh one. She draws three columns and gives each one a title: short-term, mid-term, long-term. It's important to get this right. Now that Hannah is back in her life – correction, Hannah isn't back in her life, but she will be – Ruby knows it's wise to make plans, direct the outcome. Not too much. Just enough to make sure their first meeting goes well. She doesn't want it ending up like last time.

'I won't manipulate this,' she whispers into the air. 'I won't do that.' But even as she says this she knows she'll move heaven and earth. They are going to be important to each other again. Ruby can feel it in her bones. The bones that ached as if being gnawed from the inside by the monster loss of Grant now feel as if they are healing.

'It'll take time,' she says out loud. 'The best things should never be rushed.'

But maybe she'll refuse contact with you, the voice in Ruby's head warns her. *Maybe that feeling in your bones is imaginary. Don't get your hopes up.*

This obvious truth washes through Ruby in a freezing-cold shiver and goose bumps erupt on her arms. She steadies her gaze on the paper as she waits for the feeling to pass.

Okay.

Okay. So maybe Hannah won't want to have contact with her immediately. That's understandable. And that's exactly why it's important she gets this right. She has to guard against frightening Hannah off because that's the last thing she would ever want to do. She'll start small. She writes 'do nothing' in the short-term column, then she sits back, pleased with this. She'll continue to watch Hannah on camera, just as she's done these last few months. Looking out for her – that's what Ruby's been doing for this girl since she first saw her at the bus stop. In the very same way as she does for other members of the public. All that's different now is that she knows who this girl is.

That's all.

Mid-term. After a month or so she might go to the restaurant where Hannah works. She'll keep a low profile. She'll sit in the corner and watch. Not in a creepy way – she isn't a stalker! But just in an interested way.

Establishing the lie of the land. Hannah probably won't recognise her but it would be deceitful of Ruby to mislead her, so she will have to be prepared to introduce herself.

And long-term? Long-term they'll be in frequent contact. Hannah might even move in with her, save herself money on rent and then, when the time comes, Ruby will help her to buy her own place.

Her mobile rings several times before Ruby registers the intrusion because she's deep in the folds of her imagination, happily projecting ahead. She's shopping with Hannah – Ruby's treat. They're trying on clothes in adjacent changing rooms in one of the boutiques in George Street. Hannah is excited and Ruby is allowing herself to be swept up in the fun of it all.

'Did I wake you?' Celia says.

She looks at the clock. It's after six. Where have the last three hours gone? 'No, I've been up for a while.'

'I'm just organising my diary; you know it's Mum's birthday next month?'

'How could I not?'

'Don't be like that. Listen.' She pauses and Ruby waits, running a finger over HANNAH, then lifting the notebook off the table and pressing it to her heart. 'We've plenty of time to plan. But I'm thinking, how about we have afternoon tea for Mum, at my place, with the kids, less pressure that way.'

'If you think it's a good idea.'

Celia is a talker and while she tells Ruby how important it is to 'forgive and forget', to 'move on' because bearing a grudge hurts the person who's doing it much more than the person it's directed at, Ruby rummages in her fridge. It's a double-doored American fridge with enough space for a family of six who eat like kings. It's almost completely empty apart from a few odds and sods that are bunched together on the middle shelf: an open bar of chocolate, a bottle of rosé, a stick of wilted celery, a clear plastic box of decaying blueberries speckled with white fungus, a ready-meal that expired a week ago and a withered avocado that is losing its shape and spreading onto the glass beneath it. And right at the bottom, in the salad drawer, she has a present for Lennie.

'I'll make a cake. I thought you might like to bring some savouries,' Celia is saying. 'But remember she's seventy this year so make them special.'

'I'll go to M and S,' Ruby says. She breaks off a square of chocolate and closes the fridge door. She's not really hungry. She's only looking for food from force of habit.

Grant was the cook. He wasn't a Lennie – Grant's food was simple: fish or chicken, and vegetables or salad – but he liked to be involved in the preparation. He had the vision and Ruby was his commis chef. She chopped; he finessed. 'Grub's up!' he would say and they'd sit down at the table, always the table, because Grant didn't watch TV.

'It's for the masses,' he told Ruby. 'And box sets are for when you have children and you're stuck indoors marking time before they leave home and you can start living again.' He kissed her across the table, standing up to reach her mouth. 'Let's never do that to ourselves.'

Grant didn't want kids.

Ruby didn't want kids.

They shared a love of skiing and hiking, theatre and bijou hotels. They didn't suffer fools, they weren't dinner party people, they didn't want to holiday with other couples. Their exercise bikes were still side by side in the rec room next to the double garage where they would cycle virtual country roads that unravelled on the screen before them as they pedalled furiously through France or Italy or even the Grand Canyon.

They were a match made in heaven. Everyone said so.

'And by the way, Tom says he has a client who's interested in buying your house.'

'I haven't decided whether I'm selling yet,' Ruby says.

'Well, think about it.'

Ruby hears the sound of the loo flushing in the background. 'Have you been on the toilet all this time?'

'How can you even want to live in that part of town? Surrounded by houses that have been divided up or converted into care homes for old fogies,' Celia says. 'Your house could easily be split up into four units, six even!'

Ruby registers the sound of a tap running and vigorous hand washing. 'You are in the loo!'

'You're not the only one who can multitask.'

'Charming,' Ruby says.

'There must be reminders of Grant everywhere you look. That won't be healthy, moving forward.'

Celia was right about that. Everywhere Ruby looked triggered memories of Grant, leaning against the breakfast bar when he was cooking, breathing kisses into her neck as she chopped vegetables, or sitting on the edge of the bath as she soaked in thirty-pound-a-bottle bubble bath that released an aroma of essential oils into the air where it lingered for the whole evening. Her mother thought it was a scandalous waste of money, and secretly Ruby did too, but Grant liked to spoil her and so she let him.

'Selling up is the best way to move yourself on, Rubes.'

Now she imagined Hannah here. Hannah on the sofa. Hannah admiring the artwork. Hannah asking who chose the kitchen units, marvelling that at the press of a button – ta da! – a food mixer appears or the swivel of a panel reveals a microwave.

Grant earned money easily, as if it were the most natural thing in the world to have a yearly salary that climbed into six and even seven figures. And just like some people are incapable of holding on to money, Grant was incapable of losing it. He was her very own Midas and that meant she was now quite rich.

More than quite.

As Celia pointed out, there was really no need for Ruby to have such a tiring, antisocial job. 'I like working,' Ruby says. 'I wouldn't know what to do with myself if I didn't have a job.' She needed to lose herself in other people's lives; it was time out from her own. 'I like being useful.'

'You can still work!' Celia doesn't get it. 'But let's set up a business. I've got loads of ideas.'

Ruby listens until she can listen no more. 'I'm going to see Lennie on the way to work,' she says, and that sets Celia off on another tack because as soon as Lennie's name is mentioned she starts on about her getting a dog again. 'I'm off now,' Ruby says. 'Bye!'

Lennie's home situation is the polar opposite of Ruby's. Every available space in his three-bedroom maisonette is taken up with possessions or people. The hall is littered with girls' shoes from Doc Martens to ballet pumps, coats bulge four or five deep from the rack, and on each of the stairs there are piles of clothes, loose make-up, books and bags.

Not for the first time it occurs to Ruby that Lennie and his family should be living in her house where they could spread out to their hearts' content.

'You look well,' he says. 'Better than I've seen you in a while.'

'Sleep,' Ruby says. 'I was out like a light.'

'Lucky you.' His tone is wistful. He's winning if he gets to bed at all, never mind fall sleep. Teenagers slamming doors, dogs barking, phones ringing. 'Ear plugs, eye mask, sleeping pills. You name it, I use it, but it doesn't shut out the noise.' She follows him through the hallway and into the kitchen. 'Beware of killer dogs.'

Small balls of white fur stagger towards Ruby's feet and topple onto her shoes, wrestling and chewing at her laces.

'Ruby!' Trish comes towards her and kisses somewhere close to her cheek. She's dressed in a loose top that doesn't quite hide the swell of her stomach. 'Doing okay?' She asks Ruby this while looking down at the puppies and making chirruping sounds through her teeth.

'Yes, thanks—'

'Well, I mean … apart from Grant … and what not.' She gives Ruby an apologetic, preoccupied smile and lifts a puppy off the ground to hug him to her neck.

Lennie sighs and Trish glares across at him. 'He's a right grouch, my husband.' Her mouth is tight. 'I don't know how you put up with him, Ruby, night after night.'

Discord crackles between them and Ruby averts her eyes, finds a photo on the wall to stare at: four blonde, blue-eyed daughters, almost identical apart from the width of their smiles, squint into the sun.

'This way, Ruby,' Lennie says.

They go out into the garden where three wooden huts take up most of the space. An electricity cable runs just above head-height from the back of the house to each of the huts. The little green space that's left is taken up with a circular washing line. Shona, one of Lennie's daughters, is haphazardly pulling T-shirts and trousers off the line to dump into the basket at her feet.

'You've added another hut since I was last here,' Ruby says.

'Dad calls the garden his Vietnamese village,' Shona says. She grins at Ruby and the piercing on her tongue glints in the sunshine. She's wearing a skin-tight top with spaghetti straps and the shortest shorts Ruby has ever seen.

'Hop it,' Lennie says. 'You've got homework to do. And could you put some clothes on, please?' he shouts after her.

'Oh, to be young again,' Ruby says.

'Jail bait, that one.' Lennie sighs. 'And believe me, Ruby, that's not something a man wants to say about his own daughter.'

Ruby follows him into the newest hut. There's a tired easy chair with frayed covers in one corner, and a table and upright chair in the other. The walls have photographs and printouts covering them. One wall is all Einstein, the other recipes and articles about all things foodie.

'Welcome to my man cave,' Lennie says, gesturing right and left towards the chairs. 'Take your pick. Each of the chairs is uncomfortable in its own way.'

Ruby goes for neither chair. She waits until Lennie meets her eyes before saying. 'Is Trish ... Is she pregnant?'

He gives a short, mirthless laugh. 'Either that or she's had too many fish suppers.'

'Lennie ...'

'Aye, well. Breeding seems to be what she does best. Although God only knows how she even fell pregnant – we're not exactly at it like newlyweds. And how we're going to manage a new baby is another imponderable but it seems I'm the only one who worries about that.'

'The girls are at good ages to help.'

Lennie snorts. 'Fat chance.' He thinks about it. 'Tina might, I suppose.'

'How old is Tina again?'

'Eleven. The other three are caught up in their own lives. And who can blame them?'

'I'm sorry, Lennie.' She reaches out and touches his forearm. She hasn't looked at him – *really* looked at him – for some time, and now that she does she sees the strain. His hair is thinner, his eyes dark-rimmed and heavier. He's gained weight and it's in all the wrong places. But while his body seems almost defeated, his mind is forever active.

'I should have got the snip. Chickened out at the last minute. More fool me.' He rubs his hands together. 'Anyhoo, no point in dwelling. What have you got for me?'

Ruby hands him the container of truffles and Lennie lifts a couple out onto his hand, reverently, as if they might fly away. 'How much did these set you back?'

'The guy owed me a favour.' They cost Ruby well over a hundred pounds but she would have spent three times as much just to see the gleam in Lennie's eyes.

'Perfect.' He sniffs them, then holds them up to the light like a man who's struck gold. 'A fungus like no other. The diamond in the kitchen.'

'If you say so.'

'I'll store these three in the freezer. And this one' – he shows it to Ruby for her to admire – 'I'll store in a jar of Arborio rice and then I'll prepare us a risotto for our next midnight feast. You'll be able to taste the difference the truffle makes.'

He returns them to the container and stands in front of the wall of recipes, scanning the sheets until he finds the one he's after and pulls it off the wall. 'What's that funny look on your face?' he says.

Unguarded, Ruby is drifting off into thoughts of Hannah. Within the next couple of hours she'll see Hannah heading up the High Street to work. Ruby is anticipating that moment. She can't wait. She knows that she won't be able to resist zooming in so that she can see the expression on Hannah's face. It doesn't matter what her expression is: thoughtful, moody, amused. It doesn't matter. All Ruby wants is to get to know her.

'Tell me you're not thinking of Call-me-Al?'

'Of course not!' Ruby laughs. 'Just ... happy in the moment, that's all. Watching you with your truffles.'

'It's got a posh name now, that living in the moment,' Lennie tells her. 'Mindfulness. They're forever re-inventing the wheel.'

'Aye, you're right there.'

Ruby went to mindfulness classes, years ago, before they were called that, before they were trendy, before she met Grant. The woman who ran the class told her to forget about the past: 'The past is a pound spent, the future is a promissory note, today is the only hard cash you have so spend it wisely.' The woman repeated this mantra at every class and it meant little to Ruby at the time.

But now she gets it. She understands what it means to experience each day as a new beginning. She has the chance to shape her future and it feels like a gift.

She leaves Lennie to his menus and heads to work. For the first time in weeks she isn't tempted to take a detour, stand in the cemetery surrounded by the dead and make herself late for work. That soul-destroying habit that has twisted her heart into knots has been knocked sideways by seeing Hannah again.

She lets the bus drive by and walks all the way to the CCTV centre because the weather is mild and she relishes the time to think and dream and linger. Every so often her inner voice reminds her not to get carried away, and she acknowledges this with a nod of her head. She's not a fool. She knows she needs to act with caution but what's the harm in dreaming?

She arrives at the centre with a light step and time to spare, and on the way to the control room she stops in front of the noticeboard. A new 'Missing' poster has been pinned up alongside the two 'Wanted' posters already on the board, strategically positioned at eye-level, an in-your-face reminder of persons of interest at loose in Scotland's capital. Ruby takes time to stare at the faces of the recently missing.

There are four of them: two men and two women – the photographs taken by family or friends, happy snaps from better times. The men are both middle-aged, one slightly balding, the other with a straggle of curly, grey/brown hair. One of the women is also middle-aged and has distinctive hooded eyelids. The other is close to thirty with large pale eyes and freckled cheeks.

Four new faces to watch out for on cameras where the image quality could be poor, eyes will be averted and they'll most likely have their heads concealed inside a hat or a hoodie. A person's walk is often idiosyncratic but all Ruby has is a photograph and so the odds of spotting any of these people are stacked against her. The last time she recognised a misper was purely by chance. There was an incident at the top of Leith Walk; the water mains was leaking water all over the road, creating an ever increasing puddle that soon turned into a pond, stopped the traffic and drew spectators. While she directed the police to the scene, her eye was drawn to a man at the edge of the gathering crowd who had the slightly jerky, eyes-lowered demeanour of someone who didn't want to be noticed. When he turned his head and she was able to zoom in on his face, she recognised him. He had a scar on his lip scar and almond-shaped eyes that sparked her memory. She alerted the police to question him on arrival, something they did with a casual interest so as not to send him running. It turned out he had left home more than a year previously, having lost himself in a spiral of debt. He'd been sleeping rough the whole time. When the police persuaded him into hostel accommodation, he agreed, and, as far as Ruby knew, he was still there.

Ruby stares at the photographs and waits. She's allowing time for a nudge of recognition but when it doesn't come she walks into the control room. Fiona has already arrived and is sitting on the edge of her chair watching the door. As soon as Ruby comes into the room she stands up next to her, and Freddie comes across to give them the handover. He's a man who takes pride in doing everything by the book, the sort who came out of his mother's womb with a clipboard and pen in his chubby fists and an expression of disapproval on his face.

'News about the cameras at the pubic triangle. Dodds has been in touch.'

'Detective Chief Inspector Dodds,' Ruby says for Fiona's benefit.

'They've changed the cameras' sequencing. Got one of their team undercover. We've been asked not to reset them.'

'No probs.'

'Accident on Princes Street, nothing major, two buses and a tram, all evidential feed has already been down-loaded. And a five-year-old boy was lost for twenty minutes up near the Meadows but we picked him up quickly enough. He'd got himself across the road and was halfway to Tollcross.'

Fiona is taking notes, her pen scratching across the paper. When Freddie's finished telling Ruby about the result of the inquest into a suicide on the Calton Hill most of the day shift have headed off. 'Still no coffee machine,' he says. 'But there is some instant now. Donations in the jar on the windowsill please.'

'Great. See you in the morning.'

He heads off out the door and Fiona says, 'The pubic triangle? Did he mean public triangle?'

'No. Pubic it is. Prostitutes, lap dancing, peep shows. Burke and Hare pub behind the Art College?' Fiona's eyes are wide. 'Or you can reach it from the West Port, along from the Grassmarket.'

'I didn't know Edinburgh had anywhere like that.'

'Every city has somewhere like that. I'll show you on the cameras. Neon-lit, you can't miss it. It's a magnet for stag dos.'

Ruby's nights without Lennie are never as enjoyable but for the first time she doesn't care. All she needs to do is manage Fiona and then she can concentrate on watching out for Hannah.

'Have a seat, Fiona,' Ruby says. 'Put your headset on so that we can hear the police radios if anyone needs a camera. Only cover one ear and then you can hear what's going on in the room too.'

Fiona does as she's told and they sit side by side while Ruby sets up her spot screens before saying to Fiona, 'Let's go over the basics. Tell me what you've learned so far.'

'CCTV is not big brother,' Fiona says at once. 'Its main function is public order.'

'And what's the difference between monitoring and surveillance?'

'Monitoring means that no more than ten per cent of the screen should be taken up with one person. If we zoom in for more than three seconds it becomes surveillance.' She takes a breath and listens, distracted by the chatter on her headset. 'Whisky Alpha – is that for us?'

'We're Whisky Romeo. Carry on.'

'Surveillance is illegal without a warrant or an honestly held belief that would stand up in court.'

'Good.' Ruby nods. 'Of course, this is real life and the gulf between theory and practice can be wide but we always work within the law.' She flicks some crumbs off her desk and into the bin. 'Sometimes we sail pretty close to the edge but we won't drop off as long as we remember that this is about public order. It's not about you or me or anyone we might know. Capiche?'

Fiona nods.

'Now, do you know how many people go missing in the UK every year?'

'About three hundred thousand.'

'That's right. I'll give you an example. Last month in Edinburgh, a fifty-year-old man went out for a packet of fags and never came back.'

It was a Sunday morning. He wasn't a church-going man and ordinarily he went to the shop and returned with a newspaper, half a dozen white rolls and his cigarettes for the week. The cameras clocked his habits like the watchful eye of a parent. But this particular Sunday, he went into the corner shop; one minute and thirty-four seconds later he came out again. The CCTV feed catches him hesitating, looking to the right, where the house he'd lived in for the best part of thirty years was situated. He looked to the right but he didn't turn right. (*Did he see someone? Did he have a light-bulb moment? Was there a final straw?* Afterwards, neither his wife nor his workmates were able to shed any light.) He turned left instead of right. He walked through the Edinburgh streets, three miles to Waverley Station, cameras tracking him as he walked. He bought a ticket for King's Cross but he didn't get off at the London station.

'He was lost somewhere between York and Nottingham. No cameras picked him up.'

'How come?'

'Some people are camera-aware. They avoid sightlines and move through the shadows.' Ruby glances at the clock. Hannah will be climbing off the bus any minute. 'For now, the mystery is unsolved. His name was added to the misper list and that's longer than the longest arm, so no one's holding their breath.'

'And his relatives?'

'They're left in limbo.' Ruby rubs her hands together. 'Why don't you take five minutes to look at the noticeboard in the corridor? Study the faces of the recently missing and the wanted. Memorise what you can. Beginner's luck – you never know.'

As soon as she leaves the room, Ruby brings Camera 35 down onto her spot screen. Hannah usually gets off the number 23 bus on George IV Bridge. Ruby drums her fingers on the desk as she waits, impatiently counting down the seconds until she sees the bus round the bend and come to a stop. A tall man, a woman with a buggy and ... then ... there she is. It's Hannah. Warmth spreads through Ruby's chest and brings a smile to her face.

She uses the joystick to zoom in closer. This particular

camera is one of the new HD units and the image is as clear as watching television.

Hannah's lips are moving. There are earphones in her ears and she's walking with a brisk step. Ruby uses the joystick so that the camera follows her as she moves. She is dressed in jeans and a short biker jacket. Her red hair dips down over her right eye and she pushes it back with her fingers. Her nails are long and painted pillar-box red. She glances up twice as if she suspects rain and both times Ruby sees her eyes are as deep brown as Celia's, as her own. Hannah stops at the junction and waits for the green man, hands in pockets. An elderly lady next to her says something and Hannah removes her earphones, smiles at her, listens and then points down the Mound. When the green man lights up, she takes the elderly lady's arm and they both cross the road.

'She's kind,' Ruby says, out loud. 'Caring.'

Hannah delivers the elderly lady onto the pavement opposite and watches her retreating back for a moment before she heads up the hill to the restaurant. Ruby watches until the restaurant door closes behind her and then she replays the feed. She replays it six times, memorising Hannah's features, the way she walks, the way she listens and talks, before she hears Fiona returning.

'I've taken notes,' Fiona says. 'I'll do my best to spot one of them.' She settles back in her chair again.

Ruby is smiling because of Hannah, because she can't help it, because she's happier than she's been in years.

'Is it a joke?' Fiona says. 'Because you're really smiling and—'

Ruby shakes her head. 'Sorry. I was thinking … Okay.' She straightens her back. 'Has anyone shown you the dead man's switch?'

'Freddie mentioned it. I've heard the alarm go off but …'

'So, just in case anyone gets past the keypad at the front door, every half an hour an alarm goes off and if one of us doesn't flick the switch, the cavalry will arrive to see whether we've been immobilised.' Ruby shows her the switch under the desk. 'All the desks have a switch in exactly the same position so that you can feel with your fingers and know it's there. I usually switch it off just before it sounds. When you've worked here a while, you know when it's coming.'

'Has anyone ever got past the keypad?'

'Not here but it's happened in other cities. There's barely a crime nowadays where the prosecution isn't helped by CCTV footage.'

Fiona thinks about this, swivelling gently in her chair, her eyes on the floor, before she says, 'Shouldn't there be a code or something to switch it off? I mean, if we *are* being raided, then those men could just hit the switch, couldn't they?'

'The idea is that we've all been knocked out, not that we're being held hostage.' Ruby smiles at her. 'You've got a point though.' She makes a mental note that Fiona isn't daft. Not like the last trainee who wouldn't have been able to recognise a flaw if it had poked him in the eye.

Ruby tunes in to the voices in her ear. 'This is for us.' She points to Fiona's headset. 'Put it on.'

There's the sound of running footsteps and heavy breathing. 'Whisky Romeo. I'm on the High Street, past St Giles. Red shirt! Red shirt! Can you see him?'

Ruby brings three camera feeds down on her spot screens and zooms in on different people until she spots the policeman and the man running thirty metres ahead of him. 'He's gone down the close from the High Street to New College,' she says.

'I see him.' More running and shouting. 'Lost him again.'

'He's running down the steps off the Mound towards the galleries,' Ruby says, glancing across at Fiona, whose eyes are popping.

Another voice: 'We'll cut him off.'

Ruby and Fiona watch a police car arrive at the foot of the hill; two cops burst out and position themselves at the bottom of the steps. The man in the red shirt sees them coming and considers retracing his steps but the first policeman is almost behind him now. He glances over the wall onto the pathway below but decides against it, as the drop would, at the very least, break his legs. Resigned, he raises his arms and accepts his fate – handcuffed and in the back of a police car. It's all over in less than two minutes.

'That was exciting!' Fiona's face is flushed. 'It's amazing how much you can see from here.'

The dead man's alarm starts to beep and drowns out Ruby's reply; Fiona jumps. Ruby reaches across to press the button. 'You'll get used to it.'

Lennie and Ruby never turn on the alarm when they're on shift together because it's a nuisance. They trust each other enough to know they'll not let anyone in the building, and the likelihood of someone disabling the keypad and getting through a steel door is remote. But it's company policy to keep the alarm on so Ruby does it with Fiona.

Ruby goes through more procedure with Fiona, finding her a quick learner. 'The tapes are overwritten in thirty days, to the exact second, so any evidence has to be downloaded before that time is up.'

'What if it isn't?'

'It's almost impossible to retrieve. It would take an engineer weeks to get the recording back, on the off-chance it might be useful, and nobody has the money for that.' Ruby switches the camera feeds on her spot screens to the neon-lit triangle, seen from three different angles. 'Edinburgh's red light district in all its glory,' she says.

Fiona leans forward to see the men better, already well-oiled, outside on the pavements, laughing, hands in their pockets, as they look around at the opposition of pubs and clubs, making their minds up about which one to go into first.

'Lap dancing, pole dancing or straightforward stripping,' Ruby says under her breath. 'The choice is theirs.'

Fiona has an interested but puzzled look on her face. 'I don't get it,' she says. 'Why men like this sort of thing.'

'Testosterone,' Ruby says. 'Balls, bragging and bravado.' She smiles. 'That's men according to Lennie.'

'My dad told me I might see things that'll upset me.' She looks shyly at Ruby. 'I don't mind that. I just want to do well.'

'Good for you, Fiona,' Ruby says. Her eyes flick to the clock on the wall. 'You should go and eat now. Take a full half-hour. It'll help you stay awake through the night.'

'I've brought myself a sandwich.'

'Be warned,' she says. 'Lennie likes to eat proper food. You won't be getting away with sandwiches when you're on duty with him.'

'What's Lennie like?' Fiona says. 'He seems a bit … scary.'

Ruby laughs. 'You couldn't meet a nicer man. Four daughters. Gruff exterior but heart of gold.' She thinks for a moment. 'Would do anything for anyone,' she says to Fiona's retreating back. 'No better friend.'

No better friend. Ruby hears herself say this and feels guilt turn in her stomach. She's been lying to him for months; she's been meaning to talk to him, but the timing hasn't been right.

The timing will never be right.

She cuts off that thought. She's not about to argue with herself – where has that ever got her?

And now there's Hannah. Another secret. Secret number two – or is it three? She's starting to lose count.

She returns to the screen like an addict to the needle and watches Hannah leave the restaurant. She is texting on her phone, looking up every five or so metres to check what's going on around her. Ruby drinks her in. Her features are now exquisitely familiar and if she had a pencil and paper, Ruby reckons she could draw her as accurately as a photograph. But for now Ruby is content to observe the moods that flit across her face as she reads the replies to her texts. Her face moves from smile to frown and back again and then she's openly laughing. It makes Ruby laugh too and she is completely caught up in Hannah's happiness until Hannah suddenly glances upwards, her face once more a frown.

She stares directly at the camera and Ruby draws back as if stung, as if the camera works both ways and Hannah sees Ruby watching her. Hannah's unflinching expression is like an accusation and it holds Ruby still for several long seconds, seconds that stretch taut and then tauter.

And Ruby doesn't move; she doesn't breathe.

Even when Hannah's attention has dropped back to street level, still Ruby is stuck to her seat, frozen, shocked, empty of air, until heat flames her cheeks and she takes a breath, turns her face away from the screen, and from the shame of a voyeur who has been caught in the act.

'But she can't know that I work here,' Ruby says into the empty room. 'Staring up at the camera like that, it's just … it's just a coincidence.'

She thinks of the Einstein quote, *Coincidence is God's way of remaining anonymous*, and remembers that hearing the quote validated her decision to follow Hannah in the first place.

Ruby paces the room, her expression worried until she talks herself into a justification. Bottom line: she isn't harming anyone. She isn't watching Hannah with a view to upsetting her – quite the opposite, in fact. No one could ever accuse her of not wanting what's best for Hannah. And if ever there comes a time when she should back off, she will. She makes this promise to herself.

And then she feels better.

When Fiona's break time is up, Ruby is re-sequencing the cameras close to Murrayfield. She shows Fiona how it's done and talks for an hour or more about what the police expect, and what the CCTV service is able to provide.

'You were in the police once, weren't you?' Fiona says.
'I was.'

'Why did you leave?' she says, then quickly bites her lip when she sees Ruby's expression. 'Sorry, is that a personal question? I was just …' She trails off. 'I was wondering.'

'No great mystery.' Ruby's tone is dry. 'I was ready for a change. My husband was a high earner. I didn't need the stress.'

'I heard about your husband.' She holds up a hand.

'Not that he earned a lot but that he passed away. I'm so sorry.'

Ruby doesn't reply. Instead she turns to her screen and lets Fiona deal with her own discomfort. She's beginning to like the girl but she has never been one for over-familiarity. Women like to share; it's all part of getting to know each other, but Fiona is half her age and Ruby knows that while they'll make reasonably good colleagues, they'll never be friends.

It's five years since Ruby resigned from the police service and she has barely discussed it with close family, never mind her small circle of friends. The memory is a scab she never picks because it hides a wound that is bone deep.

It was a Wednesday in February, a freezing cold morning that meant she was scraping the frost off her windscreen when the text message came through. She wouldn't have responded to it anyway because she was preoccupied with thoughts of her arrest the evening before. She had spent the night in the cells and been released that morning without charge. But that didn't mean it was over.

So although she didn't see her colleague's warning text, she walked into work expecting the worst. 'The big man's after you,' her colleague told her, his eyes lowered. 'And he's not happy.'

She nodded her thanks and carried on walking in the direction of the boss's office. She liked her boss; better still she respected him. He had been a cop for thirty years and aside from the odd lapse into old-school male banter, he was beyond reproach: intelligent, perceptive and straight as a die.

'Get your arse in there, Romano!' He was outside his own office, pacing the floor. 'Now!' She walked in ahead of him

and he slammed the door behind them both. 'What the holy fuck.' His voice was low. 'Explain yourself.'

Her head offered her two options: deny it or brazen it out. She chose neither. She spoke from her heart when she said, 'I couldn't help myself, sir. I'm sorry.'

His voice dropped even lower. 'One of my officers using confidential information for their own ends.'

'I'm sorry,' she repeated.

'Sorry?' He stood in front of her, hands on hips, an imposing figure at six foot three and built like a brick shithouse. 'Sorry for what, Romano?'

'Sorry for letting you down, sir.'

'Oh, I see.' He nodded, as if wise to her. 'You think that's going to make it okay?'

'No, sir.'

'Why didn't you come to me?'

'I …' She was staring down at her feet. 'There's nothing I can say.'

'Damn right!' He marched around the room a few times, then threw up his arms and shouted, 'So what now, Romano? What happens now? Because there's no way you can continue in the force.'

'Yes … I know …' There was a stretch of tears behind her eyes, held taut like a rubber band about to snap. 'I'll hand in my notice.'

'Fuck's sake.' His sigh was heartfelt. 'You're lucky they don't want to press charges.'

'I know, sir.'

'I'll do my best to keep the gossips quiet.'

'Thank you, sir.'

'You had a good career ahead of you, Ruby.' She dared to look up and saw him shake his head with regret. 'You'll be missed.'

She nodded her thanks and walked away before the tight band behind her eyes snapped.

And here she is, at it again, Ruby thinks. She is crossing a line into the danger zone. Because, however she tries to justify it, she has Hannah under surveillance and that's illegal. If Ruby's found out she won't simply be fired. She could quite easily be prosecuted and imprisoned.

But this isn't history repeating itself.

This is something else entirely.

Chapter Four

Does Ruby believe in God?

Sometimes. When it suits her. That's the crux of it. She turns to God when she needs something that is beyond her control, something that only a deity can make happen. At times like these, she chooses to believe there is a strength, a purpose and a power beyond herself. A power with the ability to direct events. Direct them in Ruby's favour. Well, she deserves it, doesn't she? After all the pain of the Grantless months, the emotional anguish that went along with losing him. If the tide is turning for her now, then she wants God to know that she's grateful. And if He could make sure that when Ruby does initiate contact with Hannah, as she knows she will, as she knows she'll be compelled to do, then Ruby prays that Hannah will be pleased.

The second Sunday after she sees Hannah she goes to St Mary's Cathedral. She's missed morning mass because she was asleep after a night shift and it's early yet for the evening service. The cathedral is empty apart from a few people either sitting on pews or standing in front of the candle holders.

Ruby prays. She's down on her knees, her hands clasped together, her eyes closed. Whenever she does this she's instantly transported back to her childhood.

Every Sunday the four of them – Mum, Dad and the two girls – came up Leith Walk to Catholic mass. Ruby was

*usually holding her dad's hand, Celia her mum's. Celia was
forever the chatterbox, while Ruby and her dad walked mostly
in companionable silence, only broken by observations such
as, 'Did you see that car, Ruby? It's the new model.' Or
'Could we have an ice cream after mass, Dad? I've brought
my pocket money.'*

*Celia and Mum would talk the whole way to the cath-
edral and back. Busy, loud chatter that would've hurt Ruby's
ears. And her dad's ears too. Ruby knew this without it
having to be said.*

*When they reached St Mary's, their mum would straighten
their skirts and make sure their faces were clean and then
she would place lace mantillas over their hair because their
mum was Irish and their dad was Italian and respect for
the Church was important.*

Ruby feels she must have spirited her mother up from
her memory, because when she's finished praying and
she opens her eyes, her mum is standing beside her.
'Mum?' She frowns, questioning, as past and present
collide.

'I'm taken aback to find *you* here, Ruby,' she says.

Ruby stands up and they hug, awkwardly, because it's
been months since they've seen one another and there
is so much unspoken between them.

'How are you?' her mother says.

'Good, yes.' Celia's words about 'forgiving and forgetting' and 'moving on' ring in Ruby's ears but she can't
bring them into her body, nor is she able to translate
them into words. 'I'm seeing you on your ...' She hesitates. Did Celia say it was a surprise party?

'At Celia's, on my birthday.' Her mother nods. 'It's
not a surprise party, Ruby.'

'I didn't think it was.'

'I was lighting a candle for your dad. It's five years today since he died.' She gives Ruby a look that says she hasn't forgotten the events that led up to his death and that she still holds Ruby responsible.

As if Ruby didn't love her dad more than Celia and her mum put together.

As if Ruby wouldn't give her right arm for him still to be alive.

As if Ruby would ever forgive herself.

'I know it's the anniversary. That's why I'm here … as it happens,' Ruby says. Her mum sees through her but she keeps it up. 'I was remembering Dad in my prayers.'

'That's good,' her mother says. She glances at her wristwatch, taps the face with her finger. 'Running slow … I'm due to meet one of my friends in a minute.' She almost smiles. 'Unless you want to have a coffee somewhere?'

'I'm heading to work, Mum.' She bites her lip. 'Sorry,' she adds and instantly regrets the 'sorry' because her mum doesn't look remotely disappointed. In fact she looks relieved.

They part without another word and Ruby tries not to hold on to her anger because if God is sending Ruby messages then she can't pick and choose.

She'll make an effort at the party. She really will. 'Cross my heart and hope to die,' Ruby says, crossing herself as she walks to work.

She watches Hannah every day. She doesn't always manage to catch her on her way to work but she's usually watching when she comes out of the restaurant at the end of her shift because that's when Lennie is in the staff kitchen warming up the meal for them both – truffles really do make a difference to a risotto – and Fiona likes to eat just before midnight, so that leaves Ruby on her own with the cameras.

Not much changes. Sometimes she's with leather jacket guy, who Ruby surmises must be her boyfriend. Ruby zooms in on him. He has a kind face and the bluest of eyes. He walks up the hill to meet her when her shift is over. They kiss at the bus stop and most of the time he boards the bus with her. Otherwise, he walks down the Mound and onto Princes Street to catch the number 16 heading north, not south as Hannah does.

Once, Ruby misses seeing Hannah walk to the bus stop because both she and Lennie have to assist the police on a car chase on the city bypass. They don't finish with the pursuit until well past midnight, by which time Hannah is already on her way home. Ruby watches the recording so she knows Hannah makes the bus but she feels the lack of live, visual contact like a physical blow. A physical blow that makes her feel dizzy and panicky. She's set up a dependency in herself. She knows this; it worries her. But now that she's begun, she's unable to stop. It's not just that seeing Hannah after all this time is an unexpected delight. Seeing Hannah again is visceral for Ruby. The feeling is in her bones, in her blood, in her heart.

A month goes by. Ruby has bided her time. And now she needs to, wants to, move on a step. She had considered going to the restaurant but she is more curious about where Hannah lives. There are several cameras watching the bus stops further along the route but Hannah doesn't get off at any of those stops. Ruby surmises she can't be living in Tollcross or the other side of the Meadows. She knows that Hannah was brought up in Linlithgow, twenty miles west of Edinburgh, but clearly she's not living there any more. Ruby's best guess is that she's living in one of the tenements in Bruntsfield or Morningside. Over a dozen of the bus stops are out of sight of the cameras. There are eyes at Holy Corner and at the junction in Morningside where Comiston Road begins, but no cameras in between, nor further out of Edinburgh. It's unlikely Hannah's living at the end of the bus route as it's all family homes up there but Ruby can't rule it out with any certainty.

The only way to find out exactly where Hannah lives is to be on the bus when she gets off.

Simple.

Or at least, from a practical viewpoint it's simple. When Ruby worked in the police service, following a person of interest was run-of-the-mill. Nevertheless, she plans carefully because she doesn't want to be seen. Lennie and Fiona are on night shift and she knows Lennie would spot her in an instant, just as she would spot him. And Fiona is proving to be sharp-eyed too. Sure, maybe they'll be busy looking elsewhere, but why risk it? Ruby won't be doing anything wrong even if she were seen, but she knows that, next day, Lennie will ask her what she was doing, where she was going, why she was up near the castle at that time of night. He's a friend taking an interest – no big deal. But in her mind she can hear him saying it and it makes her feel anxious. It's her business and it's far too soon for her to share.

From an emotional viewpoint it's anything but simple. It feels momentous. It feels like she is stepping from a place of relative safety into a minefield where at any moment she could be blown to pieces. So Ruby does her best to talk herself out of it. *This is about more than curiosity. This is about obsession. This makes her a stalker.*

She is 'illegally following and watching someone over a period of time'. She is breaking the law.

So why is she doing it?

Because she must.

Because every fibre in her being tells her that she must. Because her heart yearns and her bones ache and rationale means nothing.

She joins the bus at the beginning of the route, all the way down in Trinity. She takes a taxi to Lennox Row and then gets on the bus at twenty to midnight. She sits downstairs, right at the back. She's a woman of almost forty, wearing no make-up, jeans and a plain jacket. Nobody would look twice at her. There's a camera on the bus but Ruby keeps her head averted and stares out of the window. She's not trying to avoid being seen but there's no point in making it easy. They could trace her movements if they wanted to, of course they could. But she's not a criminal and anyway, who are *they*? And why would they be interested in her movements?

Still, years working as a cop means 'secretive' is her default mode. Grant could never quite grasp why she was this way. It caused friction between them but Ruby couldn't help herself. She didn't like other people knowing her business. As far as she was concerned, blabbing and blubbing were signs of weakness. She keeps her own counsel. For better or for worse.

The bus route passes close to the cemetery where she has spent many an evening torturing herself. Grief is natural, she understands that, but now she has replaced one heart's fixation with another. From Grant to Hannah. And perhaps she should lend more weight to her head than her heart but she's never been that way inclined and no amount of wishing will make her so.

Over a dozen people join the bus at the last stop in

Hanover Street before the bus snakes up the Mound. They've been on a night out and they're full of laughter and banter. If Ruby had any presence at all, she's completely lost it now and she knows it would take a trained eye to see past the happy drunks and spot her at the back.

Ruby is holding her breath when the bus tips across the Mound and down George IV Bridge. She watches as Hannah gets on board, briefly holds her bus pass over the pad in front of the driver and then walks forward. She doesn't look towards the back of the bus; she climbs the stairs to the top deck.

Ruby lets out her held breath and tries to relax. Her eyeballs ache and her feet are numb. The bus rumbles along, stops outside the old Royal Infirmary, passes where Goldbergs used to be, the King's Theatre, Bruntsfield Links. Ruby waits, her eyes sliding from the window to the bottom of the stairs and back again until just before Holy Corner when Hannah comes down the stairs. Someone has already pressed the bell and the bus is slowing to a stop. There are three people standing in the aisle and Hannah goes ahead of all three. Ruby waits for a moment before standing up and following the last person onto the pavement. She takes her mobile out of her pocket and holds it up to the side of her face, pretending to take a call.

All the shops are long closed for the night but the street is well lit. Coffee shops, boutiques, an estate agent, a bookshop – none of them are a window-shopping distraction to either Hannah or Ruby. Hannah walks with purpose, moving easily across the road to pause at an island in the middle and wait for a white van to drive by.

Ruby remembers her police training and keeps a

distance of more than thirty metres. Twice, when Hannah glances behind her, Ruby talks into her mobile, her chin low in her collar. Ruby can't be sure, but it seems as if Hannah's eyes don't linger on her for more than a split second before she stares back in the direction she is travelling, leaves the main road and hurries into a side street where tenements tower up on either side. Ruby rounds the corner just in time to see Hannah go into one of the stairs.

'Third on the left,' Ruby whispers to herself as she approaches. There's a streetlamp directly outside and the stair door is a battered, faded blue that someone has sanded down, ready to paint. The number 15 is written in chalk on the stone wall to the right-hand side of the door and it looks as if a brand-new entryphone system has recently been installed. There are eight flats in the building but names have yet to be printed next to the buttons.

Ruby crosses the road to stand in the shadows. Her heart has doubled its beat and is pushing against her ribcage like a trapped animal. She feels simultaneously excited and nauseous. Her conscience reminds her that this is stalking. But her heart tells her that this is loving.

The living room light comes on in one of the flats two floors up. Ruby can make out Hannah's shape as she takes off her jacket and throws it behind her – onto a chair, perhaps? Ruby doesn't know because she needs to be higher. She needs to be looking down. That's what she's used to. There are cameras closer to the centre of town where they can peer into people's windows but this flat is off the main road and too far from the centre to merit a watchful eye.

Ruby leans up against a closely trimmed box hedge that stands shoulder height in the tiny front garden next to her. She waits there for almost ten minutes but although the light is on and the curtains, if there are any, are left open, she doesn't see Hannah again. She's about to walk away when the door behind her opens, startling her, so that she gives a sharp intake of breath. A man comes out. He's being led by a small dog on a lead who barks at the sight of Ruby.

'Cut it out!' the man tells him and the dog stifles his bark to a soft throaty growl. 'Sorry to give you a fright,' he says to Ruby. 'Barry doesn't expect to meet anyone at this time of night.' He nudges the dog to one side with his foot. 'Apart from the lassie over the road,' he adds. 'She often works late.'

'Hello, Barry.' Ruby bends down to stroke his head and his tail starts to wag. 'You're not scary at all, are you?'

'Likes to pretend,' the man says. He's holding the door open behind him. 'You going inside?'

'No, I don't live here,' Ruby says, falling immediately into a lie. 'I used to, but I've lived away from Edinburgh for a while and I was just passing—'

'Just passing?' the man says, the door clicking shut behind him. 'It's gone midnight.'

'Jet lag,' Ruby says. 'I'm looking to buy around here. Or rent.' She looks up at the building. 'Anything going that you know of?'

'They rent out the top two, right enough.'

'In this building?'

'Aye. You have to like stairs, though.'

'They don't trouble me.' Ruby feels opportunity well up inside her. 'You wouldn't happen to know who the letting agent is?'

'The one in the front street. You cannae miss it.' The dog starts to pull on the leash. 'You're quiet, are you? Because we're fed up with students.'

'Very quiet.'

'You might be lucky then.' He starts to walk on. 'Maybe see you again.'

'Maybe,' Ruby says. 'Thank you!'

She retraces her steps back to the main road and stands in front of the estate agent's window, scanning the letting section for photographs of the flat round the corner. There's no sign of it but that doesn't worry Ruby. As Grant always said, 'Money gives you the opportunity to negotiate. It gets you in the game.' She's never been one for flashing the cash but she'll do it if she has to.

And then … and then she could bump into Hannah by accident one day, couldn't she? That would be a good way for them to meet. Of all the streets in all of Edinburgh, the fact that they ended up living in the same one would be like fate pushing them together.

But you would have engineered it.

Ruby ignores that intrusive thought and steps out to hail a cab.

Chapter Five

She is still sleeping when her mobile rings.

'Where are you?' It's Celia, hissing at her. 'It's two o'clock. Mum will be here in an hour. I want to have all the food laid out before she arrives.'

'Of course.' Ruby sits up and rubs her face. 'I'm running a bit late but I'll be there in half an hour.'

'You forgot, didn't you?'

'No!'

'You sound sleepy. Have you just woken up?'

'I work nights, remember? I'm entitled to be in bed at two in the afternoon. And if you get off the phone I'll be able to move more quickly, won't I?'

She hears Celia sigh before the line goes dead. She showers, dresses, grabs her bag and drives to the super-market, all done in double-quick time. So it's not until she's piling every canapé and finger food she can find into a trolley that she thinks about Hannah. She needs to call the estate agent. She'll do it as soon as she gets to Celia's. But in the cold light of day the happiness she felt last night as she imagined living opposite Hannah is now tinged with anxiety. Is it wrong to want to be close to her? Is this a step too far? When they bumped into each other – could she really pass it off as coincidence?

She doesn't have an answer to any of these questions and she has no time to think about it because as soon as she arrives at Celia's, her three nephews and niece grab hold of her. Strong arms and legs wriggle and squirm and pull her one way and then another. 'Auntie Ruby's here! Auntie Ruby's here! *Mum!*'

Celia appears from the kitchen, both hands full of cutlery and plates. 'Don't wind them up.' She leans in to kiss Ruby's cheek. 'They're high as kites already.' She kisses her other cheek. 'You got the nibbles?'

'And some,' Ruby says.

'All of you.' She stares at her children. 'Help carry in the bags of food from Auntie Ruby's car.' She holds up the cutlery. 'I'm setting the table in the conservatory. I'm not going to risk eating outside with those clouds.'

It's a whirlwind. Twice Ruby tries to escape to call the estate agent but both times she's hijacked by the children, who insist on taking her for a bounce on the trampoline and then, of paramount importance, showing her their latest Lego model.

And then her mother arrives, Celia comes out of the kitchen, and there's no escape. Ruby has already placed a present on the birthday table. It's the last one her mother opens, after tickets for the ballet, afternoon tea in Dalhousie Castle and an assortment of flowery-handled garden equipment from the children. Her mother carefully picks up the box and views it from every angle. 'Beautifully wrapped.'

'I can't take credit for that,' Ruby says.

Her mum flashes her a look. 'Can I return it if I don't like it?'

'Of course.' Ruby feels Celia tense beside her. 'I can give you the receipt.'

The children are watching the adult faces expectantly.

'Open it, Granny.'

'Save the paper, Granny. Cos it's really pretty.'

'Quick, Granny. I need to wee!'

Celia takes hold of Joseph, the youngest. 'You've only just been to the loo. Be patient.'

Her mother doesn't tear off the paper; she unpicks it slowly, smooths it flat and lays it to one side. Only then does she look at the designer logo on the box. 'You must have money to burn, Ruby Romano.'

'What is it, Granny?'

'When I bumped into you in the cathedral your watch was playing up,' Ruby says. 'So I thought ...'

'Put it on, Granny.'

'Well ...' Her mum opens the box and stares at the watch, lying on a bed of white satin. 'It's very ... shiny.'

'The strap has extra links if you need them.'

'I really think that the cost—'

'Mum.' Celia can no longer contain herself. 'Seriously?'

'You should say thank you,' Joseph announces. 'Even if you don't like it. That's what Mum says.'

'You're absolutely right, Joseph. I'm forgetting my manners.' Her mum looks directly at Ruby. This doesn't happen often and Ruby takes a step backwards. 'I do like it, as it happens. I like it very much.' She removes her old watch and clips the new one around her wrist. 'And look, children! It's a perfect fit.'

'You still haven't said thank you,' Joseph reminds her.

'Thank you very much, Ruby.' She comes towards her and kisses her cheek. 'Very thoughtful of you.'

Ruby's niece claps excitedly and Celia catches Ruby's eye. 'Well done,' she mouths and hands her a glass of something fizzy.

'If you want to swap it for a different model,' Ruby says, 'I won't be offended.'

'Not at all. It's really very elegant,' her mum says, holding her wrist out so that the children can examine the watch.

'It's gold.'

'And silver.'

'And it has small diamonds all around.'

They poke and prod until Celia pours them some juice and they drift off, clutching their tumblers, into the garden.

'How's work, Ruby?' her mum asks. 'You still on shifts with the lovely Lennie?'

'Cutbacks and what not, but yeah, Lennie and I are still working together. He's trying for *Mastermind* although he's such a good cook, I've been suggesting *MasterChef* to him.'

Her mother starts to tell her about a friend of hers who was a runner-up in *MasterChef* and how much all the neighbours enjoy being invited for dinner. 'She tries her recipes out on us.'

'Lennie does the same with me.'

She lets her mother talk. She's been doing this all her life, letting Celia and her mother talk. Her dad did it too. They were listeners extraordinaire. Ruby finds herself sliding back into that role, willingly sliding back, because she wants to be on good terms with her mother. She wants them to be easy with each other because then when she introduces Hannah there won't be an atmosphere, and Hannah will want to come here. She'll want to be part of the family.

'She's making an effort,' Celia whispers into Ruby's ear when she next wafts by with a plate of cocktail sausages to take to the children.

'So am I,' Ruby mutters. 'There's really no need for you to shepherd us, Celia. We're not infants.'

Ruby thinks afterwards that therein lay the problem with getting along with her mother. She was lulled. Lulled into a false sense of security. And that made her think that they were normal, that they were a mother and daughter who could share confidences without judgement.

She isn't eating much and so the drink goes straight to her head. The room is swimming, a little, not a lot, and she rests her glass on the table, rams two salmon blinis into her mouth. Celia is constantly on the move and Ruby can hear the clatter of dishes from the kitchen. She'll be loading the dishwasher now. Ruby admires her sister for her sense of purpose and order and sheer bloody-minded control. She lets nothing get away from her. She is on every detail and every mood change of every player in her life, like the fairground owner walking on the moving floor of the merry-go-round, setting a child up straight, laying a safe hand on the rider's back.

The garden is divided into three sections. At the front there is the trampoline and the sandpit, the paddling pool and the garden toys. The middle section is a vegetable patch: 'The children need to know that food grows in the ground. That it needs soil, sun and water. It doesn't just appear, ready-wrapped in plastic on a supermarket shelf.' The back third of the garden is a quiet place to sit, an arbour of climbing roses framing a wooden bench. There is a small brass plaque on the bench; the inscription reads: *Gino Romano 1950–2013*.

Her mum is sitting on the bench to one side of the plaque, staring straight ahead. She acknowledges Ruby's presence with a twitch of her lips that could be mistaken for a smile. 'I'm just taking a breather. Joseph's a right little lad now, isn't he?' She really is smiling, Ruby realises. Is that all it took? *A watch?* 'Your dad would have been besotted.'

Celia needs to appear right now, Ruby thinks, but she doesn't and so Ruby blurts out, 'I saw Hannah.'

'What?'

'I saw Hannah.'

'Hannah who?' her mum says and then Ruby watches as the penny drops and her indifferent expression dissolves into alarm. 'How could you have seen Hannah?' She stands up. 'Did you go to Linlithgow?'

'No. I saw her by chance, at a bus stop.'

'When you were watching on the cameras?' She moves in close. '*Ruby?*'

'Of course not!'

'Because that *cannot* be legal.'

'I didn't see her on a camera! I saw her at a bus stop.' Ruby gives a theatrical sigh. *Why did she open her mouth?* 'Fucking forget it! I'm only telling you because I thought you might be interested.'

'Did you speak to her?'

'No.' *Celia, where are you?* Ruby glances behind her but there's no sign of her sister. 'Of course I didn't.'

'Ruby!' She turns back to her mother. 'How can you be sure this girl was Hannah?'

'She looks like me. Well, at first I thought she looked like Celia but of course Celia and I are practically identical.' Ruby laughs, closes her eyes, lets the alcohol lengthen seconds that are made up of sweet, irresistible longing. 'She has my eyes and my smile and—'

'*Stop this!* Stop this now. A stranger with a resemblance does not make ...' Her eyes fill. 'Jesus, Mary and Joseph, Ruby! *Do not* do this.'

'Do *what*? I'm not *doing* anything! I'm not *going* to do anything! What do you take me for, for fuck's sake?'

'Do not ...' Her mother turns towards the bench and touches the inscription. 'Your father ...'

'Why did I think you would understand?'

Her mother stares at the inscription as if she is gathering

strength from it. When she looks back at Ruby, her expression is contorted and Ruby flinches. 'Ruby Romano, what would your father say?' Her face is ugly with reproach. 'What. Would. Your father. Say.'

'Time to sing happy birthday!' It's Celia's voice. 'Come inside everyone.'

'She has Dad's eyes too, Mum,' Ruby says quietly. 'Dad's. Eyes.'

Her mother pushes past her and heads towards the house. Ruby waits a moment then follows her, sees her stride past Celia, who is standing at the door, her mouth open.

'Tell me you haven't been arguing?' she asks Ruby.

'We've been arguing.'

'*What?* I left you alone for five minutes!' She flicks Ruby with the dishtowel. 'You're worse than the kids.'

Ruby walks towards the side gate and Celia follows her.

'I need to make a phone call,' Ruby says.

'What did you argue about?'

'The usual.' The usual … and more. Should she tell Celia about Hannah? Should she confess that she has spent more than a month watching her, and is now contemplating renting a flat opposite where she lives so that she can bump into her 'by accident'?

No. She won't tell her. Not here. Not now. Not with the children milling around and her mother ready to spit in her face.

'Nothing will ever be right,' she says, more to herself than to Celia.

'What do you mean?' Celia says.

Ruby's hands are fists and she holds them to the sides of her temples. Why is she such a fool? Now she won't be able to ease Hannah into the family as if they met through a moment of serendipity because her mother knows that Ruby has seen her. 'Do I never learn?'

'Ruby.' Celia is looking increasingly alarmed. 'What's going on? Who said what? Was she talking about Dad again?' She moves towards her. 'Are you okay?'

Ruby backs off and brings her mobile out of her pocket. 'I really do have to make a call.'

'Make the call and come back inside. Please.'

'I'm best heading off. The phone call will take a while.'

'Ruby …' Celia's face falls. 'You've got me worried now!'

'You know me, Celia. I'm destined to disappoint the people I love.' She throws her arms out. 'It's what I do! You know that! I know that! And our mother sure as fuck knows it!'

'That's not true! You shouldn't say things like that.' Celia shakes Ruby's shoulders. 'You'll end up believing it.'

'She stopped short of telling me that Dad would be turning in the grave I put him in, but she was heading there.'

'Why don't we go upstairs and talk?'

'Please, Celia. Just let me go?' She is on the edge of screaming, of tearing at her own hair or just going back into the house and letting her mother have it. Really letting her have it. 'I'm controlling myself, Celia, because of your kids. Because those precious, happy little moppets don't need to know how fucked up their auntie is.'

'Okay. Okay.' She hugs Ruby and then releases her, grabs her to hug her again. 'But don't beat yourself up. Whatever she's been saying, Mum's not always right about you, Ruby. You do know that, don't you?'

'Yes, I know that.'

Does she? Does she know that? Ruby isn't sure. She

wants her dad. She wants Grant. She sits in her car. She's not going to drive; she's not that drunk or foolish. It's not just because she would be caught on five cameras on her way back home. It's because she avoids causing accidents. Proving her mother wrong. Always trying to prove her mother wrong and in the trying, only ending up proving her right.

'Ruby is an accident waiting to happen.' Her mother said that to her dad when Ruby was eighteen. Her mother said a lot of things about her, now that she comes to think of it. Her mother said to whoever was listening – teachers, the priest, neighbours – that Ruby was an imaginative child. 'She builds whole castles in the air. Sometimes she doesn't know the truth from a fairy tale. She can convince herself of anything, that one.'

Like having an imagination automatically makes you a liar.

It stands to reason her mum doesn't believe her now because her opinion of Ruby is fixed in stone. But Ruby is thirty-nine, not nine, not nineteen, not thirty-four, the age she was when her father died and she temporarily lost her sanity. She was grief-stricken. *Is that a crime?*

Today, in the here and now, Ruby is completely sure of the ground she walks on. Ruby knows who Hannah is. And not for a moment does she doubt herself.

She calls the estate agent from the car and as soon as she's put through to the right person, she gives him the address of the flat she wants to rent.

'It'll be vacant next month,' he says. 'But I already have a couple lined up for it.'

'I want to live in that flat.'

'We have some other properties we'd be happy to show you?'

'I don't want to live in another property. I want to live in that one.'

'We have a ground-floor flat in the same street that's about to come up for rent.'

'I'm an artist and I need the light from the top floor. Can't you offer the ground-floor flat to the couple you have in mind for this one?'

'Well … I could certainly try.'

'I can pay you a deposit and six months rent up front. A year if necessary.'

'But you haven't viewed the flat?'

'No. But I've seen photos of similar flats on your website.'

'Well … let me first of all speak to the couple.'

'I can make it worth their while financially.'

'That's not normally the way we do business, Mrs? Miss?'

Ruby gives him her name and address. She tells him where she works. All of it true because she knows that they will follow through with credit checks. 'Tomorrow,' Ruby says. 'I'll come into your office first thing in the morning.'

She doesn't live far from her sister, just over a mile, and she finds herself jogging most of the way home. When she comes into her kitchen, she catches her breath because for a moment she thinks she sees Grant sitting there, on the chair in front of the glass doors, in his work suit, tie slung across the arm of the chair, his black, polished shoes on the floor beside his feet.

But it isn't him, he isn't there, it's only shadows and light playing tricks on her. She stands in front of the sink and drinks from the tap, her whole face under the stream of water so that when she finishes drinking she has to dry her face.

Hannah.

Ruby knows they'll meet soon. She can feel it in her bones. She closes her eyes to imagine.

'Hannah?' She holds out her hand. 'I'm Ruby. I'm your mum.'

Chapter Six

Hannah is in bed with Jeff when her mum calls. She calls three times: at two in the afternoon, at three fifteen and then at four thirty. First time: 'Remember it's Nana and Grandad's diamond wedding party on Sunday. You are coming home, aren't you, Hannah? Catch the bus with one of your cousins and then you won't be on your own.'

Second time she asks her if she knows where the sleeping bag is. 'Did you take it to the flat with you, Hannah? We'll need it for the weekend.'

The third time? She just wants to talk to her about arrangements, running all the different options past her. Chocolate or coffee cake – Grandad likes coffee but Nana likes chocolate. Sit-down meal or buffet – has to be a buffet because there are thirty family and friends coming and we don't have enough seats or a large enough table for a sit-down. Finger food or a hot meal?

'Honestly, Mum.' Jeff reaches across for the TV remote, his lips grazing hers before he settles back down at her side. 'Whatever's easiest.'

'Yes, but …'

She tunes out and starts filing her nails. Her mum should have adopted half a dozen children, a whole brood of bairns who constantly run back to her knee for advice. She has so much love to give. More than

Hannah can handle. She had suggested fostering but her mum said she wouldn't be able to part with a child once she had bonded with them.

'Remember Pat's allergic to nuts,' Hannah says. Jeff has found a football match and she senses contentment radiating off him in waves. 'Cashews are the worst.'

She has twelve cousins and they're all coming. She lost her virginity to one of them and he seems to think that gives him the right to avoid her as if she's going to ask him for it back. When she comes into a room, he scuttles out like a runaway crab. Is he embarrassed? Ashamed? Afraid? One of these days she's going to ask him.

'Surely everybody eats chicken.' Her nails have been splitting since Clem persuaded her to have a vibrant red shellac manicure, the removal of which has turned her nails to mush. 'You make a good curry.'

'Well, I have to consider Aunt Dee ...' Her mum's sister has been creating merry hell again. 'If only she'd asked me first ... because of Pat ... doing without ...'

'Don't pander to her, Mum.' She stops filing her nails because it's making them worse. They look like she's chewed them to the quick. 'She's not a vegetarian any more.'

'Pat's chronic fatigue is playing up again and ...'

'Uh-huh.' She's reached the eye-rolling stage. 'Absolutely.'

'I'll let you get on, Hannah,' her mum says quickly, sensing boredom in her tone. 'Love you, darling.'

'Love you too!' She makes exaggerated kissing noises. 'And Dad. Bye!'

Hannah tosses the phone onto her bedside table and sighs. She needs to get out, shake off the feeling of hopelessness that often descends on her after she's been talking to her mum. She nudges Jeff with her shoulder. 'Why is the word smother just mother with an s on the front?' She waits for a reply but the forwards are running with the ball. 'Jeff?'

'What?' He slides his hand under the duvet and she immediately draws up her leg so that his hand hits her thigh and goes no further. 'Shutting up shop?'

'I'm sore.'

'Can't take the pace?' He drags his eyes from the screen and gives her his goofy I-want-in-your-knickers smile. His chest is lean and freckled, his hair a curly, dirty-blond mop that really does look like you could wipe the floor with it. It's his eyes that grab her, though. They are friendly, sky blue, mesmerising. As her mum said when she met him, 'He could go places with eyes like those.'

He's been in her bed since midnight. Sixteen hours. They've had sex eight times. (Some people would describe it as fucking but not Hannah because that makes it sound mindless. Okay, so she's not sure she's in love with him but she's not an animal either.)

'Smother and mother,' she says. 'I mean why?'

'Why what?'

'Oh, for fuck's sake.' She sighs again and rolls out of bed, starts picking up clothes from the floor, dressing herself and throwing his onto the bed. 'These are yours. And these. And this.'

'You chucking me out?'

He dodges a shoe and it rebounds off the headboard onto the duvet. 'I've served my function, have I? Used and abused.'

'You can watch the end of' – she looks at the screen – 'whatever team that is.'

'Arsenal.' He stares at her sideways as if she might

have just landed from outer space to be so clueless about the Premiership. It's the first time his expression has been anything other than lustful or sleepy. She slaps the other shoe down onto the back of his hand. 'Ow!' He chucks it back at her. 'She's got you in a right bitchy mood.'

'Just be out of my room when I come home. I'll be tired!'

'Got it.' He reaches for the remote and turns up the volume. 'Are you working tonight?' he shouts after her. 'What time will you be back?'

'In a couple of hours!' She doesn't listen for any more. She checks the time on her mobile, takes the stairs at a run and dashes round the corner for the bus. She's lucky – the driver isn't out to make life more difficult, and so he waits a couple of seconds for her to catch up before pulling away from the kerb.

'Cheers for waiting.' She smiles at him, scans her pass and climbs the stairs to sit up front.

The bus takes its time, wending its way along the streets and stopping frequently for passengers or for traffic. She loves living in Edinburgh. It's vibrant and colourful, and nothing's in your face but everything is classy. Sweet FA happens in Linlithgow. Absolutely nothing. Everything is small and nit-picky: who has bought a new car, whose child bit the other one at nursery. And the weather – always the weather – bit nippy today, where has the wind come from, rain again? When will we ever get a summer?

Edinburgh gives her privacy. Apart from the nosey old bloke across the road who walks his dog at midnight – so he can catch her out, fire twenty questions at her, glance down her top if her coat's open – few people know she exists. She can move through the city without meeting anyone who will ask her how her mum and dad are or did her nana have her op.

Anonymity. She loves it.

Clem told her she would be in Starbucks for half an hour if she wanted to join her, and sure enough there she is, not yet inside the café but standing outside on the corner of George Street and Hanover Street with a girl of about eighteen who is staring down at her stamping feet. Hannah hangs back, unwilling to interrupt, while Clem talks to the girl, but it's clear the girl is nervous. She seems to be pleading with Clem, her expression pained. Clem takes her arm and persuades her along the pavement and Hannah goes into Starbucks, buys herself a coffee and waits.

Clem runs a charity that helps adopted children and their birth parents connect. Hannah first met her five years ago when she was fifteen. She contacted the charity for support after her own birth mother showed up out of the blue. She knew she was adopted, but what she didn't know was that her birth mother would just show up one day, ranting and raving like a mad woman. Hannah had never seriously considered initiating contact with her mother. Of course she had imagined meeting her – most adopted children do. And in her imagination her mother was apologetic, so profoundly sorry to have given up her baby. She would explain the circumstances to Hannah, and Hannah would completely understand. She would be sweet and kind and respectful of Hannah's feelings. She would let Hannah take the lead.

Her birth mother's entry into and exit from her life was nothing like that. It was most definitely not what dreams were made of and it had left Hannah with a bitterness that simmered deep inside her chest like the pot that never boils.

The door opens and Hannah's face lights up at the sight of Clem. 'That seemed to go well.' Clem sits down opposite her, smiling.

'I saw you outside with the girl,' Hannah says. 'Was she meeting her mum for the first time?'

'Yeah. She was nervous, but as soon as they laid eyes on each other they were fine.'

'Like *Long Lost Families*?' Hannah says. Clem's expression tells her she might have got that wrong so she adds, 'Or not. Because nothing is ever like it is on the TV.'

Clem nods. 'I'm sure the footage is edited to show the story from a particular perspective.'

'My mum always changes channel when programmes like that come on.'

'She protects you.'

'You're right. I used to think it was because she found all the emotion embarrassing,' Hannah says. 'But she's just protecting me.'

Clem stands up. 'Another coffee?'

'I'm okay.'

Hannah watches Clem as she waits at the counter for her order. She's one of those people whom everyone responds to with a smile because her attitude is inclusive and interested. Non-threatening. She's been making time for Hannah since she first approached the charity, alone, confused, the whirlwind of her birth mother's intrusion into her life something she couldn't discuss honestly with her parents. Clem was there to pick up the pieces.

'So tell me,' Clem says when she comes back to the table. 'How are you? Your mum and dad? Jeff?'

'My parents are party-planning. And that seems to involve my mum trying to please everyone. She's on a hiding to nothing but there's no point in telling her that.'

'You are ever the optimist,' Clem says, gently teasing.

'Jeff stayed last night. I'm thinking of dumping him.'

'Why?' Clem licks froth off her top lip. 'Last time you told me he kept you cheerful.'

'I suppose ... but I'd quite like to be with someone who I could actually have a conversation with. Jeff has one thing on his mind. Well, two things: sex and food. That about covers it.'

'He's in a band, isn't he?'

'Music, as well then,' she concedes. 'And football.'

'So what do you want him to talk about?'

'I'd just like him to be curious! I mean, for example, I said smother is mother with an s on the front and he was like – what? With a duh expression on his face.'

'Hannah! He's only twenty.'

'It turns out that the words have different roots. Mother comes from the Germanic *modor* and smother is—' She stops speaking and folds her arms. 'Now your eyes are glazing over.'

'He's twenty,' Clem repeats. 'His instincts are mostly basic. That's perfectly normal.'

'Yeah.' She thinks for a second. 'You're right!' She laughs and shakes her head. 'Just ignore me.' She's always been geeky with English – a word Nazi, as one of her cousins calls her – and she doesn't expect Jeff to join in. She has no intention of dumping him; she likes the fact that he's straightforward. What you see is what you get with Jeff and that suits her fine.

'Sometimes we don't know what's good for us,' Clem says.

'Jeff *is* good for me,' Hannah agrees, and is immediately reminded of something that's been bothering her. 'Is that how it is for you and Dave?'

Clem's eyes cloud and clear in the same second. 'Yes, it is.'

Hannah doesn't believe her but the moment is lost as Clem changes the subject to Hannah's university application. English or history? Hannah can't make up her mind and they discuss the pros and cons of each before Clem glances at her watch. 'I better get going. Make sure mother and daughter are managing.' Hannah stands up too and they hug. 'I'll see you soon.'

Clem blows her a kiss before she leaves, and when she's out of sight, Hannah buys another coffee and sits down to watch the world go by. People going about their business: walking, chatting, laughing, arguing, kissing. She searches for mothers and daughters. It's been her habit for longer than she can remember. And like so many of her habits, she can't seem to help herself. She keeps looking until she spots an obvious pairing. They have similar characteristics – long limbs, high foreheads, curly hair – but one of the women is clearly twenty-odd years older than the other. They are standing at the bus stop, metres from the entrance to Starbucks. They are talking, glancing at each other, looking along the street then back to each other. Smiling, not smiling. Idle chat, comfortable silences. Nothing intense. The easy, ordinary communication between them draws Hannah in. It ignites a procession of feelings inside her: jealousy, loneliness, despair, anger. And yet she keeps watching.

Five years ago when her birth mother turned up at her house, she registered a flash of brown eyes – eyes just like her own – staring up at her. She's never forgotten that moment. It still makes her heart chill.

Her mobile is on the table and the screen lights up every minute or so with an alert. When the mother and daughter climb onto the bus, she gives the mobile her attention. There are several alerts from people who are commenting on her blog, a text from Jeff saying he's leaving the flat now and will he see her tomorrow? Then there's a text from a number she doesn't recognise. **I have something to tell you about your birth mother. I wonder whether we could meet?**

At once her heart quickens and she draws a startled breath. What the fuck? *Who* is this? *What* is this? And for the text to arrive now, *right now*, when she's only just been thinking about her birth mother. She glances around the coffee shop expecting to see someone staring at her, someone holding a mobile and making it perfectly clear that they are the messenger.

But no one is paying her any attention. Plenty of customers are staring at screens but they are lost in their own worlds. Hannah is nobody to them. If they look at her at all, they see a young woman with wide eyes and bitten nails. She frequently, often obsessively, thinks about her mother but nobody knows that. There are no mind readers here.

She reads the message again and again and again, willing the words to be dulled by repetition. And when that doesn't happen she deletes the message and walks home across the Meadows, her feet pounding the path, each step an attempt to march her thoughts out of her system.

Adoption.

The fact of her adoption sits on her shoulder like a demon that sleeps little and wakes with a glint in his eye.

Why can't she accept it?

Why does she allow it to dominate her life?

She remembers the lure of the razor blade – cutting – a teenage habit, and one of the few bad habits that she has managed to put behind her. But only because she's replaced it with something else.

She was recently promoted to deputy manager at the restaurant and is just back from a training weekend where the course leader began with a getting-to-know-each-other game. Each participant had to share three statements about themselves: two truths and one lie. Then the other participants would guess the lie, and ice would be broken because they'd shared something of themselves.

When it was her turn she stood up and said, 'My name is Hannah.'

'Hi, Hannah!' twenty-five people said at once.

'The three statements about myself are …' She was planning on saying, 'I'm adopted' to these strangers who didn't know her and didn't matter and would never be in her company again but she couldn't get the words out. She choked. She desperately wanted to speak the truth casually like it was of no consequence but she couldn't say it at all. Instead she said, 'I … I represented Scotland in gymnastics, I play the piano to grade 6 and my dad has won an Olympic medal.'

Almost everyone thought the Olympic medal was the lie. (Her dad won a bronze medal on the shooting range.) Others plumped for her not being any good at gymnastics. (She proved herself afterwards by performing a drunken sequence of backflips and cartwheels across the lawn.) Both of those facts are true but the piano playing? She has no musical ability and gave up the piano within a couple of months.

Perhaps she should have said, My name is Hannah and I used to be an Internet troll. Would they have believed that?

Because she has been the sort of person who commentators discuss on *Woman's Hour* and TV magazine shows. There are worse things – psychopaths, paedophiles, megalomaniacs – but Internet trolling is cowardly and cruel. Her user name was French96. She's not French – obviously – and she wasn't born in 96. You're a fool if you frequent the websites she did and you give away identifying characteristics.

It began simply enough – an urge to hit out at people she saw as pathetic – but then it became more than that. She was quickly banned from the forums that allow adopted children to talk to each other because her comments 'did not conform to community standards'. Moderators swept in to stamp out negativity because God forbid the adopted don't know how lucky they were not to be suffering the misery of frequent foster homes.

She dived deep into the web where forums are unregulated and the pro-anorexia, pro-self-harm, pro-anything-that-is-destructive-and-unhealthy websites breed (for the record, she would never advise anyone to stop eating or to self-harm). It's dark down there. It's harsh and it's bleak. The conversation that takes place is soul-destroying and she found herself watching as a young girl was encouraged to self-harm to the point of suicide.

She reported the website to the police. Anonymously. And she never went there again. She stopped trolling because she came to realise that no one was more pathetic than her. She needed to try to understand herself, not pick on others.

When she arrives home the flat is empty. Jeff has left and her flatmate Anna is studying abroad for most of the year. She's glad she told Jeff to leave because he doesn't approve of drug-taking, which for a musician is plain naff but he's not for turning. She gets down on her hands and knees in front of the sink, 'praying to the god of oblivion,' she says out loud. She buys pills from a dealer in the local pub – she knows what she likes – tried and tested, 'Years of experience, me.' The plastic bag is wedged behind the waste pipe; her hands are shaking as she feels for it and brings it out onto her lap. The drug squad, should they come looking, would find her stash in seconds but not Jeff, nor Anna, who thinks taking paracetamol along with a Lemsip is living dangerously.

She swallows 30 mgs of amitriptyline and opens a bag of crisps – she has to eat otherwise she'll feel nauseous. Then she pours herself a glass of water and sits down in front of her computer screen.

She is still, at last, and the demon on her shoulder whispers in her ear.

I have something to tell you about your birth mother. I wonder whether we could meet?

Who? What? How?

Should she have replied?

Should she?

Should she?

Was the message from her mother, resurfacing after five years to have another try at weaselling her way into her life?

Hannah grits her teeth. Her anxiety levels are pushing nine out of ten but she knows … give it half an hour … and well-being will filter through her limbs like sand through a sieve. And her mind will settle. And she'll be able to sleep.

Better than cutting.

She thinks so, anyway.

Before she logs on to her blog, she visits a couple of forums, both of them for adopted children or parents of adopted children looking for advice. French96 was banned from both these forums but Hannah has other usernames

– catlover81 this time. She keeps up to date with what people are posting but she rarely comments. Janet from Manchester wants advice on how she should meet the half-brother she never knew she had. Should she plan a whole weekend? Start slowly? What should she do?

Comments flood in – supportive, encouraging, touchy-feely. People share their experiences and seem keen for her to learn from their mistakes. Janet has replied to several of the comments, her tone less nervous and more excited. And then a negative comment pops up, Commander99 telling Janet she should stop whining and just get on with it. 'You'll be lucky if your brother likes you. You sound like a right moany little bitch.'

Within minutes, the moderator will block this comment but in the meantime Janet reads it and replies. 'I'm not moaning. I'm genuinely seeking advice. You don't understand how important this is to me.'

Commander99 is typing … Janet clearly hasn't heard the expression 'never feed the trolls' and now she's dropped herself right in it. There's nothing a troll likes more than knowing they've got through to you. He has Janet's attention and he goes in for the kill. Hannah starts reading his reply, then moves on out of there before she starts to pity Janet.

If Janet was to ask Hannah, an ex-Internet troll, for advice she would tell her to beware of being too honest, stay off forums where you bare your soul if your mental health matters to you. Be careful. Ask yourself, Do I know these people well enough to invite them into my living room? If the answer is no then stop talking to them online. Now.

Right now.

Hannah logs on to her own blog and rereads the post she uploaded last night before she reads the comments.

Adoption – Part IV

Let's begin with the pregnant woman you should have called Mum. That woman who pushed you out, or had you cut out of her, that woman doesn't raise you.

What could be the reason?

1. She might be dead – that's fair enough, then.

2. She might be terminally ill or have MS or some debilitating disease that means she can't lift you out of your cot and so for your own safety you have to be adopted. But, like a Hollywood movie, her heart will be broken and she'll die very quickly afterwards.

3. She might not even be a woman, she might be a child herself – fourteen or fifteen years old. She doesn't even know which end of a baby is up and so you really are safer elsewhere. And you understand that – just.

4. She might have been raped. Not good. Not good at all. Who could blame a mother for not wanting that baby?

My birth mother was the age I am now: twenty. She wasn't raped. She wasn't ill. She wasn't dead. She's in a category of her own. This is a mother who gives you away because ... well, because you're an inconvenience. A fidgeting, flailing bundle of baby that squawks and squeals and hijacks her life, and most parents are okay with that because of the love, the hormones, the rush of protection. But not my mother.

Social workers bend over backwards to support young, unmarried women. And most of those mothers will rise to the challenge.

But not my mother.

My mother gave me up.

Before I go any further, I should state for the record that my adoptive parents are lovely people. They are generous and wise. They are intuitive and kind. At a cellular level we are similar – we share human biology – but we don't share DNA.

And that's not nothing.

One good parent is a gift. And children who are raised by two happy-ever-after parents have won the lottery. Take my boyfriend, Paul. He has the confidence of a much-loved child. He is like the ready brek advert and his warmth fills the space around him.

Ellie tells me that two good parents are two good parents. It doesn't matter whether they're biologically yours or not. So why do I hanker after something deeper? Does that something deeper even exist? Or is it just something I've persuaded myself of because I'm insular, self-absorbed, a narcissist?

My brother Mark keeps his head busy with rules and equations. Who knows what his heart longs for?

Let me know what you think.

Her blog is anonymous and she intends to keep it that way so she seeds through lies that will throw her adoptive parents off the scent should they ever come across it; Luddites both, it's unlikely, but then the unlikely does happen – she speaks as one who knows.

She is an only child, but blog-Hannah has a brother called Mark and a friend called Ellie. Mark is five years older than her and the story she's spun is that their parents adopted him when he was two. He'd been in foster care since birth because his mother was an addict. She described imagined photos of him. He was tiny, wide-eyed, cute as a button. Unlike her, he turned out to be some sort of genius and is an avid academic. He's completing a PhD in molecular science.

Ellie is the friend she created to show the other side of adoption: the happily adopted child who lends no weight to biology and sees her parents as her parents – end of story. Ellie is partly based on real-life Clem (Clem's generosity of spirit rather than the details of Clem's upbringing, which is punctuated with neglect and abuse) and she balances blog-Hannah's rants. Ellie offers up an alternative to her one-sided angst.

So on the one hand her blog is make-believe. But on the other hand, it reveals more truth about Hannah than she could ever express in 'real' life. The truth lies in the emotions and the understanding, not in the particulars. Her blog saves her from saying what she really thinks to the people who are actually in her life. Her current parents don't deserve to be criticised or hurt, not by Hannah, not by anyone. They are her 'current' parents because the first couple who adopted Hannah died. The circumstances of their deaths had a Roald Dahlesque feel except that you couldn't – wouldn't – make it up. Hannah blamed herself for their deaths because she had nagged them for an ice cream and so her father stopped the car and they all climbed out to buy some. Hannah had run ahead into the shop and missed being struck at forty miles an hour, as they were, when a man mounted the pavement in his car. He'd had a heart attack. It was bad luck that her parents were there at the time. That's what the policeman told her.

Bad luck.

She spent the next two years in a series of foster homes. She doesn't remember much about the homes except that she refused to speak and she cried a lot. Then her current parents came along and adopted her. She was seven years old. Her eczema was rampant and she had begun to wet the bed. That didn't put them off. She's not exaggerating when she says they're good people.

She reads through the comments, deciding whether or not to publish them. There are ten: two are supportive, six are sparky and critical, two are obnoxious. She bins the two obnoxious ones, publishes the others and begins to answer them.

Linda204 takes issue with her self-absorption. **You need to spend more time being grateful! Take a leaf out of Ellie's book.**

BecauseIcare34 has commented on her blog before. She likes to point out the obvious. **You seem really selfish to me. You even admit to being a narcissist! If your parents are so nice, what's your problem?**

TRO123 has also commented before and likes to push her to explain herself. **How can you be sure your mother gave you up because she couldn't be bothered keeping you?**

This is the hardest comment to respond to because she wants to tell him some of the truth but not all of it. After five minutes of typing and deleting, she settles for: **She made no secret of it and told several people at the time. I have no reason to disbelieve those people.**

She sits back and stares at the screen as she waits for him to reply but he doesn't and by now the drug has taken hold. Her muscles, her organs, the very bones of her have softened to cotton wool. All thoughts of adoption and text messages and blogs have drifted downstream.

The demon on her shoulder has flown the coop. She goes through the motions of getting ready for bed but she's blissfully, overwhelmingly shattered and can barely put one foot in front of the other. She doesn't bother cleaning her teeth and slides under the duvet into the foetal position. Within moments sleep takes her hand and carries her off on a cloud until morning.

Chapter Seven

Next day Hannah wakes up to a question. It's five in the morning but the question is urgent enough to startle her from sleep, knocking at the inside of her skull like a woodpecker to a tree.

How did the texter get her mobile number?

She's not going to think about the message – she's going to focus on working out how this person got her number because this is solvable. She never gives her number to insurance companies or shops. She hasn't registered it on any social media sites. She's not a great socialiser and if people other than her family, Clem or Jeff want to contact her, they do so by email. She can count on the fingers of two hands the names of the people who have her number. Stands to reason, then, that the texter must have been in touch with one of them.

She decides to start with Clem and drops in to see her on her way to work. Clem runs the charity from an office space in the Grassmarket, two floors up a narrow, winding staircase. The huge windows, draughty in winter, overlook the bustle of the Grassmarket, and if you crane your neck to the left you can just about catch sight of the edge of Edinburgh Castle brooding on the ancient rock. There are three rooms: a waiting room, the office and a meeting room. None of the rooms are more than a few metres across but they're fit for purpose.

Clem never mentions the events that brought Hannah to her door five years ago. Sometimes Hannah wishes she would talk about it and then there would be an opportunity for her to find out what Clem knows about her birth mother because Clem and Hannah's parents kept the details from her. 'Not to upset you.' That's what they told her at the time, and for her to bring it up now when she has feigned disinterest for the past five years would shine the spotlight squarely on her and she's far too secretive for that.

But still, she can't quite let go of Clem because, despite the unbalanced nature of their friendship, Clem helps her to feel normal. Before she came here, Hannah had never met anyone else who was adopted and it was a revelation to see how other people dealt with it. She no longer felt quite so alone – still weird, still angry, still disconnected – but not alone in that.

Clem is reading through a case file when Hannah comes into the office. 'Hello you! This is a surprise.'

'I was just passing,' Hannah says.

'Perfect timing. I need a cuppa.' Clem puts her arm through Hannah's as they walk across to the kettle. 'It's been one thing after another in here today.'

While the kettle boils and then Clem dunks the teabags, they talk about Clem's cat who has had an operation for a swelling above his eye. 'I'm hoping he'll be well enough to come home this evening. Dave's on his way to the vet's now.' She glances at Hannah and smiles. 'And talking of Dave, he was saying last night that you should come to our summer party this year.' She names a date and time. 'And Jeff too, of course. I know you couldn't make it last year.'

She hadn't made it last year because she didn't trust herself. She didn't think much of Dave. Correction, she couldn't stand him. It wasn't just that he was punching way above his weight with Clem. He was a bully and she couldn't help but want to pick a fight with him.

'Thanks for the invite,' she says. 'I'll do my best to come.'

'Great!' Clem looks genuinely pleased. 'Fingers crossed the weather will be fine and we can have it in the garden.'

She goes back to chatting about her cat and then when she pauses to drink her tea, Hannah says, 'While I'm here, Clem, I've got this … well … yesterday I had a text from a number I didn't recognise and I wondered whether you'd given out my mobile number?'

'Given it to whom?'

'I don't know.'

'I would never give your number out, Hannah.' She frowns. 'Not without speaking to you first.'

'I didn't think so but …'

'What did the text say?'

'I don't remember the exact wording but it was something to do with my birth mother.' Clem waits for her to say more. 'I wasn't tempted to reply,' Hannah adds. 'I never think about her.' She swallows down the urge to say, She's dead to me. Dead and buried. Or at least, that's what I want her to be but in actual fact I think about her every day. Sometimes every hour of every day. How crazy is that? Oh, and by the way, did I mention that I hate her?

Clem touches her upper arm. 'It's your journey, Hannah. It's not for me nor anyone else to tell you what to do, what to feel, how to react.' Hannah tries for a smile. 'Would you like me to reply for you?'

'I deleted it.'

'Well, if it happens again and you want my help,' Clem says, 'I'm here for you.'

'I know.' Hannah gives her a hug. 'Thank you.'

They hold the embrace for a few seconds before, 'Not interrupting, am I?'

It's Dave.

Hannah freezes at the sound of his voice but what's worse is that, for a split second, she feels Clem freeze too.

'I thought you were on your way to the vet!' Clem is across the room and kissing her boyfriend before Hannah can prepare her smile. Clem had a black eye once; Hannah has never forgotten that. When she'd asked Clem about it, she'd mumbled something about sliding on spilt water into an open cupboard door.

'And how are you, Hannah?' Dave says, managing to sound as if he cares.

'Good.'

'Popped in for a chat?'

'Something like that,' Hannah says.

He gives her a wide, false smile; he is a bad actor auditioning for the 'good guy' role in the play.

'Clem was telling me about the party,' Hannah says.

'We're hoping you're able to come this year.' He's holding the smile. 'No pressure, though. Might not be your scene.'

'I can definitely make it,' Hannah says, watching his jaw tighten.

Clem is looking from one to the other, her eyes lingering on Dave. She changes when she's around him. She becomes fidgety and overly alert as if she's trying to anticipate what he will say, and do, and want. It makes Hannah wonder at the power some men have over women. Clem is a perfectly sensible grown-up woman who manages a difficult role, liaising with professionals, using her insight to right wrongs, but when it comes to Dave she turns to water, yielding at every turn.

'Weird,' Hannah says under her breath as she walks up the hill to work. 'Weird and sad.' She wishes she could help her but the balance of their friendship would have to shift and Clem is always very protective of the details of her private life. She is the one who gives the help and advice. She's not the one who receives it. Or if she is receiving advice, then it's not from Hannah.

Hannah arrives at the restaurant in good time and catches up with the staff on the evening shift. Most of them don't have English as their first language but they know the task-specific vocabulary they need and are willing to work hard. She checks in with the chef to make sure all the deliveries have arrived. He gives her the thumbs up and then she steps outside to make a phone call to her parents. They like her to talk to both of them at the same time and automatically put her onto speaker. They tell her how their party preparations are coming along – everyone's having parties, Hannah thinks. Two in quick succession will definitely be a record for her – and are five minutes into the conversation when her dad says, 'Should you not be at work?'

'I'm here. First booking's not for twenty minutes.'

'We'll let you go then, love ...'

'Before I go, I wanted to ask whether either of you gave out my mobile number?'

'No,' her dad says. 'Not me.'

'Me neither,' says her mum. 'Oh! Unless you count Clem.'

'Clem?'

'Well, not Clem herself, but her secretary. She had lost your contact details.'

'Right.' Clem doesn't have a secretary. She can barely

afford to pay herself. Everyone else who works there is a volunteer.

'I didn't do the wrong thing, did I?' her mum says. 'You are still friendly with Clem? If you've fallen out with her or something—'

'No, no. It's fine, Mum. Clem and I are good mates.'

'That's what I thought.'

Hannah ends the call and leans against the wall to think. At times like this she wishes she was a smoker but she has to make do with biting her nails. She'd tried smoking once, with the same cousin who took her virginity, but not only did it make her feel sick, she didn't get much of a hit from it. As drugs go, it was a minor high and not worth the money.

So … She stares upwards, at the ancient stone walls that rise four storeys above her, all shades of grey shot through with silver streaks. The Royal Mile has social history embedded in the very walls, centuries of construction, pre-dating the Reformation and stretching forward in time to Queen Victoria and her relentless empire-building. A hotchpotch of culture writ large and small through every hand that laid a stone. She's been thinking about studying Scottish history at university; she's been reading about Edinburgh's past. About the evolution of architecture, creation and re-creation, as fire, flood and plague stole along the streets.

And now the twenty-first century is all about preservation. Building control and regulations, security cameras, attached to the walls, so high as to be resolutely out of reach, but low enough to spy. She shields her eyes from the late evening sun and stares up at one of the cameras, perched like an eagle on the lookout for a scampering mouse.

So … the mystery person who has something to tell

her about her birth mother is a woman. One who has no problem confidently impersonating a secretary. And while her mum isn't exactly cautious, she's not a pushover either. The woman must have been convincing enough to talk her mother into giving out her daughter's number.

Who, then? How would she even know about Hannah's relationship with Clem? Who could she be?

The anger that simmers in Hannah's chest thickens and boils. It has to be her birth mother. The woman who caused havoc five years ago, who approached her illegally, who frightened her, shocked her, caused her to spiral into confusion, that woman is back for more.

Still playing games.

Bitch.

She works four evening shifts at the restaurant – four in a row – which leaves no time for Jeff as he works in the daytime and is often gigging with his band in the evening. Twice he meets her at the end of her shift and they walk to the bus stop together but she doesn't invite him back to hers because she's tired. That's what she tells him, but really it's because she needs to go online and roam around, read posts and connect with like-minded people.

One of those evenings she meets the dog walker on the pavement ahead of her. She gets the feeling he's been hanging around, waiting for her to turn the corner, and as he's closer to the stair door than she is, there's no way for her to avoid talking to him. His terrier regards her with disdain, then carries on sniffing at the base of the lamppost. She doesn't much like dogs but she pretends to because good people, nice people, trustworthy people like dogs, don't they? It says something about a person if you like dogs and dogs like you. But they can sniff out the phoney human and when she bends down to stroke his wiry fur his tail doesn't wag.

'A woman moved into the top-floor flat today,' nosey bloke says. He points upwards at the flat across the road from her. 'Says she's not bothered about the stairs. She's after the light.' Hannah keeps walking towards her stair door and he falls into step beside her. 'She paints. I'm not sure whether it's landscapes or portraits or something more modern.' He gives a dismissive snort. 'Time will tell.' The dog cocks his leg on the lamppost outside the stair door, watching Hannah as he does so, daring her to tell him off. 'She doesn't have that much furniture but there was a delivery of canvases. Big ones, small ones and all the sizes in between.'

'That's nice.'

'You doing okay?'

'Never better.'

'I see your boyfriend coming and going.' She twists her key in the lock. 'Entry pad up and running now?'

'Yes.' She walks inside the entrance to the stair and briefly looks back at him. 'Goodnight.'

'Don't forget to put your bins out.' His foot is wedged in the gap, preventing the door from closing. 'They'll be here by seven.'

'Thank you.' She climbs the stairs quickly and as she turns the key in the lock, she hears the main door slam shut. One of these days he'll follow her up the stair and then she'll have to tell him to piss off. 'Creep,' she says out loud, kicks off her shoes, drops her coat onto the sofa and sits down in front of her computer screen. She's written another post: Adoption Part V. She uploads it onto her blog, then has a shower and a tidy up. The flat is blissfully quiet. She used to be lonely when she was alone. Used to feel the lack of friends as a personal failure. She had some friends at school but they all moved on, one way or another, university mostly. She lost touch with them apart from on social media where they're all having wildly exciting times, leading popular and busy lives.

Or are they? Hannah thinks probably not. She thinks most of what they say is nothing more than an exaggerated snapshot, isolated fragments of their lives magnified and amplified. It seems to her that most of them exist on the brink of loneliness and failure because they're so desperate to be 'liked' and 'followed' and 'shared'.

Hannah hasn't felt lonely for a couple of years now, partly because of Jeff but mostly because she's self-sufficient. She's resilient. And she's learned to pat herself on the back for that.

When she's finished tidying up and returns to her computer, there are several responses to her blog post. She takes her time to answer them, lets midnight become the witching hour before she heads to bed. She hasn't had another text and she doesn't expect to.

The bitch didn't try very hard. Hannah doesn't know whether to feel angry or relieved.

And I'm definitely not disappointed, she tells herself. Not in the least.

Her dad is dressed in a checked shirt and brown cords. He is stockily built and his stomach grows a little year on year, meaning he's had to adjust the waistband to sit underneath the bulge. He has faded blond hair and grey eyes – both her parents do – and 'Scottish skin' – pale, freckled and blue-veined. It's blindingly obvious that she's from a whole other gene pool. Her eyes are dark and her skin is a rich cappuccino. Aside from her copper-coloured hair, she looks like she belongs in the Mediterranean and so she wasn't surprised when she found out that her mother was an Irish/Italian Scot. Her birth mother, that is, because the woman standing in front of her is most definitely her mother. As soon as she hears the sound of her daughter's voice at the front door talking to her dad, she is beside them in a flash, drying her hands on her apron before reaching out to hug her.

'Lovely to have you home, darling.' She squeezes Hannah's shoulder. 'I've made some carrot cake for you to take back with you. It's just for you and Jeff. I've hidden it at the back of the kitchen cupboard so that none of your greedy cousins find it.'

'I'm not sure they're hankering after cake,' her dad says, smiling. 'They're outside getting stuck into the beers.'

'Outside?' Hannah says.

'We saw the weather forecast and we thought we'd attempt a barbecue.'

Her mum shakes her head. 'I tried, Hannah.'

'Nana and Grandad are sitting in comfy chairs close to the barbie, blankets over their knees and as long as the rain doesn't tip it down we'll all be fine,' her dad says, grinning. (He's always cheerful, her dad. No matter what. 'As long as nobody's dead.' That's his benchmark. 'Anything else we can cope with.')

She moves through the house, saying hello to relatives, and ends up in the garden where she chats to her nana and granddad for half an hour before going back inside to help her mum finish the preparations. Several people are in there supposedly helping, including her Aunt Dee who is leaning up against the sink, and she can tell from the set of her mum's shoulders that she's already getting on her nerves.

'How's the restaurant going?' Dee asks her.

'Busy.' Her mum wordlessly passes Hannah a cucumber and she starts to chop it.

'You're bound to be busy when you're so close to the castle.'

'We get passers-by coming in, but people also book months in advance.'

'You still working the evenings?'

'The manager works lunchtimes.'

'I would worry about you going home at that time of night.'

'It's fine.' She tips the cucumber slices into a bowl. 'I've had the odd guy harassing me at the bus stop—'

'You didn't tell us that!' her mum says.

'It wasn't worth mentioning. Just a drunk being an ars—' One of her small girl cousins is staring at her, listening acutely as she shovels peanuts into her mouth. 'Drunk,' she says. 'A drunk being a drunk.'

'Not an arsehole then,' her dad says into her ear. 'Well saved.'

She hands him the bowl of cucumber. 'Who's in charge of the cooking out there?'

'Alex is rising to the challenge.'

Alex and Hannah have been thrown together since they were small because Alex is her dad's favourite brother's son. There are seven brothers and sisters on her dad's side, and on her mum's side there are four sisters – a veritable glut of family. Only her parents were unable to add to the baby count as, year in and year out, cousins were born.

Alex is the cousin she slept with and he's been pretty much avoiding her ever since – not so that other family members would pick up on it, but he went from seeking out her company to giving her a wide berth. So hours later, after everyone's eaten their fill and she's drunk two triple vodkas and two glasses of wine, she takes a six-pack from the drinks table and follows him down the side of the house. 'Well done on the barbie,' she says.

He is sitting on the low wall that borders the neighbour's garden and he immediately jumps to his feet. 'I'll be ...'

'You'll be what?' Hannah challenges, blocking his way. 'Five years not long enough?'

'What do you mean?'

'Why do you avoid me?' she says.

'I don't.'

'Not much.' She nods towards the garden hut, which is just visible at the end of the path. 'As first times go it could have been worse.'

He says nothing, pulls a packet of cigarettes from his pocket.

'Was it that bad then?'

'No! Of course not, but ...' He offers her a cigarette. She shakes her head and passes him a beer. 'Awkward, you know. With what happened afterwards and ...'

A bulb lights up inside her brain. 'That wasn't because of you! That was because ...' Was there any part of her life her birth mother hadn't infected? 'That was because my ...' She had taken time off school, been 'under the doctor' as her nan would say. 'It wasn't you,' she repeats.

He watches her face for a second then laughs. 'You were determined to tell me all about spiders,' he says.

'I was.' She sees he is remembering and lets herself remember too.

She was sitting on the lawnmower waiting for him. He'd gone to pinch some booze from behind the adults' backs.

While she waited, she watched a spider repair her web. She liked spiders. She still does. Common as muck yet gifted with genius, they weave seven kinds of silk: one to wrap prey, one to wrap eggs and five to construct the web itself. Each type of silk comes from a separate set of spigots in the spinnerets and can be strong and super-stretchy, or strong and inelastic, or stretchy and sticky. So-called dragline silk, used to anchor the web, has a higher tensile strength than steel.

When Alex came back into the hut with a plastic cup of lukewarm wine for them – 'Best I could do,' he said – she pointed to the spider.

'Did you know the silk's strength comes from the way the amino acids are joined together and—'

'Right.'

He held the plastic cup to her mouth and she drank half of it before pulling back to finish her sentence. '... scientists are trying to copy the structure.'

He finished the wine and placed a finger to her lips. And then his hands were inside her T-shirt and down the front of her trousers and it felt good – better than good – it felt exquisite and vital and intense. She was experiencing each second with a clarity that she'd never felt before, and she forgot about spiders and parents and being adopted.

Bliss.

'We should be friends, Alex,' she says, cracking open a beer.

'We should,' he says. 'Although you are a bit scary.'

She turns to face him.

'But I can overlook that,' he adds.

'I'm scary?' She makes a face. 'How?'

'It's the way you are.' Her eyes widen and then he shakes his head. 'Not because you're adopted. It's because you're kind of ...' He stops talking until he comes up with the right word. 'Enigmatic. That's what you are. I never know what you're thinking.'

'Do you ever know what a girl is thinking?'

'Fair play.' He laughs. 'But you?' He points the can at her before tipping beer into his open mouth. He takes time to swallow, making loud, unnecessary glugging noises as it goes down his throat, before running the back of his hand over his mouth. 'You're harder than most.'

'You've drunk too much.'

'Aye.' He burps. 'Maybe. But that doesn't mean we're wrong.'

'We're wrong?' A chill settles on her shoulders. 'Is that what everyone thinks then?'

'Not everyone. Just me,' he back-pedals. 'I meant me.'

'Aunties, uncles, cousins. Nobody gets me because I'm the cuckoo in the nest?'

'No!' He gives an exasperated sigh. 'Fuck's sake, Hannah. Why do you make everything about adoption? It's got nothing to do with that! It's to do with the way you are. You're secretive; you keep yourself to yourself. And you're downright unfriendly sometimes, like you're looking down your nose at all of us.'

She stands up and he immediately looks regretful. 'Hannah. Don't go.' His tone is soft. 'Sit down. Please.'

Pity is so corrosive. She feels it burn inside her heart like acid on skin.

'Sit back down.' He reaches for her hand but she slaps him away. 'I'm not meaning to offend you, Hannah, but you are fucking weird sometimes.' He smiles, trying to make light of it. 'Weird in a good way. Like you don't give a shit. That's awesome.'

It's not awesome because this is her family and she does give a shit. She wants to bawl like a three-year-old.

She wants to run upstairs and throw herself onto her childhood bed. She wants to kick him in the teeth.

She walks away.

'What the fuck! Come back, will you?'

Her heart pounds and words tumble through her mind, every one in capital letters. Words like MISFIT and LONER and LOSER. She goes back inside and almost walks into the kitchen but stops just short of it when she hears her Aunt Dee's voice.

'She was *so* good at English at school,' she says. 'You really should encourage her to do better.' Hannah's mother mumbles something she can't make out. 'And is she still friendly with the girl at the adoption charity? That can't be healthy, can it? Not with everything that went on. You must worry about her mental health, surely?'

'Enough, Dee.' It's her dad's voice, quiet but firm. 'Hannah is our daughter and we're very proud of all she's achieved. I'll thank you to keep your opinions to yourself.'

Hannah knows her aunt will flounce out of the room now that she's been told off so she quickly sidesteps into the living room and waits there until she hears the click-clack of her aunt's heels on the lino.

'I'm sure I didn't mean to offend!' Dee shouts back. 'Always so sensitive in this house.'

Alex and now Dee. Hannah tries to take a deep breath but her ribcage is rigid and she has to force in the air until it hurts. She tips her head right and left and feels tension in her neck, and when her head is at an angle she sees something shiny under the chair. She bends down to pick it up, slides it into her pocket just as her dad comes into the room, his fingers spread wide with the stems of upside-down wine glasses.

'Here you are, Hannah! I'm just putting the posh glasses back.' He opens the display cabinet and carefully arranges the glasses on the shelves. 'We bought enough of the plastic ones and your mum's worried these'll get smashed.' He takes her arm. 'Fancy a game of table tennis? Uncle Bob's set it up.'

'I can't, Dad. I have to go.'

'What?' His pale eyebrows sag with disappointment.

'It's Jeff. He's hurt his hand and is in A and E.' She lets tears fill her eyes. 'They might have to operate.'

'Oh no, love.' He hugs her. 'What a shame for the lad!'

Her dad's hugs should be bottled and sold to the public; he'd be a rich man. He can't give her a lift back to Edinburgh because he's had a drink but he insists on paying for a taxi for her. Her mum packs up the carrot cake. 'Text us later and let us know how Jeff is.'

As she says her goodbyes, she's aware of Alex shaking his head from the sidelines. And she's also aware of her Aunt Dee, who is wandering around asking people whether they've seen her bracelet. 'It must have fallen off when I was washing my hands.' She waves Hannah across to her. 'You haven't seen it, Hannah, have you?'

'No. Sorry.' She kisses her cheek. 'Good to see *you*, though.' She kisses her other cheek. 'Thank you for worrying about my mental health but I assure you I'm fine.'

'What?' Guilt flashes across her sunbed-tanned face but she quickly recovers. 'Now Hannah ...'

Hannah walks away.

When she arrives home she texts her parents: **I'm at the hospital now. Hopefully no operation. We're just**

waiting for the consultant. Jeff says thank you for the cake!

They both answer at once with comforting, kind messages. She replies with kisses and sets her mobile aside. Her bedroom is sparsely furnished: a king-size bed, a fitted wardrobe and a small bureau that her parents bought her as a present when she left home. They were surprised she wanted a bureau – her mum thought a dressing table would be better – but Hannah wanted a lockable space.

She feels for the key underneath the mattress and unlocks the front of the bureau. Inside there's a shoebox containing a disparate assortment of things. She takes everything out and lays the pieces on the dining table: a pen, a feather, a bookmark, a small porcelain cup, one hoop earring, a miniature photo frame, an ivory piano key, a spider key-ring, a plastic banana … and so on. She has collected all these pieces at critical moments that punctuate her life.

She adds Dee's bracelet to the collection. It's silver-plated, not worth a lot but Hannah expects her aunt will never let go of the fact that it's missing and her mum will have to move furniture, look under rugs, peer into drains most probably.

This is her other secret habit. Collecting small, mostly insignificant things that belong to other people. Technically that makes her a thief but, in her defence, she takes things that other people won't miss. For the most part anyway. Tonight she broke that rule but that was Alex's fault because his observations unnerved her. He has to be the least observant person she's ever met so if he has clocked her as a lonely, secretive loser then other people who are a lot smarter than him will be thinking the same. And saying she makes everything about adoption. Does she? Well, yes. She does. She's willing to admit that to herself. But she had no idea that everyone else knew it too.

She gathers all her memorabilia back into the shoebox. She knows each of the pieces by heart – the shape, the feel, even the smell. She places them carefully in the box, adding the bracelet last. She'll remember this day for ever now. This is the day Alex and Dee gave her insight into the way the family view her. It seems she's fooling nobody. And by the sounds of it Dee is expecting her to go the same way as her mother – a ranting, crazy woman who gets carted off in a yellow van.

She takes a sleeping pill, then sits down at the table to write another blog post. It's her preferred route to catharsis. (Dee was right about one thing: she really is good at English.)

Adoption Part VI

I haven't had a good day today. It should have been a good day. I wanted it to be a good day. The whole family were gathered to mark my mum's sixtieth birthday. She was looking lovely in a twinset and pearls – don't mock, she suits that style.

Ellie came with me. She loves my parents and they love her. Who wouldn't love Ellie? My regular readers will know that despite her impoverished beginnings, she is made from sunshine. She was two when she was adopted. She had been neglected since birth and was finally removed from her mother's 'care' when neighbours called social services. Her mother was out on a pub-crawl and Ellie's nappy was so water- and poo-logged that it was flapping halfway down her legs. Her pyjamas were stained with ten-day-old tomato ketchup and grease. She was lifted out of that squalor into the world of tree-lined streets and private education, ballet lessons and holidays in the Maldives. She was a straight A student and she's in her third year at medical school.

Apart from hanging about with me, Ellie is perfect. She has an enviable ability to ignore all the negative stuff while my antennae are alert to everything that makes me feel excluded. I don't think my family even know they're doing it. 'You're just like Mum,' an aunt says to my dad. 'She always loved a lemon meringue pie.'

'Isn't the baby lucky to have inherited his mum's eyes and his dad's smile?' someone else says about a new-born cousin. 'Perfect combination.'

'Uncle Pat was always a natural swimmer.'

'It's all in the genes,' my uncle says. He even looks at me when he says it. Like the reality of my adoption doesn't exist.

Like I don't really exist.

It gets worse – no good ever comes from listening at doors. I should have known better but I came inside to go to the loo and heard my name being spoken. 'We can't know with her, though, can we?' my aunt was saying. 'The little we do know about her background isn't particularly good. What with her mum and ...'

'We'll just have to keep an eye out,' my dad says. 'And if she shows any signs of going the same way as her mother then we'll do something about it.'

I walk into the room then and demand to know what they mean about my mother. At first they don't want to tell me but when they do start talking it's a shock.

In a nutshell – my mother is crazy. I've suspected this for some time but I haven't wanted to believe it.

Mental illness is often inherited, isn't it? Or not

always, but whatever has triggered her could also trigger me, couldn't it? Does that make me a ticking time bomb?

What say you, readers?

She uploads the post onto her blog and climbs into bed. The pill has kicked in and it makes her too tired to wait for comments. What does she actually remember from five years ago? A lot, actually, but she doesn't want to examine the details. She doesn't want to rehash the whole sorry tale over in her mind because she's depressed enough as it is.

She hears a text arrive and drags herself out of bed to see whether it's another one from her parents. If she doesn't answer them, they'll send more messages and then they'll call and if she still doesn't answer, they'll be knocking at her door. She's not exaggerating – they've done it before.

The text isn't from either of them. It's a second text from the unknown number. **Sorry to bother you again but I need to talk to you about your mother.**

Surprise forces her wide awake, her heartbeat booming in her ears. She types: **WTF? Who are you?** Her finger hovers over the send button but she changes her mind and deletes it, writes instead: **If you have something to tell me, just get on with it.**

This time she does press send. And then she types some more: **If it's you who's texting me, Ruby Romano, insane as you were, are, will be, with your crazy eyes and your banshee screaming—**

Before she sends this message, a reply comes back. It's a man (apparently). He tells her that he's a friend of her mother's. He asks to meet her so that **I can give you the details.**

She sits on the edge of her bed and stares at the screen. Adrenalin demands fight, flight or freeze. And at first she is frozen, in body if not in mind. There is a choice to be made and she feels, she knows, that this is one of those significant moments that will direct the course of her life. Flight is not an option – she can't run away – not from this. These last five years she's been marking time, treading water in life's enormous swimming pool, waiting for a moment like this.

'Fight then,' she says out loud. 'I'll fight.' She smiles into the air. 'Bring it on.'

I'll meet you, she texts back.

Then she climbs back into bed and is asleep in seconds.

Chapter Eight

She wakes up to half a dozen comments on her blog. They can be divided into the empathetic, the reality-checkers and the trolls.

Ratty1166 is the empathetic sort: I feel for you. I've been in a similar position as yourself. She goes on to tell Hannah what she did and how much the Samaritans helped. And she ends with advice to approach one of the agencies that helps adopted children come to terms with the facts of their parenting. She even finds an address for Hannah in Manchester (blog-Hannah lives in Manchester). It's an organisation similar to Clem's charity.

TrishaTen20 is pushing for her to widen her view. I've read your blog posts with interest and I'd like to speak out as the mum of an adopted child. FYI – There are adoptive parents who feel like they got a raw deal. It's the luck of the baby draw and in their private moments, they wonder why they bothered. Your parents have invested heart and soul and a great deal of cash into raising you and all you can do in return is to bleat on about genetics and someone who never cared for you. Think about your parents, for once. You're very immature and lacking in perspective.

BecauseICare34 is back. Get over yourself! YOU are obsessed with the fact of your adoption, YOUR FAMILY ARE NOT.

TRO123 is also back. Sometimes she thinks he's more troll than commentator but she likes his way of thinking. You sound like you're in love with Ellie. Are you sure you're not a lesbian?

And then we move on to the trolls: The sooner you lose your shit the better. Then it'll be one less person clogging up the Internet with self-pitying bollocks.

Your mother gave you away because she knew you'd end up like this – a whingeing whore with no friends.

She bins the trollers' comments and uploads the first four. She answers each one with the same sentence: I'm searching for like-minded souls, someone who gets the essential me. I'm not sure you do but thank you for taking the time to comment.

Another text arrives. He gives her details of a time and place to meet. She has a couple of hours to kill first and is just thinking that Jeff could be the answer when the bell goes.

'It's your neighbourhood sex pest,' Jeff says, heavy-breathing into the microphone. 'Let me in at your peril.'

She presses the buzzer to release the main door and then she hangs over the banisters to watch him bound up the stairs. 'I was just thinking about you,' she says.

He gives her a quick kiss. 'You think of me and I appear, oh goddess.' He holds up a litre of milk and a packet of chocolate breakfast cereal. 'I've been hunting and gathering.'

'You can come in then.'

He walks past her into the kitchen and takes a couple of bowls from the cupboard. 'I bumped into that old guy with the dog. He said you didn't put your bins out last week.' He rips the top off the cereal packet and fills the bowls. 'He'll be reporting you to major crimes if you're not careful.'

'If anyone's the sex pest, he is.' She starts to pour the milk into Jeff's bowl and he dips a spoon into it before she's even finished. 'He almost followed me into the stair.'

'Don't give him an excuse to make a citizen's arrest.'

'I'm serious,' she says, sitting down opposite him. 'He gives me the creeps.'

'I'll have a word with him.'

'Don't. You'll make it worse.'

'Man to man.' He pushes out his chest. 'I'll take him down an alleyway and threaten him.'

'And his dog hates me.'

'Then I'll have a word with his dog too.'

'But you love dogs!'

'Not as much as I love you.' His eyes capture hers to tell her he means this and when he has her in his thrall, he takes advantage of her dreamy, grateful expression to swap his almost empty bowl for her almost full one. 'Just give me the word and sex pest won't know what hit him.'

'Actually. Listen. I do have something to ask you. If you speak to my parents, or they come into the shop, you'll need to continue with the pretence that you injured your hand.'

'What pretence?' He holds up both his hands and turns them over, looking for faults. 'Did I say I'd injured my hand?'

'No, you didn't, I did. I needed an excuse to leave the party yesterday and it was the first thing that came into my mind. I couldn't take any more of cousins and aunties and the usual family shit.'

'Fair enough.' He shovels more cereal into his mouth and crunches it quickly before saying, 'So what exactly did I do to my hand?'

'I didn't say.'

'Was there blood involved, do we think? Should I wear a bandage?'

'I said it was touch and go whether you needed an operation so you could have a bandage handy just in case they do come into the shop.'

Jeff works in a music store in town. He plays the guitar and he's in a band – it's his passion – and her parents supported him through a crowd-funding project when the band needed sound equipment. Whenever they come into Edinburgh they drop by to see him. For them, Jeff is a window into their daughter's life. Her boyfriend is creative, easy-going and handsome. This is reassuring and she is automatically elevated in their eyes.

'And my mum made you a carrot cake but I left it in the taxi.'

'I'll tell her it was delicious.' He stands up and rubs his stomach. 'Woman! Come with me.' He pulls her to her feet and steers her to the bedroom. They're good at this – clothes off, into bed, energetic sex. He's not a porn watcher so he doesn't expect anything beyond straightforward bonking and that's just as well because she lacks experience. He's the only real boyfriend she's ever had and he's so confident in his own straightforwardness that he carries her with him – not just sexually, but in every way. He doesn't notice she's weird. And when she's with him, she doesn't notice she's weird either. With Jeff she feels close to normal.

But for all their physical closeness, he's easy to keep at an emotional arm's length because he believes what she tells him and rarely pushes to know more. He knows she's adopted but he doesn't know she has a problem with it. He's not suspicious. He trusts her, takes her at face value. He's someone who has never been hurt or deceived or felt unloved. The universe and everyone in it are his friends.

She can't imagine what that must feel like.

He leaves at lunchtime to rehearse for a gig and Hannah gets dressed again. She takes a chemical boost to help her along – amphetamines, this time. Her parents would be appalled if they knew – Hannah is *taking drugs*? She can only imagine the soul-searching that would follow. They blame themselves for every negative thought and feeling she's ever shared with them – or they have found out about – so is it any wonder that she stopped sharing her feelings when she was about ten? Apart from a need for privacy, it upset her to see them upset.

Within twenty minutes everything is sharper. She has twice the energy and focus that she normally has. She feels ready for anything. The only downside is an ache in her temples but she can handle that.

She gets to the café a few minutes early, orders a coffee and sits right at the back so that she can watch the front door. Her heart is racing – and it's not just the amphetamine: she's nervous. This is an important moment and she doesn't want it to go wrong because she hasn't considered all the options. She's already decided that if a woman who looks like she might be her mother walks in, then she will leave through the kitchen – it's easy enough to get behind the counter; she can't see anyone stopping her – because there's no way Hannah will meet her mother in a café. If – when – they ever meet it will be on Hannah's terms. No negotiating that one.

A family comes in and orders two coffees and two milkshakes. They sit in the window where the world moves by outside in a stream of traffic and people; everyone is headed somewhere. The parents spend most of the time on their mobiles while the children drink their milkshakes, and when the straws become clogged, they suck and blow and make each other laugh.

Three women – good friends who never stop talking – order pots of tea and a plate of cakes and sit in the opposite corner to Hannah.

Finally, a lone man comes through the door and glances around. He's wearing jeans and a pale blue shirt. He's ordinary-looking, quite old, old enough to be a dad. His eyes are piercing and as Hannah's mum would say, he has a strong jaw.

'Hannah?'

'Yes.'

He shakes her hand. 'You look well,' he says.

'Have we met before?' she says.

'No.'

'So how do you know I look well?'

He smiles. 'I don't. It's just an expression.' He digs around in the pocket of his jeans for some money. 'You want another coffee?'

'No thanks.'

Okay, so she's tense and he isn't. She watches him as he chats to the girl behind the counter. He is at ease with himself. It's clear that interaction comes naturally to him. Not that this impresses her. For all she knows it's a veneer that's only skin deep. He's a nice guy while he's in control and it's all going his way, and then someone scratches his surface and the ugly underneath is exposed.

She could be wrong, but she's no Jeff. She doesn't give people the benefit of the doubt. Doubting someone is a human instinct that has evolved over thousands of years, and for a very good reason – self-preservation. As far as Hannah's concerned, people would do well to have a healthy respect for that.

When he returns to the table he's carrying a glass of fizzy water and a long baguette bulging with brie and grapes. 'Would you like some?' He has a knife poised ready to cut it in half.

'No thanks.'

He cuts it in half anyway and stifles a yawn before he bites into it.

'You're tired?' she says.

'My partner is pregnant.'

'Oh, okay.'

'With twins,' he says.

'Babies, eh? Who'd have 'em?'

He stares at her then, chewing slowly on the bread. His expression is interested, kind even.

This man knows my mother. That's the thought that comes to her suddenly. It's a thought that is heavy with significance and is accompanied by a spike in her emotions that makes her want to say, *Ask her what it felt like to give up her baby. To walk away from me. Ask her.*

She places her hand over her mouth.

'Are you feeling ill?'

She shakes her head.

This man has sat opposite her mother, most likely on many occasions. He has looked into her mother's eyes and now he is looking into hers. She wishes she could see what he sees. *Do I look like her? Is my voice like hers? Does she want to meet me – is that why you're here?*

'Hannah?'

She glances up. 'What?'

'I think your mother may be about to contact you,' he says.

So it is that, then. She stares down at the table while a storm of feeling swirls inside her chest. She thinks about the girl, just days ago, who Clem helped to meet her mother. It seems a parent is entitled to show up in a child's life when all the hard work is done. Just re-appear when it suits them. And all is forgiven.

Not.

'I know she tried to make contact with you a few years ago and that she was warned off by your parents.'

He makes it sound mild. Her parents had to call the police. She was banging on the door in the middle of the night, totally off her head, ranting and raving.

'What she did was wrong. She realised that afterwards.' He eats some more of his baguette. 'She was at breaking point. Her father had died and that made her vulnerable.'

'Why are you here?' Hannah says, her tone aggressive. 'If my mother wants to get in touch with me, she can go through the proper channels. Then *I* decide' – she places a flat hand against her chest – 'whether I want to see her or not. And it's all dealt with without work colleagues or friends or whatever you are getting involved.'

'Are you high?' he says.

'Am I *what*?' she replies.

'You seem wired.'

'Wired?' She suddenly becomes aware of her feet tapping on the floor. She's pulling at her hair with one hand, shredding a napkin with the other. Her eyes dart around, from window to wall to his face. 'First of all, you don't know me. Second of all, guess what? You don't know me. Third, Mister I'm-doing-you-a-favour-by-coming-here, you don't fucking know me.'

'I—'

'I was anxious coming here today, and I'm still anxious because I had no idea who would turn up. You could be anyone. I don't even know who gave you my number because I've done some detective work and my mum tells me she gave my number to a woman pretending to be a secretary. So who is that woman? Did you ask her to get my number? Is it my mother?' She doesn't wait for him to reply but rushes on: 'And, when I'm anxious, I talk fast and I fidget. Do you have any idea how hard it was for me to come here today?' He starts speaking but she talks over his reply. 'No you don't! You have no idea because you're not me and instead of putting yourself in my shoes you accuse me of taking drugs.' She sits back and folds her arms.

He takes another bite of his sandwich before saying, 'Methinks the lady doth protest too much.' Gives her a small smile before adding, '*Macbeth.*'

'It's from *Hamlet*,' she counters. 'And you've misquoted. The methinks comes last.'

He smiles widely this time and then he laughs. 'You're like her, you know? You have an answer for everything.'

She stands up and the chair falls backwards behind her. The three women glance across at them, waiting to see what will happen next. She expects they're the sort of women who will rush to her aid if it looks as if she's being threatened.

'Please, Hannah.' He lays the remains of his sandwich on the plate and stands up to set her chair upright again. 'Please.' He points to the seat. 'I'm sorry I offended you.'

He sits back down and she reluctantly does the same because she knows that if she follows her inclination and storms out she'll regret it. 'Get to the point,' she says quietly. 'I can't be doing with this.'

'She's been watching you.'

'What? When?'

'I don't have exact details.'

'Who told you?' She throws out her arms. 'Did she tell you?'

'No, she didn't tell me. I have …' He hesitates. She can see he's unsure how much he should give away. 'She doesn't know I know.'

'She doesn't know you know and yet you do?' She screws up her face. 'So someone close to her told you?'

'That's right.'

'Does she know where I live?'

'I don't think so, but … she's resourceful.'

'You know … I don't really understand why you're telling me this. What's your motive? It seems like you're her friend but you're here behind her back and you don't know me from Adam – or Eve.' She laughs and it relieves the tension just enough for her to take a breath. 'So what's going on? Why are you here?'

'Because I feel you have a right to know.' He tries to look earnest but as far as Hannah's concerned he's failing in the attempt. 'Five years ago it was tough on you, her turning up the way she did, and I thought that if it were to happen again then you deserved a warning.'

She doesn't believe him. She trusts her gut and her gut tells her that this man has an agenda. She doesn't know what it could be, but she's not about to believe he has her best interests at heart.

'I heard she was in the police,' Hannah says.

He nods.

'That was the reason my parents didn't press charges. They didn't want to get her sacked.'

'They spoke to you about it?'

'No, they're protective.'

'So how did you find out?'

'None of your business,' she says. She watches the family leave, milkshake stains on the boy's T-shirt, the mum and dad each holding a child's hand before they join the rush of people on the pavement. 'Is she still in the police?'

'No, she had to leave after the way she behaved. Using her position.' He shakes his head. 'It was an abuse of trust that couldn't be tolerated.'

'Are you a policeman?'

'No.'

'Well, you're acting like one.' She sighs up at the ceiling before gathering her thoughts and saying, 'So the upshot seems to be that my mother is watching me, possibly with the end game of introducing herself, and you came here to warn me.'

'That's right.'

'Well, cheers for that.' She stands up. 'Good luck with your new babies.' She's opening the door before she remembers to ask, 'You didn't tell me who gave you my mobile number?'

He doesn't reply at first and when he does it surprises her. 'It was your grandma.'

She walks back home wondering why her nana – none of them ever call her Grandma – would impersonate a secretary to disclose her number to a strange man who claims friendship with her birth mother. For one thing, her nana rarely speaks on the phone because she's forty per cent deaf and she always says her hearing aid is uncomfortable. But more to the point, she already knows Hannah's number. She wouldn't need to ring anyone to get it.

And then the penny drops: he means her birth mother's mother.

She has a grandma.

She lets this truth paddle around in the shallows of

her mind for a minute or two to see what it feels like. She has never thought much about wider members of her birth family. Occasionally she wonders about her dad, what he might have looked like, was he a one-night stand or was she in a relationship with him? Did he want to keep the baby? Did she even tell him she was pregnant?

So, she has a grandma. She feels her heart harden at the thought because she suspects she was involved in the decision to give her up. When she discovered her mother's surname was Romano – sounds Italian … Catholic? – she wondered whether she had been put under pressure to give her up for adoption. Would that vindicate her a little?

No. No, it wouldn't. As she said in her blog post – social services are there with a safety net as wide as a football pitch. There is really no reason for a woman of nineteen to give up her baby unless she wants to.

By the time she gets back home the drug is wearing off and she's beginning to flatten out as her mood rebounds and the pendulum swings towards introspection. So when this grandma of hers got her number, why not just ring her herself? Why rope in the bloke with the pregnant partner and his I-know-something-you-don't attitude?

Hannah isn't afraid of meeting her birth mother – quite the reverse: for years she's been anticipating the opportunity to confront her. And now she's been gifted an extra layer of ammunition because this woman has been watching her. Spying on her. Stalking her. Is she a customer at the restaurant? Does she watch her when she leaves work? When she arrives home? Does she know where she lives?

There have been times when Hannah has felt the hairs

on the back of her neck stand up. Sometimes when she's walking home, she feels it. She explained it away as an overreaction because she was bothered by a drunk some months ago and it made her extra vigilant. Turns out she was right to be wary.

Online – the font of all wisdom. Her birth mother might have been a policewoman but that doesn't give her a monopoly on detection. Hannah logs on and begins a basic search, made easier by the fact that Romano is an unusual surname.

There is only one person called Ruby Romano living in Edinburgh, in a district Hannah's unfamiliar with. At another click of the mouse, Ruby's postcode and directions to her house arrive on Hannah's mobile. It's two o'clock in the afternoon; there's no time like the present.

She pops a pill. She'll need a razor-sharp focus if she's to get through this without screwing up. She needs to be in the moment, experience every second as it happens, not allow herself to drift off on a thought or a feeling because if she gets emotional she'll fold.

She checks which bus will get her there and she heads off. With any luck her mother will be at work and she'll be able to poke around the house uninterrupted. Snooping behind her back is no more than she deserves.

The bus journey takes for ever and Hannah's stomach churns so that she holds a hand against her middle. She has a bottle of water and a packet of mints in her pocket and by the time she gets off the bus she's crunched the mints into tiny pieces and swallowed them down with the water.

Her mobile app tells her that the address is about one hundred metres from the bus stop. She starts walking, her head up as she takes in every home she passes. The street is wide and exceptionally well-kept. The word that springs to mind is affluent. This area is wealthy beyond the ordinary. Every house is a Victorian mansion. Some of them are divided into several smaller units and many of them have stayed as one large house but have signs out front advertising that they are care homes for the elderly. Nevertheless, wealth is written into every recently forked gravel driveway and newly pointed stonework.

She's expecting to find that her mother – no, not her mother, Ruby. She'll call her Ruby, because when she thinks of her mother she sees the face of the woman in Linlithgow, most probably in the back garden with her dad weeding next to the path, or walking back home after taking Hannah's grandparents a hot meal.

Hannah expects to find Ruby living in the smaller flat in a divided house, but she isn't. Her house is huge. And before Hannah walks through the gates she stands and stares. This is a family home, surely? This is a place where it's easy to imagine children playing hide and seek, sleeping in tree-houses and building cushion and blanket dens in a sunny playroom. And yet, she got the impression that Ruby was childless. In fact, it's more than an impression. Five years ago she was definitely childless. She heard her parents talking about this after Ruby had shown up on the doorstep and the police had been called.

'I feel so sorry for her,' Hannah heard her mum say. She was sitting in the dark shadows on the stair, her knees pulled up to her chest. 'We know what it feels like to long for a child, George.'

'She had a child, Morag,' her dad replied. 'She gave that child up and now that child is ours and we love her and we care for her. Hannah doesn't need this woman interrupting her life.'

'Are we sure?' Hannah could tell her mum was crying.

'*I know Hannah has never asked after her birth mother but—*'

'*Our responsibility is to Hannah. Not to Ruby Romano. If Hannah wants to get in touch with her when she's of an age to do so, then she can. That will be her decision. And that's where we need to leave it, Morag.*'

'*You're right. Hannah can choose to contact her birth mother if she wants to,*' her mum said, her voice so quiet that Hannah almost missed the rest. '*I hope she doesn't, though, George. I know it's selfish, but I hope she doesn't.*'

Hannah hesitates for a split second before she pushes open the tall iron gate and walks up the curved driveway to Ruby's front door. There's a car in the driveway so maybe Ruby is home. Or maybe she has a husband who works from home. Whatever. After all these years she will come face to face with her mother, and she has a lot to say.

She takes a deep breath, feels the fist of anger steady in her stomach and her mind balance on one still point of focus.

Then she rings the doorbell and waits.

Chapter Nine

Ruby secures the tenancy on the flat without any difficulty. The weekend before she moves in she doesn't sleep; she works overnight as usual and packs in the daytime. She isn't taking everything. She doesn't need to because she hasn't yet decided what she's doing with the house, and she can always pop back for forgotten items. She'll only be thirty minutes across town.

She has loud music playing and is packing kitchen equipment into a large cardboard box when her sister walks in on her. 'Celia?' She starts back. 'What are you doing here?'

'I rang the bell. Twice,' Celia says. 'I thought you might be lying dead in your bed!'

'Ever the dramatist.' Ruby takes her door key from her sister's hand and Celia follows her as she walks out the front door to put it back in the magnetic holder hidden under a pipe.

'You force me to be dramatic,' Celia says. 'And why do you keep a key out here anyway if you don't want people just walking in on you? It's hardly secure, is it?'

'I often forget my key. You know I do. And I still have the Busy Bee Cleaners once a week.'

'Well, I've called you three times in the last few days. You must have seen the missed calls? Joseph wants you to come to his play and Mum still refuses to tell me what you argued about on her birthday. She's gone very quiet on me. So that makes two of you.'

'I'm not taking responsibility for Mum's moods.'

'I'm not asking you to.' Celia follows her back into the kitchen. 'But I don't like being left out.'

'No one's leaving you out, Celia.'

'So what's going on?' She stares around the kitchen. 'Are you moving?'

'I'm … clearing and tidying.'

'But these are removal boxes.' She points to the company name along the side of the box.

'Yes.'

'So you are moving?'

'Not exactly.'

'You're sending some things into storage?'

Ruby considers lying but the interrogation would only be delayed. Better to be economical with the truth. 'I've rented a flat.'

'What? Why?'

'I need a change of scenery. You're right about living here – there's no sense of community, no neighbours to speak of. It's dragging me down.' She takes a breath before saying. 'I … Well …'

Celia lifts the kettle, senses there's enough water in it and flicks the switch. 'Well what?' She folds her arms, her interest piqued. 'Tell me.'

'I want to paint.'

'Paint? Paint what?'

'Pictures. People. Scenery. I don't know.' Ruby shrugs. 'Just something creative. Something different. And I was good at it, remember?'

'Were you?'

'I got an A for GCSE.'

'So did loads of people!'

'Thanks, Celia.' Ruby glares at her and walks around in a circle, sighing as she goes. 'And you wonder why I didn't tell you?'

'I'm sorry.' Celia rushes over to hug her. 'I'm just surprised, that's all.' She smiles and shakes Ruby's shoulders. 'I'm excited for you! I am!' She reaches into a cupboard. 'Have you packed all your mugs?' Ruby lifts a couple of mugs out of the box and hands them to her. 'So where is this flat?'

'Up near Holy Corner.'

'Why there? You could have rented one of the conversions in the old Royal Infirmary.'

'Quartermile? I don't fancy it.'

'Why not? The flats at the back have views over the Meadows and Arthur's Seat.' She takes some teabags from the box on the work surface. 'I'm sure the sunsets must be fantastic if that's what you fancy painting. Tom has a client who lives in one with a rooftop garden. And it's not like you couldn't afford it.' She stops talking and glances across at Ruby. 'What?'

'Sometimes I think you need to listen to yourself.'

'Meaning?'

'I'm thirty-nine years old and you're still telling me that you know better.'

'I'm taking an interest. You're my sister!' She walks to the fridge and opens the door.

'Say nothing,' Ruby warns her.

Five seconds pass before Celia closes the fridge door and brings her hands together in the prayer position. 'I'm saying nothing.' She stands in front of Ruby. 'I'm sure it's not necessary to have milk in tea. Or food in the fridge.'

They hold eye contact until they both begin to smile and then Ruby says, 'Tea *is* better with milk. But where are the shops around here?'

'I know. If only supermarkets would deliver.' She affects a thinking face and Ruby laughs. 'Oh, wait a minute. They do!'

Friends again, they sit down on the easy chairs by the sliding doors and drink mugs of black tea. 'Tell me about my nephews and niece,' Ruby says and Celia talks. She runs through each child from eldest to youngest and when she gets to Joseph she tells Ruby that he is a tortoise in the play and he wants his auntie to come and watch. Celia has made the costume with a cardboard box painted green, 'And I really want Mum to help me with the head but she's in such a mood.'

Ruby doesn't take the bait. She listens as Celia progresses from Joseph to Tom, his prospects of promotion and whether they should move to Glasgow. 'You can't possibly move to Glasgow.' That's all Ruby has to say for Celia to embark on a long list of pros and cons.

'But anyway,' Celia says at last, bringing a hand down onto her sister's knee. 'I know you're keeping me talking so that I'll have to go and collect the kids from school and you can hold onto your secrets for another day.' She waits for Ruby to answer and when she doesn't: 'Were you just going to move house without telling me?'

'I'm not really moving. I'll be back here all the time. I want more of a work-space than anything else.'

'And will we be invited round?'

'I was planning on inviting you all round when I had something to show you.'

'Like a painting?'

'Like a painting,' Ruby agrees.

'Okay ... well.' Celia stands up, stretches her arms above her head and wiggles her fingers at the ceiling. 'We should start going to yoga together. Like we used to.' She does a couple of half-hearted lunges and then her attention is drawn to the dining table where Ruby's papers and letters are piled high. 'What's with all these unopened solicitor's letters?'

'I've fallen behind with all my admin.'

'Call this falling behind?' Celia holds up more than two dozen unopened envelopes. 'Do you want me to help you?'

'Definitely not.' Ruby realises just in time that the notebook with HANNAH written in capital letters is lying on the other side of the table. She walks round and picks it up before Celia homes in on it. 'I'll get round to it in my own good time.' Celia isn't listening. She tears open one of the envelopes and Ruby instantly grabs it and lobs it back onto the pile. 'I mean it, Celia. Keep your nose out.'

'For goodness sake! You just can't accept help, can you? You have to do everything your way, singlehandedly, like there's virtue in struggling. Grant was right when he—' She sucks in her lips.

'Grant was right when he *what*?'

'Nothing. Nothing.' She rubs Ruby's shoulder. 'I wasn't going to say anything.'

'You're just being a bitch.'

'I'm just being a *sister*. Where's your sense of humour?' She softly punches Ruby's upper arm. 'Anyway, I can't afford to fall out with you.' She makes wide eyes. 'Who would I get to babysit?'

Most people would be lightening the mood when they said this, not meaning it, not meaning it at all. But Ruby knows that Celia isn't joking. There's a downside to her organised, family-focused nature. She's an interferer. She directs Tom and her children's lives and she would happily extend that to Ruby's life too if she would let her. But they aren't teenagers any more and Ruby has no intention of allowing Celia to start playing her like a puppet and then dropping her when the going gets tough.

Ruby stands a metre from the window. All her canvases are stacked against the wall, apart from a medium-sized canvas that rests on the easel. Watercolour paints are laid out in tubes on a table beside it. She is good to go. She'll have to get something on the canvas before Celia comes to visit or she'll be accused of being a fraud. She could pay an art student to come here and get started for her or she could do it herself. Perhaps she really is a painter? Stranger things … And it would be good to have something creative to show to Hannah when they finally meet because she really doesn't have a lot going for her. Apart from money. She has money. And she has a family. Celia and the children – well, especially the children – would welcome Hannah into their lives. Lennie's eldest daughter is not much younger than Hannah. Perhaps they could all spend time together, fill the house with footsteps and laughter. She could learn to cook family meals. Hannah could come to yoga classes with her and Celia. She could take up cycling again.

Ruby is used to being up in the Edinburgh sky although normally she is viewing it through a camera. This time, however, there is no lens between her and her daughter. She stares across the street and down into the flat opposite. The angle is perfect and the light at this time of the evening allows Ruby to see right into the living room. Hannah came home over an hour ago and logged straight onto her computer, which is on the table close to the window. She is staring at the screen, typing and reading, her right hand lingering on the mouse. Ruby can't see the expression on her face. She could see her expression, but she would need to use binoculars and that is a step too far. Then she really would be spying and she's not a spy. She cares, and that makes her want to be close to her daughter. But she's under no illusions as to how her interest would be perceived by other people. Even if they didn't know about her meltdown five years ago, they would surely see her behaviour as obsessive and potentially dangerous.

They're wrong.

She continues to watch Hannah on the cameras at work. Twice she is almost caught. Once when Fiona comes back early from her break, and the second time Lennie is behind her before she even realises he's come into the room. She has zoomed in on Hannah's face at the bus stop. She is with her boyfriend; Ruby is now sure they are going out because she's seen him in the living room with Hannah. He has a crown of blond curly hair and an open smile.

'What's got your attention?' Lennie says and she jumps, draws back the camera's focus.

'I thought he might be bothering this girl. Remember she had trouble with a drunk a few months back? We almost called it in.'

'Right.' Lennie sits down. 'I don't recall that, but shall I tell you what I do notice?'

'Yes.' Ruby's heart beats faster but she keeps her face expressionless. She expects Lennie to say that the girl looks like Ruby, to ask her if she might be a relative. She's holding her breath as she waits for it, waits to hear him say the words so that she can casually deny it. She might even zoom in again and make a show of pointing out that the girl's nose is completely different or her eyes are the wrong shade of brown.

'The jacket she's wearing is this season's must-have

according to Shona. She's been trying to persuade me to buy it for her. The iPad has been shoved under my nose every day this week.'

Ruby laughs, more from relief than anything else. 'Will you give in?'

'I might use the purchase as leverage. That's if Trish doesn't give in first.' His expression falls. 'The girls know their mother's a soft touch.'

'How's the pregnancy going?'

'Don't ask.' He shakes his head multiple times as if all is lost.

'Whisky Romeo.' The voice on the radio is loud. 'Potential suicide on the North Bridge.'

Ruby and Lennie snap into action. It takes moments for them to pull the relevant camera feeds down onto their spot screens. Two police officers are out of their car, standing about twenty metres from a man who has climbed onto the edge of the bridge. He is completely still, facing down towards the drop. His eyes are shut; his lips are moving.

'It looks as if he might be talking to himself,' Ruby says to the cops.

'It's possible he's praying,' Lennie adds. 'Go easy.'

While the policemen discuss their approach, a second police car arrives. The officers climb out and usher a group of late-night revellers away from the scene.

'Hopefully we'll have time with this one,' Lennie says to Ruby, briefly turning away from his microphone. 'As long as he keeps praying, he won't jump.'

Ruby is less optimistic and her heart is sick with the knowledge of what they might be about to witness. They have three cameras focused on the man and there are four officers at the scene. He needs to lift his head and look around him to see he's not alone.

The first policeman approaches him from the side, talking as he walks. As per the manual, he speaks slowly and Ruby is able to lip-read what he's saying: 'Excuse me, sir. My name is Mike Chambers, PC Chambers. Could I ask your name, sir?'

The man's eyes open.

'His eyes are open,' Lennie says into the microphone. 'He can hear you.'

The policeman neither moves nor speaks; Lennie and Ruby stop breathing. The man adjusts his feet and Ruby glances at his trainers – not the most expensive but not the cheapest either. This man doesn't have obvious money problems. He is handsome enough, clean enough. His hair is neat; his clothes are smart-casual and well-fitting. He's an ordinary man who's got himself into an extraordinary situation.

'Should I approach him further?' the policeman whispers.

Lennie glances at Ruby. She shakes her head and mouths, 'I don't know.'

In the next second her attention is caught by a car travelling down the cobbled High Street towards the Tron Kirk.

Five seconds later, the car jumps the lights and turns left. 'Car approaching at speed,' Ruby warns the policemen at the perimeter. The car drives the thirty yards down onto the North Bridge, heading for the two police cars that are half blocking the road.

Five seconds more and the cops are in the middle of the road waving the car to a stop. Ruby watches the man on the bridge, sees his eyes widen as he tunes in to the screech of brakes. He turns. He recognises the car and a look crosses his face that says it all. Ruby shivers. 'Oh God,' she whispers.

A further five seconds, and a woman has climbed out of the driver's seat. She's shouting, her face contorted with anger. One of the officers holds her back from the bridge, talking all the while in an effort to calm her down.

Four seconds later, the man jumps.

He doesn't fall – most people fall – he doesn't. He jumps. He literally jumps into the air and drops, his body still, no arms or legs fighting the velocity, no change of heart, just a curved downward trajectory onto the road below.

Lennie bangs the desk with his fist; Ruby screams. They watch as the first police officer looks over the bridge and then at his colleague, shaking his head against the truth of what's just happened before he radios it in.

And the woman? She is struck rigid, staring into the space where the man once stood before she covers her face with her hands and collapses onto her knees.

Lennie opens his desk drawer and takes a tissue from the box before passing the box to Ruby.

They don't watch the clean-up. The cameras record the man's broken body being recovered from the road but they don't watch. They each have to write a report and they give one another the time and space to do it. They don't speak to the officers again that evening – they won't speak to them until the next day when they have all submitted their own version of events. There are the what-ifs and buts – and as far as Ruby is concerned, if the woman hadn't arrived when she did they had a fighting chance to stop him from taking his own life. No guarantees, but her arrival definitely precipitated his jump. The cameras will back this up. Ruby downloads the footage and adds it to the file.

It's almost five in the morning before Lennie and Ruby are both back in their seats, their moods reflective.

'Remember the talking bus stops?' Lennie says. 'Do you think if we had been able to talk to him it might have helped?'

'I doubt it,' Ruby says. 'My guess is that he phoned the woman from the bridge to tell her what he was about to do and she called the police before driving there.' Lennie is nodding. 'Whatever was going on between them ...' Ruby trails off.

The talking bus stops had been a pilot project. For six months the cameras were linked to a dozen bus stops. If the CCTV operators witnessed illegality or distress, and wanted to give a warning or show support, they could talk to people on the street. The problem was that people were shocked when they heard the disembodied voice and that made their reactions unpredictable. The project was terminated when a woman was so spooked she ran out onto the road and narrowly missed being hit by a car.

'Thank goodness it was you and me on duty tonight,' Ruby says. 'Fiona would have found that difficult to deal with.'

'We'll be offered counselling.'

'I'd rather eat my own hand,' Ruby says. 'I could do with a drink, though.'

'I have a bottle of vodka hidden at the back of the freezer for just such an occasion. You're welcome to join me?'

They sit in the hut in Lennie's garden. Ruby is on the tattered armchair; Lennie is on a garden chair that is only inches off the ground. They have been drinking for over an hour, both of them staring out into the garden where sparrows squabble on the bird feeder. The sun is yet to reach the small patch of dew-glistened grass, and the puppies are in a makeshift run outside the back door, squealing and practising their barking.

They talk about what they just witnessed, the finality of death, the impotence they felt just sitting there watching the event unfold when what they needed to do was take action, the sheer courage – or is it cowardice? – involved in taking your own life. 'Talk about seizing the moment,' Lennie says, topping up their glasses with more vodka than Coke. 'God knows my life's a trial at times, but suicide?' He shakes his head. 'Brutal.'

'People need something to live for,' Ruby says. 'You've got your girls and your passions. It's not the same for everyone.'

Lennie slumps down in the chair, his head at an angle, his legs stretched out before him. 'You make that sound like you're one of the everyone.' He squints across at her. 'You're not, are you?'

She hesitates for a moment before saying, 'I've been there. I've never climbed onto a bridge but I've been close.' She takes a drink and winces. 'Breakdown or breakthrough – that's what I was told by one of the other patients.' She drinks another mouthful. 'Psychiatric hospital wasn't like I thought it would be.'

'Ruby, I'm sorry,' Lennie says quietly, reaching his fingers across the space between them but falling short of the chair so that his hand lands on the floor next to the vodka bottle. 'I never knew you'd spent time in hospital.'

Ruby shrugs. 'There were so many people who were far worse off than me.'

'I'm no shining example of mental health,' Lennie says. 'If it wasn't for this' – he gestures to the right and left where Einstein facts and quotes shout out from one wall, food facts and recipes shout out from another – 'I'd be depressed. No doubt about that.' He stares down at his feet. 'The irony isn't lost on me by the way.'

'What irony?'

'*MasterChef*, *Mastermind* and me master of nothing.'

'Stop it! Your mind is more active than most people half your age.' She frowns across at him. 'And you have a family who adore you. It's a lot more than I have.'

'Aye.' He scratches his neck. 'And here I am in the garden hut.' He laughs. 'Don't get me wrong, I'm not complaining. We all need a reason to get out of bed in the morning.'

'Or late afternoon in our case,' Ruby says and they both laugh.

'Hospital though, eh?' Lennie says, his tone reflective. 'Not easy.'

'It was five years ago,' Ruby says. 'I was sectioned for my own good.' She bites her lip, remembering. 'My dad died and then I did something unforgivable. I had to resign from the police service otherwise I'd have been pushed.'

Lennie nods. 'I'd guessed you had to leave.' Drink is loosening both their tongues. He doesn't remember them ever being so frank with each other. 'But you didn't break down, Ruby, did you? You broke through.' He stretches further this time and slaps her knee. 'You're stronger than you know.'

Strong? Ruby doesn't feel strong. She's walking a path that is deceitful. If – when? – Hannah finds out that Ruby has rented a flat that looks directly into her front room, what will Ruby say? It's not as creepy as it looks; I'm watching you because I care?

And despite her promise to herself, Ruby has already

broken her own rule about binoculars. The second time Hannah took a box out of the bureau in her bedroom, Ruby couldn't resist seeing what Hannah had inside. They were small mementoes – a key ring, a bracelet, a small notebook – individual pieces of memorabilia that clearly meant something to her because she held them in her hand and stared at them closely as if each item triggered a thought.

'How come I never knew about your troubles?' Lennie says. 'Here I was thinking we were good pals.'

'We are good pals.' She smiles across at him. 'It's just me, Lennie. It's the way I am. I avoid talking about my feelings. I bury my head in the sand and hope it will all go away. Maybe that's my downfall.'

'What downfall?' Lennie demands.

She thinks about Celia's words, when she implied Grant had an opinion about Ruby's inability to seek help.

'It's not your fault Grant got cancer,' Lennie says.

Ruby's eyes flick sideways. 'How did you know I was thinking about Grant?'

'Because you look sad.'

'Well, that's because … About Grant …' She takes a breath. 'Grant, he—'

'Aye, aye,' Lennie interrupts. 'Here comes trouble.'

Shona appears at the door to the hut. She's dressed in jeans torn at the knees and an oversized sweatshirt. She has a bag slung over her shoulder and is holding an iPad. 'Hi, Ruby! Do you like this jacket?'

She thrusts the screen in front of Ruby's face as Lennie says, 'Why are you not at school?'

'Free periods.'

'Then you should be in the library.'

Shona ignores her dad. 'What do you think, Ruby?'

'Very nice, yes.'

'See, Dad? I told you.'

Lennie gets up off his chair, laboriously, so that Shona sniggers and Ruby reaches out a helping hand, accidentally knocking over the vodka bottle. 'What are you doing drinking at this time of day?' Shona says. 'And you've got the cheek to judge me!'

'We had a difficult shift,' Lennie says, pushing her ahead of him into the garden. 'And I'd thank you to take yourself off to school before I drive you there myself.' He chases her into the house, both of them complaining all the way.

Ruby sighs, disappointed that she didn't get the words out. She wants to tell Lennie about her relationship with Grant. And about Hannah. She wants to share the fact that she too has a daughter. She would love to say 'my daughter' out loud and to another human being, someone other than her mother, who won't throw it back at her. Her head and her heart are full to bursting with doubts, unanswered questions, regrets, love. Mostly love. That's what she wants to be left with. When the fat lady starts singing, that's what Ruby wants her overriding emotion to be. Love.

Lennie is gone for over thirty minutes and when he returns he has two plates of food with him. 'Thought I'd whip us up a little something,' he says. He lays a plate in front of her – blueberry pancakes, maple syrup and some streaky bacon. He sits back down in his chair, balancing his plate on his knees. 'Trish says she'll bring us out some coffee when she's finished on the phone.'

'You getting on better again?'

Lennie goes on to tell Ruby that he's accompanying Trish to the hospital today for the latest scan after 'being accused of not taking enough interest'. They'll have to shop for more baby equipment and Ruby tells him that Celia is giving equipment away because Joseph is three now. She wants to bring the conversation back round to herself, to the baby she gave birth to and gave away, but the moment is lost and Ruby allows herself to be drawn into other people's lives, the way she's been doing for years.

Chapter Ten

Later the same day, Ruby wakes up with a fist of melancholy wedged in the pit of her stomach. She hasn't slept well. The image of the man falling off the bridge plays back in her mind's eye, rewinding and then repeating, a loop she's unable to interrupt, and she's forced to keep reliving those few horrific seconds.

She's been here before. It's not the first death she's witnessed and she knows that, in all probability, it won't be the last and she'd like to push the incident to the back of her mind, cover it up with activity, with thoughts of Hannah and wishes for their future. She stands at the window in the flat, off to one side, so that if Hannah does glance up she won't be able to make her out. She will be nothing more than a shapeless, grey shadow. A ghost of a person.

Hannah is in the living room sitting in front of her monitor. She twirls her hair with her left hand as she reads what's on the screen. Every so often she moves the mouse with her right hand and then uses the keyboard. Usually the sight of her daughter lifts Ruby's spirits but not today. The aftermath of what she witnessed is too strong. Too destabilising. She sets off for work and is in no better a mood when she gets there. Details are coming in about the man: forty-five years old, father, husband and son. Turns out he was unhappy in his job, his relationship with his wife was in crisis and his brother had recently died. Three events in quick succession that quite literally drove him over the edge.

Fiona has got wind of what happened and is writing about the event in her training folder. 'Did the police try to talk him down?' she asks.

'They did, but it all happened too fast.'

'I wish I'd been on duty,' she says, then she catches Ruby's expression and immediately adds, 'because dealing with the incident would be good experience for me.'

'Trust me,' Ruby says. 'You don't want to watch someone die.'

'I know. But it's a fact of the job, isn't it?'

'Yes, not very often, but it will happen.' She holds up her hand. 'I strongly advise you not to replay the footage.'

'I've seen worse.'

'How could you have seen worse?'

'You see worse on YouTube.'

There's no answer to that. At thirty-nine, Ruby feels old. 'If you want to know how to complete an incident report, I'll go over it with you. Then you can tick off another objective.' She points at the bank of screens on the wall in front of them. 'This is real life we're watching, Fiona. And it's serious. Real life, real time, real people.'

'I know. I—'

'The man's name was Alastair Robinson and he was desperately unhappy. This morning, two children have lost their father. A mother has lost her son.'

'I—'

Ruby leaves Fiona to think about what she's said and goes into the breakout room to make a cup of tea. Perhaps she's being hard on her but she needs to realise that there are times when learning takes second place to having due respect for the event. It's good that she's gaining confidence but she also seems to be forgetting her humanity.

Suicide, a desperate, life-denying action, is sobering and has made Ruby question herself. What is she doing? What is she *actually* doing? Tempting fate – that's what she's doing. Because the last time she made contact with her daughter, her dad had just died. Her mother wasn't wrong. Her dad's death was precipitated by Ruby finding out about Hannah. That is the bald, unarguable truth. She didn't cause his death but she did set the wheels in motion.

She shouldn't have moved into the flat. She shouldn't be spying on her daughter. She has allowed herself, persuaded herself, that it's okay because she means Hannah no harm. But bottom line, it isn't okay. It's never going to be okay.

She dunks the teabag in the hot water and makes a plan. She has to retrace her steps. She'll stop watching Hannah on the cameras. She'll go back to her house. She'll open her solicitor's letters and get her life in order. She'll sign what needs to be signed and then she'll sell the house. And when she's in an honest position to approach Hannah, she'll do so through the proper channels.

'Ruby?' Fiona is standing behind her. 'Sorry to bother you but there's a police officer on the phone who needs to speak to you.'

Ruby acknowledges Fiona with a nod, goes back into the control room and puts on her headset.

'Ruby? It's Steve Wilson.'

'Steve. How's it going?'

'Same old, same old. I hear you and Lennie witnessed a suicide last night?'

'We did.'

'You okay?'

'Yup.' She sighs. 'It makes you think, but that's no bad thing.' Fiona is ear-wigging and when Ruby glances across at her, she turns her face away and shuffles papers on the desk. 'What can I do for you, Steve?'

'We're in the middle of an operation and we need an entrance watched.' He names one of the closes that lead off the Royal Mile not far from where Hannah works. 'The suspect is camera-aware so we need to fix more than one camera if possible, leading up to and down from the entrance.'

'Okay.' Ruby brings several cameras onto her spot screens and checks the sightlines. 'Three of the cameras will be of use to you. I'll remove them from the sequencing now. You can get the paperwork to me when you have time.'

'Perfect.'

Ruby ends the call and signals to Fiona to come across. 'Let me show you how to re-sequence the cameras.'

'You've shown me before.'

'Have I?'

'The ones around Murrayfield.'

'So I did.' Ruby nods. 'You have a go then.'

Fiona pulls her chair in close and is about to lay her hands on the keyboard when she hesitates. 'We have authority to do this?'

'We wouldn't be doing it if we didn't,' Ruby says lightly. 'Go back to the fundamental question, what is the purpose of CCTV?'

'Public order.'

'Exactly. So if a detective in major crimes informs us that they're running an operation and they need eyes on a particular place then we have the autonomy to take the camera out of the moving sequence and fix it in one direction. It's often the best way to gather evidence against drug-dealers. And there's also the issue of terrorism, catching members of cells communicating with each other and so on.'

'You mentioned paperwork.'

'I did. Steve will get the request to us when he has a moment.'

'Shouldn't we wait for that?'

'Strictly speaking, yes. But I've worked with him before and I know he'll deliver.'

Fiona pulls back. 'I think we should wait for the formal request.'

'I understand,' Ruby replies. 'You're new to the job and it's important you follow procedure.' Fiona stares at her and Ruby stares back. 'I've known Steve for years.'

'I've been told by Al that I should ...' She hesitates. 'We should ...'

Ruby knows she can't quite say the words because she's realising the gulf between management and those who actually do the job. She's sitting with Ruby and so she has to go along with what Ruby decides but Ruby's hackles are up. Fiona's eyes are on her as she removes three cameras from the sequencing and programmes them to remain still. She's in no doubt that Fiona will report her. Loyalty to management above her colleagues. She's coming to the end of her night rotation and Ruby makes a mental note to talk to Lennie before she writes her supervisor's report, see whether he senses the same traits in her.

The night passes without further incident. Ruby doesn't watch out for Hannah; she can't do this anyway now that the cameras are fixed on the entrance to the close, and she wonders at fate's intervention.

She finishes her shift and walks back to her house,

not the flat. Her feet are heavy and her eyeballs ache
with unshed tears. Failure sits on her shoulders, bearing
down on her like the leaden grey sky above. She opens
her front door and goes inside. Never has the house felt
quite so barren, lifeless as a morgue, a huge, empty
mausoleum of a place. She climbs the stairs, holding
onto the banister as if she has aged thirty years. She has
a choice of sleeping pills and she opts for the strongest
before pulling off her clothes, throwing on a nightdress
and crashing out on her bed.

She slides into a deep sleep. A couple of times during
the day she is almost aware of noises around her but
not enough to properly rouse her. When, at last, she does
get out of bed, her mouth is dry and her head aches.
She pulls a cardigan on over her nightdress and pads
about the dimly lit kitchen in her bare feet, moving from
the sink where she drinks a glass of water, to staring
into the empty fridge. There is an assortment of past-
their-best ingredients but no combinations that constitute
a meal. She finds a tin of tomato soup in the cupboard,
uses the tin opener attached to the wall and empties it
into a small pan.

It's while she's waiting for the soup to warm that the
hairs on the back of her neck stand up. She rubs her
neck but it doesn't help. She opens her eyes wide and
listens; her pulse begins to race. There's someone else
in the room. As surely as she knows her own name, she
knows this.

She swivels around too quickly and experiences a rush
of dizziness that fizzes inside her head and sends flashing
lights before her eyes. As her vision clears, she begins
to make out a shape sitting on the chair by the patio
doors: shoulders, head, the outline of a body waiting in
the shadows. She holds onto the edge of the work surface

for support. She could run. She could hide. She grabs for a knife and it slides from her hand, clattering onto the work surface and spinning away from her. A voice speaks. 'Ruby?'

For a prolonged moment she thinks she must be hearing things.

'Ruby?' he repeats.

His voice is familiar, more familiar, in fact, than anyone else on the planet apart from Celia and her mum, and yet she hasn't heard it for months.

'How have you been?' he says.

She shivers and pulls the cardigan around her.

He stands up and walks towards her, his gait loose. 'I bumped into that yoga teacher of yours,' he says. 'She was sure I was dead.' He clenches and unclenches his right fist, staring down at his hand as if he doesn't fully recognise it. 'Do you have anything to say?'

Ruby takes a step away from him. There are times when Ruby is afraid of Grant because he's always known exactly how to control her. She doesn't want this to be one of those times.

'Ruby?'

She takes another step backward so that she can't be seduced by the heat of him, pulled back into his orbit like a lesser star. For the first few years of their marriage he made her heart beat faster and she lost all sense of herself. The power of sexual attraction, the rush of hormones that made her giddy and giggly and so unlike herself that sometimes it took days to crawl back to a place where she could think logically and exist independently. A friend, back in the day when she had friends, told her that Grant was her poison, and that she should run away and never look back, no matter how much she wanted him to want her.

'Struck dumb?'

'I can't control what people think,' she says.

'You *told* her I was dead,' Grant says, shaking his head at the absurdity of it. 'I mean, what the fuck, Ruby?'

Did she tell people he was dead? She doesn't think so. She just didn't deny it. Her mum and Celia knew that he wasn't dead, that he had left her for someone else. But other people … she'd let them think what they wanted and somehow because people knew he had cancer, they jumped to conclusions, and she let them. She probably used words like 'gone' and then didn't correct them when they associated gone with dead.

'I know you were pissed off when I left you but to say I was dead?'

'I've never told anyone that you're dead. You had cancer. People make assumptions. They put two and two together and get twenty-two.'

'You told the yoga teacher I was dead,' he repeats. 'She was sure of it.'

'Well, you know what, Grant? You *are* dead to me,' Ruby says, her arms tight to her chest as if to restrain her anxious heart. 'You are out of my life. You are relegated to the past tense, wholly and completely.' She meets his eyes. 'And by the way, I wasn't pissed off at you leaving. I was gutted. Deeply hurt. To the core.'

'Ruby …' He reaches for her shoulder.

'Don't. Touch. Me.'

The soup is bubbling on the hob and a splash of tomato-red lands on the soft skin of Ruby's forearm.

'Ouch!' She pushes Grant out of the way, her eyes smarting, and goes to the sink. When the cold water lands on her skin she feels the pain subside and breathes more easily. Grant takes the soup off the hob and walks across the room. He switches on the light. Ruby is at first dazzled and she squints against the rush of light but within seconds her eyes grow accustomed, and she sees that Grant is idly glancing through the bookcase, acting as if he still lives there.

'Could you not?' Ruby says loudly. 'Those are my books.'

He moves to the dining table, glancing at the piles of mail and stray paper. She knows her notepad with HANNAH written in large letters is on the table somewhere but it doesn't catch his eye. Like Celia, he is more interested in the unopened solicitor's letters.

Ruby watches him, her arm still under the running water. Even through his shirt she can tell his six-pack has lost definition. He has gained weight around his middle – at least a couple of kilos – and there are bags under his eyes. And his hair has thinned a little. Trouble in paradise? She stares down at her bare feet, enjoying the temptation to smile.

When she looks back at him her expression is neutral. 'Are you well?'

'You know the cancer was only stage one,' he says, a sigh in his tone. 'There was never any suggestion I was going to die from it.'

More's the pity. She doesn't say that; she only thinks it. And then very quickly regrets it because death is so final. And she wouldn't wish that on anyone, even Grant.

'Why are you here?' She turns off the tap and wraps a dishcloth around her forearm.

'I think you know the answer to that.'

'Enlighten me.'

'Violet saw you outside our house.'

She shrugs. 'I've been going to the cemetery to visit my father's grave.'

'Your father's grave is on the other side of the cemetery.'

Ruby inclines her head because there's no point arguing with that.

'Stalking is an offence.'

'I haven't been stalking her.'

'I know you've been following us,' Grant says.

'I haven't been following *you*.' She laughs. 'Or at least not very often.' She has her compulsion under control. In fact, since she discovered Hannah, she's barely thought of Grant. She did go through a phase of following him – and Violet – mostly Violet, and that often made her late for work. The day that Al came to the centre to give them a briefing, Ruby had seen them go into the museum and she'd followed them inside, both fascinated and hurt. Grant had never even suggested they go to a museum so Ruby had thought it must have been Violet's idea but when she saw them in front of a display, it was Grant who was the animated one, standing before an ancient Greek statue and talking about it knowledgeably, or so it appeared. It made her feel confused, as if someone else had taken possession of his body.

'Ruby, we were married for fifteen years. I know when you're lying.'

'Sixteen.' She pauses. 'And I hate to break it to you, but we're still married.'

'Exactly.' He gives her a weary smile. 'And that's the other reason I'm here.' His eyes focus on hers. 'Please sign the divorce papers.' He drifts across the room again to lift the solicitor's envelopes off the dining table and wave them in her direction. 'You haven't even opened these yet.'

Her shrug says – so what?

'My offer is generous, Ruby. You can keep the house. I'm happy to pay for anything you want. You don't need to work. Money isn't an issue. You know that.'

Bearing in mind how much money he makes, his offer

is patently ungenerous but Ruby isn't going to argue that point either. She runs her tongue around the inside of her mouth. 'Do you want a drink?' she says.

'I suppose,' he concedes. 'If you're having one.'

Ruby knows she's being weak, pathetic even, but she's longed to have Grant back in their home. That's the real reason she left the spare key outside where they had always kept it. And now he's here she might as well make the most of it.

Don't, the cautionary voice inside her warns. *You'll only end up hurting yourself.*

She makes them both a double gin and tonic. 'No lemon, I'm afraid.' She slides his glass along the work surface and when it's within his reach he catches it. She takes a long, slow mouthful before saying, 'You go to dinner parties now.'

'I … yes. Sometimes.'

'But when we were together you hated dinner parties.'

'People change.'

'Do they?' She's drinking too fast. 'I wonder what else you do with her that you didn't do with me.'

He sighs. 'Do we really have to go over this?'

'I know. I know,' she says, her expression sarcastic. 'You want me to sign the papers and then you can leave. Make Violet happy. Marry her before … Well, before …' The words can't be said. She drains her glass and pours herself another generous measure. 'It's still a couple of hours until I'm due at work,' she says, more to herself than to him.

'Ruby, let's just do this thing,' he says, Mr Reasonable. 'Let's not hate one another.'

She nods, thinking. She sees him nod in response, mirroring her body language, convinced he's got through to her.

And then she says, 'Nobody has brought me higher than you and nobody has taken me lower.' She frowns because the second the words leave her mouth and hit the air she knows this isn't true: giving away her daughter – that was her lowest point. She didn't know it at the time, of course. That realisation crept up on her as the years rolled by and the magnitude of her actions gripped her in a vice of regret and self-loathing. 'Correction,' she says, pointing a finger at Grant. '*I* have taken myself lower. Giving up Hannah, that was my lowest point.' Her lip trembles. 'And seeing her again, that was my highest.' She smiles as she visualises her daughter's face.

'This isn't going anywhere,' he says.

She raises the glass in his direction. 'To my dead husband.'

'Fuck you.'

She laughs. 'That really has got under your skin.' Her blood has a fast-flowing stream of alcohol running through it, bending and shaping her emotions like a magician. 'Have you cheated on Violet yet?' She stares at him, her eyes aglow with a simmering hurt that quickly becomes malice. 'Lucky old Violet, with her posh frocks and her kitten heels. Does she shop in Harvey Nicks? Have champagne lunches with her friends? Well, no … not champagne, not at the moment.' She shivers. 'Does she know you sleep around?' She widens her eyes at him. 'Does she know about your unregistered phone? Has she found it?'

'This isn't going to work, Ruby,' he says.

'You still haven't located your conscience?'

'Oh, I have a conscience.' He moves towards her. 'But you can't guilt me into feeling shame because I don't care what you think. I don't love you,' he says flatly. 'I haven't done for many years now.'

She knew he didn't love her but to have not loved her for *many years*? To deny the good memories, the memories she felt proved their marriage hadn't been a complete waste of time and energy. It's a bull's-eye straight to her heart and the ripples reverberate through her chest. She clutches the edge of the worktop. He moves in closer and she thinks he's going to help her. He might even take back the words.

'Sign the papers,' he says.

Can her heart really drop any further? It seems it can. She sits down on the floor.

'Stand up.'

Just breathe, she tells herself.

'For Christ's sake!' He hauls her to her feet and half carries, half drags her to a chair where she slumps, head to chest, arms dropped by her side.

'Ruby?' He shakes her hard.

'Not today.' She's drooling; she wipes the back of her hand across her mouth. 'I can't sign anything now.' She shakes her head. 'I'm exhausted.'

'Too exhausted to lift a pen?'

He shakes her again and she screams, 'You can't make me!'

'I will make you.' His tone is cold. 'Sign the papers and then I'll stay out of your life.'

'You're already out of my life.'

'That's not the way your family sees it.'

Ruby squints up at him. 'Celia?' The light is behind him, a saintly halo over his head, and she wants to laugh at the irony of it. And then there's Hannah. She thinks she sees Hannah standing in the corner staring at her. She smiles and sits up straighter, feels the pull of her daughter's presence lighten her load.

'Ruby?' Grant says.

Ruby blinks and Hannah is gone. 'Imagining it,' she says.

'What?'

'I thought … nothing.'

'Have you looked at yourself in the mirror lately?'

'Have you?' she barks back.

'You're a mess! No wonder your family's worried.'

'My sister likes to talk. She talks about everyone.' What was it Celia said to her, right on this very spot, surrounded by the packing boxes? *Grant was right when he*— And then she'd stopped talking. It was something to do with Ruby not being able to accept help. 'Did she get in touch with you?' Bloody Celia, taking interfering to the max. When Ruby went on Facebook to see whether Hannah had a page – she did, but it was set to private – Ruby saw that her sister and Grant were still 'friends'. 'Celia knows nothing about me,' Ruby says.

Ruby hasn't confided in her sister for years. Celia knew she'd given birth to Hannah and given her up for adoption. She knew that much, but she didn't know the rest. She'd been busy having babies when their dad died. She barely had time to dress herself never mind keep up with Ruby's life or their dad's death. She didn't visit Ruby when she was in the psychiatric unit and she chose to gloss over Ruby turning up at Hannah's door and then having to leave the police. 'Put it behind you,' she instructed her. 'No point in dwelling.'

Dwelling? *Dwelling?*

'They're worried you're heading for another break-down,' Grant says.

He's using a tone that Ruby recognises – silky, faux-sympathetic – a perfect accompaniment to his words which are meant to make her anxious, doubt herself, wound. 'My life has never been better,' she states.

'We know you better than you know yourself.'

'That must be where I'm going wrong then.' She gives a short laugh. 'Clearly, I'm not fit for purpose. Wife, daughter, sister ...' She looks around for her glass but it's on the kitchen counter, out of reach. 'Mother ...'

He leans on the arms of the chair, staring down at her, his presence so overwhelming that Ruby hears herself whimper. 'Why would your daughter want to have anything to do with you?' he says. 'How can you expect anyone to love you when you look like this?'

From somewhere deep inside herself she summons up a reply. 'Go fuck yourself, Grant.' Gin-bravado talking? Most probably, but the words give her strength. 'Go fuck yourself!' she says again, louder this time.

He leans back, shaking his head before coming in close again. 'Just do it, Ruby,' he says, his spit landing on her cheek. 'Next week. Or else.'

'Or else what?' she murmurs.

'Or else I'll destroy you.' His voice is a whisper. 'You know I can.' He drops a hand between her legs and she gasps. 'Is this what you want? You want me to fuck you?'

His fingers probe inside her and she tries to pull his hand away but his grip is too strong. 'Get your hand—' She screams as he squeezes tighter. Her vision blurs; there is an unravelling of time. She tries to gasp for air but Grant's face is kiss-close and he steals the breath from her mouth.

'*Don't* cross me.' He tightens his grip and she moans. 'Are you enjoying that, Ruby?'

She's not enjoying it. Her head is loud with dizzy, chaotic screams that drown out her thoughts. Bile rises in her throat and at the same time her limbs freeze, from her torso to the tips of her fingers and the ends of her toes. Her feet can't kick him; her arms can't punch him.

She has lost her body and she feels close to losing her mind.

He holds her like this for seconds that are longer than hours before he lets her go and she manages to choke down some air while shielding herself from him, turning her body sideways and cupping one frozen hand between her legs. He has made her bleed. Sticky, warm blood stains her nightdress.

'You'll meet me next Wednesday, four o'clock, outside The Hub. The papers will be signed and you'll stay the fuck away from me and Violet. Is that clear?'

She nods, keeps nodding into the empty space, empty because Grant is already leaving.

'And stop telling people I'm dead, you mad bitch!' he shouts from the hallway before the front door slams behind him.

Ruby rests her head on the table and cries weak, soundless tears. She is defeated. Defeated by Grant, by the life choices she's made, by her own loneliness. She has no strength left. She has nowhere to go. She remembers the man on the bridge. She visualises his face, set with determination and resolve. He'd come to the end of the road. She gets that. She *really* gets it. How comforting death could be. A welcome embrace. A hot bath when the nights are drawing in and the draughty air brings shivers to your skin.

She stands up, wincing at the burning pain inside her. Grant's fingers dug into her body, as if he hated her, as if she were dead flesh, not a live, breathing human being. Not the woman he's been married to for the last sixteen years. She looks down and behind herself and sees the bloodstain on her nightdress. She should change it but she won't. There's no one else to see it.

She washes the blood off her hands and goes upstairs

to her bathroom. She dumps the contents of her medicine cabinet into the dry sink. She tips out every bottle and watches the colours and shapes muddle together like a bowl of children's sweets. She gathers up two handfuls and makes her way downstairs again and into the kitchen where she lays them out in a haphazard row on the work surface. She stares at them while she pours a large glass of water and then she chooses the first one – a small, blue diazepam – places it at the back of her tongue and swallows it.

Chapter Eleven

Hannah rings the bell half a dozen times but no one comes to the door. She looks back at the car and then at the house, frowning. So Ruby doesn't take her car to work. Maybe it's like one of the television dramas her mum watches. Ruby has a partner of the *Scott and Bailey* variety who comes to collect her in the morning, and then they drive off together to solve Edinburgh's crimes even though they end up spending most of the day discussing their broken relationships.

Except that the man in the café, Ruby's so-called 'friend', told Hannah that Ruby no longer worked for the police, not after the stunt she pulled five years ago. So where is she? Living in a house like this, she can hardly be desperate for money. She doesn't need to take a minimum wage job. By the looks of things, she doesn't need to work at all.

It's not an easy house to break into. Hannah walks around the perimeter, trying the handles on the doors and looking for open windows. There is an alarm box above the front door so even if she does find a way in, she expects all hell to break loose but it's worth a try. She also looks for cameras – she noticed them on several other houses in the street; it seems obvious to be security-conscious when you're living in a house like this but she can't see any sign of an electronic eye.

She peers through a window. Most of the house looks

unlived in. The living room is vast, white-walled with pale grey furniture. Two enormous, slate-grey leather sofas are placed in an L-shape in front of a wood burner, with a sheepskin rug filling the L but barely covering the acres of wooden floor. Hannah calculates that she could do five or six cartwheels before she would reach the opposite wall.

The kitchen-dining room is at the back of the house. It's the only room that looks lived in. The table is piled with unopened letters, magazines and papers. There are clothes on the chairs and a mug and glass on the work surface.

'She's not the tidiest ...' Hannah murmurs, the sound of her own voice almost startling her in a neighbourhood where quiet reigns supreme. There are no noises suggestive of people going about their business, no playing children or barking dogs; all she can hear is the distant hum of traffic, but she has to listen very hard to tune into that.

She wanders to the rear of the well-kept garden where there is a self-contained office. She peers through that window too, half expecting to see eyes staring back at her, but there's no one there. Turning back towards the house, she can't help but admire it. She knows what her parents would say if they saw it. 'There's been money thrown at this place' – that's what her dad would say. And her mum: 'Imagine living somewhere like this! All this space. I call this living like a queen.' And then she would think and add, 'Could be lonely, though.'

Just as she's about to give up and go home it occurs to her there might be a spare key hidden somewhere. Her own parents keep one under a huge granite stone, close to the back door. She begins at the front of the house again and runs her hand along the edges, under and over the windowsills. Finally she feels a magnetic box on the underside of one of the pipes that comes from the upper floor down the outside wall.

'Bingo!' she says, sounding like her nana. She slides the key into the door and holds her breath as she waits for the beep, beep, beep of an alarm. It doesn't happen and when she glances at the panel inside the porch it's obvious that the alarm is switched off.

She returns the key to where she found it and comes back inside, closing the door quietly behind her. The first thing she notices is the smell – a blend of ginger and lilies and a deeper, spicy note she can't place. The scent of money, no doubt.

She slides off her shoes and walks from the hallway to the living room. Her progress is soundless because there are no creaky floorboards like in her parents' home. Nothing to trip over. Nothing to offend the eye. It's like something from *Homes and Gardens*.

She walks into the living room and performs a cartwheel and another and then another before her foot nudges the rim of a glass coffee table and that brings her to a stop. There are art books on the table, in pristine condition. Just for show, probably. Like a lot of the house. An interior designer was likely given permission to do as he or she pleased; none of it says anything about the people who live here.

Hannah knows she's going to steal something – a keepsake, a reminder – something small enough to fit inside the box in her bureau; but the books are too large and the blue glass paperweight on the table is too heavy and too obvious.

At the entrance to the kitchen there are several photographs on the wall. A mum, dad and four children: three boys and a girl. The woman looks like … well, she looks like me, Hannah thinks. Same eyes, same skin, same texture and shine to her hair and almost the same smile. It can't be Ruby, surely? Five years ago Ruby didn't have any children and from what she's seen of the house so far, she doesn't have any now either. Her sister then, maybe. Hannah's aunt. And these children are Hannah's cousins. She already has a lot of aunts and cousins – she doesn't need any more. This is what she wants to feel, to believe, but there is a deeper pull from her heart that says, Wouldn't it be interesting to meet them? To stare into eyes that mirror yours? To clock the family traits?

In the kitchen Hannah stares out into the garden through windows and doors that cover a full wall. Louvred cupboard doors are built in at right angles to the windows and are positioned along the length of the back wall. Then there's the breakfast bar and modern kitchen with light-reflecting units and a minimalist feel because most of the equipment is hidden. Hannah enjoys herself for a few minutes, pressing buttons that make all sorts of things pop out, from electric sockets to a micro-wave.

The dining table is next. And this is when the first what-the-fuck moment punches Hannah in the gut.

There is a letter from Ruby's employer, a company called Spectra. Ruby watches CCTV for a living. *She's been watching you* – that's what the man in the café told Hannah. Hannah thought he meant half a dozen times in person, not this, not on camera. She thinks about how many CCTV cameras she walks past every day. The Royal Mile has no end of CCTV: leading up to the restaurant, on all the streets to and from the restaurant, outside the restaurant. She could be watching her every day.

Hannah collapses back into a chair. She stares straight

ahead, her expression moving from confused to disbelieving to angry. Ruby joined Spectra after she left the
police service. Was her choice of second career deliberate? Has she been watching Hannah all this time? Is
there a camera in the street where she lives?

Who does that?

Hannah's throat is tight and she reaches up to loosen
her collar but she isn't wearing a collar. The tightness is
inside her.

*Spying on her ... day after day ... while she kisses
Jeff at the bus stop ... while she texts on her phone ...
has she been to the restaurant? Would Hannah recognise
her?*

Her teeth are chattering. She doesn't know why. She
isn't cold. She's strangely numb. She'll call Jeff – no,
her parents. No – Clem. She'll call Clem.

Her fingers shake as she presses the screen. Clem's
mobile rings half a dozen times then goes to voicemail.
'Clem, it's me. Hannah. Please call me as soon as you
get this.' She bites her lip. 'Please. It's important.'

She ends the call and stands up. Her legs wobble. She
flexes her knees and walks to the windows, then returns
to the dining table and reads the letter again.

Fuck.

Ruby really is crazy. And obsessive. And secretive.

Ripples of fear travel along Hannah's spine but as the
seconds tick by her overriding emotion strengthens into
anger. She is gut-churningly angry. And vindicated.
Because all this time she has hated her birth mother and,
as it turns out, she was right to hate her. She gave her
up because she couldn't be bothered caring for her and
now she's creeping around, spying on her, following her
movements like some sort of pervert.

She should call the police. Now. Immediately. Her

finger hovers over her mobile just as 'Clem' flashes up on the screen.

'Everything okay?'

'Not really, I'm ...' She'll have to play it down a bit otherwise Clem will insist on coming round and fixing it. 'Remember the text? Well, it was my birth mother. And she's been in touch again. It's making me mad as hell.'

She doesn't need to say any more than that. Clem tells her that her anger is completely justified but to remember that, 'Fear is the primary emotion from which all other destructive emotions flow.'

Hannah holds the phone a few inches from her ear. Her gut tells her that while this might be true in theory, in the heat of this moment it means sweet FA.

'Because we crave security and control; it's what keeps us alive.'

Hannah doesn't agree with this. As far as she's concerned, what's kept her alive is luck and grit and the kindness of strangers.

'You need to be in control and your birth mother is not respecting that.'

This isn't helping. 'Thanks, Clem. I have to go.'

'Hannah, I—'

She ends the call and decides that the way forward is to keep it simple. If someone treats you badly you're entitled to be angry about it. It's called sticking up for yourself. It's got nothing to do with being afraid. It's about having self-esteem and resilience. It's about valuing yourself.

She thinks again about reporting Ruby to the police.

She could get her sacked. She's pretty sure there will be a law against using cameras to stalk members of the public. It would teach her a lesson.

Wouldn't it?

Probably not, Hannah admits to herself. She needs to be cleverer than that. She needs to show this woman that she wants nothing to do with her, that she needs to stay the fuck away.

Hannah walks towards the front door to step back into her shoes. And then she stops. She hasn't been upstairs yet. Ruby could have a room with photos of her all over the wall, a shrine even. The extent of her obsession could be wider than simply watching her. It's worth taking a look.

The first room is a guest bedroom, and so too the second and third. Perfectly made beds with plump pillows and themed décor. The door to the fourth bedroom is ajar. Hannah surmises it must be the master bedroom. She pushes the door wide and the light from the cupola floods across the carpet and onto the bed. Ruby is lying there, on her back, splayed across the bed like a starfish. Hannah stops dead, stock still and shocked, until her brain shifts gear and she retreats away on tiptoes, slowly retracing her steps, breath held, until she's in the hallway.

What the fuck? Ruby has been in the house this whole time. Fast asleep. Out for the count.

Hannah leans back against the wall next to the bedroom door. Her whole body is shaking, from her toes to the roots of her hair. She can hear the thudding of her pulse in her ears.

She lets a minute pass and then she goes back into the bedroom, half expecting to find Ruby's eyes open, but they aren't. A white pill pot sits on the bedside table. Hannah reads the label. It's a drug she's heard of but never taken, a powerful sleeping pill that explains why Ruby has slept through Hannah nosing around her house. It's not available on prescription in the UK so she must have a supplier. Hannah can hardly criticise her for that.

The wardrobe doors are open and she glances inside. There are no men's clothes in there. In fact most of the rails and shelves are empty. Ruby could be a lesbian but there are barely enough clothes for one woman never mind two. She rummages through Ruby's jewellery box, then goes into the en suite bathroom and looks inside the cabinet. She could be running a pharmacy; there are so many pots of pills, bottle after bottle of uppers and downers. Hannah does a quick count – twenty-four! Ruby is even more of a pill-popper than she is.

Hannah pockets a couple of the more expensive drugs and returns to the bedroom. She stares down at Ruby. The tables are turned, Hannah thinks. The watcher becomes the watched. This small, thin, unhealthy-looking woman is her obsessive, selfish and secretive mother and yet she appears to be no threat to anyone. She looks like me, Hannah thinks. If I were twenty years older and I'd let myself go.

Hannah watches the rise and fall of Ruby's chest. She leans in towards her, her hands inches from her neck. How easily her life could be snuffed out. She doesn't look like she has the strength for much of a fight back. She would be dead before she even knew she was under threat.

Hannah leaves the bedroom, goes back downstairs and into the kitchen. She pulls open drawers that glide on smooth, silent runners and contain every conceivable implement from avocado slicers to graters. Without thinking too hard, Hannah pockets two items. And then she crashes and bangs about the kitchen, opening and closing doors, hoping to be heard. She wants Ruby to wake up and then she'll confront her, hold the letter under her nose, demand to know how long she's been watching her.

And she'll tell her she's deluded if she thinks Hannah will ever play mother-and-daughter-happy-ever-after in this great fucking morgue of a house.

And then she'll tell her what she thought, what she *felt*, at fifteen when her mad mother showed up at her door.

And she'll finish by telling her to take her money and stuff it where the sun don't shine.

She hears a key slide into the front door lock.

She freezes only for a moment before she runs to the other side of the kitchen, opens one of the louvred doors and hides alongside the vacuum cleaner and the ironing board. There is just enough space for her to stand upright, elbows pulled in. At first she holds her breath as she watches through the slats. A man comes into the kitchen. He has a cursory look around and, clearly feeling at home, makes himself a cup of tea. Even in this low light, Hannah recognises him as the man from the café. He sighs when he sees there's no milk in the fridge, then sits in the armchair by the patio doors.

When he's settled in the chair, Hannah begins to breathe more easily. If he hasn't sensed her presence now, it's unlikely that he will. She gradually adjusts her body, one small movement at a time, until she's in a more comfortable position. Her phone is on silent and she'll just have to wait it out, see what happens next.

Half an hour goes by before Ruby comes into the kitchen. Hannah watches her yawn, her eyes half closed as she stands by the sink drinking water. Hannah doesn't get it – why isn't her friend speaking up? Ruby is by the hob when she suddenly spins around and stares across at where the man is seated. The man speaks and Ruby freezes. Even from a distance Hannah sees her reaction and is confused by it. When he walks towards her, she backs away. Hannah presses her face up as close to the slats as she dares. This man isn't Ruby's friend – he's her husband.

She's not sure what happens next, what exactly Grant does to Ruby's arm, because his back is obscuring her view, but Ruby suddenly cries out and pushes him away from her to run her arm under the cold water. He stands there for a moment holding the pot before putting it to one side.

And then Hannah listens as Ruby talks about 'giving up Hannah, that was my lowest point.' Her lip trembles. 'And seeing her again, that was my highest.' And then she smiles. It's a smile that lights up her sad, tired face.

She's sincere.

She's not playing to any crowd.

She's not saying it to annoy him.

In fact, as she says it, it's as if she's only just fully realised it herself. Or perhaps she's known it all along but this is the first time she's been able to articulate it.

Her mother loves her.

She loves the idea of a daughter. She doesn't know you. So how can she love you?

On a visceral level, her mother loves her. Has always loved her.

That doesn't excuse her.

Grant raises his voice and hauls Ruby over to one of the dining chairs and when she lifts her face, she looks afraid.

Hannah opens the louvred doors. She does it without thinking; she can't help herself. Ruby's eyes focus on hers and Hannah flinches, slips back inside the cupboard, annoyed. Should she be surprised that Ruby's marriage is so messed up? She hasn't come here to lend support; she's come here to confront her. But Grant has got here first so she'll just have to wait it out.

'Go fuck yourself,' Ruby says to Grant.

And then the mood changes. Hannah feels it even from several metres away. The air thickens with tension. And then violence. She watches through the slats as Grant grabs Ruby between the legs.

I'm not going to help her. I'm not.

She's not going to help Ruby. She's clearly got herself into this mess and she can get herself out.

She watches Grant hurt her.

She watches Ruby suffer.

He makes her bleed.

She should feel bad.

She doesn't feel bad because this woman, *her mother*, gave up her baby and then decided she wanted her back. Fifteen years later! Five and a half thousand days later she decided she wanted her back. And now, again, she has been creeping her way into her life like a snake.

She doesn't deserve forgiveness.

'I'm not helping you,' she whispers. 'I won't help you.'

Hannah counts the seconds until Grant lets Ruby go. She watches Ruby recoil backward, holding on to herself, protecting herself. She hears Ruby agree to meet Grant the following week and then, when he leaves, she drops her head onto the table and starts to cry. It's a sound that Hannah has rarely heard before. It's the sound of hopelessness.

Hannah puts her hands over her ears and shuts her eyes tight.

She won't feel sorry for Ruby. She absolutely fucking won't. She'll cover her ears until the crying stops. She'll block out what's happening on the other side of the louvred door because it doesn't concern her.

Finally … eventually … Ruby stops crying and Hannah can breathe again. She watches Ruby cross over to the sink, clutching her hand to her snatch as if her insides are about to fall out. She washes the blood off her hands. She's still crying – soft, weak sobs that cave in her chest.

When she turns from the sink, Hannah sees her expression. And as soon as she sees it she wishes she hadn't. She's only seen that expression on a face once before.

Her own.

In the mirror.

Before she learned to cut herself.

Something loosens inside Hannah's chest, a heavy brick that she thought was too entrenched to shift. She feels the beginnings of a sensation that isn't hate or anger's cousin. It's lighter than that.

She stares down at her feet, her jaw tense, and when she looks up again the kitchen is empty.

She waits for a few minutes until she hears Ruby climbing the stairs, then leaves the cupboard, puts on her shoes and opens the front door to go home.

Chapter Twelve

Adoption Part VII

Today I met my birth mother. It was unexpected. I never imagined I would meet her. I've thought about it a lot but never with the intention of making it happen.

So, how did it happen?

It was Ellie. My one-time friend. I say 'one-time' because how do you forgive someone for springing that on you? She asked me to meet her at an aunt's house. So along I go, lamb to the slaughter, and the woman who opens the door is not Ellie's aunt – no, she is my birth mother. At first I'm completely shocked because well, a) I didn't expect it, b) it was like looking at myself in an ageing mirror and c) she acted like this was all completely normal.

And then, when I stop being shocked, I think, What the fuck is going on? Because, wait for it, she's been watching me. She's been watching me on CCTV cameras, following me to and from work …

Hannah hesitates – that's too close to the truth and she doesn't want the details to catch her out. So she deletes her last paragraph and writes:

And the point is not the detail, it's not the he-said-she-said, or in this case she-said-she-said. The point is

– the question is: is a crazy, deluded birth mother better than no birth mother at all?

Because she is crazy. Not only is she a ranter and a raver, a drug taker and a drunk, she thinks we can pick up our lives where we left off – me a few days old and her a nineteen-year-old. She thinks that it's okay for her to step back into my life when it suits her. But it seems to me that being a parent is all about showing up. Showing up every single day, no matter whether you feel like it or not. My time on the planet – seven thousand, two hundred and ten days, give or take. She's been in my life for four of them.

And in case you're wondering – yes – that still makes me angry.

Will the anger shrivel or expand if I get to know her?

Will I be able to forgive her?

Should I just walk away and never look back?

Help me. Please.

She uploads the post and gets herself a drink. She feels marginally better for writing the blog. It puts some distance between her and what she just witnessed in Ruby's house. What she witnessed and what she discovered.

She gulps the wine and stands by the window, staring up and across the road. It's already dark so she can't see much but she wonders if there are CCTV cameras on the tenement opposite her. She doesn't have any curtains. Ruby could have been spying on her at home too, watching her in the living room, in the bedroom, having sex with Jeff.

She feels sick at the thought.

The dog walker is on the pavement below, his dog sniffing every lamppost and hedge. He looks up at the flats, catches sight of her and waves; she waves back and as she does, she has a sudden flash of insight. He's not a creep; he's lonely. He's probably a widower who doesn't see many people. If he has any kids, they've left home and can only see him once every so often, and that breaks his heart because he loves being a dad and a granddad.

Hannah's first job was in a shop round the corner from her parents' house – an old-fashioned ironmonger's – but she couldn't bear it because every day the lonely elderly came in looking for conversation. It felt too close to the bone for Hannah. The only reason she isn't one of the Beatles' 'lonely people' is because she is still young enough to work and attract a man. But she doesn't see herself getting married and having kids. Hannah wouldn't trust herself to be a good mother. She doesn't want history repeating itself.

Hannah's mobile rings. It's Clem. 'Just checking you're okay.'

'I'm fine.' Hannah forces an upbeat tone. 'Sorry for worrying you.'

'You're sure?'

Hannah tells her that she's asked her birth mother to leave her alone and she thinks she will respect that. 'But listen! It's your party at the weekend! What shall I bring? Snacks or booze? Both? I can do both.'

When Clem finishes chatting Hannah sits down on the sofa to think.

Ruby is a basket case.

Grant is violent. And he is a liar.

Hannah wishes she'd never met either of them.

But she has.

And, like it or not, Ruby is her birth mother.

The watching, the stalking. Hannah shivers.

Perhaps she sees herself as a guardian angel of sorts, watching out for her daughter.

Or maybe she's just crazy. And maybe the craziness will get worse and—

What's Grant's game?

He let Ruby think it was her sister who'd been in touch with him when it was her mother. And he said nothing about meeting Hannah.

What would it mean to him if mother and daughter got to know each other?

He wouldn't have any control over what might happen next. And men like Grant need to have control. You don't make lots of money by being a nice guy. You make it by manipulating other people's behaviour in your favour. And that includes your wife, even when she becomes your ex because it suits you that she's a casualty. And wasn't Grant a hero for putting up with her for so long?

Wouldn't he just love it if she were sacked again? Then she would have to fall on his mercy, sign his papers and put up with any shit he threw her way.

She takes her mobile from her pocket and sends Grant a text: **I'm wondering whether you'd be willing to meet me again? Now that I've had time to think, I have a few questions to ask you about my mother.**

She's barely put her mobile back when there's a reply: **Of course. I'd be happy to.**

I bet you would. It'll be another chance for you to go behind Ruby's back. Well, I'm ahead of you there, Hannah thinks. They make arrangements to meet on Monday. She's struck by the thought that Grant could be her father but then she remembers what he said to Ruby: 'We were married for fifteen years. I know when you're lying.' If he'd known Ruby since they were teenagers, he would have said as much.

Hannah hears the ping of mobile alerts as responses to her blog start to arrive but she ignores them for a moment and begins an online search for marriage records. Within half a dozen clicks she has discovered that Ruby Romano married Grant Stapleton in October 2002.

She googles Grant Stapleton and follows a trail. Companies House informs her that he is the director of four businesses: three insurance companies and one selling bespoke sports equipment.

She searches for him on Facebook and there he is, his arm around the shoulders of a woman called Violet – she looks much younger than Ruby. She can't be more than thirty. Hannah scrolls back through 2018 and 2017 paying particular attention to his photos. Friends offer profuse congratulations on their engagement. (Hannah shakes her head at this; does Violet know he's still married to Ruby?) There's a photo of Violet holding her ring out to the camera, the diamond so large and heavy that her finger is barely thick enough to support it. And then there are the pregnancy congrats. Her belly grows larger in each photo and she even posts her black and white scan-grab with digitally added love hearts all around the perimeter.

She wonders whether Ruby stalks Grant online, whether she's a masochist. Childless Ruby's husband has got another woman pregnant with twins. Did Ruby not want kids? Did giving birth to Hannah put her off?

There is no Ruby Romano living in Scotland registered on social media, and, as far as Hannah can tell, Ruby has no online presence. Not as herself at any rate, Hannah thinks. Of course if mother is anything like daughter she'll have a pseudonym.

Celia PeacockwasRomano is a friend of Grant's and

Hannah raises an eyebrow at this. It doesn't strike her
as very loyal to Ruby to still be in contact with her ex,
especially when he left her for someone else. Celia's
profile is full of gifs of cute puppies and kittens, and
short videos of her own children being even cuter.
Hannah finds herself smiling as she watches the youngest,
Joseph, sing a song about being a tortoise who wins the
race. He's wearing a green costume made of corrugated
cardboard and a lopsided hat. He sings with a childish
disregard of vanity and it makes Hannah want to hug
him.

When she's had enough sweetness, she checks out the
comments on her blog. Ratty1166 is the first to write
and, as usual, it's all empathy and advice: What a shock
that must have been for you! Have you taken arnica?

BecauseICare begins with: Your mother is trying to
make amends, for God's sake cut her some slack!

BecauseICare likes to think she's someone who 'says
it as it is' but Hannah sees her as someone who thinks
she's always right. She's probably powerless in real life.
She most likely has teenage children who ignore her and
a husband who watches porn when she goes to bed.

TRO123 is back with his particular way of seeing
things: As usual you're asking the wrong questions –
the thousand dollar question here is – who's the daddy?

This brings Hannah up short. It's not that she never
thinks about who her dad might be, more that she doesn't
feel it's particularly relevant. Her birth mother is real;
her father has always been an imaginary character,
someone who opted out after the initial act of conception.
She's sure a great dad is an asset to any child's life –
she's experienced this herself – but most childrearing is
done by women. It's not discrimination. It's biology. It's
like saying an orange and an apple are the same. They

aren't. They're both fruits, but in almost every other respect they are different.

She asks Jeff to come with her to Clem's party. 'Who is Clem again?' he says.

'I told you. She runs the adoption charity.'

'What adoption charity?' He always frowns when he's in the process of actively thinking, which she finds both endearing and irritating. 'Are you looking for your mum?'

'I found her already.' *And it's strange and I still can't dwell on it because if I do it sets off emotions inside me like tiny detonations, firecrackers that run along a wire and will eventually accumulate in a massive explosion.*

'You've found her?' He sits up straight, suddenly interested. 'How?'

'The usual way.' She reaches for him.

'Is she nice?'

'Not especially.'

'Oh, I'm sorry.' He cuddles her into him. 'Are you disappointed?'

'Nah. I already have a mum and dad. But' – she puts her hands on his cheeks and pulls his face towards hers – 'whatever you do, don't tell them I've found her. They'd be really hurt.'

'I won't.' He kisses her. 'You can count on me.'

She can count on him for company, but because he lacks curiosity he doesn't ask her any more questions. They have sex again and then again so she ends up being late for the party. Jeff stays at the flat to watch a film and Hannah would stay with him except that she doesn't want to let Clem down and, even more so, because she knows her turning up will piss Dave off.

And going out will take her mind off Ruby.

Her face.

The sadness.

Hannah is not without a heart; she'd just rather not lend it to her mother.

Clem and Dave live in a quirky property on the south side of the Forth, right underneath the rail bridge, so that the colossal metal structure looms over the garden like a prehistoric monster. The iron girders are a sight to behold and she stands for more than a minute staring up at them before she takes a deep breath and goes inside.

It's not the sort of party where you show up whenever you fancy. It's one of those parties where everyone is there by eight and it's now half past nine so most of the guests have already eaten and are drinking and chatting. Drug-taking happens discreetly so as not to offend (she passed a couple smoking dope in the garden) and all the snacks are at the very least vegetarian, if not vegan. Dave is holding forth about women's rights (really?) when Hannah arrives and Clem is so captivated by him that it takes her a while to notice Hannah.

'You made it!'

'It's organic.' She passes her the bottle of wine. 'From Kent, would you believe, so the carbon footprint is low too.'

'A hint of raspberry notes with a fresh floral bouquet,' Clem says, reading the label. 'Sounds delish.'

Clem introduces her to most of the people in the room. 'This is my good friend, Hannah. We've known each other for ever, haven't we, Hannah?'

They're interested, inclusive people. Champagne socialists to a man, they talk about poverty and deprivation as if they know, really *know*, what that means, when they've never been homeless and they all have jobs in the university or the arts. Hannah drifts from group to group, from discussions about the increase in food bank numbers to social housing initiatives, and then she goes outside to join the dope smokers.

They smile at her and wordlessly pass her the joint. She takes a long drag before giving it back. They are easy company. At first they ponder on the beauty of the moon and then they discuss a recent story in the press where a woman murdered her partner. 'She said she always goes crazy when there's a full moon.'

'There's crazy and then there's crazy,' one of them replies.

'He had a history of violence towards her.'

'There's only so long anyone can put up with that before they snap.'

'Full moon or no full moon.'

Hannah thinks about Ruby and what she's been putting up with from Grant. It would be enough to drive any woman to extreme behaviour. And yet he was the one who left her. Clem would say Ruby must have low self-worth to live with a violent man for all those years. Maybe Hannah should be cutting her some slack.

Dave appears at the door and, as if on cue, the dope-smoking couple pass her the end of the joint and go inside.

'I thought you'd left,' he says.

'I'm admiring the moon.'

'You're not enjoying the conversation inside?'

'I'm not very political.'

He reaches for the joint. 'You going to share?'

'Be my guest. There isn't much left.'

He sucks on it with the fervour of a man who's done this many times before. Although not recently, because he's cleaned himself up for Clem, become the sort of man who takes out the rubbish without being asked, and knows the f word stands for feminism not fuck.

'We're all actors, playing a part,' she says quietly. 'Even Clem.'

He ignores this. Instead he looks Hannah up and down, measuring her attractiveness. If it's meant to intimidate her, it doesn't.

'Most friendships are unequal and, believe it or not, there's something Clem can learn from me,' Hannah says.

'And what would that be?'

'Thing is, Dave – I don't get what she sees in you.'

He laughs.

'I'm not sure why Clem hasn't clocked how manipulative you are. But she will.'

'Thing is, Hannah,' he says, mimicking her tone, 'I think you're a closet lesbian and now your nose is out of joint.'

'Yeah, that must be it,' Hannah says. 'But I'm going nowhere. And I've known her a lot longer than you. And when you're long gone we'll still be friends.'

'You think you know it all,' Dave says.

'Here you are, you two!' Clem comes down the back steps and walks across the grass towards them.

'We're marvelling at the moon,' Dave says, pointing upwards to where the full moon hangs heavy in the sky.

'No strings attached,' Hannah says.

'What's that?' Clem says.

'The moon,' Hannah replies. 'It looks like it should fall down on top of us but it doesn't.'

'There's a message in there somewhere,' Dave says. He puts his arms around Clem's shoulders and turns them both towards the house. 'Let's join our friends inside.' He looks back at Hannah and gives her a smile that says, Look! I've won.

'Good party?' Jeff says.

'No.' She pulls his shirt up over his head. 'Well, it was okay but ...' She sighs. 'Oblivion. That's what I want. Can you help me out or not?'

He helps her out and then he falls asleep with his arm around her. She closes her eyes, post-orgasm relaxed, snuggles down and waits to drift off. She waits, but sleep eludes her. She can't relax because when she closes her eyes Ruby's face leapfrogs to the front of her mind.

She wriggles out from underneath Jeff, pulls on a long T-shirt and stands by the window. She's trying not to think about Ruby, because thinking about her doesn't help make anything clearer. But after being in her home, hearing her declare her feelings at giving up her baby and then finding her baby again, watching her being attacked by Grant, listening to the sound of her tears: she is now the ghost in the corner of Hannah's eye.

Except that she's alive.

And she wants to make contact.

So how can Hannah not think about her?

February, five years ago, ten o'clock in the evening, and she was in bed already because she had an exam the next day. The rain was battering down outside and she was tucked up, a bug in a rug. She loved her bedroom, and her bed. She wasn't a normal teenager; she was a homebody. She loved her parents and grandparents; spending time with them was high up on her list of happy ways to spend a weekend. They were kind, natural people, salt of the earth. She still remembered her parents from when she was adopted the first time round, the couple who took her in her when she was a baby and died because she wanted an ice cream. She didn't blame herself for that any more. Or not very often. Occasionally, when she was feeling premenstrual and weepy she thought about them, and hated herself. Her greed had led to their deaths. One pivotal moment when she should have kept her mouth shut and she didn't.

'Please, open the door! I only want to talk to her. Please!'

She sat bolt upright in bed at the sound of the woman's voice.

'Please! It's important.'

She pulled on her sheepskin slippers and opened her bedroom door.

'I need to speak to Hannah! Just for a moment.' *Her mouth was at the letterbox.* 'I'm begging you.'

Hannah was halfway down the stairs when her dad said, 'Go back upstairs, Hannah. And stay in your bedroom.'

She turned around at once because she'd never heard that tone in his voice before, a tone that implied there was danger outside.

'Please, just give me a minute,' *the woman pleaded.* 'I promise you, I'll leave after that.'

Hannah closed her bedroom door and sat behind it with her knees drawn up.

'I need to see my daughter.'

'I have no intention of letting you in,' *her dad said.*

'Please! You can't stop me seeing her!'

'I'm calling the police,' *he said.*

There was a loud keening sound like someone who is grief-stricken and then fists hammering on the door. 'Let me in, you bastard! Let me in!'

Hannah clapped her hands over her ears and tried to ignore the thoughts blowing a storm inside her skull: This was her mother? Her birth mother? At the door?

Hannah sat on the floor, arms wrapped around herself,

until her bedroom turned blue with a searchlight that pene-
trated the curtains and made patterns on the wall. She looked
out of the window and saw two police cars in front of the
house, lights flashing on the roofs. A woman was being taken
down the path and she wasn't going easily. She was strug-
gling against the two officers, twisting her body round to
shout back at Hannah's dad, 'I have to see her! Hannah!
Hannah!' She stared up at the window and caught Hannah's
eye. Hannah gasped and moved back into the shadows. She
wanted to stop seeing but her eyes wouldn't close.

'I just want to talk to Han—'

The woman was bundled into the car, and a police officer
climbed in next to her. Hannah's dad walked along the path
and spoke to one of the remaining officers, rain falling hard
on both their heads. Her dad usually stood with his hands
in his pockets, but now his arms were moving through the
air to emphasise his point. At the end of the conversation,
the policeman held out a hand and they shook on it before
her dad came inside again.

Hannah drew back from the window and opened her
bedroom door a crack. Her dad was in the living room
talking to her mum. She stood at the top of the stairs, holding
her breath and straining her ears to hear what was being
said.

This woman really was her mother.

She had already phoned twice and turned up in person
once when Hannah was round at a friend's.

'She gave up her baby because she didn't want to bring
her up,' Hannah's dad said. 'And now, when she's fifteen –
fifteen! – she wants her back. It's not happening.'

'We don't know that, George. We don't know why she gave
her up.'

'We do know, Morag. We know perfectly well. She was
given every chance to keep her. The social worker told us.'

'I know, but, well ...'

Hannah listened to her dad say that Ruby had never wanted her baby, that the baby was an inconvenience. There was no record of a father's name on the birth certificate because she'd had a one-night stand.

'She seems to be having a nervous breakdown,' her mum said.

'I know. And I feel for the woman. But we told her the other night that she was going the wrong way about it.' He sighed loudly. 'We can't have her around Hannah.'

'No,' her mum said. 'You're right, George.'

Hannah went back to her bedroom and climbed into bed. At first she was too shocked to feel anything. She lay in bed, legs and arms straight, eyes wide to the ceiling, and it wasn't until her pillow was wet with tears that she rearranged herself into the foetal position and hid under the duvet.

Although Hannah is five minutes early, Grant is waiting for her when she arrives at the café. 'Thank you so much for meeting me again,' she says. He stands up and holds out his hand. She can't take it. Not when she's seen how cruelly he can use it. She breezes past him. 'Can I get you another drink?'

'I have one,' he says.

Hannah goes to the counter to buy a coffee. Her heart is still. It feels hard in her chest. Like steel.

'I was surprised you texted me,' he says when she returns to the table. 'I didn't feel like we parted on the best of terms.'

'I'm sorry. It was a lot to take in.'

'The whole business must be hard on you.'

'Well ...' She sips some coffee and then stares directly at him. 'I thought maybe you could tell me about her. Forewarned being forearmed and all that. If I know her

better then I'll be more prepared if she does approach
me.'

'Fair enough.'

'How long have you known her?'

'Must be about seventeen years.'

'You met at work?'

'We met in a bar.'

'Is she a big drinker?'

'I wouldn't say so.'

'You said something about her father dying.'

'That was five years ago.' He looks regretful. 'They
were close.'

'And that was why she came to my parents' house?'

'It was the catalyst. She was grieving.'

Hannah nods without breaking eye contact. 'You don't
happen to know who *my* dad is, do you?'

'I'm sorry, I don't. She said he was a one-night stand.'
He makes an attempt at a sympathetic face. 'You were
a mistake.'

'I heard as much when I was fifteen,' Hannah says,
and the nub of anger that's been germinating inside her
since she watched him hurt Ruby doubles in size, because
– imagine saying that to someone? What if she hadn't
already known that about her father? Grant could have
said that he didn't know. There was no need to be so
blunt.

'Sorry to say,' he adds.

Hannah shakes her head as if it doesn't matter. 'Is she
married?'

'In the process of getting divorced, I believe.'

'So what's her husband like?'

'He's a good bloke ...' He trails off, not quite able to
expand on the lie.

'And they didn't have any children together?'

'They didn't.' She watches him grow uncomfortable but he keeps the smile on his face. 'Why don't we talk about what you'll do if she approaches you?'

Hannah takes a slow sip of coffee before passing the buck back to him. 'What do you think I should do?'

'Well ... I think you should avoid meeting her. I think you should, perhaps, nominate a go-between who will tell her that you know she's been watching you.'

'And warn her off?'

'Exactly.'

'Would you do that for me?'

He moves his head from side to side, weighing this up like it's a tough choice. And then he takes a breath before saying, 'I would.' He nods. 'I would do that for you.'

Hannah frowns as if a thought has just occurred to her. 'But she could be good for me, couldn't she? We could be good for each other.'

'Hannah.' He doesn't like this. He holds up his hand – that hand. 'Hannah, Ruby is unstable. Trust me. I know her.'

'Perhaps she's only upset because I'm not in her life. If I was in her life then—'

'Hannah!' His tone is urgent. 'This is the woman who gave you up. This is the woman who crashed into your life at fifteen and is creeping into your life now. Stalking you.' He leaves a significant pause. 'Stalking you, Hannah.'

His words are simply an echo of her own thoughts but coming from his mouth? 'You really hate her that much?' Hannah says.

'Of course not!' His face is a mask of insincerity. 'Of course I don't hate her!'

'It's about control then? Is it?'

'Hannah, I ...' Hand to chest. That hand. 'Believe me when—'

'I tell you what, *Grant*.' She says his name very deliberately. 'Why don't we just stop the bullshit? I googled you. I know you're Ruby's husband. And I know you're divorcing her.'

'Okay.' He nods several times, quickly recovering his composure. 'Even better. Now we can be honest with each other.'

'Honest?' She scoffs. 'You couldn't be honest if someone held a gun to your head.'

He looks shocked at this, as if she completely misunderstands him. 'I didn't tell you I was Ruby's husband because I wanted to keep things simple for you.'

'Bollocks.' She raises her chin to him. 'I don't know what your game is; correction – I think I do. You're a bully. And you're not done with her yet because you have to make sure she can't make any trouble for you. Does Violet know you're a cheat?' Hannah hears these words come out of her mouth, almost the exact words Ruby used, and realises she's hit upon the crux. 'You've reinvented yourself with Violet, haven't you, Grant? You don't want Ruby to be strong because she might have too much to say for herself. Too much to say to Violet.'

'You don't know what you're talking about.' He stands up.

'The truth hard to take?' Hannah stands up too. 'You don't like being crossed, Grant, do you?'

His lips are tight. 'You think you know everything?'

'I know you're—' *meeting my mother on Wednesday. And I saw the way you treated her last week. Bastard.* That's what she wants to say but she makes do with, 'I know you should keep your nose out of my business.' She glances at his hand then up to his face. 'And your filthy hands to yourself.'

When she arrives back home she goes online again and lets her alter ego trawl around but within minutes she is dissatisfied. She's tired of pretending to be someone she isn't: blog-Hannah with her imaginary friend Ellie and her imaginary brother Mark. That worked while she wanted to sound off because, up to this point, her posts had never been about the exact nature of events.

But now she feels the need for change. Confronting Grant has shifted her perspective. She unmasked him and it felt good. Better than good – it felt illuminating, challenging, honest. It felt honest, and she could do with some of that in her life. Hannah wants – needs – advice. She wants to draw back the curtains. Expose herself. Be honest. With someone. Anyone.

Short of finding herself a decent counsellor, her only recourse is online because a) Clem won't get it. b) Her parents are literally the last people she can be honest with. And c) Jeff has no idea what's going on inside her. Not only would he struggle to give good advice, he would be deeply shocked that the Hannah he knows is so very different from the Hannah he doesn't (or so it seems). And then he would go all quiet on her, stare at her with a serious, pent-up expression, when he thinks she isn't aware of his eyes on her. (It happened once before when he caught her taking a cocktail of drugs – no big deal in her eyes, but he turned it into an I-thought-I-knew-you conversation that was exhausting.)

She could approach one of the commentators on her blog. They had a proven track record of being interested in her story and some of them even gave good advice.

What could go wrong? she asks herself.

Everything! Is the answer that comes straight back at her.

Why? She won't give her real name. She won't say anything that could pin her to a time or place. She will continue the pretence that she lives in Manchester. All these measures will protect her from being identified.

So really – what could go wrong?

The answer still comes back – *everything* – but Hannah ignores it because what was life without a measure of risk?

She doesn't need sympathy or motherly advice and she knows to avoid anyone who has a personal axe to grind or confuses meanness with plain speaking. She decides to approach TRO123. She has often found his comments thought-provoking.

She sends him a private message: I like the way you think – could we have a chat?

He's back at once with: Yes.

We keep it between the two of us, yeah?

Sure.

I don't have a friend called Ellie or a brother called Mark. I do have a boyfriend but he's not called Paul. I pretend to be someone I'm not.

Why?

Because it adds distance, like I'm playing a game.

I get that.

But now I want to be honest because I have a real problem to solve.

Go on.

Their conversation continues long into the night until Hannah has given up all her feelings to this person.

TRO123 tells her his (her?) name is Jo. Man? Woman? She has no idea. And it really doesn't matter. All she knows is that now her load is lighter because someone is on the journey with her.

Chapter Thirteen

'So what happened to you last night?' Lennie says.

'I was sick,' Ruby replies. 'I made it into work by midnight. Freddie ended up staying on until then. It gave him an opportunity to get to know Fiona and to lord it over me.'

'Well, I hope you're up for a treat tonight.' He brings a Tupperware box out of his bag. 'Slow-cooked lamb shanks, mustard mash and purple sprouting broccoli.'

'Sounds delicious,' Ruby says. 'If it wasn't for you I'd die for want of a decent meal.'

'And sticky toffee pud for afters. Get some fat on your bones.' He walks off towards the kitchen. 'Keep an eye on Thistle Street, will you?' he shouts back.

'Will do.'

When Lennie leaves the room, Ruby points her face in the direction of the screen but her eyes don't focus. What she sees instead is a picture that plays out in her mind's eye. It's a rerun of what happened: Grant in her house, questioning, demanding, threatening her, hurting her.

The line of pills. A wobbly line of colours and shapes that would, had she swallowed them, have stopped her breathing.

She would have died. No doubt about it.

This reality is sobering. It makes her hands shake and her mouth dry.

'You watching Thistle Street?' Lennie is back. 'You look like you're in a daze.'

'Sorry.' Ruby snaps out of her thoughts and brings three feeds down onto her spot screens. There has been a run of robberies in Thistle Street. People leaving pubs and having their pockets picked. Classic distraction technique: two perpetrators, one bumps into the victim, holds his attention by making a show of apologising while the other one calmly lifts a wallet or mobile from handbag or pocket. Easy to drive away in several directions, so despite the fact that the police have watched hours of footage they have yet to isolate the suspects.

Did she really intend to kill herself? Yes, in that moment, she did. She was perched on an emotional precipice and now that she's stepped back from the edge, she feels altered. She can't quite put her finger on it yet but she likens it to coming to the end of a long road that has a steep drop at the end of it – and she has the choice to fall down and hit the bottom or attempt to fly.

'How are you finding Fiona?' Lennie says. 'Her probation's almost up; we'll have to write our assessments.'

'I'm not sure about her,' Ruby says.

'Oh?'

'She's a good worker. She's strangely naïve in some ways and in other ways hard as nails.'

'Immaturity and ambition,' Lennie says. 'You going to put that in her appraisal?'

'Maybe. You?'

'She's sharp. She's a quick learner and she has some skills but ...' He shrugs. 'Do you remember back when you were a cop and you'd be partnered up with someone who on paper should be great, but you knew as soon as you met them that you could never trust them?'

'Aye. I've been there.'

Lennie raises his eyebrows. 'That's her.'

'Well put,' Ruby says. 'Sums her up perfectly. I've a feeling she could sneak on me and not give it a second thought.'

Ruby likes that she and Lennie are in tune with each other and it makes her feel uncomfortable that she hasn't been truthful about Grant. How had that particular lie got so out of control? She can't even remember saying he was dead but that's what everyone believes so she must have said it. She'd like to tell Lennie the truth now. She'd like to tell Lennie about Grant leaving her for pregnant Violet. She'd like to tell him about the cathartic way she spent her morning. She finally opened all the solicitor's letters on her dining table and read every one. Grant was clearly lying when he said he was making a good offer. The house is less than ten per cent of the assets.

And she'd like to tell Lennie about Hannah. But this was neither the time nor the place for such a conversation. 'You fancy going out for a drink one evening?' she says.

'One evening as in one morning?'

'Sure.' She laughs. 'Whatever suits you and Trish.'

'We could meet up in my back garden again? No one uses the hut but me.'

'You're on.'

'I'll cook us a little something. I've got my eye on a recipe for flatbreads.'

They agree to meet the following week. By then she will have given Grant the divorce papers to return to his solicitor because he doesn't trust her to hand them in herself.

And then it will be done.

And then she can move on.

They have a quiet night with little to report and when Ruby arrives home in the morning she finds her mum standing in the front drive. 'Mum?'

'I'm sorry to disturb you.'

'You're not disturbing me.' Ruby takes her arm. Her mum looks worn out and thinner than she was when they last met. She is usually a neat and tidy woman, not a pound over- or underweight, her greying hair well groomed, her make-up subtly applied. Today her hair is unkempt and her blouse looks as if it hasn't been ironed.

'Mum? Are you okay?' Ruby feels a fluttering panic. 'It's not Celia, is it? Or the children?'

'No, no. Nothing like that. I just wanted to have a word with you.'

'Okay.' She smiles and unlocks the front door. 'You haven't been waiting long, have you?'

'No, I just … I know it's the morning and you need your sleep.'

'I never go to bed straight away. I need time to unwind for a bit.' She throws her keys and coat on the dining table. 'Coffee?' As she says this, she remembers there won't be any milk in her fridge. She opens it anyway and is surprised to see one whole shelf stacked with groceries: milk, jam and butter, cheese and yoghurt, some apples and raspberries. I actually have food in the house! Her eyes fill with tears. Such a simple gesture. A caring gesture. Who? Certainly not Grant. Celia, then. Celia must have shopped for her. But she *could* believe, couldn't she, that it might be Hannah? Would that be so crazy?

'I have something to tell you,' her mum says.

Ruby realises that it must be about her health – the weight loss, the air of distraction. This is the sort of atmosphere that precedes a disclosure, a parent breaking the news that they have cancer and the prognosis isn't good. 'Sit down, Mum,' she says.

They sit opposite each other at the dining table. Her mum puts her hands on the table, clasped together, and

Ruby reaches to hold them. Her mum seems shocked at this and almost pulls them away but stops herself. 'After Celia's birthday party, I was very upset.'

'I know. I shouldn't have told you about seeing Hannah. I regretted the words as soon as they were out of my mouth.'

Her mum nods at this admission. 'Hannah has become a tricky subject for us.'

'No harm done,' Ruby says. She has rarely seen her mum so uncomfortable. She squeezes her hands. 'Let's not mention it again.'

'We have to talk about it, Ruby, because I shouldn't have reacted the way I did. I was so upset with myself, and with you, that I did something I shouldn't have.'

'Oh?' Ruby tries to smile.

'Well... I sat on it for a while. But, I wanted to make it better.'

'What better?' Ruby pulls her hands into fists by her sides.

'Your relationship with Hannah,' her mum says, as if it's obvious. 'And so I called Hannah's parents. I still had their details from before.' Ruby's mouth falls open. 'Remember when you were ill and you asked me to check that Hannah was okay and I went round there?' Ruby is unable to nod. 'So I got Hannah's mobile number from them. I thought they wouldn't give it to me if they knew why I wanted it but then I remembered that, back then, they told me Hannah was having help from a charity, and on the off chance the charity was still...' She takes a weighty breath. 'So I had to pretend—Well, anyway... I got the number and I approached Grant,' she blurts out, loudly.

'What?' Ruby shakes her head as if there's water in her ears. 'You *what*?'

'I told Grant you had seen Hannah, that you were watching her.'

Ruby shoots to her feet but her legs are made of jelly and she falls back against the wall. 'Say that again?'

'You heard me, Ruby. And I'm sorry but you really pressed my buttons. You know you did.'

'Grant? You approached *Grant*? Why? *Why?* WHY?'

'Because I was concerned that you were heading towards making another mistake.'

'I *told* you I wasn't. I *told* you I had it under control.'

'I could *not* see you in psychiatric hospital again, Ruby. I could *not*. It took its toll on you, and on me.'

'So you speak to Grant? *Grant*, of all people?' Ruby's hand reaches down involuntarily to between her legs. She's still sore from when he hurt her. 'If you really had to talk it through with someone then why not Celia?' She pulls her hand back to her side. 'Why Grant?'

'Because despite what you might think, I know Grant is a good man who has your best interests at heart.'

'And you know that how exactly?'

'I know that because of the way he's cared for you over the years.'

'Cared for me? You have no fucking idea!'

'I've seen it with my own eyes!'

'Have you? Have you really? Expensive bubble bath and holidays in the Maldives? Is that your idea of caring?'

'Now you're being ridiculous!'

'If you were really using your eyes then you would have seen that he wasn't good for me. He was manipulative. He made me feel useless.'

'That is simply not true!'

'Dad saw it, but you never would because you were taken in by the fact that he went to a good school and found it easy to make money.'

'It's not as simple as that, and well you know it.'

'And his sodding charisma! Always charming you with his listening skills. Another manipulation, by the way.'

'You're making me sound like a fool.'

'This is the man who never wanted babies and gets another woman pregnant, with twins. Twins!' Ruby shouts. 'I longed for a baby, Mum. I longed for and dreamed about and yearned for a baby!'

There is a flicker of understanding at this. 'I know that my speaking to him must feel like a betrayal,' she admits.

'It feels like a betrayal because it is a fucking betrayal!' Ruby shouts.

Her mum sighs and stares up at the ceiling. 'I came here to tell you this, Ruby, because I made a mistake and I know your dad would have wanted me to be honest about it, but if you're going to swear and shout then the message is lost.'

Cold.

Ruby goes from spitting fire to ice-cold in a split second.

'Fine. Good for you. I appreciate your honesty,' she says, and then laughs because she sounds so reasonable and polite when every fibre in her being is raw and spent and bloody. 'And what has Grant done with the information you gave him?'

Her mum swallows nervously before saying, 'He met up with Hannah.'

Ruby takes a very deep breath. 'To tell her what?'

'Just ... Well ...'

'To tell her that her mad mother was on the prowl again?'

'Ruby! Of course not! We just didn't want her upset, that's all.'

'But it's fine to upset me? To talk about me behind my back? To approach my daughter. My' – she bangs her chest – 'daughter behind my back?' Ruby walks to the front door and holds it open. Her mum follows more slowly.

'I understand that you're angry with me, Ruby, but I—'

'No, you don't,' Ruby says flatly. 'You understand nothing.'

'Do you really want us to part like this?'

'Yes. I want you to leave my home and never come back.'

Her mother walks through the doorway and Ruby closes the door behind her.

She doesn't sleep. She spends all day awake, thinking, remembering, endlessly mulling over the past, turning it over in her mind like a baker kneading dough. And like dough left to prove, the injustices of the past double in size. She feels sure she's willing to accept the blame for her own mistakes. She acknowledges that her decisions aren't always good ones. But for her mother to tell Grant that Ruby was a threat to Hannah? And then for Grant to approach Hannah?

It's too much.

Was it her fault for letting them get away with it? Was she always too much of a pushover? Past conversations come back and are relived.

Married for a couple of years, they'd gone to the Maldives for a holiday, escaping the Scottish winter. They spent the time lying by the pool, strolling hand-in-hand along the beach and having luxurious, prolonged periods in their room. It was after they'd just made love that she said to Grant, 'How about we try for a baby?' This wasn't the first time she'd brought it up but he'd always managed to deflect her questions: the phone rang, he had a meeting to attend, he was too tired to talk.

'A baby? Why would we want a baby?' He started to tickle her. 'We'd have to wave goodbye to times like this.'

'No, we wouldn't!' She laughed, holding his hands at bay. 'My mum and dad would help. And we can afford a nanny.'

'I love having you to myself.'

'Babies do sleep.' She put a finger to his lips. 'And they grow up and they go to school.'

He kissed her fingers and brought her hand down onto his chest. 'Your life's no longer your own.'

'But there are so many joys to having your own child.' She spoke about the happiness of watching them pass each milestone, the pride in their achievements, the overwhelming love. 'Of course, up to a point, we would be sacrificing our freedom but we would gain so much more.'

'It's a good sales pitch but—'

'Please, Grant. I'd love us to be a family. I really would.' She smiled through the trembling of her lips. 'I've been longing for a baby for a while now.'

'Says the woman who gave her baby up for adoption!' His tone was half jokey. 'You should be the last person who wants a baby.'

She knew that some people must think this of her, judge her actions in black and white terms, but to hear it spoken so bluntly by her husband was a punch to the stomach. She nursed the hurt through the rest of the holiday, a protective hand hovering over her solar plexus.

She should have left him then.

She should have known that if he wouldn't even discuss whether to start a family without prioritising himself and judging her harshly in the process, then what hope was there for an equal, respectful marriage.

*But she didn't leave him because when she visited the
darkest, harshest corner of herself she knew he had a point.
She had held her baby daughter in her arms and then passed
her off to someone else. That was the truth. She didn't want
her. The baby had spent nine months growing inside her only
to be rejected at birth.*

Grant was right.

Ruby didn't deserve a second chance.

At two o'clock, and still wide awake, she gets out of bed
and stares into the fridge. The food is still there, and
that feels like a miracle. She makes herself a sandwich
and eats it in the still of her kitchen. She watches blue
tits and sparrows hop about on the grass outside, tap,
tap, tapping to fool the worms into surfacing. She can
still feel her mother's presence in the room. Have they
ever got along? Ruby thinks not. There's been friction
and misunderstandings for as long as she can remember.
She sifts through conversations in her head until she
lands on one in particular. Her dad had been dead six
months, and Ruby was just out of psychiatric hospital,
jobless and vulnerable. Grant was working abroad so
she was staying with her mum.

*'Cup of tea, Ruby,' her mum said, setting a mug down on
the table beside her. 'And some fruitcake.'*

*Since she had come out of hospital Ruby had spent time
catching up with her thoughts because the drugs she'd been
prescribed had switched off her ability to focus and concentrate. She'd been numb for weeks. She couldn't have lined
up a train of thought if her life had depended on it.*

'Are you all right, darling?' her mum said.

*Ruby was staring down at her feet. Faults, like blessings,
only exist if there is someone to notice them. She hadn't fully*

understood her own faults, her own failings as a nine-teen-year-old. Nor had she seen the blessing, the miracle of a baby, not understanding that giving her daughter away would become a mistake so monumental that no matter how much life blossomed around her there would always be this gaping hole at the centre, a hollow space that could only be filled with her baby.

She hadn't had any more children because Grant was set against it and had refused to discuss it further, but she knew that even if she had given birth to more babies, she would never have forgotten Hannah. She would have thought about her every single day, no matter what.

'No one told me that I didn't have to be the greatest mother on earth,' she said quietly. 'Nobody told me that I could do it. Nobody.'

'Oh come on, Ruby! It was fifteen years ago. Do we have to go through this again?'

'Why did nobody tell me I could be a mother?'

'People did tell you!' Her mum sat straight-backed in the chair opposite, regarding Ruby with a mixture of impatience and confusion. 'Dad told you! I distinctly remember you both sitting on the window seat and talking about it.'

'I don't remember it that way.' Ruby's mouth was firm but her lip trembled and she pushed away the thought that this decision was one hundred per cent on her, that she had been given advice but not taken it. Her dad would have been on her side. She knew this as surely as she knew her own name but she couldn't think about her dad because the pain of his death made her feel bleak to the point of collapse.

Did she have any real understanding of what she was doing when she gave Hannah up? She had thought she could have another baby. That's what she had thought. So, aged nineteen, she gave her baby girl to a couple who desperately wanted her and would place her squarely in the centre of their lives. Unlucky people who weren't able to have their own baby – she made their day, week, year. She made their life. She gave her brand-new daughter away as if she were an unwanted gift. Pass the parcel. 'Here you go! You have her.'

'The social worker told you that you'd be given help to manage. I remember. I was there,' her mum continued.

'That's not what happened.'

'It wasn't 1950s Ireland, Ruby! You had every opportunity to be with your baby. Your father and I—'

'Couldn't you for once in my life just take the pain for me?' she said, looking up from her feet at last, and shielding her eyes from the light coming through the window. 'Isn't that what parents do? Don't they save their children from pain?'

'What pain?'

'The pain of trying to please everyone.'

'You were a grown woman!'

'I was nineteen!'

'We were disappointed that you were pregnant but we weren't judgemental. By the time the baby was due we were looking forward to being grandparents.'

'Don't you dare,' Ruby said, her tone a low growl.

'Don't I dare what? Challenge your opinion of yourself?'

'I will not allow you to rewrite history. Not this history.'

Her mother had been ashamed of her. Only her father's strength and good sense had prevented her mum from throwing her out.

'Oh, for goodness sake! Drink your tea before it gets cold. And eat the fruitcake. You need the calories.'

Ruby's hand shook as she picked up the mug. The milk was forming a skin on the surface and she had to hold back the urge to retch. She put the mug back down again.

'Surely you want to be better for Grant coming home?'

She didn't answer because her thoughts moved on to how she ended up in the hospital. She remembered telling the psychiatrist that it wasn't one thing. It was a series of happenings coming together, fate orchestrating events that led her to Hannah's front door. She was a policewoman, and by sheer chance she had been given a case that was normally outwith her remit. If she hadn't been on that case, she would never have been looking into road traffic accidents back in 2003. And if she hadn't been checking through all the RTAs that had occurred in Edinburgh during that year, she would never have come across the couple who had died when a car mounted the pavement. The couple who had a daughter aged five, a girl who had originally been adopted. So while Grant and Ruby were on holiday in the Maldives, at the very time that she was asking Grant if they could start a family, her own daughter was back on the adoption register and living in a foster home.

If only she had found out then. If only it hadn't been a further agony of years, and Hannah now fifteen, before she had found this out. The nineteen-year-old girl Ruby was and the thirty-four-year-old woman she became were a hundred miles apart but separated only by a whisper – the thinnest membrane that was punctured by the collision of facts. And so she ended up tracking Hannah down. Banging on her front door. Losing her mind on the doorstep. She knew she'd behaved badly and she'd most likely frightened her daughter. But it was love. Not spite or anger or jealousy or any of those other emotions that drive people to do crazy things. How often as a cop had she gone to a domestic where the motive was love?

Never.

The following week Ruby's blood is still boiling. She's meeting Grant at four o'clock outside The Hub on the

Royal Mile and she intends to have it out with him. She let far too much go when they were married and look where that got her. Undermined and unfulfilled. Childless and divorced in her fortieth year.

She crosses over the cobbled street and walks up past St Giles' Cathedral to wait at the pedestrian crossing. She looks down to her left and along George IV Bridge where she first spotted Hannah as she waited at the bus stop. It was only days before that she'd followed Grant and Violet into the museum, stalked them no less.

But all that was weeks ago now, and circumstances have spun her around one hundred and eighty degrees. Her life is no longer about the past, about Grant and being left, but about Hannah and looking forward. One door closes and another one opens. Well, not quite open. And it isn't a door she's entitled to push against; she has to leave that to Hannah. But all Ruby craves is possibility, a sense that her life can change. And while she waits for that change, she can exist in a limbo of hope and imagination. She really can. For however long it takes. She can do that.

The Edinburgh wind is, as usual, doing a good job of dropping the temperature. She stands outside The Hub and stamps her feet, glancing at her watch then up at the camera, which is facing in the opposite direction, fixed on the close across the street, rendering her invisible. Grant's late – he does this. She's never worked out whether it's a conscious ploy on his part or an unconscious one. But she recognises that it's another way he controls his environment and the people in it. With some people, it's better to be early and catch them off guard. If he is late for Ruby he knows that it will take the wind from her sails. Her mother will have reported back to him, told him that Ruby knows he met Hannah. He will expect her to vent her anger.

He's a player, if ever there was one, that's what Lennie said when he first met him. He didn't mean it harshly; he said it with a smile. And Ruby knew that he was right. Grant was usually two or three moves ahead of everyone he came into contact with.

She sees him coming. She watches him walk towards her and wonders what madness it was that meant she loved him and wanted him for so long.

'Ruby.'

'Grant.'

'You've signed the divorce papers?' he says.

She glances down at the A4 envelope under her arm. 'Before we get to that, I want to know what you said to Hannah?'

'I thought you might bring this up.' He scratches his cheek. 'Your mum asked me to help and I helped.'

'You never do anything unless it benefits you.'

'Perhaps. But what benefits me usually benefits others.'

'Aren't you generous? When it suits you,' she says with a sarcastic smile. 'I don't share your view of yourself.'

'I wouldn't expect you to.' He inclines his head. 'But the fact is, Ruby, that we judge ourselves on our intentions and we judge other people by their actions.' He pauses to let this sink in. He loves to make this type of statement as if he's the only man on the planet who has a handle on human dynamics. 'I'm sure you felt your intentions towards your daughter were good, but your actions were not.'

'You have no right to judge me.'

'That's as may be. But the facts remain.' He points at the envelope. 'Anyway, it doesn't matter what either of us thinks. When you give me the envelope we part company and we need never meet again. If your mother calls me, I'll ignore her and if she calls me again I'll block her number. How's that?'

'How's that?' Ruby repeats. 'Well, I came here today thinking you might at least apologise for speaking to Hannah and also for hurting me the other day.' She searches for guilt in his eyes but sees none. 'You might even make me believe you meant it, help me to understand your motives. But I'm not worth that?'

He shrugs, so she begins to walk away, and as soon as her back is turned, he whips the envelope out from under her arm and looks inside. 'The papers aren't in here?' His tone is incredulous. She smiles and keeps walking. He grabs her shoulder and swings her round to face him. 'Don't you dare walk away from me!'

'Ten per cent of the assets? Generous? Really, Grant?' She sidesteps him and heads into the close that leads towards Princes Street Gardens. It's a narrow, winding lane with buildings rising high on either side. He follows her and blocks her path so that she is forced to back against the wall.

'I've been patient with you, Ruby.'

'As I have with you.' She leans in towards him. 'You approach my daughter. You hurt me. You make me bleed. And you have nothing to say?'

He looks down into her eyes and she can tell he doesn't like what he sees. 'You were damaged goods when I met you,' he says.

'And you exploited that.'

'I stuck by you through thick and thin.'

'You got another woman pregnant.'

'Our marriage was well over by then.'

'Does Violet want you to marry her before the babies are born?' She's able to say it this time, to say the word 'babies', and it makes her proud of herself. 'And I'm supposed to fade out of the picture and not bother you again, is that it?'

Ruby is watching him closely. His eyes have darkened; his mouth is tight. She knows that he will suddenly grab her and she is primed to stop him but she is distracted by a man walking towards them. Grant stares at his feet, then as soon as the man passes them both he seizes Ruby's throat. 'I warned you not to cross me.'

His jaw tightens and so too does his grip, his fingers squeezing the air out of her windpipe. Ruby trained in self-defence when she was in the police service – how to subdue an assailant, how to deal with an aggressor – but it's been a while since she has practised any of her moves and she knows that with her back literally against the wall, his strength will very quickly overwhelm her. But after the other day, she made sure she was prepared for this. Her right hand is in her pocket and as it closes over what she's searching for she becomes aware of a presence next to her.

Hannah.

Hannah is by her side before Ruby even clocks that she's come into the close. And then time seems to both slow and accelerate as several things happen simultaneously: Grant looks at Hannah, Ruby looks at Hannah, Grant's grip loosens on Ruby's throat, Ruby brings her hand out of her pocket, Hannah's eyes are Ruby's eyes and when they meet, Ruby's heart leaps with a remembered joy. As the knife goes in beneath Grant's ribs, Ruby feels ... nothing.

Nothing.

And then.

Grant is moaning. His right hand fumbles for the knife. 'Bit-ch. Bi–'

Ruby pushes him against the wall. 'Go!' she says to Hannah.

'Fuck! No!' Her face is ashen. 'He's bleeding! He's really bleeding!' She tries to pull the knife from his chest but Ruby's hand is in the way. 'We need to save him!' Hannah says. She pushes Ruby aside and pulls at the knife but the handle is already slick with blood. 'He's dying!'

'Give me your jacket,' Ruby says.

'*What?*'

Ruby pulls Hannah's jacket from her shoulders and uses it to wipe the blood off Hannah's hands. 'Listen to me!' Ruby tells her. '*Listen!*' she shouts, and Hannah's eyes snap from Grant to her. 'You have to ensure you're not caught on camera.'

She reels off the places to avoid and Hannah stares at her, her expression alarmed, her eyes wet with tears. 'How can you—' She looks sideways at Grant and shivers. 'He's ... I mean ...'

'Do not get on a bus,' Ruby says. 'They all have cameras. Walk across the Meadows.' She pushes Hannah with her shoulder, to avoid touching her with bloody hands. 'Go! NOW!'

Hannah hesitates for a second and then she runs away. Ruby feels a momentary relief. Hannah doesn't belong here. She has no part in this mess. Ruby did it. And she will be the only one to take the fall.

Jesus Christ, what have you done? What have you done?

Ruby tries to ignore her inner voice, to breathe around it, to think.

Think. *Think*.

She stares down at Grant, her husband, the man she promised to love, honour and obey, 'till death do us part'. He has slid down the wall to the ground. One of his shoulders rests on the cobbles. He is half coughing, half panting, his lungs a frantic wheezy bellows. His hands feel blindly for the knife but his jacket has closed over his front and his fingers can't find a way to open it. Rich, scarlet blood pulses out of his body and pools around him. So much blood, Ruby thinks, remembering what she learned as a child – eight pints in an adult body. There have to be two or three pints on the ground already.

There's a whimper in her throat and she grits her teeth against allowing it out into the open air where it will surely double, triple in size. The enormity of what she's done will sink in later but for now she has to decide what to do. There's no point calling an ambulance because with blood loss like this he is beyond saving. She saw the aftermath of several stabbings as a police officer and she's sure that Grant is close to death.

No sooner does she think this than his chest is still, no gasping, no reaching for air. His eyes are open but they are glassy, lifeless as a landed fish.

She stares down at herself: blood on her trousers and a splash on the hem of her top, blood on her hands and wrists, sticky, warm blood. She tries to wipe it off her hands and onto her trousers but it's thick and gluey and congeals almost at once.

Is she going to call the police? Does she see herself going to prison? Because if she calls the police that's what will happen.

She glances up and down the close. There is no one coming in either direction. *Grant is dead. Grant is lying dead beside you!*

She senses the beginning of a plan knit together in her mind. It's not fully formed, not yet, but for now she needs to get out of the close.

Evidence. Every contact leaves a trace. Her DNA will be on his hands, his clothing. No doubt about that.

And so will Hannah's.

First step, she has to take the knife with her. She grits her teeth and pulls it out of Grant's chest. Even more blood rushes out and tears fill Ruby's eyes. She blinks them onto her cheeks and wraps the knife inside Hannah's jacket, folding it into a tight oblong so that no blood is showing. Then she goes through his jacket pockets: two phones and a wallet. She drops them into her own pockets and, keeping her bloodied hands hidden inside the jacket, she runs to the end of the close, the opposite direction from Hannah, down into Princes Street Gardens.

She forces her feet to walk at a normal pace and blends in with the other pedestrians, knowing where the camera sightlines are and avoiding them as much as she can. There's a bottle of water in her pocket and as soon as she reaches the gardens she finds a corner and pours the water over her hands and wrists before drying them with the blood-free inside of Hannah's jacket. She expects at any moment to hear a police siren or the weight of a hand on her shoulder telling her that she is under arrest.

It doesn't happen.

She crosses Princes Street and goes inside one of the clothing chains. She buys a white top, a pair of navy trousers and a pair of running shoes exactly like the ones she's wearing, and pays her 5p for a carrier bag. Then she goes into the loo and washes her hands, wrists and face thoroughly. Next, into a cubicle to swap clothes; she puts the bloodied ones in the carrier bag along with Hannah's jacket, Grant's wallet and both the mobiles.

She hesitates, thinking. She should keep the knife, put it back in the knife rack in her kitchen. She takes off her socks and doubles them up, then puts the knife inside and drops it into her pocket.

Another minute passes and she hasn't been arrested so she takes the next step. She walks three-quarters of the way down Hanover Street, turns left into Thistle Street and finds a bin at the back of a restaurant. She checks there are no private cameras in sight and pushes the carrier bag deep into the bin.

Every minute or so she is reminded of the reality: *You have fled the scene of a murder. Grant is dead. You have killed your husband.* When she remembers this she feels the weight of remorse sink deep into her stomach. It stops her breathing; it makes her panic.

She has to keep moving.

She walks in a circuitous route, not avoiding cameras this time but instead allowing herself to be seen. An hour passes and it's time to head to work – relief – where she can slide into her routine. When she gets there, the day shift are just leaving and, as Lennie arrived first, Freddie is giving him the handover. Ruby waves a hello, opens her locker and takes off her coat. She rummages past her winter boots and a discarded blouse and finds a spare pair of socks. She takes them out and then forces her coat right to the back, making sure the pocket containing the knife is hidden in the folds of the coat and won't be felt by anyone casually searching her locker.

She turns the key in the locker door and buries it deep down inside her trouser pocket. The knife is in there, she thinks. *The knife that has just killed Grant is in your locker.*

She's surprised her legs still work because they don't feel like her legs. There is an absence of feeling in her limbs, as if she has spent too long in very cold water and she no longer has any sense of her muscles. She walks by force of habit alone. She goes into the toilet to put on the socks, shuts herself in the cubicle and feels a tidal wave of panic flood up from her stomach. She tries to ride it out but it's impossible and she vomits into the toilet.

Keep it together, keep it together, keep it together.

You have a plan. Be strong.

When her stomach is empty she pulls on her socks and goes to her desk, lifting her headset as if it's any other evening.

'Sleep well today?' Lennie says.

'Not bad.' She manages to look at him. 'You know how it is sometimes.'

Chapter Fourteen

Hannah runs. And then she stops running. *Don't make it look as if you're running away from something*, that's what Ruby told her. Slow down. Act normal. Be normal.

Just be normal.

She's chilled to the very marrow of her bones and not just because her jacket is gone. Her mum would tell her she's in shock and she needs to lie down with her feet up. Her nana would recommend sweet tea, a warm blanket and a cuddle. The blog commentator Ratty1166 would advise her to take some arnica.

Shock and horror. Those words are associated with films, with Stephen King and *Nightmare on Elm Street*, Freddy Krueger and Pennywise the dancing clown. A rite of passage for teenagers, and when she was thirteen she scared herself half to death with friends on sleepovers watching films that were too old for them, clutching at each other and screaming, and then sleeping with the lights on.

Now she has witnessed real horror and she is shocked to her core. All five of her senses are overwhelmed by what just happened: there was the sweet but metallic smell of blood; the touch of it, slick and warm on her hands; the sight of life's spark, essence, call it what you will, as it prepared to leave him; the sound that came from his throat when he was stabbed, a dull groan as his chest was punctured.

And the taste. She can taste it. She can taste death and it makes her want to retch. She holds her hand over her mouth and walks back to her flat, questioning, questioning, questioning too much.

Is he dead? Is Grant dead? How could he not be, but then, there's still a chance, isn't there? If Ruby has called an ambulance, he could still be alive, couldn't he?

And what of Ruby? What will happen to her? What sort of a woman is she? How could she react so calmly? This woman who is her birth mother and didn't so much as flinch as the knife plunged into her husband's heart. This woman who is able to compartmentalise her feelings to such an extent that, as he lay there dying, she was able to give Hannah a detailed description of how to avoid cameras.

She doesn't want to think about pregnant Violet, at home, with no idea that her partner is lying in a close bleeding to death. She doesn't like people like Violet, all that social media showing off, but for Violet to lose her babies' father before they're even born? Hannah wouldn't wish that on anyone.

She feels jittery and jumpy and when she bumps into a woman on Bruntsfield Links who asks her if she's okay, she screams at her, 'Leave me alone!'

She took a couple of amphetamines just two hours ago, before she left the flat. Have they made her more shocked, more panicked, than she would otherwise be? She's not sure. She only took them because she thought they might keep her sharp and prevent her being spotted by either Ruby or Grant.

What possessed her to follow them? What did she think she was playing at? When she was hiding in the kitchen she heard Grant say when and where they were to meet but that wasn't an invitation for Hannah to join them.

What a mess she'd made of everything.

She runs up the stairs to her flat, ready to bury herself under her duvet, to wail and punch the pillow, but Jeff is in the house.

Fuck.

'I'm going in the shower,' she shouts.

'I'll join you!' he replies.

Hannah locks the bathroom door and switches the shower on to full blast. The noise of the pump fills the bathroom so that when Jeff tries the handle, finds it locked and bangs on the door, she can legitimately pretend not to hear him. She strips off and climbs into the bath to stand under the running water, eyes closed for a long time before she reaches for the shower gel. There is a cut on her right hand and everywhere she touches she leaves a bloodstain behind. It's a long, narrow cut that follows the lifeline on the palm of her hand. She knows when it happened because she felt the pain at the time. When she pushed Ruby aside and tried to pull the knife out of Grant's chest, the knife was slick with blood and her hand slipped down onto the blade. She wraps a flannel around her palm and presses hard but still it doesn't stop bleeding.

Pressing on the cut makes it more painful but she welcomes the pain. This is familiar territory for Hannah, although she hasn't deliberately cut herself for a while, and she would never have used the blade somewhere so obvious. The outside of her thighs are where the memories are, silvery-white lines of scar tissue, most of them about two centimetres long. She had a favourite razor blade that she hid in a small tear inside her mattress.

Back then, the secrecy, the pain, the control – it gave her a high.

When she comes out of the shower, she finds Jeff

lying on her bed waiting for her. 'I tried the door. Why did you lock it?'

'Did I lock it?'

He instantly spots the blood seeping onto the towel. 'What's happened to your hand?'

'I don't know … I was …'

'What's going on?' Jeff sits up, concerned. 'You don't look well.'

'I'm …' Her hand is aching and she winces. She holds it out towards him.

'Geez! This is bad!' He jumps to his feet. 'We should take you to hospital.'

'No, no. I'm not going to a hospital.'

'But, Hannah.' He dabs it gently with the towel. 'It might need stitches.'

'Could you go to the chemist and get me a bandage or something?'

'The hospital will have bandages.'

'I can't face going out again, Jeff.' Her eyes fill. 'If it's still bad tomorrow then we can go.'

'Okay.' He looks doubtful but she knows he'll go along with her decision because he can't bear it when she cries. 'I'll get you some painkillers first.'

She sits down on the edge of her bed and shuts her eyes, then opens them again because behind her eyes the film of what's just happened plays out in hideous technicolour with sound effects and smells.

But when her eyes are open her mind is flooded with questions and she feels like her head will explode. Is he dead yet? What will Ruby be doing now? Has she called the police? Will she tell the truth? If she knows how to avoid the cameras, has she also worked out how not to be seen? What will happen when the police find his body? Will they check his phone? Will they see Hannah's number? Their text conversation?

'Swallow these.' Jeff is back with two capsules and a glass of water. She takes the capsules from his hand and swallows them. 'What happened, Hannah?' His tone is gentle. He sits on the bed beside her and she feels his concern as a disabling force. 'Did someone hurt you?'

'I …' She's afraid to speak in case the whole story spills out of her in a rushing torrent of words that will lead to Ruby. And how can she do that? How can she drop Ruby in it?

'It wasn't the old guy, was it?' Jeff says, frowning.

'What?' She thinks he means Grant. She shakes her head and mumbles, 'He's not that old.' She has a flashback to Grant's lifeless body and the taste of death rises up from her stomach into her mouth. She rushes into the toilet to be sick.

As she vomits into the pan, Jeff holds her hair out of the way and strokes her back. 'I don't see the painkillers coming back up so hopefully you've absorbed them already,' he says.

When she's emptied her stomach she curls up on the bathmat and he asks her again. 'Please, Hannah, tell me what happened?'

She closes her eyes against his questions. She appreciates his kindness. She wants him to hug her and never stop but that affection comes at a price and she can't be honest with Jeff. But she does need to be honest with someone – TRO123? He already knows part of her story: what happened when she broke into Ruby's house and her second meeting with Grant.

Jeff talks and Hannah tries to listen. He's working out what has happened to her and although he's completely off base with his assumptions – he decides it must be the dog walker who has upset her, perhaps because

Hannah recently described him as a sex pest – she allows him to jump to this conclusion so that he will stop talking.

When he leaves the flat to go to the chemist, she stands up on shaky legs and, holding onto the wall for support, makes her way to the living room. She sits down at the table and logs on.

Are you there?

TRO123 answers at once. **Yeah. You okay?**

No. I've got more to tell you.

I'm listening.

She tells him everything. She starts with watching Ruby and Grant when they met up and finishes with her running out of the close. And because of the cut on her palm, she has to type the whole thing with only her left hand. She doesn't hold back on any of the details and when she's finished, she waits for him to comment. Minutes tick by …

Are you still there? she types.

I'm thinking.

Thinking what?

It's a lot to take in.

Gut feeling?

She waits, sitting up straighter when she sees – typing …

You need to go to the police.

This isn't what she expects him to say and she immediately deflates. She wants him to tell her something profound, something that would shed new light on what happened. She wants him to say that it isn't her problem and that sometimes tragedies can't be avoided.

To put it bluntly – she wants to feel better about the fact that a man is now dead. She logs off, just as Jeff comes through the front door. He is carrying a bag from the chemist but he throws it aside to say, 'It wasn't the dog walker who upset you, was it?' He paces up and down in front of her, clearly harassed. 'Was it?'

'No, but—'

'So why did you tell me it was?'

'I didn't tell you it was,' she says tiredly.

'But you didn't say it wasn't! Fuck, Hannah! I had a real go at him just now!'

'I'm sorry.' She touches his arm but immediately pulls her hand away again because it's still bleeding. 'You didn't hit him or anything, did you?'

'As good as! I had him up against the wall and told him he had to stop bothering you.' He pulls at his hair. 'He was scared shitless, Hannah! I'll be lucky if he doesn't report me to the police.'

'Fuck. I'm really sorry.' *But compared with witnessing a man die?*

She watches Jeff pace up and down and realises that she's very attached to him. Whether that's love or not she isn't entirely sure but what she does know is that she doesn't want to be without him. Jeff is normal. Jeff is good. And when Jeff is on her side everything is better. 'I saw something,' she blurts out. 'I saw a homeless guy getting attacked in the Meadows. Two young men, teenagers really, were kicking him in the head and punching him. And when I went to help, I cut my hand. I don't even know what I cut it on—'

Jeff's eyes are wide. 'One of them must have had a knife.'

'Maybe. That could be it. I'm not sure.'

'Did you call the police?'

'Someone else called them.' Her eyes fill again. 'I ran away.'

'No wonder!' He comes across to hug her and she softens against his chest. 'That's a horrible thing to see happen.'

'I'm sorry I didn't tell you straight away.' She looks up into his face. 'It really upset me and ...'

'You were in shock.' He strokes her hair. 'I'll look after you.'

'Thank you.'

'I'll see if I can get another guitarist to fill in for me tonight.' He reaches for the chemist's bag. 'Let's sort your hand out first.'

Next day, Jeff goes to work and Hannah spends the morning online. First things first. She has a nagging feeling that she gave too much detail to TRO123 but she is reassured after a brief conversation.

Any more thoughts on what I told you? she asks.

Our world is in chaos, and though the weak sometimes survive, it's only the strong who are able to thrive.

Bearing in mind what she's confessed to him, she's not sure what he means by this but it sounds suitably TRO123-like and she feels better knowing that he's not freaked out by their message exchange.

The rest of the morning she spends reading news reports to find out about the 'late' Grant Stapleton. As is the way when someone is dead, he has become a paragon of virtue.

'Grant Stapleton sustained a single fatal stab wound to his chest.' In the accompanying photograph, Grant is smiling. It's one of the photos he has on his social media page. Violet is standing next to him, her head on his shoulder, but she has been mostly cut out of the photo apart from her hair, which is just visible at the edge of the shot. Grant was a local businessman 'of some repute'. And one of his friends is quoted as saying, 'Everything Grant touched turned to gold. But more than that, he was one of life's gentlemen. None of his employees ever had a bad word to say about him. He will be sorely missed, both in the business world and by his fiancée Violet who is pregnant with twins.'

On live, rolling news, a police inspector with a serious expression makes an appeal for witnesses. 'Although the close itself is infrequently used, the roads either side are not. We are appealing for anyone who may have seen Grant Stapleton walking up the Royal Mile at around four o'clock yesterday afternoon to please come forward. Any information, however seemingly insignificant, could aid us in our enquiries. This would appear to be a violent, unprovoked attack and it is important that the perpetrator is found and apprehended.'

She thinks about Ruby telling her to avoid the cameras. Hannah is sure that the police will be checking the CCTV footage, trawling through hours of film to trace the murderer. Hannah has no idea whether she will have been caught on any cameras. She supposes that she might have been but will they know who she is? Should she delete the texts Grant sent her? But then the police can find these things out anyway, can't they?

When the buzzer sounds, Hannah's heart does a somersault. Have the police found her already? She tiptoes to the window and stands at the corner to look out. She can't see who's at the door but there aren't any police cars in sight and she doesn't imagine they'd arrive on foot. The buzzer sounds again, several times – push, push, push. She goes to answer, praying it isn't her parents – she really couldn't handle them right now.

It's not her parents – it's Clem. Clem never normally comes to the flat, and Hannah is immediately suspicious. After a hello hug, Clem points to Hannah's hand, which is now heavily bandaged and resembles a boxing glove. 'What happened?'

'I was chopping veg and the knife slipped.' She smiles. 'It's not as bad as it looks. Jeff has gone to town on the bandaging.' She waves an arm behind her. 'Come in.'

'Cheers.' Clem goes ahead of Hannah into the living room. 'I wanted to speak to you before you saw the news.'

'Oh?'

'Yesterday, a man was killed in one of the closes off the Royal Mile.'

'I heard about that. Grant Stapleton was his name, I think.'

'Yes.' She gestures towards the sofa. 'You might want to sit down for the next bit.' She sits down and Clem sits beside her. 'Grant Stapleton was married to your birth mother.'

It's on the tip of Hannah's tongue to say, I know. I'm way ahead of you with this one, Clem. But she doesn't speak and she knows her face is letting her down – shocked and frowning would be good but she just sits there, almost expressionless.

'Hannah? Did you hear me?'

'I heard you, but ...' Clem's two front teeth overlap a little bit and Hannah has always found that attractive because she has – or had, before she met Dave – such an obvious lack of vanity. But now she is wearing braces. 'Did Dave want you to fix your teeth?'

'The braces?' Clem touches the metal on her front teeth. 'They're a bit teenage, I know. I wanted to get the invisible ones but they were too expensive.'

'Why do it at all?'

'Hannah ...'

'No really. Tell me.'

'Hannah,' she repeats and then she reaches across to take her hand.

Hannah knows what she's thinking – she's thinking that Hannah is deflecting because she can't deal with the news.

'Bearing in mind that your birth mother has been in touch recently, this news is bound to be doubly shocking for you.'

'Actually, it's not.' Hannah allows her hand to be held. 'I already knew that man was her husband.'

'Oh. Okay … '

Clem means well; she cares. But still this feels like an intrusion and Hannah bites back, 'What do you see in Dave?'

'Hannah.' Clem sighs. 'I know you and Dave haven't got off to the best of starts.'

'You should leave him.'

'What?' She frowns. 'Why are you saying that?' Her tone is disappointed. 'I know this must be a difficult day for you.'

'Really, Clem. You should leave him while you still can.'

'Stop it.' She pulls away this time, dropping Hannah's hand. 'Why are you talking about Dave?'

'Because I know what sort of man he is.' This has to be said. 'That black eye you had a few months ago. How did you really get it?'

Clem stands up and Hannah does too.

'Tell me he didn't give you the black eye. I'll believe you if you say it wasn't him.'

'I won't say it, because I don't need to say it.' Clem's eyes are cold. 'And I'd prefer you not to comment on my relationship with Dave.'

'Why not? You comment on my relationships.'

'I'm going to leave now,' Clem says. 'We can forget about this conversation or we can discuss it later. Your call.'

Hannah closes the door behind her and goes into the kitchen. Her stomach feels concave, shrunken and bitter with acid. She needs to eat. She makes herself a sandwich, spreading butter thickly on both sides of the bread before squashing a banana in between the slices. She stands by the sink, taking man-sized bites and hardly allowing more than a couple of chews before she swallows the lumps.

She wouldn't be willing to watch Jeff walk out of the door. She would fight for Jeff. But Clem? Hannah can't keep pretending to see Clem as the wise one.

She goes back to the sofa and nods off, wakes up again just a short time later with Ruby at the forefront of her mind. She's tempted to make contact with her but she doesn't have her mobile number. She could go back down to Ruby's house but she doesn't know what she'll find there. The police might be questioning her, and if they haven't yet, they will soon. She's bound to be a suspect because the police always look at close relatives first. She knows this from TV dramas.

She has been back to Ruby's house once since the first time. After she'd witnessed Grant and Ruby in the kitchen she bought food for her fridge – she can't easily explain to herself why she did that but no doubt Clem would have her theories; all Hannah knows is that she's not so dissimilar to Ruby. She recognises herself in her mother's behaviour. They're both secretive, for one: she would bet that Ruby's family and friends don't know that she has a cabinet full of drugs. And for two, they both tell whopping great lies: the business of Grant being dead, for example. That was quite a monumental deceit.

And now Grant really is dead. Every time Hannah thinks about this it makes her heart race and mouth dry. She goes to her bureau and takes out the shoebox. The pills and the two items she took from Ruby's house were still in her jacket pocket and so they're lost to her but she does have something else of Ruby's. She holds the hoop earring up to the light and lets it swing from her finger. She found the earring on the garden path when she was fifteen, after Ruby had the meltdown at her front door.

The day after her birth mother was carted off in a police car, Hannah got up to go to school as normal. She had an exam during the extended first period – French, not her favourite. She hadn't slept well but she pretended to her mum and dad that she had because it was clear they were both tiptoeing around her, their eyes wide and watching. Her dad set a place for her at the table and her mum made her favourite scrambled egg with tomato chunks. She managed to act as if it were just like any other day until her dad said, 'We can chat about last night, if you like.'

'I don't want to talk about last night.' She gave a bright, false smile.

'Did you hear your dad and me talking at all?' her mum asked, her voice abnormally high-pitched. 'We were up quite late.'

Hannah shook her head and shovelled egg into her mouth. Both her parents nodded, determined to believe her, and she helped them out by adding, 'I have a French test today so I fell asleep dreaming in French.'

'Je rêve en français,' her dad said, smiling.

'Oui,' Hannah repeated. 'Je rêve en français.'

It was when she was walking along the front path that she spotted the glint of gold on the grass. It must have been recently dropped because it lay on top of a layer of frost. She knew her parents would be watching her from the window so she bent down quickly to pick it up and slip it into her blazer pocket. She didn't get it out of her pocket until after the exam – which she failed spectacularly because she could no more concentrate on translating English to French than she could build a rocket to the moon. She excused herself from maths by telling her male teacher that she needed to go to the loo and 'you can't ask me why'. He waved her aside and she stood in the girls' toilets – alone – with the earring in her hand. She washed it under the tap and dried it with toilet paper. It was a circular hoop made from expensive, mellow gold. She held it at eye level and stared at it. And then she wrapped it in more toilet paper to nestle deep inside her pocket.

When she got home, she went straight to her bedroom and added it to the small collection inside her shoebox, but not before she examined it again, treating it with the sort of reverence that people bestow on photos of much-loved dead relatives or new-born babies.

Ruby.

What to do about Ruby?

Hannah locks the shoebox back inside the bureau but she keeps the earring out. She wants to show it to Ruby, to let her know that she's kept it all these years as a reminder of that night her mother came looking for her.

Chapter Fifteen

'They found a body in one of the closes off the High Street,' Lennie says, sitting down at his desk.

'Oh? Man or woman?'

'Man. Look.' He brings the camera feeds down onto his spot screen. A section of the Royal Mile, from The Hub to the junction with George IV Bridge, is closed off. Forensic vans are parked on the cobbled street and two people in white disposable boiler suits are walking back and forth with evidence bags in their hands. The entrance to the close is police-taped across so that people leaving and entering need to duck underneath. Several plain-clothes detectives are chatting to each other while a couple of uniformed officers stand at the entrance, shooing any member of the public away if they stray too close.

'Three cameras were taken out of sequence,' Lennie says. 'So unfortunately we didn't have eyes on the entrance.'

'That was me,' Ruby says. 'Steve Wilson asked me to keep the cameras fixed on the close across the street. Drugs, I think.'

'Sod's law.' Lennie nods. 'They'll want to track back on footage leading to and from the scene. We'll see what request comes through from the SIO. I expect we'll hear from him before the night is out.'

Ruby calculates what cameras she could have been

caught on. It's in her nature to be camera-aware so, even on her way to meet Grant, she might not have been seen. What she has to decide before she is questioned – and she's bound to be questioned – is whether or not she will admit to meeting him at all. Violet most likely knew about their meeting, so Ruby could say that she was going to meet Grant but then decided against it. Normally in situations like this, Ruby would advise that it's important to keep the lies to a minimum. She interviewed many a criminal, and the smart ones were the ones who stuck as close to the truth as possible. So many suspects were tempted to over-imagine and over-embellish their lies and that made them easy to trip up. The truth tends to be mundane and straightforward. She needs to keep that at the forefront of her mind.

'Fancy an early supper?' Lennie says. 'It's bound to get busy later on.'

'Good idea.'

'Beef bourguignon,' Lennie says. 'And I'm serving it with soda bread. Not your standard recipe, though. You'll need to guess the secret ingredient.'

While he's in the kitchen warming up the food, Ruby decides to check through the footage leading to and from the Royal Mile, before and after the crime; time of death will be easy to establish as Grant's body was found so quickly. She searches back through the recordings, looking for her own image. She quickly discovers that she's only in one shot, and that's over a mile from the High Street. And it's almost an hour before the murder. She isn't picked up again until she's on her way to work two hours after the murder.

Hannah, on the other hand, is in several shots leading up to and on the Royal Mile; Ruby's heart sinks. Why did Hannah even come? Why was she following Grant?

Or was it Ruby she was following? What was in her mind?

And after the murder, Hannah is visible on multiple cameras, multiple times. To begin with, she followed Ruby's instructions and so she isn't picked up immediately. But when she's about two hundred metres away from the scene she must have forgotten what Ruby told her and she starts to run. In one of the shots further on, she's seen bumping into a woman then shouting at her.

Ruby reminds herself to think like a cop. Are there any links between Grant and Hannah?

1) Grant will likely still have Hannah's mobile number. But if Ruby knows Grant at all, she knows that he will have called Hannah from the pay-as-you-go model. And he won't have registered it. Both his phones are now at the bottom of the bin behind the restaurant. As long as the bins are emptied in the morning then the evidence will be lost.

2) Ruby's mum knows that Grant met Hannah. Will her mum be questioned? Ruby thinks not. Or, at least, not in the first instance. She might step forward voluntarily but Ruby doesn't think so. Family matters are kept within the family. She's unlikely to share information unless she has to.

3) Did Violet know about Hannah? Ruby can't be sure but as Grant was a law unto himself she would err on the side of her not knowing.

4) Has Hannah ever been arrested? If so, her DNA will be on record and will be matched with that found on Grant's clothing.

5) If Hannah is brought into the frame, then it will quickly become apparent that she is Ruby's daughter.

But surely the most pertinent question for any

investigator would be: what motive could Hannah possibly have for killing him? The obvious murder suspects are herself and Violet – old wife and fiancée. Does Violet have an alibi? Have they ever argued in public? Is Grant still having affairs?

Ruby found out about his first affair six years into their marriage. A smarter woman would have sussed more quickly than she did, and maybe Violet is the smarter woman.

Lennie comes back in and they eat their supper. Ruby doesn't guess that the secret ingredient in the soda bread is treacle. She's trying her best to act normal but she can't manage it and finally Lennie says, 'What's up with you? You're usually bolting down your food.'

She should tell Lennie that Grant didn't die from cancer, that he has, in fact, been alive until today. The clock is ticking and at any moment they'll find out the name of the dead man and Lennie will be horrified and confused.

'Lennie?' She stares down at her plate. 'I need to tell you something.'

'Yeah?'

'I hope we'll always be friends.'

'What?' He frowns. 'What does that mean?'

'In a minute you're going to find out that I've been lying about something, something major. And I don't want it to affect our friendship.'

Silence. Ruby counts to five and then Lennie says tersely, 'Spit it out.'

'Grant isn't dead. He left me for someone else. Her name is Violet and she's pregnant with twins.' She looks across at him. He's chewing slowly, his eyes wide. 'I didn't want to deceive you but somehow I have and I'm really sorry about that.' Lennie swallows his mouthful and puts his plate down on the desk. 'I tried to tell you. I ... Fuck.' She shakes her head. 'I don't have any excuse.'

Lennie stands up, takes both their plates and leaves the room. She waits for him to return. It's a long three minutes and when he comes back she daren't look at him. He sits down next to her and is watching the screens when he says, 'Trish has always said you're the still waters run deep type and it looks like she was right. I'm not going to pretend I understand why you lied. And I'm not going to pretend that I'm not hurt.'

'I almost told you,' she says, her tone pleading. 'Last time we were in your hut, but Shona came in and—'

'I hardly think Shona can be blamed.' He starts typing, his attention on the screen. 'Not in this instance anyway.'

'And I hoped to tell you when we went for that drink but that hasn't happened yet and—'

'What does it take for you to speak up, Ruby?' he shouts. 'The stars to be aligned? A missive from the Pope? A fucking fanfare?' He looks across at her and she shrivels back into her seat. 'And you know what it makes me think?'

She shakes her head.

'If you lied about that what else are you lying about?'

'Fair point,' she says quietly. Deep breath. 'I found my daughter.'

He swivels his chair towards her. 'What daughter?'

'When I was nineteen I gave my baby up for adoption I saw her five years ago when I found her illegally I used information gained when I was on a job it was why I had to leave the force.' She blurts this out in one long flow of words before stealing a glance at Lennie to gauge his reaction.

He is listening intently, his expression uncharacteristically serious. 'Go on,' he says.

'A while back, I spotted her on a camera. She'd finished her shift at the restaurant where she works and was standing at the bus stop.'

'Have you been watching her?'

Ruby nods.

'Fuck, Ruby!'

'I know. I know,' she says. 'But I haven't …' She sighs and rubs her forehead. 'I've broken the law; I accept that. But I haven't actually …' She's about to say 'done any harm' but she thinks twice about voicing that because she must have done harm otherwise Grant wouldn't be dead. If only she hadn't told her mum about Hannah because then her mum wouldn't have told Grant. If she'd eaten something at the birthday party, she wouldn't have been so drunk and her tongue wouldn't have loosened. She should have kept Hannah a secret and then she wouldn't have been so angry with Grant for interfering. She would have signed his papers and he'd still be alive.

'Have you made contact with her?' Lennie asks.

'Not exactly.'

Lennie stands up and walks around the room shaking his head. 'So Grant is alive, although it turns out he's a shit and he left you. And you had a baby girl.' He thinks on this for a second before saying, 'Is there anything else?'

'One more thing,' Ruby admits. 'But it's better you don't know about that.'

'Better for whom?'

'For you. You need to be surprised.' She tries to breathe but her chest hurts. 'Shocked. You need to be shocked.'

Lennie stares up at the ceiling, shaking his head. 'Aw

fuck. This sounds ominous. Too fucking ominous.' He points a finger at her. 'Tell me. Tell me *now*.'

'Trust me, Lennie, it's better if I don't tell you.'

'Trust you?' He bangs his fist on the table and Ruby jumps. 'Haven't you insulted me enough?'

If looks could kill, Ruby would drop down dead. They don't talk for over an hour. They both pretend to be absorbed by what's on the screens and when Ruby feels like she might explode from the palpable tension between them, Lennie reaches across and pats her hand. 'I'm sorry about your daughter. That must have been tough for you.' He doesn't say anything else but when a tear slides down her cheek, he passes her the box of tissues. 'It'll be all right, Ruby,' he says. 'Just give it time.'

It's midnight when the two detectives show up. Lennie answers the door and leads them down into the control room.

'Ruby Romano?' one of them says.

'Yes.' Ruby stands up.

'I'm DS Livingstone and this is DC Markie. You're married to Grant Stapleton?'

'Yes … we're separated but, yes, legally we are still married.' She hazards a smile. 'Why?'

'We're sorry to inform you that Mr Stapleton's body was recovered from a close in the High Street. He was stabbed.'

'What? He …' Lennie says. 'How could …' He glances across at Ruby and her eyes silence him at once.

'Grant's dead?' Ruby is making a good job of looking shocked because it is shocking to hear the reality of Grant's death spoken out loud like this.

'Did you arrange to meet Mr Stapleton earlier today, Ms Romano?'

'Yes. We did arrange to meet.'

'We'd like you to come to the station with us to answer a few questions.'

'Why? Do you think I can help?'

'We'd like to eliminate you from our enquiries.'

'Okay, but is it really necessary for me to come just now?' She points towards the bank of screens. 'I finish at seven in the morning. I could come along then.'

'I understand you were in the police service yourself?'

Ruby nods.

'Then you'll know that it's important we don't let the grass grow.'

Ruby could prolong these moments, she could refuse to go with them, but the look on Lennie's face – utter disbelief, confusion and panic – is a look she has to get away from because it will make her weak and remorseful and they won't have to prod very hard for her to confess to everything.

'Can I get my bag?' Ruby says.

'Of course.'

She opens her locker. The knife is in there, burning a hole in her coat pocket. She's lucky they didn't come with a warrant. She takes her bag and locks the door, then returns to the control room.

'Two of my colleagues will begin gathering footage,' DS Livingstone is saying to Lennie. 'They'll be here by about one. You okay with that?'

'Yes,' Lennie says. 'Except that – Ruby?' He comes across and takes her arm. 'I can ring Al. Someone should be with you.'

'I'll be fine, Lennie, really. I'll be back before you know it.'

She smiles.
He doesn't.

When they arrive at the police station they leave her in a room on her own for fifteen minutes and while it might increase some people's anxiety, Ruby is grateful to be given the time to gather her thoughts. She comes up with a plan. She'll keep her lies to a minimum; she'll keep her wits about her. She is innocent until proven guilty, that's the law. And the innocent and the guilty behave differently when they are questioned.

The innocent begin by wanting to cooperate. They have nothing to hide, after all, and so helping the police is the right thing for a law-abiding citizen to do. But as time goes by the innocent get tetchy, often tearful, upset that they're not being believed, annoyed at the repetition, keen for the police to get out there and catch the bad guys.

The guilty, on the other hand, they like to project a justified anger. They like to make it known that they are helping, and therefore they should be treated well, not kept waiting, not kept hungry or thirsty. They are far more demanding because in that way they create a distracting bubble of activity and modulate their emotions according to that bubble. But bubbles can be pricked with a pin and a good detective will do that.

The same two detectives come in and sit down opposite her. They have three bottles of water with them and pass one to her. Livingstone is still the one doing all the talking. He sets the tape to record, states the names of all present and then he asks her whether she'd like legal counsel. She says no. He glances down at the sheet of paper in front of him and says, 'So let's begin, shall we?' He smiles. 'Talk us through your day today, Ms Romano.'

'Please call me Ruby.'

'Ruby,' he says obediently.

'Well.' She takes a moment to remember. 'I sleep during the day because I work nights. I got up at about three and left to meet Grant because we're in the process of getting divorced and he wanted me to sign the papers and give them to him so that he could pass them on to his solicitor.'

'And did you meet him?'

'Very briefly.' She shrugs, looking embarrassed. 'I hadn't signed the papers because I didn't want to make it easy for him.'

'Was he angry about that?'

'Yes.'

'Where did you meet?'

'Outside The Hub.'

'How long for?'

She tells him their meeting lasted less than a minute. 'Then I walked around town until I was due at work.'

'So you didn't walk with Grant into a close off the Royal Mile?'

'Which close?'

'Would it matter?'

'No, I'm just wondering but … No. I didn't go down a close with Grant.'

Ruby knows that the man who walked past them could come forward and, if he's sharp-eyed, he could identify her in a line-up but she gambles that he won't. He was very preoccupied. His eyes were on his shoes as he walked.

'Did you kill your husband, Ruby?'

She knows she will be asked this several times and she looks Livingstone in the eye when she replies, 'No, I didn't kill him.'

'Do you always walk to work?'

'Not always.'

'But you did yesterday?'

'Yes.'

'Your husband has been living with the woman he left you for. Is that right?'

Ruby nods.

'How did that make you feel?'

'Hurt.' She purses her lips. 'Angry, gutted ... ashamed.'

'Would you say you were on good terms with him?'

'No.' She frowns at this. He wants her to state the obvious, dig deep into her pain, and it almost unsettles her. 'No, I wouldn't say so.'

'Violet is the woman's name. Violet James,' he says.

Ruby acknowledges this with another nod.

'She told us that you've been watching them.'

'Grant also accused me of this.' She sighs. 'They live opposite the cemetery where my father is buried.'

'And following them.' His face is sympathetic when he says, 'Did you follow them?'

'Once or twice we were in the same place at the same time. Edinburgh isn't such a big city.'

'She says it was many more times than that. About a dozen times, she said.' He raises surprised eyebrows at Ruby. 'She described your behaviour as stalking.'

'Stalking?' Ruby gives a short laugh. 'She must have reported me to the police, then?'

'She didn't do that.' He pretends to look at his notes. 'She felt sorry for you.'

'Look ...' Ruby takes a deep breath. 'I'm not going to pretend I liked my husband, I didn't. Perhaps I did follow them a couple of times. But that was all I did.' She looks them both in the eye when she says slowly, 'I didn't kill him.'

DC Markie is writing everything down and he reminds Ruby of trainee Fiona as his pen scratches across the paper.

'Your husband was a successful businessman,' Livingstone says.

'Are you asking me or telling me?'

'Asking you.'

'Yes, he was.'

'And he was generous. He was giving you a good divorce settlement?'

Ruby doesn't argue with this because she's not about to hand them a motive. Even if Grant changed his will in favour of Violet, Ruby is legally still his wife and is therefore set to inherit considerably more than ten per cent.

'And yet you wouldn't sign the papers?'

'I told you why.'

Markie holds up the notepad and points to a sentence for Livingstone to read aloud. 'I didn't want to make it easy for him.'

'That's right.'

'Did other people feel like that about Grant?'

'In what way?'

'Wanted to make his life difficult?'

'I don't know.'

'Sometimes men in his position attract enemies. Do you think this could be the case with Grant?'

Ruby knew this would be one of the questions and she decides to answer it honestly. 'He was a fair boss.'

'He worked hard and he played hard?'

'He worked hard but he didn't play hard. We led a fairly quiet life, although I believe he has changed since he left me. He's become more social, dinner parties and whatnot.'

'Does that bother you?'

'A bit, yes.'

'Hell hath no fury?'

Ruby sighs. 'I'm not a killer.'

The door opens and a woman pops her head in. She signals to Livingstone to go with her. He speaks for the benefit of the recorder, pauses the tape and is gone for five minutes. In that time neither Ruby nor DC Markie speak. Markie is staring at his notes and Ruby is pre-occupied with thoughts of Hannah. She wonders what will happen if Hannah is brought in for questioning and whether she will crack under the pressure. Ruby has been on the other side of this table and so that gives her the advantage of familiar ground, familiar questioning. And yet even she is finding it slightly unnerving. And she knows there's more of the same to come. They will loop backwards and repeat some of their questions to test her veracity. They will probe and poke and they will rely on their gut to push harder when they sense a chink in her story.

Livingstone comes back, resets the tape, and the questions begin again. 'So tell us about the job you do.'

'I work in the CCTV centre,' Ruby says. She goes on to explain her role. And while she talks they both stare at her, their expressions deadpan. She finds it off-putting and brings her explanation to an end. 'So that's it, really.'

'You haven't mentioned the fact that you are able to control the sequencing of the cameras?'

So that's what leaving the room was about. Ruby thought it might just be a pretence. 'That is something we do. But you must know that already.'

'Explain why the camera sequencing excluded the entrance to the close.'

She explains that it wasn't about exclusion so much

as focusing on the close opposite. 'Steve Wilson is running an operation. You can check with him.'

'We will.' Livingstone nods. 'We are contacting a member of his team as we speak.' He sits back and smiles, suddenly all-inclusive. 'You used to be in the police service?'

'Yes.'

'How did you find it?' His tone is friendly.

'Mostly good, sometimes not. You know how it is.'

'You resigned?'

'Yes.'

'And why was that?'

'Stress.' This is easy to explain. There isn't a cop in the service who hasn't suffered from stress. She tells them she'd seen one too many stabbings, one too many abused children, domestic violence where the wife won't prosecute, and so on. 'There was no point in struggling on. My husband earned enough for both of us.'

Livingstone folds his arms and turns to his colleague. 'I thought I heard a rumour of something else.' He frowns. 'Did you, Pete? Or have I got that wrong?'

'No, sir,' Markie says. This is the first time he's spoken and so it feels significant. 'I heard something too.'

Crafty, Ruby thinks. She'd have done the same if she was leading the questioning. 'What did you hear?' she says.

'I heard that you left before you were pushed.'

'Crossed a line,' Markie says. 'That's what I heard.'

Ruby stares down at the table. She isn't as concerned with this line of questioning as she would be if they pushed her on Violet's pregnancy, or probed her with questions as to what sort of husband Grant was. That might make her crack. But this? This was manageable as long as they didn't connect her with Hannah and then match Hannah with the girl on CCTV.

'Well, you heard right,' Ruby says. 'I was stressed and I crossed a line. I mishandled some information and was hauled over the coals.' She shivers, remembering. 'And then I ended up being sectioned. I was quite doolally for a while.' She gives a wry laugh. 'The job can do that to you.' She stares each man in the eye, one after the other. 'Did Violet tell you about Grant's affairs? Or was she leaving that to me?'

Two more hours of questioning and then they ask for a sample of her DNA. She agrees because innocent people cooperate. She knows her DNA will be on Grant's suit but that doesn't make her a murderer. And if she refuses that will only light a flame under their suspicion and she doesn't need that. She wants their questioning to remain as low-key as possible. No big reveals, no sudden confessions.

It's five in the morning when they drop her back at work. Ruby is more tired than she's been in years. She places her thumb on the keypad, types in the code and expects the door to open but it doesn't. She tries again but still the door won't budge so she presses the buzzer and speaks into the entryphone: 'Lennie, it's me. The door won't open.'

'I'll be right up,' he says.

Moments later the door opens and Lennie is standing there, his face creased with worry. 'How was it?'

'It was okay. They have to ask their questions. You know the stats. Most murders are committed by the nearest and not so dearest.' He's blocking the doorway and she squints up at him. 'You going to let me in?'

'I had to call Al,' Lennie says. 'You know it's against the rules for me to be on my own.'

'I know.' Ruby nods.

'He called Fiona in. She wouldn't have been my choice, but …'

'It's okay, Lennie. Really.'

'And, Ruby, I'm sorry but you're not allowed to be here.'

'I'm what?'

'It's company policy. Al told me to tell you that you're suspended on full pay until the investigation into Grant's death is concluded. It's because of access to the cameras, tampering with evidence and—'

'Guilty until proven innocent?'

'I know it's bollocks but …' He's watching her face, looking out for telltale signs. 'Because you had nothing to do with it.'

'They haven't charged me with anything.' She's staring down at her feet. 'They'll have to look a lot further than me.' She takes a breath before saying, 'He had affairs, you know? Short-term shags with whoever took his fancy.'

'Ruby, I'm sorry.' His head drops onto his chest. 'I had no idea he was such a bastard.'

'Why would you? I was too ashamed to tell anyone.' She's thinking about the knife in her locker. She has to get it out of there in case the police come with a search warrant. 'So, am I going to be allowed in to collect my things?'

'Sure, of course.' He moves off to one side to make way for her.

'Then you can escort me off the premises,' she says, walking ahead of him down the stairs.

'Don't say that,' Lennie says. 'I'm gutted about this.'

'I know, Lennie.' She turns and hugs him. 'I'm sorry. I'd only just told you Grant wasn't dead.' She opens her locker door. 'Who would have believed it?'

'But you knew, didn't you?'

'What?' She tries to look innocent. 'I knew that he was dead?'

'It was the thing I had to be shocked about?'

'God, yes.' She forgot she had said that to him. 'Yes, I knew.'

'How?'

'My mother called me. She's friendly with someone who works in a restaurant on the High Street.' She brings her coat out first and puts it on. The weight of the knife is heavy against her thigh and she's glad of it. 'He'd been in there for a meal.' She shovels the contents of her locker into a couple of plastic bags, her head averted as she lies to Lennie. 'The body was found by a member of staff outside having a fag.'

There's a weighty pause while Lennie digests this. Ruby knows that he can, and will, fact-check but her priority is to get the knife out of the centre before she's caught with the murder weapon because then she really would wave goodbye to her freedom.

'Do you think they'll have you in again?'

'I suppose it depends on the evidence, forensic, CCTV.' She closes the locker door, leaving the key in the lock. 'Talking of which – are the police technicians here?'

'They've just arrived.'

This time Lennie leads the way and they go into the control room. Fiona is there with her pen and paper, scribbling away, clearly excited that she has been called in. When she sees Ruby she comes across. 'Al says you're not supposed to be in here.'

'Wind your neck in, Fiona,' Lennie warns. 'This is my control room, not yours.'

'If you don't mind I'd like to get my things from my

drawer,' Ruby says, smiling at the girl. 'Could you move out of the way, please?'

Fiona moves aside and Ruby goes to her desk. There are two technicians in the room, busy pulling camera feeds down onto the spot screens and rewinding back in time. The one who is seated at Ruby's desk slides to one side to make room for her to open the desk drawer and bundle the contents into one of the plastic bags. As she does this, she glances at the screens. The technician is gathering together persons of interest; on two of the screens there are two men who Ruby doesn't recognise and, on the third spot screen, there is an image of Hannah.

Ruby's heart plummets and accelerates simultaneously. She hesitates only for a second and then she follows Lennie to the front door.

'Stay in touch,' he says. 'Hopefully they'll put this to bed within the next couple of days and you'll be back here pronto.'

'Aye,' Ruby says. 'Hopefully.'

The door closes behind her and she begins the walk home. Just because they're flagging up Hannah's image, it doesn't make her a suspect. They will be gathering more footage than they know what to do with. They will be flagging up forty, fifty, one hundred people who were in the High Street at the given time.

Ruby tells herself this but still she can't help but worry. When she arrives home she takes the knife from her jacket pocket and runs it under the kitchen tap. Blood has dried on the handle and there are small stains on the blade. She spends a good five minutes using bleach and then soapy water to ensure every trace of blood is gone. Then she returns it to the empty space on her knife rack. It is the middle size of five knives, lined up in a row, waiting for peppers, onions or carrots to chop.

Or meat to carve.

Ruby feels despair gather at the back of her eyes. She pours herself a gin and tonic and sits in front of the patio doors, watching black sky thin to grey.

She knows what her next step will be.

It won't be easy. But she'll do it.

Chapter Sixteen

Accept nothing, believe nobody, challenge everything.

Although he was no longer in the police service, this was still Lennie's mantra. Because, like Ruby, Lennie was once a cop. But unlike Ruby, he left of his own accord. Four growing girls and never at home, and when he was at home, his mind was often on the job. He had seen too much of the dark side of humanity: the aggression, the violence, child abuse, murder. Police work was a pendulum-swing of the mundane, day-to-day call-outs that demanded nothing more than a calm demeanour, interspersed with the truly appalling cruelties that made his heart sick and painted his days a hard, stony grey.

And when his eldest daughter found him on the sofa one morning, having lain there all night in a drunken stupor, he knew he had to make an either-or choice: job or family? There was no competition.

He joined the CCTV department back when there were fewer cameras and fewer TV programmes peering behind the scenes of the emergency services. He'd been there long enough to watch the service grow and change, prove its worth and continue to earn its keep. The day Ruby came along was a good day for him because she was of like mind and they became the sort of colleagues who relied on each other, shared banter, had each other's backs.

And now this.

He wasn't happy with Fiona; she could barely contain her excitement at being called in. 'Ruby's been arrested?'

'Not arrested. Her husband has been murdered and she's helping the police with their enquiries.'

'But I thought her husband was dead?'

'Well, you thought wrong.'

And when the day shift arrived she got to them before Lennie did. It was no surprise that Freddie was Fiona's natural ally and they were whispering in the corner when Lennie came out of the loo.

'She lied about her husband being dead and now she's accused of his murder?' Freddie repeats. 'Fuck a duck!'

Fiona says something else, her voice too low for Lennie to make out each word, and Freddie responds with, 'She was always a moody cow, but this is another level.'

Lennie goes over to them both and says quietly, 'If you're going to have such disloyal thoughts about Ruby then have the decency to keep them to yourselves.'

'Oh, come on—' Freddie says.

'*I* knew Grant wasn't dead,' he says, pointing into his own chest, and Freddie responds with one of his pop-eyed, surprised faces. 'And I'll say it again, Fiona. She's not been accused of his murder. She was simply helping the police with their enquiries.'

'Well, we all know what that's a euphemism for,' Freddie says.

'Is that right, Freddie?' Lennie moves in closer. 'What would you know about being a cop? You been one?' He points a finger in his face. 'No, you haven't and so I'll thank you to keep your mouth shut.'

The rest of the day shift have gathered behind him and Lennie turns to eyeball each one of them in turn. 'I know you've all heard about Ruby's late husband. And I know it's easy to judge. But let's show some solidarity here, folks. Ruby would stand by each and every one of you, shoulder to shoulder, and well you know it, so if you can't think the best of her then keep your opinions to yourself.'

He takes the bus home with his heart heavier than he's experienced in recent times. The house is quiet because the school has an Inset day and they're all having a lie-in, apart from his youngest daughter Tina, who's in front of the television with three puppies on the sofa beside her and a couple under her feet, the flat of her foot rubbing their warm bellies. She smiles when he comes in. 'Hi, Dad.'

'They allowed in the living room now?'

She gathers the sofa puppies further onto her knee. 'Mum says.' She lifts two of them up onto her chest and they lie there wriggling like overfed furry grubs. 'They won't pee. They've just been outside.'

Lennie collapses onto the chair opposite and the puppies' mother jumps up beside him. She rests her head on his knee and stares up at him until he strokes her ears.

'You see! You like them really,' Tina says.

'I like them when they're house-trained and they don't chew my shoes.'

Tina giggles, and then she looks at him shyly. 'But you must be glad Mum's having a boy this time, Dad?'

Lennie rolls his eyes up to the ceiling. 'Your mum told you?'

'She had to because Shona really wanted to know.' Tina snuggles against the wriggling white fur. 'So are you glad?'

After they'd been for the scan they'd agreed to keep the baby's sex to themselves. But typical Trish: *he* wasn't allowed to tell anyone – he'd have been lynched if he did – but she could tell their daughters when he wasn't home and somehow that was okay.

'Dad?'

He'd prefer Trish not to be having a baby of either sex but that's not the right answer. 'I'm a girls' dad,' he says to Tina. 'I'm not sure I'll know what to do with a boy.'

Tina stares at him, her expression thoughtful, and as is often the case with his youngest daughter, he senses she sees all there is to know of him. All his indecision and weakness, his lack of resolve. He would gladly give his life for any of his giggly, argumentative girls, no matter how mad they drove him. And he'll love his son too. He hopes Tina sees all this in his actions because expressing it in words is more than he can manage.

'I could bake with you later?' she says.

'That would be a treat.' He closes his eyes and sleep swims up from his very soul to disable him. He's dimly aware of Trish coming into the room and saying, 'Oh not again! Why doesn't he make it as far as the bedroom? Always cluttering up the living space! Throw a blanket over him, Tina, will you?'

'He's had a bad day, Mum.' The blanket is tucked in around him and he welcomes the warmth. 'Something happened with Ruby.'

He doesn't remember even mentioning Ruby. He doesn't remember anything at all. He slides into the arms of Morpheus, and lets himself dream about a sturdy wee boy who enjoys kicking a football and doesn't take hours in the bathroom.

He's back at work that evening with an idea. Ninety-seven per cent of gut instinct is accurate and that's why he knows Ruby is lying. Not everything she said was a lie but some of it was and he needs to separate the two. He ignores the inner voice that tells him Ruby has let him down and doesn't deserve his loyalty. She's not the friend he thought she was. She let him believe that Grant was dead. She only told him the truth when she absolutely had to. And Grant's body was not discovered by a restaurant worker on a fag break but by a plumber taking a shortcut.

Still, Lennie has no qualms about standing by her. She's his friend and she needs his help – end of. Unless an obvious suspect is revealed within the next twenty-four hours, Lennie knows she'll be taken in for questioning again. And he has an idea as to the best person to speak to about the investigation.

He's on shift with Fiona, who is skirting around him after the ticking-off he gave her. She arrived at work with a cafetiere that looks brand new. 'My mum doesn't need it.' She makes him a decent coffee and places it by his right hand. 'You don't take sugar, do you?'

'You're not here to make me coffee,' he tells her.

'I know but …'

They're at their desks for a couple of hours; business is slow but they never say 'quiet' because it's tempting fate. 'Listen, Fiona,' Lennie says. 'I need to make a phone call. You up to holding the fort here for a bit?'

'Of course.'

'Call me if anything comes up.'

Lennie wants inside information on how the murder investigation is progressing and he knows the man to get it from. Trish's brother Connor works in the police service. It was how they met, he and Trish, all those years ago. Connor and Lennie trained together and became best mates. Falling for Connor's sister was easy because she was sunny and naïve and appealed to Lennie's need to protect other people, especially women.

Connor had stayed in the force and had been promoted year on year. Last year he made DCI. Lennie couldn't help but think that Trish was disappointed he wasn't more like her brother. The grim nature of the work never got to Connor the way it did Lennie. Somehow Connor was able to separate his own humanity from the victim's suffering. 'Too much empathy,' Lennie's boss told him when he was barely twenty. 'You'll never make a decent copper unless you develop a harder edge.'

He goes into the staff kitchen and gives Connor a call. Always late to bed and early to rise, his brother-in-law answers after two rings. 'Lennie.'

'Connor, mate. I need a favour.'

'Shoot.'

'You'll have heard about the murder off the High Street?'

'Aye.'

Lennie goes on to explain his connection with Ruby. 'I'm wondering if they have anyone in the frame?'

'From what I hear, they're leaning towards Romano as the likely perp. They're building a case against her.'

'How come?'

'According to his new partner, Violet James, she was being obstructive over the divorce. She'd arranged to meet Stapleton in the High Street with the divorce papers but Violet was doubtful that she'd have signed them. Violet also said she'd been following them both. Romano didn't deny this when questioned.'

'She has no history of violence.'

'Not true. Five years ago she was arrested for breach of the peace. Narrowly missed prosecution.'

'That was when she left the service ...' Lennie says, thinking, remembering that she told him she'd done 'something unforgivable'.

'That's right.'

'So is there any evidence she met Stapleton yesterday?'

'Well, here's the thing: she's saying she met him very briefly, and in the convenient absence of CCTV footage who knows whether she's telling the truth or not? You must know she re-sequenced the cameras so they were facing in the other direction? Tying her to the murder is currently a stretch but the investigating officers are going for it.'

'She re-sequenced the cameras following a request from Steve Wilson at major crimes,' Lennie says, trying to ignore the weight of his heart as it sinks into the pit of his stomach. 'And you could argue that because she's camera-aware, if she planned to kill her husband she would arrange to meet him somewhere with no cameras and no potential witnesses.'

'Aye, I'm sure a good advocate would argue that.'

'Knife?'

'No knife at the scene. They're searching surroundings but nothing's turned up so far.'

'Any forensics?'

'Not processed yet but she willingly gave DNA samples and didn't object to them swabbing under her fingernails. They didn't ask for her clothes as she hadn't been arrested.'

'No one else in the frame?'

'It seems he didn't have any enemies, if that's possible when you're as rich as he was. We'll keep looking.' There's a pause and Lennie is treated to loud munching on the other end of the line. 'And he was a man who liked to play away from home so other women may well come out of the woodwork. For what it's worth, I'm sceptical about the woman-scorned motive. Still, let's wait for the forensics. They might be able to build a case to take to trial. Or not, as the case may be.'

'Right.' Lennie gives an audible exhalation of breath.

'And if the knife turns up, we'll be laughing.'

'No leads there, then?'

'Not so far. If I hear anything more I'll let you know.' They don't have to mention confidentiality because it's unspoken between them.

'Cheers, mate.'

Lennie goes to end the call but not before Connor insists they have a chat about the new baby. Turns out Connor also knows it's a boy. 'You need to tie a knot in it, Lennie, before my sister goes for a half-dozen.'

'You're telling me.'

They promise to meet for a drink before long. 'Don't leave it till we're wetting the baby's head,' Connor says.

Lennie doesn't have a chance to mull over what Connor's told him because Fiona calls him through to point out someone she's spotted at the top of Leith Walk. 'I think he's one of the men on the missing poster.'

Lennie compares the man in the poster with the man on screen. Roughly the same height and build with a telltale crooked nose. 'You might be right,' he says. He's not convinced but there's no harm in allowing her to have a go. 'Call it in.'

'Can I?'

'Knock yourself out.'

Fiona can barely contain her excitement and Lennie listens as she contacts the police: 'Juliet Alpha, this is Whisky Romeo.' She tells them about the man she's spotted and who she thinks he might be. 'He's standing outside the pub at the top of Broughton Street. He's wearing a leather jacket and baggy jeans.'

They both watch as the police car arrives outside the pub and the two cops climb out. It quickly becomes obvious he's known to them and is no more a missing person than Fiona is. He lives close to the pub and is a regular when it comes to disturbing the peace. It all comes to nothing but it gives Fiona the chance to go through the process. And then write it up in her file.

'Sorry, I got that one wrong,' she says to Lennie.

'No harm done,' Lennie says. 'We all make mistakes.'

At six in the morning, Lennie's mobile rings. It's Connor. 'They have a warrant to search her house,' he tells Lennie. 'They'll be there within the hour.'

Lennie isn't tempted to call Ruby – that's not the way it works with him and Connor. But from then on he clock-watches as time ticks by infinitesimally slowly before the day staff arrive. And when they do start coming in, he excuses himself at once, telling them that Trish is laid up with sciatica and he has to get back to the girls. 'Fiona can give you the handover.' Fiona steps forward with her notebook and he leaves them to it.

He could get a taxi but he doesn't, he takes the bus, because he's just a friend stopping round on his way home from work. She's not close to the bus stop and he's careful not to run. He strolls along the wide street, for all the world like a man enjoying the wakening of the day.

Ruby is standing in the driveway, smoking.

'Since when?' Lennie says, pointing at the cigarette.

'Needs must.' She leans in for a hug. 'Good to see you.'

'What's with this?' He points to the three parked cars and one van, people milling around, their feet crunching on the gravel, from house to van and back again.

'They have a warrant.'

'Why?'

'I must be prime suspect.' She laughs and shakes her

head at the absurdity of getting herself into this situation, then takes a long drag on the cigarette, inhaling enough smoke to make herself cough. 'I'm out of practice.' She coughs again and Lennie claps her on the back. 'Behind the bike sheds is a long time ago.'

'Seriously, Rubes.' His forehead creases with worry. 'What is all this?'

'They'll be searching for the knife. The murder weapon,' she says, her tone reflective.

He has to ask because he has to know. 'And …' He pauses. 'Will they find it?'

She looks at him then, fully, no holds barred. And he sees it – the look you search for as a cop, the one that says: guilty as charged, and is closely followed in Ruby's case by a flash of fear and then remorse.

'Ruby?' He backs away.

'I cleaned the knife. Thoroughly. There's unlikely to be any traces of blood left on it,' she says flatly. 'But if they want to build a picture of me as a law-breaker, they will find other things.'

Lennie is reeling. 'What's that supposed to mean?'

'I have illegal drugs in the house.'

'For fuck's sake!' He shakes his head; this isn't the Ruby he knows. 'I—'

'Not heroin or crack. Pills mostly. Cocaine.'

'Well, that's okay then!'

'If I go to prison,' she says, taking hold of his arm, her grip tight, 'I want you to live in this house. You and your family.' Her voice is a whisper. 'Look around you. Imagine you, the girls, Trish and the dogs enjoying this garden. It's crying out for a family.' An insistent, persuasive whisper. 'Imagine, Lennie. Just imagine.'

'Snap out of it!' he says, glancing around to check that the cops are out of earshot. 'You're not going to prison.'

'Lennie, if I'm made to face up to what I've done then so be it.'

'Stop this.' He grabs her shoulders and shakes her.

'I was in denial.' She stares down at her feet. 'And now I've had time to think.'

'To think what?'

'My DNA will be on his clothes, on his hands.'

'So you met him! So what?'

'I did more than meet him, Lennie.'

'You—' Angry tears fill his eyes. 'I could slap your face, Ruby Romano! I'm so fucking furious with you.' He walks away from her, out onto the pavement to take several steadying breaths, and when he returns, his jaw is set. 'Have you got a solicitor yet?'

'Not yet. It's all happened so fast.'

'I'm calling Linus Beattie.' He gets his mobile out of his pocket. 'He's a wily, persistent bastard. He's exactly the man you need.' He finds the number in his contacts and presses the button. 'And his brother Frank is an advocate. Even more wily, if that's possible.'

Ruby waits while Lennie talks to the solicitor. He summarises events and they arrange a time when Beattie can meet her.

Lennie ends the call, grabs Ruby's arm and marches her further into the garden. 'Now you listen to me,' he says. 'And listen good. I will not watch you go down.' He takes a breath. 'Prison, Ruby. Prison,' he repeats. 'You and I have been inside prisons. We have walked in as officers of the law and we have walked back out again. But you remember the hairs on the back of your neck warning you of danger? Can you imagine what it must feel like when visitors, cops, guards, cleaners, all get to walk out of that building but you don't?' Her eyes flicker with anxiety and it spurs him on. 'You will be stuck in there, Ruby. Every move you make will be monitored. You can't take a shit without the whole world knowing about it. And there is the crux – prison is now your *whole world*. You have no privacy, no peace, no sky to wonder at, no fresh air to breathe. And it doesn't matter how much you fight or cry or beg. They lock the door on you. Every – single – night.'

Her eyes fill with tears but he doesn't stop.

'You know how many years you'll get for premeditated murder? Twenty-five. You might be out in fifteen if you're lucky but— What?' She's trying to speak. 'Say it again?'

'It wasn't premeditated,' she whispers.

'Then you'll need Frank Beattie on your side because the prosecution? They'll argue that nobody carries a knife – how long was the blade?'

'Four inches.'

'Nobody carries a four-inch blade in their pocket unless they intend to use it,' he tells her. 'And when they take you back in for questioning again, admit nothing. Do not talk unless Beattie is present.' He walks around in a circle, breathing heavily, then comes to a stop in front of her again. 'Promise me you won't confess to anything. Make the fuckers prove it.'

'Reasonable doubt,' she says.

'Exactly.' He nods. 'No witnesses, no CCTV, no real motive. They'll have a hard job.'

Quiet settles between them. The quiet of fear and anticipation, dread and despair. But there is fight too. In him, at least. And he needs to see it in her.

'Promise me, Ruby. Promise to fight.'

'I promise.'

'Louder.'

'I promise.' She looks him in the eye and he sees his friend. 'Lennie, why are you doing this?'

'We stick together. We have each other's backs. You'd do the same for me.'

'Lennie.' She tries to breathe but the cigarette has irritated her lungs and she coughs again. 'Lennie,' she repeats. 'I killed a man.'

'You don't admit that.' His expression is fierce. 'Not to me, not to anyone.'

Chapter Seventeen

Lennie lies in bed staring up at the ceiling. For once he isn't kept awake by the chatter around him but by the chatter inside his own head. He wants to help Ruby but he needs to understand what drove her to the point of killing her husband. He remembers the conversation they had in his hut after the suicide on the bridge when she talked about being an inpatient. He had no inkling that she'd ever had such grave mental health problems. Still waters really did run deep with her – but to murder Grant?

Lennie has seen more than his share of murder and he finds it hard to fathom. To take another person's life in cold blood and then come to work as if it were just another day. That's the behaviour of a psychopath. Has she been deliberately manipulating his feelings so that he stays onside?

He will never believe that of Ruby. She's no psychopath; he knows her better than that. So she's been keeping secrets, but show him someone who hasn't.

He rolls over onto his side and feels the mattress groan. He makes up his mind to think in her favour. She's a friend in need. And she must have had a reason for killing Grant. Lennie had never warmed to the man because Ruby changed when she was around him. She was quieter, didn't laugh as easily nor relax as fully. If Grant was a man who had affairs, was he also a man who bullied his wife? Was he an abusive husband? If so, it's no surprise that Ruby took the knife with her because she knew him and she knew he might threaten her. She didn't mean to kill him; she only meant to defend herself.

And it all got out of hand. Suddenly a man is dead and she has to lie. Self-preservation. There's no human instinct like it.

At four in the afternoon he gets out of bed and finds Tina in the garden with the puppies. 'I know I'm a day late but are we going to bake then?' he says.

Her smile is everything he needs to restore his faith in human nature. She comes running to his side. 'Can we do meringues or a chocolate roulade because I want to separate the eggs?'

'We can and we will.' He brings the bowls and mixer out of the cupboard. 'Eggs on top of the fridge.'

She pulls a chair across and hands him down two boxes. 'We'll have lots of yolks left.'

'We can think of something to do with those.'

'Mayonnaise?' she says. She jumps down and drags the chair back. 'I've been in your hut, Dad. I hope that's okay?'

'Of course it's okay.'

'And I was reading your recipes on the wall.'

'You were?'

She tells him what she's read, how she knows about truffles, how she wants to help him. 'You can teach me how to chop properly and then I'll be fast. I'll be a really good assistant.'

He feels a lump rise up in his throat and shakes his head against it. I really am a big softie, he thinks.

At work that evening he's tired, but filled with a sense of purpose. It's important he tries to understand where

Ruby is coming from so he calls Celia and arranges to meet her at the end of his shift. He knows Ruby and her sister see a lot of each other and if anyone has insight into Ruby's marriage it will be Celia. Is this going behind Ruby's back? Yes, but too bad. She needs help and in order to help her he has to find out how far the secrecy goes. And he'll look into what – and who – she's been watching on the cameras when he's been out of the room.

He's on duty with Fiona again. She's bubbling with a sense of possibility as Al has told her that her work is good and there should be a full-time position for her when her probationary period is up. 'Great news,' Lennie says. He hands her a printout that he keeps in his desk drawer, filed under 'tests for the newbies'. 'Something to help you with your learning objectives,' he tells her. 'It's a series of scenarios. You read each one and write down what the procedure would be.' He watches her skim-read through the four sheets. 'You have ninety minutes. Exam conditions. Sit at the table in the kitchen.'

'But what if you need me in here?'

'Then I'll shout on you.' He swivels his chair away from her and brings two cameras down onto his spot screens. 'Nothing is happening at the moment, and chances are Edinburgh will sleep the whole night, so you might as well make the time count.'

She reluctantly leaves the room and returns twice, once for a pen and the second time for the chewing gum she left on the desk. Ruby's desk. When he's finally sure she's gone, he tracks back through Ruby's viewing history. There is a record of everything she pulled down onto her spot screens over the last thirty days. If she's been watching her daughter then he'll be able to work out who that girl is. And he hopes that will help him to understand Ruby better.

It takes him less than twenty minutes to discover that she has been watching a young woman who works evening shifts in a restaurant. When he zooms in, he sees a familial resemblance and he clocks from the numbers – 06.06.18, 23.55, 4.15 minutes; 07.06.18, 23.54, 3.28 minutes, and so on – how much Ruby obsessed over this girl, night after night, when Lennie was organising their supper or taking a nap. This is targeted surveillance and is a criminal offence. But irresistible – he gets that. Ruby gave birth to this beautiful girl. The compulsion to watch her is understandable and it sets off all sorts of questions in his head, the main one being: Why did she give up her baby?

Lennie is dragged back into work mode when a fight kicks off in the West End. He spends almost half an hour on the radio liaising with the police as they chase down three suspects. Fiona would love the excitement but he doesn't call her through because he doesn't need her. When she arrives back in the room, exercises complete, and she catches the tail end of the operation she is annoyed. 'It would have been good for me to observe this,' she says.

'You've observed several like this, haven't you?'

'Yes, but ...'

He takes the papers from her hand. 'How did you get on with the questions?'

'Okay.'

'Right then.' He stands up. 'I'll go next door and have a look at your answers. You're in charge. Shout me through if you're worried.'

Lennie always makes the same observations within the first few seconds of being in Celia's company: Celia is like Ruby but she talks more, her face is fully made up and she doesn't have Ruby's savvy. Ruby is an observer. She gets people. Lennie has always bonded with her over that.

Celia has brought their mum Sinead with her. They order coffees and sit down.

'We were so glad to hear from you, Lennie,' Celia says, glancing at her mum and then Lennie. 'I can't tell you how shocked we are by this. I mean, Ruby can't have anything to do with Grant's murder, can she? But they had a warrant to search her house yesterday. Did you hear about that? And when we called round yesterday evening she wasn't there, and she wasn't answering her mobile, so now we have no idea where she is and to say we're worried is an understatement.'

Sinead lays a hand on Celia's knee and that seems to remind her to breathe so that she stops talking ... and breathes ... and falls silent.

'I've been calling her too,' Lennie says. Twice last night and twice this morning. 'She didn't answer me either. I thought she might be taking time to think.'

'But where is she?' Sinead says.

'She definitely didn't sleep in the house overnight?'

'Not that we could see.'

'She might have moved into a hotel,' he says. 'When the police turn your house upside down, it can feel like a violation.'

'So the police will know where she is?' Celia says.

'She'll have told them.' He nods confidently, his certainty an act because, with all he's learned recently, he wouldn't put it past her to go into hiding.

'I already feel better,' Sinead says. 'You have the insight, Lennie.' Her tone is unwavering but the flash of her eyes tells Lennie that she's holding herself together by the merest of threads.

'Well, I'm happy to share my insight on the progression of the investigation.' He pauses. 'And in return I'm hoping you'll help me with insight into Ruby's character.'

'Of course,' Celia says.

Lennie places his clasped hands on the table. 'My colleagues and I – we thought Grant was already dead.'

'That doesn't surprise me,' says Sinead. 'We knew she pretended he was dead.'

'Why?' Lennie asks.

'She said it hurt too much to talk about it. Grant had cancer and so people put two and two together. It was easier to let them believe that gone meant dead.'

'She was ashamed,' Celia said. 'And the fact that the other woman was pregnant.'

'Ruby is complicated,' Sinead says.

'I don't think she's complicated,' Celia says, glancing at her mother. 'Just secretive.'

'Private,' Lennie says, with a small smile. 'There's nothing wrong with that.'

'There is if you're born into a family of meddlers,' Celia says.

'We aren't meddlers, Celia.'

'We are, Mum. She accused me of it the other day.'

'Well, sometimes—' Sinead bites her tongue.

'Was Grant a good husband?' Lennie asks.

'He was,' Celia says. 'In lots of ways. But he was also controlling.'

Sinead frowns. 'I think that's unfair, Celia. Ruby was vulnerable and Grant was there for her. Someone has to take charge.'

'She wasn't always vulnerable. Not when she was a girl. She changed when she gave Hannah up for adoption.' Celia looks at Lennie. 'Did you know about her daughter?'

'She told me recently,' he says.

The waitress arrives with their coffees and they stop talking until she has gone again.

'What happened five years ago when she went looking for her daughter?' Lennie asks. 'Before she was sectioned and admitted to hospital.'

'You knew about that?' Sinead says. 'She was close to you then, Lennie, because she didn't share her story with many people.' She takes her coffee without milk and she stares down into the cup, blowing on the surface to cool the black liquid, but although she lifts the cup up to her mouth she doesn't take a drink. 'We'd had a difficult six months. Gino, the girls' dad, had died and, well …' She sighs. 'About four weeks before his death, Ruby said something to him. We don't know what she said. He wouldn't tell us and neither would she. Whatever it was, it knocked the stuffing out of him. He wasn't well anyway, and …' She shrugs. 'The spark died in him.'

'Mum, that's not fair,' Celia wades in. 'And it's one of the reasons you and Ruby don't get on – because you blame her for Dad's death.'

'I don't blame her for his death.'

'You do! You know you do! You've said it more than once.'

'I think you'll find you're wrong about that.'

Celia starts to reel off whens and wheres and what was said, and Lennie sits back to watch the verbal tennis match between them as each woman tries to score the final point. Neither will give any ground to the other and finally Lennie interrupts. 'So do either of you know if she's made contact with Hannah recently?'

'No!' Celia looks startled. 'She hasn't seen Hannah since she was fifteen. She shelved the idea that they could be reunited ...' She trails off, sensing that her mum knows something different. 'Mum?'

They both watch as Sinead swallows down her reluctance before saying, 'At my seventieth party, Ruby told me she'd seen Hannah at a bus stop.'

'What?' Tears fill Celia's eyes and Lennie has a feeling it has more to do with being left out than any sympathy for her sister. 'That's what your argument was about?'

'I was angry with Ruby for finding Hannah. I didn't want the whole bloody mess to start up again,' Sinead continues. 'Losing her job and ending up in hospital.'

'Like you always know best!' Celia says.

Pot, kettle, Lennie thinks.

'And then I did something that I bitterly regret.' Her voice wavers for the first time. 'I got hold of Hannah's mobile number.' Judging by the look on her face, Lennie guesses this was obtained by foul rather than fair means. 'And I gave the number to Grant. I told him that Ruby had seen Hannah and was going to make contact with her.'

'You did *what*?'

'Keep your voice down, Celia!'

'*You did what?*' Celia repeats, her voice even louder.

'Stop,' Lennie says, holding up his hand. 'Please. Celia. Calm yourself.'

He asks Sinead to continue and she tells him that Grant met with Hannah to warn her that she was being watched. She also confesses to having told Ruby this and being ushered out of her house. 'She was very angry with me. And with Grant.' She looks at Lennie through sad eyes. 'It could be a motive for killing someone, couldn't it? Do you think?' Celia is stopping herself from talking with the hand she has over her mouth. 'Because Celia—' She winces. 'Celia has a point when she says that Grant was controlling, and perhaps Ruby wanted to put a stop to that. Hannah was a no-go topic for all of us. And now Grant was sticking his oar in. It might have been the catalyst.'

'Okay, first, I don't think we should jump to the conclusion that Ruby is guilty,' Lennie says.

'But ...' Sinead clears her throat. 'When Ruby had her breakdown she was ... different. She lived with me for a while because Grant was working abroad and she ...'

'She what?' Celia is hanging onto her mother's every word.

'I felt quite afraid of her. She was aggressive at times. And ... A couple of times she pushed me.'

'That doesn't make her a murderer!' Celia says.

'Celia's right,' Lennie says. 'And in the absence of another obvious suspect, the police always look to the family first.'

'So it's normal procedure to obtain a warrant?' Sinead asks.

'Yes.' Both women visibly relax a little. 'They'll also have his fiancée under the spotlight. And they'll be trawling through all his friends and acquaintances. No stone unturned.' He throws out his hands. 'But *our* focus has to be sticking by Ruby. She's innocent! Why would we think otherwise?'

'Of course,' Sinead says. 'I didn't really think that she'd killed him.' She tries to smile. 'But because she's not answering her mobile.'

'You don't want it to be your fault,' Celia says quietly.

'Unhelpful, Celia,' Lennie says. She stares at him, her expression part defiant and part sulky. 'Anything constructive you want to add?'

She doesn't answer immediately. 'Well ... Only that

...' She's drawing out the suspense. 'Only that, I know where she might be.'

Her mum falls back in her seat as if she's been pushed. 'How can you?' She is incredulous.

'You're not the only person Ruby confides in.'

'And you've kept this quiet?' Sinead says, even more incredulous.

'Well, I don't know where she is *exactly*,' Celia says. 'I only know that she's renting a flat up near Holy Corner.'

'Well, why didn't you *say anything*? We've had – *I've had* – hours of worry!'

'I'm saying something now, aren't I?' Celia has the decency to look apologetic. 'She was packing boxes a couple of weeks ago, talking about having a dedicated space to paint.'

'Paint? Paint what?'

'Pictures.' Celia shrugs. 'I don't know! I asked her if we could come to the flat but she said not until she had something to show us.'

'Do you know the address?' Lennie asks.

'All she said was that it was near Holy Corner.'

'Nothing else? She didn't mention whether she was renting privately? Through an estate agent? Top floor? Garden flat?'

Celia tries to think back. 'No, that really was all she said.'

'But her house is more than big enough,' Sinead says. 'She has a studio in the garden that she could paint in. She has umpteen bedrooms and a family room the size of my whole house!'

'My thoughts exactly,' Lennie says, mulling over why Ruby would feel the need to move.

'She was fed up with the house. There were too many

memories of Grant and it's not exactly a lively area. She never has any milk in her fridge! She needs local shops.'

'I cannot believe this!' Sinead says. 'How could you, Celia? How could you keep this information to yourself?'

'How could *you*, Mum?' Celia snaps back. 'How could *you* betray Ruby's trust and get in touch with Grant?'

'Okay. Listen!' Lennie says. 'You're both stressed and upset. Understandable.' He points a finger at Celia. 'Stop tearing at each other's throats. We have to support each other. And we have to support Ruby. And both of you' – his finger moves to include Sinead – 'need to stop bickering. This is *serious*. Save your arguments for when Ruby is no longer a suspect. And in the meantime, solidarity.'

They both nod.

'Have you told the police about the flat?' he asks Celia.

'No. Should I?'

Lennie shakes his head. 'They might already know about it, but if not, don't say anything unless they ask you directly. I'll have a gander up there myself and see whether the local estate agent can give me any clues.' He stands up. 'I need to go home for a sleep first. Don't start arguing when my back is turned.' His eyes warn each of them in turn. 'You're on the same side, remember.'

Sinead inclines her head, and Celia says, 'I can see you're the father of girls.'

And so they part on a smile.

He sleeps for two hours then gets the bus to Holy Corner, so called because three churches sit close to the junction. It's an expensive area of town, what with the Grange and Morningside a stone's throw away, and Napier University attracting thousands of students, keen to offload their loans in the local pubs. And that reminds him – somehow Shona's got herself into Glasgow Uni to study biology. She can't wait to escape the confines of home. He'll worry about what she might get up to when the time comes.

For now, it's Ruby he's concerned with. He only wants to know she's safe. He's tried calling her, he's left increasingly irritated voicemails but she's not replied. He's trying not to be hurt about that, but *really*? She can't just let him know she's safe? He only hopes she'll keep her appointment with Beattie.

She needs to. She bloody well needs to.

There's an estate agent on the main street. His police ID would make questioning the staff straightforward but he had to hand that in when he left the service. He can't rope Connor in because it's not a line they cross. So he'll just have to get creative, wing it a little.

There's a lone woman behind one of the desks. More girl than woman, she can't be much older than Shona. Her face is a waxy colour – thick foundation covering up a bad case of acne. The other three desks are empty. She glances up when Lennie comes in. 'My colleagues are out showing at the moment, but I might be able to help.'

'Sure thing.' Lennie taps his fingers on her desk. 'The wife, she's a bit of a fussy one (Trish would kill him if she heard him say that but he's playing a part) and I've been sent on ahead to rent a flat.'

She jumps to her feet. 'I can show you the ones we have on our books at the moment.'

'Great. But actually ...' He looks up to the ceiling as if he's just thought of something significant. 'A friend of ours, she started renting a place from you a couple of weeks back and the wife, well ...' He nods his head from side to side. 'I'm not saying she's competitive but if I could see the one Ruby rented then I'd be able to go one up.'

'Oh, okay!' She laughs. 'What's your friend's name?'

'Ruby Romano.'

'I remember her. And the flat she rented because I've still to input everything on the computer. She paid cash,' she adds, then scrabbles around in a low cupboard. 'Here we are.' She hands him a property details sheet. 'That's the one your friend has. And take this too.' It's a current list of all properties for rent. 'There are loads of photos online.'

'Cheers. You've been a great help.' He should really tell her that giving out confidential information is a gift to an estranged partner or a stalker. Hasn't she been on any training courses? 'Thank you for all this.'

'Hope you make your wife happy!'

Fat chance, Lennie thinks, but – hey – go, Lennie! He should be back in the force. Piece of cake. He has the address and it's just around the corner.

Ahead of him a young couple are talking to a man, a white and tan terrier by his side. When Lennie draws close, the dog strains on the lead until he's allowed to sniff at Lennie's trousers.

'Barry!' the man admonishes his dog. 'Don't get in the gentleman's way.'

'It's no bother,' says Lennie, bending down to stroke him. 'My wife breeds dogs. I'm well used to it.'

'Barry must be able to smell them,' the young woman says.

Lennie's neck heats up. The tone of her voice is familiar to him. He feels like he's moving in slow motion as he turns in her direction.

And there she is. Ruby's daughter. He could have picked her out in a crowd. She looks like her mum –

hair, eyes, smile. And she sounds like her mum. No denying it.

Painting, my arse, Lennie thinks. Now he knows why Ruby moved here.

Later, at work, Lennie sits back in his seat, lingering over Tina's chocolate mousse – you can have too much mayonnaise but you can't have too much mousse. He's waiting for Fiona to be busy elsewhere so that he can scrutinise the footage from before and after the murder. Because he has a hunch – a policeman's hunch – and that's never to be underestimated. When Fiona disappears to fill out a questionnaire for Al, Lennie pulls up the footage. He watches it through once, and then twice, and then a third time, just to be sure.

He doesn't want to be proved right, not really. It makes him feel both relieved and disappointed.

When his mobile rings, and he sees it's Connor, he answers at once, anticipating that Connor will be about to tell him that the investigation has reached the same conclusion that Lennie has.

But no.

'Early forensic results have come back,' Connor tells him. 'Romano's DNA is all over the deceased's jacket. But worse than that – traces were found on his skin, one centimetre from the incision site.' Lennie's heart contracts. Not great news. 'There are five separate DNA samples, three of them at present unidentified.'

'Well, that's something,' Lennie says.

'And meanwhile, Romano's done a runner,' Connor says. 'Sorry, Lennie, but when they find her, she'll be formally charged with murder.'

Chapter Eighteen

Ruby feels the urgency of a life that has to be lived in a few days. She imagines this must be what it's like when you're given a terminal diagnosis. There is the urge to pack everything in, fill each day with experiences that you will cherish during the next stage, be it your deathbed or, as in Ruby's case, a prison cell.

Prison. It's not a reality, not yet. And so she guards against thinking about it too much. But every now and then it catapults to the forefront of her mind and dread rises up from her stomach in waves.

And death? Well, she tried that, didn't she? Suicide. Not for her, as it turned out.

She walks through the Meadows, criss-crossing the pathways to stroll under the trees that have been growing there since before her own childhood. She walks past the Commonwealth Pool where she learned to swim and to dive. She climbs higher than the yellow flowering gorse, onto the Radical Road that takes her around the Salisbury Crags and then to the top of Arthur's Seat where the Edinburgh panorama she knows so well stretches out all around her.

She makes this journey three days in a row. She knows the police will be looking for her and that it's only a matter of time before she's spotted on one of the cameras. She could run away, jump on a train to London and disappear into the crowd. She could pull that off; it wouldn't be hard for her. She has all the necessary skills – but where would she go? She doesn't want to start again. She doesn't want always to be looking over her shoulder. No, she feels better keeping the emotion out of it – a man is dead; society demands justice. And justice is what keeps humanity on the right side of civilised.

So, she will be caught.

And she will be imprisoned, but in the meantime she'll have a few days to herself and she will take these three days into prison with her because Lennie was right when he talked about how it would be. She'll need the most colourful, lively, heart-warming memories so that when she closes her eyes the prison will cease to exist and she will be outside again, enjoying the sunshine and the fresh air, the rain on her cheeks and the view from the top.

When she isn't walking, she stays in the flat. The police haven't discovered this second address of hers. It seems that she hasn't been living there long enough for her details to filter through to the right places.

She surprises herself by shopping for food. She fills her fridge with luxury dinners and every evening she eats her body weight in steak and chips, or shepherd's pie or battered fish with mushy peas. Then there's rhubarb shortbread or raspberry mousse or rice pudding for afters. She eats by the window, sitting in a comfy chair that faces outside. The windowsill is low off the ground and so her view is unrestricted. She stares down into Hannah's front room. She watches her daughter work on her computer and lie on the sofa watching television, her head on her boyfriend's knee.

Snooping, spying, stalking.

Ruby knows that's what she's doing. And she's fine with it.

On day three she stays outside for the sunset and

when she returns she finds Lennie sitting at the top of the stairs. 'The man with the dog let me into the stair,' he says. 'I told him we went to art class together.'

Ruby laughs. 'It's good to see you, Lennie. I hoped you would find me.' She walks past him, unlocks the door and leaves it ajar behind her. 'Did Celia tell you about the flat?'

He nods and follows her inside, goes straight to the window to stare down into the homes opposite. Few curtains are drawn, rooms are lit and people are moving around inside. 'What are you playing at, Rubes?' he says quietly.

'Making memories for when I'm in prison.' She switches on the oven. 'Will you share a meal with me?'

He pats his stomach. 'Be happy to.'

'I'll cook for you for once.'

'Your daughter lives opposite, I see.' He watches the muscles in Ruby's neck tense. 'I'm not going to say anything. I haven't come here to make trouble. I just think in times like this two heads are better than one.'

Her lips tremble. 'The die is cast, Lennie.'

'You sure?'

'I am.'

She serves them both sea bass on crushed potatoes. 'Crispy skin on the fish, rosemary and garlic on the potatoes,' Lennie says. 'So you can cook.' He swallows another mouthful. 'How many more secrets have you been keeping?'

'I can paint.'

'Can you really? I thought that was just your cover story.'

Ruby puts her fork down. 'I'm not going to get emotional but, I just want to say that you're the best man I've ever met, Lennie Williamson, and I hope your girls know how lucky they are to have you for a dad.'

He thanks her, and briefly touches her hand before saying, 'So tell me about Hannah.'

On day four, she's out to greet the sunrise. She hasn't done this for years. The earth's spin towards the sun and the light show that follows will be lost to her when she's in prison. No doing what you fancy when you fancy. So she climbs once more to the top of Arthur's Seat and waits for the seam of pink to crack open to the east of her. And when it comes, she sits down with her back against a rock and admires the raspberry hue as it spills across the sky.

Around nine o'clock she begins to walk back the way she came. Yesterday she loitered outside her nephews' and niece's school, not so anyone would notice – she pretended to be on her mobile – but close enough that she could watch them playing at break time. She decides she'll do that again this morning and wouldn't it be just perfect if Lennie came for dinner again? She'll buy a leg of lamb and stud it with anchovies the way her mother does.

Or maybe not.

She sees the police car at the bottom of the hill, close to the Scottish parliament. Both officers are outside, leaning against the side of the vehicle, staring up in her direction. They must know she's there and they've saved themselves the climb, despite the fact that there are several ways down should she choose to run. She's not worthy of a helicopter but she might be if she made a run for it.

She doesn't run. That's never been her plan and all she'd be doing is delaying the inevitable. She follows the path down towards them, neither rushing nor dragging

her heels. She was up early so it must have been the
night shift who spotted her. Lennie would never blow
the whistle on her. Fiona then. It'll be Fiona. She'll have
enjoyed that. Another learning objective ticked.

She doesn't know either of the arresting officers and
that's a relief. This isn't personal for them so there's no
awkwardness.

It's a fair cop.

Ruby meets solicitor Linus Beattie within two hours of
her arrest. Linus is mild-mannered, softly spoken and
meticulous. He takes note of everything Ruby tells him,
writing it down on his legal pad in a neat, even script.

Frank Beattie, his advocate brother, comes to see Ruby
on the following day. Ruby recognises his type. He is
the sort of man who gives advocates a bad name. He
doesn't care if his clients are guilty, he doesn't care about
right and wrong, he doesn't even care about justice.
What he cares about is winning. Biggest, fastest, strongest
– that's his *raison d'être*. She can see why Lennie recom-
mended him; to have him on your side is an invitation
to win.

'I am your mouthpiece. I will amplify your story when
needs be and minimise your story when it serves you
better,' he tells Ruby. 'Do you understand what I mean
by that?'

'You'll shine a spotlight in the right places.'

'Exactly. I'll ensure the illegal drugs the police found
in your house are inadmissible. And your mental health
problems from five years ago?' He shakes his head.
'Inadmissible.' He glances at the briefing in front of him
again before saying, 'Rumour has it your leaving the
police service was precipitated by a fall from grace. Is
that right?'

'I – yes.'

'It matters not a jot. What I will amplify, however, is your excellent police record up to that point.'

'Right.'

'What possessed you to go AWOL?' Ruby opens her mouth to reply and he holds up his hand. 'Don't answer that. The truth is of no consequence. But your actions will make it impossible for you to get bail as you'll be seen as a flight risk.'

He likes the sound of his own voice, a handy trait for any advocate. He talks for almost an hour and Ruby does little more than nod. The irony is that she can only afford his astronomical fees because she was married to Grant. Ruby imagines the newspaper headline: DEAD MAN PAYS FOR HIS MURDERING WIFE TO GET OFF SCOT-FREE. He would be turning in his grave – were he in one. There is yet to be a funeral as his body is still in the morgue.

'They have enough evidence to go to trial,' Beattie tells her. 'DNA, some circumstantial evidence, weak motive.' His expression is dubious. 'I don't anticipate a problem. I've won against odds like this before.'

'Even with the DNA?'

'Juries like solid facts, Ms Romano. The prosecution has no murder weapon and no CCTV.' He starts gathering his papers together. 'Steve Wilson has corroborated the fact that he asked you to re-sequence the cameras.' He glances across at her, his expression shrewd. 'He was only sorry he hadn't got the paperwork to you immediately.'

'I shouldn't have gone ahead without it.'

'And let criminals deal drugs on our High Street?' He stands up and holds his hand out for her to shake. 'Keep your head down.' He walks away from her and opens the door, looking back at her just before he leaves the room. 'Remember, Ms Romano – no loose talk in prison. Speak only if you have to and keep your answers short. Talking is overrated.'

Coming from him? Ruby smiles for the first time since she was arrested. She wishes Lennie was with her. They would have shared a laugh.

The food isn't as awful as she expects it to be, and almost every time she eats a meal, she thinks of Lennie and it makes her smile because she can hear his voice, like John and Gregg on *MasterChef*, critiquing the taste and the quality of the cooking. 'Over-boiled, under-seasoned, could have done with a sauce.'

Ruby sleeps in the Vulnerable Prisoners Unit because if any of the prisoners were to suss out that she used to be a cop, she would be made to suffer for it. Her case isn't getting much press at the moment; that will happen when – if – the case goes to trial. And then the shit could hit the fan: EX-COP MURDERS HUSBAND WITH A KITCHEN KNIFE.

They all eat together in a communal dining area. The other women know that she's been arrested for her husband's murder and it gives her a certain notoriety and respect. On the morning of her first breakfast she sits down in the corner, and within minutes a woman comes over to sit opposite her. Ruby doesn't look up.

'You murdered your man?' the woman says, her Glaswegian accent as thick as the porridge they're both eating.

Ruby is tempted to say a number of things from 'he wasn't my man' to 'I didn't do it' but she says nothing.

'Respect,' the woman says and she raises a fist. Ruby almost ducks until she realises the woman wants to bump fists with her. Ruby obliges and the woman moves back to sit with her own gang.

Ruby knows that in reality prisons barely resemble those portrayed in television dramas. And it's not much like high school either, but there is a pecking order and most of the power resides with the woman who approached Ruby at breakfast. She's called Sandra and she is late thirties/early forties, short hair, wide hips, overweight but not obese. She is surrounded by four other women who hang on her every word. They stick together throughout the day, bestowing attention on some of the others but only if the mood takes them.

Ruby watches as the other women vie for that attention. Many of them have mental health problems, some of them are clearly ex-addicts, all of them are needy. The gang of five ignore a whispering, mousey woman who follows them around for most of the morning until eventually she cracks, starts screaming obscenities and the room erupts: jeering, cat-calling and hair-pulling. The guards descend in under a minute and it's all over in another minute but the air buzzes with adrenalin and fear for the rest of the day.

Ruby's roommate is called Tiffany and she's only twenty but she could easily pass for twice that age. She has obvious track marks on her arms and legs, and a shake that has given her the nickname Stevens. The other women mostly avoid her because there is a strangeness about her that smacks of decay.

Within a week, if anyone asked her, Ruby would say that prison is mostly mundane with moments of brutality. The brutal moments are two sorts: a sudden outburst of violence, a kick to the kidneys or a twist of the arm; the second is being ignored, and this would mean nothing in the outside world, but, inside, loneliness and exclusion are a killer.

She lives with a constantly raised heartbeat, always

on the lookout for threat in whatever form it takes. She
knows it's only a matter of time before someone takes
a dislike to her and so, despite the monotony, there is
no relaxation. She can't breathe the way she used to.
Her breaths are short. Her lungs won't inflate. It's as if
they're stuck together with glue and prising them apart
takes more puff than she can muster. She closes her
eyes to remember yoga lessons with Celia when they
would sit cross-legged and breathe, slow and deep, their
spines straight, the crowns of their heads pulled heav-
enwards by an invisible thread, but she is so far removed
from that world now that the memories fail to reach her
body.

And now just taking a normal breath, one that isn't
loaded with regrets and emotion and the weight of what's
gone and what's yet to come, is at times impossible. She
has to place both hands on her ribcage and try to coax
it into expanding. Twice she has fallen over and been
left there until she pulls herself upright again. Nobody
steps forward to help her. One woman takes the opportunity to murmur 'bitch' under her breath and another
stares hungrily at Ruby, as a piranha fish stares at a
dipped toe, before kicking her in the groin.

As Beattie predicted, she is denied bail on the grounds
that she is a flight risk. She's been expecting this but
still it's a gnawing disappointment, momentarily allevi-
ated when Lennie comes to visit her.

'I've only got twenty minutes,' he says. 'Because your
mum and Celia are here.'

'They can wait. They've seen me already this week.'
She reaches across the table to touch his hand. 'I'm so
glad you're here, Lennie.' She hasn't smiled this wide
since she came inside.

He returns her smile but it doesn't wipe the sadness

from his eyes. 'I'm sorry I haven't made it in to see you before now. Family ...' He waves away the rest of the explanation as if it isn't worth hearing. 'And I hope you know it wasn't me who dobbed you in,' he says. 'It was fecking Fiona, prissy little madam.'

'I knew it wasn't you. But in any case I wasn't avoiding the cameras. It was inevitable I'd be spotted. Please.' She reaches for his hand again. 'I don't want to talk about me or the trial. I spend all day with me. Tell me about your girls.'

He tells her that he's teaching Tina how to cook, that Shona has got into university: 'God knows how she got the grades. I never saw her doing any work. And I don't think I told you that Trish is carrying a boy.'

'Wow!' Ruby laughs. 'It's all going on! And listen, I meant it when I said you could have my house.'

'No.' He pulls away. 'I won't have you saying that.'

'Even if I get out, it's too big for me. You'd be doing me a favour.'

Lennie shakes his head at her. 'I couldn't accept it, Ruby.'

'Think about it, please. I'd feel so happy knowing you were all there.'

Lennie promises to think about it and next her mum comes in. She visits twice a week and stays for as long as she can. Desperate as Ruby is for company, she finds her mum's visits loaded with emotion and it adds to her burden.

'I'm only staying ten minutes because Celia has a lot to say to you.' Ruby nods and her mum runs through the questions she asks every time: Are you well? Are you being bullied? Are you warm enough? Has one of the Beattie brothers been in this week? What are they saying? Is there anything you need? (There's no mention of

Hannah because Ruby made it clear to both her mum and sister that all talk of Hannah is off-limits.)

Ruby does her best to answer each question, hoping it won't lead to another question, but whatever she says, she knows her mum will leave dissatisfied. 'Very disappointing about bail,' her mum says.

'I know.' Ruby looks at her mum's hand where the watch she bought her gapes an inch or more from her wrist. 'You need a link taken out of the strap,' she says.

Her mum frowns. 'I don't have time to go to the jeweller's.'

'You could have gone today,' Ruby says. 'I don't expect you to visit me twice a week.'

'When I'm not here, I'm in St Mary's, praying for you.'

Ruby sighs.

'What, Ruby? You don't want my prayers? You don't want me to visit you?'

'I don't want you to tire yourself out.'

'Tire myself out? Jesus Christ! You're my *daughter*! And you're in *prison*.'

'I just don't want you coming here because you feel it's your duty. Or because you think Dad would want you to. Or because you think—' Ruby stops talking; her mouth hangs open. 'Mum?' Her mum is crying; her mum never cries. Even when they lost Ruby's dad, she didn't cry. But now her whole body shakes with the eruption of tears, tears that seem to be coming from the very depths of her soul. 'Mum, please.' Ruby reaches across to hold her shoulders. 'Don't cry.' Her body continues to convulse, her ribcage twisting as if expelling more than just air. Ruby looks for help from the prison officer on duty. The woman walks forward with a box of tissues, then returns to stand in the corner.

Ruby takes a handful of the tissues and puts them in her mum's hand. She doesn't know what else to do. This isn't her mum. This is someone else. This is a woman who is overwhelmed by her feelings. Ruby has never met this woman before. Ruby had no inkling that this woman even existed.

Finally the tears stop and her mum wipes her face, blows her nose and raises bloodshot eyes to Ruby's. 'I don't always say the right thing. I make mistakes.' She nods, agreeing with herself. 'Talking to Grant was unforgivable and I can't help but think it's what led to his death.'

'Mum—'

'Let me speak, Ruby. If I don't say this now, I may never say it. And these words need to be said.' She blows her nose again. 'I lost a baby the year before you were born. Did you know that?'

Ruby shakes her head.

'Also a girl. It was a difficult pregnancy. She was born three months premature and had problems with her liver. It took four days for her to die. And my heart—' Her voice cracks as she lays a hand on her chest. 'I thought my heart would break. And then I fell pregnant with you.' Her expression softens. 'I had no morning sickness. No heartburn. No varicose veins. You arrived on your due date, just as your dad finished his shift. And when he first clapped eyes on you ... well ...' She smiles. 'It was love at first sight for him.' Her gaze drifts into the past. 'It was love at first sight for me too but Gino and you, you were enamoured with each other and I loved watching you together.' She pauses to wipe at her eyes. 'And then when Celia was born? I had to make it up to her. Your dad loved her too, of course. But she wasn't you.'

Ruby can't speak. Her head is telling her that this is

her mother rewriting history to suit herself but her heart recognises the truth. Her dad did favour her. It wasn't blatant. It was subtle. His smiles were slightly wider for her. His laughter at her jokes was just a tad louder. They shared a love of Hibs football club and would go to matches together. It was always her hand he reached for when they were out walking. And when he was dying, it was Ruby he asked for.

'I love you, Ruby,' her mum says. 'Never let there be any doubt about that.' She stands up. 'Say nothing of this to Celia. If she asks why I've been crying, say I'm upset about the bail.'

'Thank you, Mum.' Ruby stands up too, her head spinning; she feels like she's been through an emotional wringer. 'I ... Thank you for telling me that. And I'm sorry.'

'Don't be.'

'I am, though. I'm sorry about the baby you lost.' She hugs her mum, feels her skin and bones through her jacket and says, 'You need to eat more.'

Her mum sighs, as if Ruby hasn't been listening at all, not to one single word. 'Dear God, how can I eat with you in here?'

There's no answer to that – or nothing that would satisfy her mum – and then Celia is sitting in front of Ruby, and she's holding Ruby's hands and talking about someone she knows who won their trial against all odds because of this and that, and Ruby mustn't lose hope because the system is on the side of the innocent and—

'The morning you came to my house,' Ruby says, interrupting her sister's story because who is the story for? Certainly not Ruby. 'When I was packing to move into the flat, you said to me Grant was right when he

... And then you stopped talking. What did you mean? Were you in touch with him?'

Celia stares across at her sister, eyes wide. 'I don't remember saying that.'

'Well, you did. So what could you have meant?'

'Erm.' Celia slumps in her seat while she thinks. 'I do remember Grant once saying to me that you found it difficult to accept help.'

'And did you agree with him?'

'Well, not really, but you know what Grant was like.'

'Yeah, I do. I do know what Grant was like.'

'He was controlling, wasn't he?' Celia says quietly. 'Did he ever ... ?' She trails off, thinking. 'I should have ... Are you mad with me?' She gives Ruby an almost-smile, the one that showcases her dimples. 'Did I let you down?'

Ruby wonders whether this is a conversation worth having. She's in prison and Grant is dead. Does it really matter if Celia was often more loyal as a sister-in-law than she was as a sister? And now, after everything her mum has told her ... Did Celia know? Did she sense Ruby was their dad's favourite?

'Tell me about the kids,' Ruby says. 'Is Joseph sleeping through the night yet?'

Celia is never happier than when she's talking about her children and Ruby will never grudge her that.

She is fifty fathoms deep, lost in a recurring nightmare where there is a blanket over her face and she's gulping for air but the material is blocking her mouth. Her body is pinned from the waist down and she's wearing no underwear – where are her pants? – and she struggles, she screams and she scratches.

And then she wakes up, in her bed, in her cell where

Tiffany snores and the air grows staler and she clutches at her own throat. Sometimes she is dizzy and sick with the emptiness inside her, the lack of life's oxygen and the sky so far away now, so out of reach. Everything is out of reach: her home, her peace of mind, her freedom to walk outside.

And then one day, there she is – Hannah – sitting at the table, waiting for her. At first Ruby thinks she might have conjured her up but when she blinks, Hannah is still there. There is a delay and they don't let the inmates into the visitors' room immediately so Ruby has time, as she stands in line, to watch her daughter and think back to the moment they first spoke to each other.

She swallows a small blue diazepam, then she picks up another, and is about to swallow that too when, for the second time that evening, she senses someone behind her. The pain between her legs intensifies at the thought of Grant coming back to taunt her but when she swivels round, it isn't Grant.

It's Hannah.

'Hannah?' Ruby approaches her daughter slowly. 'Is it really you?'

Hannah is standing by the window staring back at Ruby. She is beautiful, fragile, wide-eyed as a fallow deer.

'I broke into your house,' she says.

'Okay,' Ruby says, nodding.

'I've been in all the rooms, nosing around. While you slept. And before Grant arrived,' she adds.

'I'm sorry, I would have—'

'I almost left when you went upstairs,' she says loudly. 'But I changed my mind because I heard you say something to Grant and I want you to say it to me, to my face.'

'Of course. Whatever you want.' Anything to keep her

here. *That's all Ruby wants: to have her here, to hold a conversation with her, to see her smile.*

'You said' – *she takes a deep breath* – 'giving up Hannah was my lowest point and seeing her again was my highest.' *She breathes again.* 'That's what you said.'

'I did,' *Ruby agrees.*

'Say it to me now.'

Ruby purses her lips, thinking back. 'I said, giving up Hannah, that was my lowest point.'

'Look me in the eye when you say it.'

Ruby walks towards her daughter and stops about a metre in front of her. Rather than repeating exactly what she said, with Hannah before her, it makes sense to change it. 'Giving you up, Hannah, that was my lowest point.' *Her voice is strong.* 'And seeing you again, that was my highest.' *And then she gasps because their eye contact feels electric, as if the energy that flows between them will make walls tumble and fireworks explode.*

Hannah turns away first to stare out of the window and rub tears from her cheeks.

'Hannah, I ...' *Ruby is breathless with a fizzing joy that bubbles up from her heart.*

'I'm going now,' *Hannah says. And then she's out of the kitchen, her steps unsteady but quick, and Ruby runs behind her.*

'Will you come back?' *she shouts.*

'Maybe.' *Hannah is outside on the drive when she hesitates and glances behind her.* 'You shouldn't swallow those pills.'

Ruby draws back, suddenly remembering what she was about to do, realising how Hannah must see her – her birth mother in a bloodstained nightdress, tear-streaked face, greasy hair, about to end her own life.

'You're better than that!' *Hannah calls back and then she is gone.*

Ruby closes the door behind her and begins to laugh then cry then laugh again. She's already late for work but she doesn't care. She is energised. She dances around the kitchen, feeling the rhythm in her limbs and the beat in her heart.

She's hungry and she decides to cook something for herself, forgetting there's almost nothing in the fridge. She needs a pot and a chopping board and a knife. She notices that the middle knife is missing from the knife rack but she thinks nothing of it because there are four more. And who needs five knives anyway?

The prison officer lets the women into the visitors' room and Ruby approaches Hannah as if she were floating. Hannah stands up and leans in to kiss Ruby's cheek. 'Is it okay?' she says.

'Okay?' Ruby laughs. 'It's more than okay! It's wonderful. If I had to pick one person I longed to visit me it would be you.' Ruby's smile is so wide that surely her face will split in two. And if it did she wouldn't care.

'I brought you this.' Hannah holds up the hoop earring.

'Oh …' Hannah's hand is shaking and Ruby wants to take it in hers to reassure her, but instead she takes the earring and says, 'I had a pair like that once. I think I lost one of them.'

'Five years ago.' Hannah's expression is serious. 'I looked for the other one in your jewellery box but I couldn't see it.'

'Is it mine?' Ruby says. It could be one of a pair that Grant bought for her when they were going through the airport from Paris to the Maldives. She rubs the gold between the tips of her fingers.

'I found it on the path the next day,' Hannah says. 'And I saw you when you looked up at the window.'

Ruby's fingers grow still. She knows at once what

path and what window Hannah is referring to. 'I must have frightened you.' She looks her daughter in the eye. 'I'm so, so sorry for that, Hannah.'

'You didn't frighten me; well, you did, but only because I didn't know you and I wasn't given any information and I was too afraid to ask.' She bites her lip. 'I take things.'

Ruby nods. 'I used to do that.' She doesn't admit that she was watching Hannah from the living room window in the flat when Hannah took the shoebox from the bureau. Hannah doesn't know about the flat. And it doesn't seem important now. It will have to be cleared of her stuff and she'll ask Lennie to do it for her. Better that no one else ever knows why she moved there.

Hannah leans in towards Ruby, and Ruby does the same so that their faces are inches apart. 'I took the knife,' Hannah whispers.

'I know,' Ruby says, glancing to the right and left to make sure no one can overhear them. 'We don't need to talk about it.'

'I took it and put it in my pocket. I don't know why, it was like ... they were all lined up and I took the middle one. I normally take small things so that nobody will notice they're gone. I don't know what possessed me.'

'It's okay.' Ruby doesn't need to hear this. The knife was from her house, Grant was hurting her, Hannah was only there because of Ruby – as far as Ruby's concerned she stabbed Grant, not Hannah.

'I never meant to kill him, only to scare him, because he was hurting you. And I'd already seen him hurt you in your kitchen.' She shudders. 'I couldn't watch it happen again.'

'I understand.' Ruby is brave enough to hold her hand

this time. It's freezing cold and she rubs it between both of hers to warm it. 'Thank you. But you really mustn't—'

'You had pepper spray in your pocket, didn't you?' Hannah asks.

'Yes, I always have. Since ...' She trails off.

'I know that because I looked through your coat pockets when I was in your house. You were reaching for it when I came into the close, weren't you?'

'Ye-s, but—'

'Would that have stopped him? Would he have let you go?'

'Maybe, but Hannah ...' Ruby strokes the hair away from her daughter's eyes. 'What happened was an accident.'

'I killed a man,' she whispers, her eyes an agony of guilt.

'Ssh.' Ruby puts her fingers over Hannah's lips. 'Don't say that.'

'Why are you taking the blame?'

'Because the blame is mine. It's my fault. I married him. I stayed with him. I brought this on myself. You were an innocent bystander and for that I am truly sorry.' *And this way I can make up for giving you away as a baby. This is my redemption.* She doesn't say that because it sounds too melodramatic. But it's what she feels. It's what makes the whole thing bearable.

Hannah comes back again and again. Each time there's awkwardness between them as they make the effort to get to know each other. Often Hannah's resentment rumbles just beneath the surface of her words. 'So you never met the parents who adopted me for the first time?'

'I didn't,' Ruby says. 'I would have liked to but it wasn't possible.'

'But did you wonder?'

'Of course! And every day I thought about you. I hoped and I prayed that you were loved and thriving and—'

'That sounds like a lot of effort!' Her tone is disbelieving. 'Wouldn't it have been easier to have just kept me?'

'Yes!' Ruby's face crumples. 'Every single day I wished I'd kept you.'

Hannah stares down at her hands, focuses on her nails and picks at the cuticles with an aggressive finger.

'I made a mistake,' Ruby says quietly.

'You're not the only one,' Hannah replies. Her expression clouds as she remembers her own guilt. 'I've been thinking about Violet and her twins. They'll be born soon.'

Every visit ends with Ruby reassuring Hannah, taking all the blame upon her own shoulders, holding her daughter tight before she leaves.

Ruby asks Celia and her mum to visit at other times. She doesn't mind if Lennie meets Hannah – she would be proud for Lennie to meet her daughter – but she doesn't want them to meet until she's sure Hannah is able to see past her own guilt.

It's on Lennie's second visit that they discuss the murder. 'I know it was Hannah who killed Grant,' he says.

'What on earth?' Ruby is startled. She shakes her head. 'I don't know what's brought you to that conclusion. I—'

'I watched the CCTV footage before and after the crime. She was in the High Street just before it happened looking twitchy and anxious. And afterwards, she's seen a couple of hundred metres away, running through town, looking like she'd just supped with the devil.'

'She witnessed a murder and she freaked out,' Ruby says.

'I'm sure if you hadn't gone AWOL they'd have watched more of the CCTV footage and got round to questioning Hannah. And you didn't want that, did you? You wanted the focus to stay on you.'

Ruby folds her arms and sighs.

'We both know it's thirty days before the footage is overwritten. If you're found innocent and they're looking for another suspect, Hannah has no connection to Grant so she's unlikely to be a person of interest, especially in the absence of CCTV evidence. Was that your thinking?' She doesn't reply. 'But this is a murder investigation, Ruby, and they were thorough. They've downloaded everything within a three-mile radius: our CCTV, surveillance footage from shops and car parks, dash cams – you name it, they have it. And that evidence will always be on file, just waiting for the day to prove its worth.'

'Lennie.' She shakes her head again. 'I know you want to believe I'm innocent, and I love you for that. I really do. But Hannah had no reason to kill Grant.'

Lennie sits back in his seat and stares up at the ceiling. Seconds tick by and Ruby's mouth grows drier. 'Something interesting up there?' she says.

'I saw the forensic report.'

Ruby raises her eyebrows at this.

'There was unidentified DNA close to and inside the wound.'

'So?' Ruby says.

'I bet if they screened for genetic markers they'd find out that the DNA belongs to a female relative of yours. And then they'd go looking. It wouldn't take them long to find out about Hannah, now would it?'

Ruby goes to stand up but Lennie grabs her hand. 'I'm just asking you to *think*, Ruby. That's all.'

'That's what I have been doing!'

He keeps going. 'I bumped into Hannah in the street when I was looking for your flat.'

'*What?*' Ruby glares at him. 'You didn't tell me that.'

'By accident. Her hand was heavily bandaged. She was telling a neighbour that she had cut her palm.' His expression is deadpan. 'It's a classic injury. You stab someone, the knife handle becomes slippery with their blood and your own hand slides down onto the blade.'

'I'm guilty,' Ruby repeats.

'I get it, Ruby. I'd be tempted to take the fall for one of my girls but there's something to be said for facing the consequences of your actions. You are denying her that.'

'Grant's murder was on me.' She thumps her chest. 'No one else is to blame.'

'Hannah is responsible for her own actions.'

'But it wasn't her fault.' Ruby's voice is low and urgent. 'She only got mixed up in this because of me and you know what? I'm at peace with my decision, because I have regretted giving her away since the day after I did it. That's a lot of days, Lennie, and a lot of regret. And now she visits me every week. She talks to me and she includes me in her life. It's all I've ever wanted.'

She watches him wrestle with this, to think of a way to persuade her otherwise, but eventually he sighs his acceptance. 'And if you're found guilty?'

'I hope not to be.' She shrugs. 'But if I am, then I'll serve my time.'

'It doesn't scare you to gamble with your freedom like this?'

'Of course it scares me. But you know what scares

me more? The thought of Hannah walking into a police station and making a confession.' Ruby chokes back her emotion. 'Hannah in here and me out there? I couldn't handle it, Lennie.'

The buzzer sounds for the end of visiting hour and they both stand up. 'Can we just agree to disagree?' Ruby says.

'Only if you let me visit you every week,' Lennie says.

'Well …' She smiles. 'If you bring brownies with you next time, I might just see you.'

The fifth time Hannah visits she brings photographs of herself growing up, and Ruby sticks them on the pin-board in her cell alongside photographs of her nephews and niece. Being part of her daughter's life is heart-warming for Ruby and it goes a long way towards countering the negative aspects of prison life: the monotony, the incipient dread at being locked inside a cell, the complete lack of personal space.

The sixth time Hannah visits she wants to know about her dad. Ruby has been expecting this and so she has prepared her story. 'He was kind and funny.' She smiles, pretending to remember. 'And handsome. He was very handsome.'

'But he was a one-night stand?'

'Yes, and I know that makes it sound careless and insignificant but it wasn't.' She leans across the table and takes Hannah's hands in hers. She does this every time she comes to visit now. She senses that the contact calms Hannah down because there's no doubt that Hannah is anxious. It's difficult to keep her from talking about anything other than the murder and Ruby is glad when another topic holds her attention. 'His pinkie finger was just like yours,' Ruby says.

'I can't straighten it,' Hannah says, trying, and failing, to flatten her hand on the table.

It's all she has of her father, Ruby thinks. This tiny imperfection.

'So what happened?' Hannah asks.

Ruby's smile grows wider. 'We had a twenty-four-hour love affair. I know that seems like no time but it felt so much longer than that. And I was left with many happy memories.'

Hannah nods, pleased at this. 'What happened to him?'

'He was only in Edinburgh for the weekend and then he went back to London.'

'Why didn't you get in touch with him when you were pregnant?'

'I tried, but his name was John Miller.' She rolls her eyes. 'There are hundreds of John Millers in London.'

Is it wrong to lie so spectacularly? Ruby doesn't think so. She's only once told the truth about what happened that night and she told it fifteen years too late when the experience was set in stone and nothing could be done. It was the recounting of that fateful night that sent her father to an early grave.

Later in bed, awake after the recurring nightmare, Ruby knows that she's done the right thing. Hannah already has to live with the reality of her mother giving her up. How much worse if she knew her father raped her mother? How would that colour her view of herself? To be conceived in violence. No child should have to live with that knowledge.

It was a secret that had to be kept.

Ruby knew who he was, the man who pinned her down and covered her face with a blanket while he raped her. His name was Peter Swanson. He had been in the year above her at school, and already at university; she'd innocently returned to his student flat with him when he said he had some music she'd love to hear.

Years later she looked him up on social media. He had emigrated to Canada and there was a picture of him with his wife and two little girls, Hannah's half-sisters. She zoomed in on his wife's face to see whether there was a suggestion that she knew the sort of man she'd married. Her eyes were clear. Her smile seemed real. Perhaps he was a changed man. Perhaps he realised what he had done, and from that moment on he bent over backwards to listen and not to force. That's what Ruby hoped.

She joined the police service because she needed to have perspective on what had happened to her. She wanted to help other women. She wanted to be part of the solution, not the problem. And as a cop, she learned about the reality of sexual crimes and she felt lucky – lucky he hadn't killed her, lucky it was over in five minutes, lucky that it hadn't coloured her life, or not visibly at any rate.

And it wasn't that she blamed the baby, that wasn't why she gave Hannah up. It was more that she couldn't trust herself. What if the baby reminded her of him? Of the attack? What if every time she looked at the baby, she saw him? She couldn't be sure that she wouldn't hate the baby. And that wouldn't be good for either of them.

Better they both have a fresh start.

And so the nineteen-year-old girl came up with a simple lie.

She was five months pregnant when she was willing to face the reality of a baby growing inside her – too late for an abortion, and anyway, she was a Catholic and the thought of one violent act following on from another was too much for her. That wouldn't make it right. What would make it right would be to give the baby away to a loving couple who would raise her as their own, no danger of Ruby's memories infecting his or her upbringing.

She told her family it was a one-night stand. She insisted the baby be adopted. 'But Ruby,' her dad said when he'd got over the disappointment of her pregnancy. 'This is our flesh and blood. We'll help you look after the baby, my grandchild. Take time to think it through.'

She wouldn't listen, and had no understanding of how much her decision would haunt her. As far as she was concerned, the baby's adoption would draw a line under the rape.

Grant, with his confidence and his surety and his conviction that she was his perfect woman, came into her life when she was twenty-one and they fell in love. At work she was tough and strong, but without the uniform she was vulnerable, compliant and sweet. Exactly the sort of woman Grant liked. He didn't want to marry a woman who had close female friendships and spent evenings and weekends gossiping with girl-friends. He looked down on women whose diaries were full of beautician appointments and lunches. He wanted a woman who kept him at the centre of her world.

Ruby was that woman.

Sometimes she's lucky and the nightmare leaves her alone and on those nights her dreams are able to take flight. She is outside, up in the sky, flying above the rooftops where she belongs, gulping breaths of fresh, freezing night air into her lungs. She wakes up from these dreams, still in her cell, but nevertheless refreshed, ready for anything. Always a bonus when she's meeting with Frank Beattie.

'It's about reasonable doubt,' he tells her. 'They have some evidence but nothing that merits a solid conviction.'

'What about my DNA on his jacket and close to the wound?'

'We can get round that.' He shrugs, his confidence undented. 'You met him, he was forceful with you, you went on your way. Someone else came along and killed him. The truth of his affairs is surfacing and that makes him untrustworthy. The women on the jury will automatically dislike him. They'll know he could have had any number of enemies.'

Ruby's final thoughts as she falls asleep at night are not for herself but for Hannah. She knows that Hannah is still wrestling with what she did and Ruby worries that she might never get over it, especially if Ruby is convicted.

Chapter Nineteen

Hannah carries a list in her head. It's a list with two columns. In one column she adds up the pluses and in the other the minuses.

There is only one minus – she killed a man.

In the plus column, she has an extensive list that she adds to every week:

1. The dog walker. His name is Bill Mathison and she goes into his house for a cuppa, she helps him with his ironing – he has arthritis in his fingers – she listens to him talk. She even tries to like Barry.

2. Clem. She went to see Clem and she apologised. And now she's making more effort with Dave. She's having to grit her teeth but she's glad to do it because she knows her efforts won't count unless her pride takes a knock. And she's coming to realise that maybe Dave isn't as bad as she thought he was. He didn't give Clem the black eye – one of Clem's clients did. Clem tells her this when they are sitting in her garden under the stars. Dave has gone out and they have polished off a bottle of wine. Clem confiding in Hannah is something that's never happened before and Hannah feels the urge to reciprocate, to share her own secrets. She tells Clem she's been visiting her mother in prison. Clem sits bolt upright at once, almost spilling the last of her wine, and turns to face Hannah wide-eyed with surprise. Her interest is piqued and she demands all the details. Hannah

shares some of the truth but holds back on the part she played in Grant's death. She's not that drunk. She'll never be that drunk.

3. Her mum and dad. She's stopped lying to them. If they ask her a question, she gives them an honest answer. So when they asked to meet her in town 'for a chat' she knew it would be about Ruby. She listened to what they had to say about not judging other people and how, if you're mentally ill, it's not your fault. And when they asked if she had heard about the woman accused of murder, she told them she knew that Ruby Romano was her birth mother. And then she dropped the bombshell that she regularly visited her in prison.

They didn't take it well. Her mum cried; even her dad cried. She's called them every day since to reassure them, and she visits every weekend. She loves them and she'll keep proving it.

4. Jeff. It dawns on her one evening that she's in love with Jeff. He is a good person, trustworthy and fun to be with, and she knows that she will never again under-estimate how important he is in her life. She tries very hard to stop lying to him too.

5. She volunteers in a homeless charity, early on a Sunday morning, exactly when she'd like to be lying in bed.

6. She takes her nana out to the bingo every other Friday evening – the best evening for tips. She makes enough tips on a Friday to cover all her food and drink for the week and without it she has to penny-pinch.

7. She babysits for her neighbour – a single mum with two wild boys who eat up every ounce of her energy – for free.

8. She doesn't go on Internet forums now. Not once. Not ever.

9. She gives back Aunt Dee's bracelet. She told her she found it on the floor and was really sorry she took it. Her aunt couldn't get her head around this and wouldn't let the subject drop for a whole hour – Was it an accident? Did she mean to take it? – and Hannah tried to be as honest as she could.

She sees her list almost like a computer game where the aim is to get back to zero. If the murder is worth minus one thousand points, then every good deed in the plus column is worth plus one.

It's exhausting being this good but there's an infinity of fear inside her and she'll be sucked into the vortex unless she makes sure to counter it with light. She knows she'll be making up for the murder for the rest of her life.

So it will take her for ever. But it's no more than she deserves.

Hannah's terrified that Ruby will be found guilty. It's bad enough that she isn't being punished for what she did, doubly worse that her mother is paying the price. She visits her twice a week and it's not always easy because her anger is yet to disappear, but it's a revelation to feel so much love from a woman she's only just getting to know. Love based on the fact of her birth and then twenty years of longing. And she's started to call her 'Mum' because who else but a parent would do for Hannah what Ruby is doing for her?

On the first day of the trial, Hannah wakes up at four thirty and paces the room until Jeff calms her down, rubbing her back and making her chamomile tea. Jeff has been her rock. He has taken the whole story in his stride. But then it is a story; it's not the truth.

'You'd only just found her and now she's being tried for murder?' he asks, shocked.

'She's innocent,' Hannah says, her tone entirely without doubt.

'I'm sure she is.' He doesn't look sure but he does his best. 'Hopefully, she'll get off.'

'It's not that she'll get off,' Hannah says. 'The evidence will prove that she's innocent.'

'That's great, Hannah.' He smiles to show that he isn't arguing with her, he's just not allowing himself to be sucked into her certainty.

She doesn't like deceiving him; it doesn't fit in with the person she wants to become but she's not lying exactly, she just can't risk telling him the whole truth, so she slips a Valium into her mouth when he isn't looking and swallows it down with the tea. She'll be completely honest with him one day – just not yet.

So there is the Jeff problem, and then there are two more problems that preoccupy her.

The first is Violet. She wants to help Violet somehow because it hangs heavy on Hannah's conscience that the babies have lost their father before they even met him. Okay, so Hannah can't wind back time, she can't undo the moment when she stabbed their father – a memory that makes her shudder and then retch – but she won't forget these two babies.

The second problem is her addiction. This is something she will only be able to tackle when her mum is free. Giving up drugs, without resorting to another 'coping' mechanism, will take every ounce of her strength and she won't be able to do it until everything else is sorted.

Jeff offers to accompany her to the trial but she assures him she'll manage. She already has company because when waiting to visit her mum, she spoke to her Grandma Sinead and to her Aunt Celia. Just a 'hello' and 'how are you', both women also saying 'sorry' and hugging her. Hannah's unclear what the apology was for but it's enough for her to feel she has been accepted. They are kindred spirits, and so they sit together in the gallery and follow every word spoken in court.

There are several members of the press at the trial, and a dozen or so members of the public, but Violet isn't there because she has given birth. Hannah has been checking the notices in the *Scotsman* every day, and over a month before the trial started she saw the announcement: Twins Lucas and Holly born on 7 August ... their father sadly and dearly missed ...

Ruby sits in the dock, her expression calm but serious. She never looks up at the three women, and Hannah wonders if she's been told not to, or if to look up and see her family would hurt rather than comfort. Hannah has sent a message to let her know she will be in court every day, sitting next to her mum and sister. And that they are all rooting for her, praying for her, willing her to be free.

The jury is a cross-section of adults – male, female, white, mixed race, young and old. Fifteen strangers who are to be trusted with her mother's destiny. Hannah wants them to intuit, as soon as they set eyes on Ruby, that this woman is no killer. She stares at them, trying to transmit thoughts from her to them, but they are mostly inscrutable. Sometimes one or two of them look like they're nodding off and she wants the judge to tell them to wake up!

Every now and then he does speak to them, usually to explain a point of law. Sinead has a pen and a notebook with her and whenever the judge speaks she writes down what he says. 'You can get clues from this,' she tells Hannah when they have a recess. 'And at the end, he'll instruct the jury, remind them what's relevant and what's not.'

Hannah likes Sinead. She wears her heart on her sleeve. Hannah senses her love for Ruby is a force of nature, a storm that never sleeps.

Celia sits between Hannah and her grandma and whenever the prosecuting advocate gets up to speak, she reaches for their hands and holds them tight. She gives them both a confident smile when he's finished talking, and whispers into Hannah's ear, 'Beattie won't have any problem rebutting that nonsense!'

Frank Beattie is a contradiction, a nimble Rottweiler who leaps over legal puddles and charges at procedural gates. To be up against him in court must be maddening because, although he never quite breaks the law, he twists the truth into his own version of a legal knot. Several times the prosecuting advocate is made to look ill-prepared and frankly stupid. The prosecution have an expert forensic witness who Beattie undermines, making all his scientific surety look more like supposition. 'But, Mr Lambert, forgive me for reminding you – a moment ago you admitted to us that DNA is eminently trans-ferrable, and now, here you are, talking with certainty when you claim that the presence of my client's DNA supports the murder charge.'

'I'm as certain as I can be.'

'Is that enough? I wonder.' Beattie's face is puzzled as he regards the jury, making them feel both wise and central to the proceedings. 'Ms Romano has admitted to meeting her husband. Perfectly possible then that her DNA would be on his coat, and that her DNA could have transferred from his coat to his skin when he came up against the person who stabbed him.' Several of the jury nod and Beattie speaks for them when he faces Mr Lambert again. 'Is that not so?'

'Y-es.' Mr Lambert is torn. 'That could have happened.'

'So, let's be clear,' Beattie says. 'The DNA close to the wound *could* have been transferred from coat to wound during the act of Mr Stapleton's murder?'

'Yes.'

'So, despite the presence of her DNA, Ms Romano need not have been present when the murder was committed?'

'That's true.'

Beattie lets his eyes linger on each member of the jury before retaking his seat.

It takes five days to hear all the evidence and while the jury deliberate, Hannah waits outside the courtroom with Sinead, who talks non-stop. She tells her about Ruby as a child, about her dad, about what a wonderful auntie she is. She doesn't mention the time when Ruby gave up Hannah, nor does she remark on Ruby's marriage to Grant, or what happened when Hannah was fifteen – and that's all okay with Hannah. She's keeping it positive; Hannah gets that.

Celia returns with a selection of drinks and sandwiches and they have a few bites before nerves stop them eating any more.

'She bought me this watch, you know.' Sinead holds her wrist out to show Hannah. 'That's another one of her good points – she always buys exactly the right present. Doesn't she, Celia?'

'She does,' Celia says. 'Remember when she bought Dad the Sports Car Experience? He was in seventh heaven.'

The jury don't deliberate for long and Hannah isn't

sure whether this is good or bad. She suspects bad, and she feels so nauseous that she wants to hang over a toilet, but Celia holds her upright. 'We can do this, Hannah,' she says. 'Let's do this together.'

So the three women walk in together. Sit down together. Sinead is shaking so much that the waves reverberate along the bench and make Hannah's teeth chatter. Only Celia can watch, her jaw strong, her eyes on the judge, then the jury, then her sister. So Hannah watches Celia's face; she sees her listening, her eyes reacting to every word. And when the verdict comes – not guilty – Celia cheers, Hannah's heart expands and Sinead's relieved sobs echo around the courtroom.

Ruby looks up then, for the first time in five days, and smiles.

Trouble comes out of the blue – that's what it feels like to Hannah – but in reality she should have been half expecting it. One of her nan's favourite expressions is 'You lie down with dogs, you stand up with fleas'. Being an Internet troll is like lying down with dogs. Trusting a dog? The dog won't bite the hand that feeds him but he will bite the hand that takes his food away. TRO123 isn't happy with Hannah because she asks him to leave her be. Thank you for everything but I'm fine now.

I could use these emails against you, couldn't I? he replies.

He's put two and two together and worked out that she doesn't live in Manchester. The press have been covering the trial and Hannah foolishly let slip enough details for him to work out that catlover81 is Hannah.

Your mother's got off with it. Surely you'll be in the dock next?

He sends one message after another over a series of

days, days when she should be happy because Ruby is home and they see each other every other afternoon for lunch or a walk or a trip to the cinema. It occurs to Hannah, briefly, fleetingly, that if she can kill one man then she can kill two. But the thought no sooner crosses her mind than she recoils from it. She didn't plan on killing Grant and the aftermath has been a slow torture. Sometimes she feels as if a snake has encircled her, squeezing and squeezing, and soon she won't be able to talk and breathe at all.

It's Sunday and Ruby's been out of prison for two weeks when she has a 'freedom party'. Hannah asks friends and family to come and Ruby does the same, both of them crossing their fingers that those they love will mingle well together. A long table is set up in her garden and everyone brings a plate. The weather is breezy but Ruby's garden is sheltered by a ten-foot wall so even Hannah's nana isn't cold.

Hannah's parents are standing off to one side and Celia is chatting to them as if they've been friends for life. 'You must give me your recipe,' she says to her mum. She takes another greedy forkful. 'It's the best coronation chicken I've ever tasted.'

Hannah shows her new cousins how to perform one cartwheel after another without any collapsing legs or floppy arms. Jeff has brought his guitar and is sitting on the grass, quietly strumming a tune, small children gathering at his side to lean across his arm and pluck at the strings. Lennie's girls help with the catering and share the weight of a plump baby boy with sturdy legs and a Tintin quiff that his sisters have gelled in place.

Lennie has been accepted as a contestant for the next series of *Mastermind* and is sitting under a tree with books spread over a separate wooden table, taking notes and talking aloud.

'He needs saving from himself,' Trish says, her expression resigned.

'But he does make the most wonderful jam doughnuts,' Sinead counters. She has cut one into four pieces and is sharing it with Joseph, who's licking the sugar off his top lip.

Hannah is nervous of Lennie because she senses that he knows the truth. She remembers talking to him in the street just before Ruby was taken into custody. He's an ex-cop; he had tracked her down. And he worked alongside Ruby so he'll have seen the CCTV. But she also appreciates how fond he is of her mum and that makes her try hard with him. 'Cup of tea, Lennie? Wine? A beer?' she asks him.

'I'd love a cuppa, Hannah, thanks.' He tells her builder's tea is fine. 'None of the fancy stuff.' When she comes back with it, she asks him whether he'd like her to test him on his knowledge of Einstein. 'Go on, then.' He sits back with his arms folded. 'Everyone else has had enough of me.'

'Not Tina,' Hannah says, and they both glance across at Tina, who is grinning back at her dad as she dishes up raspberry pavlova to Clem and Dave. (Dave is there more from curiosity than anything else, Hannah thinks, but Clem – Clem is being Clem, loving and friendly with everyone.)

'You're right about Tina,' Lennie says. 'She's a gem.'

Hannah picks up one of the books and begins to question him: 'Where was Einstein educated? When was he stateless? Who did he marry?' And so on ... Lennie gets most of the questions right, and they're coming to a natural break when another message arrives from TRO123.

I could fuck you over. You know I could.

Hannah walks to the bottom of the garden and stares back at everyone chatting and laughing in the sunshine. Shona has lined the children up for a game of Sleeping Lions. Jeff has taken Hannah's place and joined Lennie under the tree. The remaining adults are clustered around the table finishing off the puddings. It's like the opening scene of a film, Hannah thinks, where life is perfect until the zombie disease erupts or a tidal wave washes away their homes or an alien ship sits above them blocking out the sun.

What does TRO123 actually know?

Everything.

She could say she made it all up.

But her messages could be traced to her IP address. And the police wouldn't have to dig very deep to uncover the truth.

He tells her he lives in Leeds, close to the station, and that she should come to see him, to thrash it out, face to face. Or else the truth will out.

Ruby is walking towards her. Her feet are bare and she has pulled her hair up onto her head in a tumble of loose strands that frame her face. She has gained a few pounds and shed ten years. Everyone tells her how well she looks. 'Hannah.' She takes her arm and squeezes it. 'It's so lovely that we're all coming together, isn't it?'

Hannah nods. She knows that Mum-Ruby is bending over backwards to ensure that Mum-Morag doesn't feel pushed out. Inviting them today, holding back from contacting Hannah too much, making it known that her home is an open door to any family members who need a bed for the night.

'I wouldn't go that far,' Hannah's dad said to Ruby. 'You'll have half of Hannah's cousins tipping up here on a Saturday night when they can't afford a taxi back to Linlithgow.'

Hannah's dad is approaching the whole situation with his usual upbeat, well-as-long-as-no-one-is-dead attitude. He's taken the changes in his stride and is helping Hannah's mum to do the same.

But of course someone *is* dead and Hannah heard her mum whisper to her dad, 'So who *did* kill Grant then, George? Somebody must have.'

And George shushing her: 'That's for the police to worry about.'

'Maybe we could do some clothes shopping next week?' Ruby says to Hannah. 'And we can try the new Thai place if you have time?'

'I'd like that,' Hannah says. She can see Jeff in the background staring at her. He's wearing his 'thinking' expression – he must have already reached his Einstein threshold.

'What's a good day for you?'

'I'm going to be busy on Monday,' Hannah says. She'll meet TRO123 and have it out with him. She can travel to Leeds and back in one day. No one will even know she's gone. 'How about Tuesday?'

'Perfect,' Ruby says. 'We can paint the town red.'

Leeds has Edinburgh's rain but none of her beauty. Hannah knows she's biased but the Royal Mile from the castle to Holyrood Palace is head and shoulders above anything Leeds has to offer.

They meet in a vegan café where Hannah settles for a liquorice tea and a sesame slice. TRO123, whose name is Marcus, orders a full meal: chickpeas three different ways, with kale and a mush of aubergine. He eats hungrily, chomping through his food like a Labrador.

His face is pale, narrow and pointed, his two front teeth disproportionately large. And he's skinny. And fidgety. His pupils are pinpoints. She knows what that means. She also susses after a brief few minutes that he won't give her up to the police. He's all bark and no bite.

'I only drink fruit tea,' he tells Hannah.

'Your body's a temple.'

'I'm a vegan.'

'No kidding.'

He snorts at this. 'Comedian,' he says. He has none of his online bravado. He's a puppy who wants to be stroked. 'I've made you come all the way here.' He has the grace to look embarrassed. 'I hate the pigs. I'd never turn you in.'

She stays for over an hour and they talk about other bloggers and commentators. It's a world she's finished with but she manages to sustain her interest just enough so that he knows he's being listened to. After seventy minutes, he grows twitchy and she realises he's having withdrawal symptoms from drugs or his screen, or both. It's a full-time job keeping track of his virtual life.

There isn't a train for over an hour and while she waits she mulls everything over. Mulling is something she does frequently now because she's constantly trying to find a solution to the fact of her guilt, a solution that doesn't involve a lifetime of good deeds and a constant looking over her shoulder. There is a part of her that is disappointed TRO123 isn't going to offer her up to the police. Now she'll have to continue living in limbo, waiting for the knock at the door.

But imagine if she was caught? Imagine if fate lent a hand and she was legitimately arrested. Well …

In the plus column: sure, she'd be denied her freedom but she would be punished and that would be the end of it. She could serve her time and then be free to truly move on.

In the minus column: she would be infamous, shamed, forever known as that woman who killed the businessman in the Edinburgh close. She'd never get a job unless she changed her name. Jeff would never stick by her, even Clem would be hard pushed. And what about her parents? Her mum and dad would be destroyed by the news. Mum-Ruby is a new person now Hannah is back in her life. And both families are just beginning to get along. All that would be ruined.

It's the devil and the deep blue sea.

She has to live with what she's done and let time take care of the rest.

This doesn't sit well with Hannah. She walks around the station concourse, kicking up her heels, impatient for a solution. She likes to do, to control, not sit back and wait for fate to take her by the hand.

If she is to stand trial for the murder then why not get it over with, tempt fate? Just this once? When she was visiting Ruby in prison, she told her that she must be careful never to be arrested because they would take fingerprints and a speculative sample of DNA. The samples would be matched with those on file and then they would have their prime suspect.

She has a choice of drugs in her pocket, brought with her for every conceivable emergency. She pops two pills and washes them down with a half-bottle of vodka. Then she staggers onto the train; reality is hazy through a heavy curtain of booze and pills. She doesn't know what she's saying but she's dimly aware of people frowning at her loud voice. She spills a can of Coke over a man, who shouts at her, so she gives him the finger. He ushers his child ahead of him to move seat. Her crowning glory comes when she vomits over an elderly woman quietly reading her book. And then the guard is there, and the man is back to complain, and Hannah has to follow the guard to another part of the carriage. Twice she falls over and crashes her knee against someone's suitcase and then her eye on the edge of a table.

When the train pulls into Edinburgh's Waverley Station the police are waiting on the platform. They tell her they will be arresting her for being drunk and incapable. And she knows what the next step will be. They'll search her, find the drugs and then she'll be driven to the police station where they can take the DNA sample. She wonders how quickly the sample will be processed. Will she have time to go to the shops with her mum tomorrow? Should she tell her mum that the police will be coming for her? Her mum will pay for Beattie and there will be another trial but this time Hannah will be in the dock. She wonders if Beattie will go for diminished responsibility due to drug addiction? Will he put Ruby on the stand to testify that Grant had been violent towards her?

The old lady she vomited over approaches the policemen. Hannah can't hear what she's saying but they all turn to look at her. The man and child are gone, and Hannah hears the guard say, 'She cooperated fine with me.'

The policemen look at each other and one of them shrugs. 'Go on, then,' he says to Hannah. 'You can thank this lady here for standing up for you.'

They walk off, and Hannah stares after them with her mouth open.

'You don't want the fuss and bother of an arrest on your record,' the elderly lady says to Hannah. 'Might affect your job prospects.' She looks Hannah up and down. 'You do have somewhere to go, dear, don't you?'

Hannah nods, wincing at the pain in her head. 'I'm sorry about being sick on you.'

'Well, I had a change of clothes with me so no harm done.' She pulls Hannah's jacket up onto her shoulder. 'There you are.' She smiles. 'Just be careful in future. You don't want to ruin your life.'

She walks home, up Cockburn Street and then the Royal Mile, shying away from glancing down into the close where Grant died. She strolls between the university buildings and Quartermile, and then across the Meadows. She smiles at teenagers playing football on the grass and cries when she sees a homeless man asleep on a flattened cardboard box. She empties her change into the tin can at his feet, tucks forty pounds into the pocket of his jacket.

Leaving the path, she picks her way across the grass to sit down on a bench. Dusk is falling, and the moon shines brightly from a cloudless sky, casting tree shadows onto the grass, softening the edges of buildings. Contours fade. A couple, hand in hand, become a single moving body and a dog chasing a ball disappears completely, his shape invisible in the gloom.

She's not meant to be punished for Grant's murder. That must be it. The lady on the train was a guardian angel stepping between Hannah and the police. Maybe life can be magical. Maybe she will get to marry the handsome prince after all.

Her mother is free; there are good times ahead.

She climbs the stairs to her flat and finds it empty. Jeff must have changed his mind about coming round. When she tries his mobile it immediately goes to voicemail. She doesn't leave a message; she texts him instead, a line of heart and kiss emojis. He doesn't text her back straight away as he normally does. Maybe he has a gig tonight? She doesn't remember him telling her that, but then she has been preoccupied lately.

She pours herself a large glass of water and sits back on the sofa. The light from her computer winks at her from underneath the table. She hardly logs on to her computer these days so she's surprised at this. She finishes the water and goes over to the table, moves the mouse and the screen lights up. There are several windows open: her blog, which she hasn't added to since before Grant died, her search history into his murder and her conversation with TRO123. More a confession than a conversation; Hannah told him everything that happened, from sneaking into Ruby's house and helping herself –

I steal things – I always have – nothing too important. I took pills from her bathroom, a magnet from her fridge and a knife.

– to killing Grant.

I didn't mean it. The knife was in my pocket. I'd already seen him hurt her and I just acted on instinct.

The alcohol and drugs are yet to fully wear off and so Hannah's mind is slow to react. She knows she didn't leave these windows open but she has time to think no further when the buzzer sounds. She presses the door-release button without asking who's there because she's sure it will be Jeff. It's when she's hanging over the banisters watching the two men climb the stairs that her welcome smile dies. The two men are in plain clothes but their ID cards tell her they are policemen.

'Hannah Stewart?'

She nods.

'We're here in connection with the murder of Grant Stapleton.'

Hannah feels the cold, stone wall slam hard into her back as she falls against it.

'We'd like you to come with us to the station.'

Hannah takes a breath and tries to speak but finds there's nothing to say. She closes the door behind her and follows the men down the stairs.

EPILOGUE

Prison isn't as Hannah imagined it. When she visited Ruby and asked her questions, her mum gave her short answers. She told her about her roommate Tiffany who 'keeps herself to herself'. Mealtimes: 'the food isn't that bad'. Being locked up in a cell 'you get used to it'.

So Hannah decided that prison would be ... boring, inconvenient, monotonous. Mostly boring, though. Occasionally scary. Every now and then, probably quite relaxing – no decisions to make, food to shop for, jobs to do.

In every respect Hannah is wrong.

She quickly discovers that monotony and boredom aren't the same thing. Boredom is downtime, too many choices and none of them stand out. Boredom is a lesson with a teacher who can't teach, or two hours stuck in front of a film that doesn't hold your attention. When you're bored you're not watching your back. You're not anxious about who to fear and who to favour. When you're bored you curl up and fall asleep, you watch clips of cute animals or reruns of *Friends*.

Monotony, on the other hand, is the meat of prison life. It's the endless tyranny of being cooped up with people who are verbally aggressive and often violent. Within four hours Hannah is punched in the face, hard enough to knock her over, because she looks at a fellow inmate the wrong way. It turns out that there's no right way to look at most of the women. What she needs to learn is not to look at them at all.

While she awaits trial, like her mother before her, she sleeps in the Vulnerable Prisoners Unit. This is down to Linus Beattie, who demands she is given a bed there because of her withdrawal from drug dependency, but even more so when he sees her black eye and swollen cheek. 'Be strong,' he tells her. 'Don't get mixed up in prison politics. Keep your head down, but not so far down that you are perceived as a victim. It's a tightrope and you have to learn how to walk it.' He takes a white cotton handkerchief from his top pocket and passes it to her. 'Crying is fine as long as you're with me or my brother or you're in your bed at night.'

'Did my mum – could my mum cope?' She holds the hankie up to her cheeks and lets the tears soak into the material. 'Did she struggle?'

'Your mother is older … wiser. Ex-police. She knew what she was walking into. You didn't.' He sighs as he reads through the papers in front of him. 'It's a great pity you confessed to all of this before we had a chance to talk.'

'I'm sorry.' Initially she felt relief telling the truth, words pouring out of her like water, a heavy weight emptying through her. Very quickly, though, one weight was replaced with another. She has seen Ruby and her parents only once and asked them not to visit for the first few weeks until she's settled into prison life because their pain and disappointment weaken her.

'The prosecution have incriminating CCTV evidence, your DNA is on Stapleton's coat and skin and they have your confession,' Frank Beattie informs her. 'Even I won't be able to get you off but we will argue diminished responsibility … or perhaps self-defence.' He frowns.

'Something for me to consider.' He shuffles the papers together and slides them into his briefcase. 'I've already spoken to your mother, who will testify to the fact of Grant's violence.' Hannah nods. 'I'll be back to see you in a week or two. If there's anything you need to discuss before then, call my brother.'

'Thank you.'

As he leaves the room, he turns back to say, 'Keep your chin up, Hannah. Nothing lasts for ever.'

It was Jeff who gave her up to the police. She doesn't blame him for this; after all, his goodness was what attracted her to him. She writes to him every day – variations on the same theme – please come and see me, just the once, so that I can apologise to you.

It's three months before he comes to the prison and that's only after she asks Ruby to go round to his house and plead her case. The sight of him makes her heart squeeze with a new kind of sadness: the loss of everything she had and everything she will never have again. She moves towards him but he holds his hand out to keep her away. 'I'm not staying, Hannah. I've come because your mum twisted my arm.' He sits down. 'Let's get this over with.'

She doesn't ask what led to him discovering her secrets but he seems to believe that's the reason she wants him to visit. 'At your mother's party Lennie gave you a wary look as you were walking away from him. It was nothing really. Or it wouldn't have been, but I already knew something wasn't right. And when you told me you were working a day shift, I called the restaurant but they said you had the whole day off.' He gives a short laugh. 'I thought you were cheating on me.'

'Jeff, I would—'

'Don't,' he says. 'Or I'll walk out right now.'

She nods her agreement, deflated. He's staring at her as he speaks but his expression is so un-Jeff-like that she feels hope shrink. She had foolishly imagined there would be a crack in his resolve but it's clear that he's all but finished with her.

'Your behaviour had changed.' He tells her that it took him a while to access her files but he got there in the end. 'I'm sure you thought I was too stupid to work out your passwords?'

'No, I—' She has to stop because that's exactly what she thought.

'When I discovered what you'd been doing, and what you'd done.' He leans in towards her, his blue eyes hard and cold. 'You would have let your mother go to prison.'

'I wouldn't have! Please.' She reaches across the table for his hand but he sits back at once. 'I'm sorry, Jeff. Truly sorry.'

'It's too late, Hannah.'

'I love you.' Her eyes fill but she sees this no longer has any effect on him. 'I love you, Jeff.'

'Love?' He stands up. 'I can do without your love.'

And then he's gone.

His visit happens at the worst possible time – the day before her trial – and the next few days go by in a blur. There's a ringing in her ears and a pain in her middle. She looks up into the gallery but Jeff isn't there and she can't bear to see the eyes of those who love her looking down, so she keeps her head lowered after that.

During her mother's trial she listened to every word; during her own, she hears only snippets: 'high on drugs', 'stole frequently', 'law unto herself'. And from Beattie 'difficult past', 'drug addiction', 'couldn't bear to see her mother ill-treated'.

The verdict comes in: she is found guilty of culpable homicide and is sentenced to eight years in prison. She doesn't hear this from the judge but from Beattie because she's tuned out of most sights and sounds. 'Eight years,' she repeats.

'Knuckle down,' Beattie tells her. 'You'll be out in five.'

When she returns to the prison she spends the first week in a daze of heartache and disbelief. Time stretches ahead of her on a continuum of aggression, locked doors, nowhere to walk and no one to hold her. A torment of seconds, minutes and hours. Hours and hours of time to fill … to kill. If she had access to drugs, a belt, a drop, then she would kill herself. But the prison officers are careful to deny her the means to end it all. They keep her on suicide watch. They encourage her to eat. They are kind; they persuade her back into prison life. Within three months she has a routine of sorts. Four months inside and she is able to organise her thoughts.

That's when she starts counting down the days.

The monotony is punctured by three life-changing events.

The first happens early on, one hundred and fifty days into her sentence. Her lifeline is a teacher who spends one hour a week with those who sign up for her creative writing class. They begin with autobiography and the imagination. Each of the women have to write down a memory, as truthfully as they can. During the second lesson, they are asked to twist the truth, take the story in a different direction so that it becomes a work of fiction. This is easy for Hannah – it reminds her of her blogging days – but it takes her further than blogging because instead of trying to manipulate the reader, she writes freely.

The teacher tells her she has a talent; she should read more. She loses herself in the reading list: Jez Butterworth, Emily Dickinson, Margaret Atwood. The walls of her room no longer prevent her from leaving the prison as the world of imagination opens up to her.

Three hundred and twenty-five days go by. By now Hannah is studying for a degree in English with the Open University. Her three parents visit her regularly. Jeff has moved on and Clem doesn't visit either. 'I can't visit you, Hannah. I'm so sorry. It brings up too many painful memories for me.' But she does write and Hannah enjoys their correspondence; they grow closer than they ever were, with Clem telling her about her childhood and her mum's frequent lapses into crime that led her back to prison's revolving door. And Hannah tells Clem that at least prison doesn't allow her to lead a double life. No more secrets and lies.

On the three hundredth and twenty-sixth day, the second event happens. The prison governor calls Hannah into her office and tells her that Violet has been in touch with her. 'Have you heard of restorative justice?' she asks Hannah.

'No.'

She explains that this is a process whereby 'the person harmed meets the person responsible. The objective is to speak the truth and repair any harm done to allow both parties to begin to move on.' She watches Hannah's face, gauging her reaction to this. 'You're not obliged to say yes.'

'I'll do it.' Hannah nods. 'Of course, I'll do it.'

'I'm really glad this is happening,' Hannah tells her friend Angie when they're having their dinner. She has an easy truce with the other women in the prison now. 'I've always worried about her and her kids.'

'And it'll go in your favour when you're up for parole,' Angie says. 'Big tick.'

'That's a bonus.' She dips a spoon into her yoghurt. 'It's not why I'm doing it, though.'

'Play the game.' Angie is serving her third sentence for drug-dealing and knows the prison system inside out. 'Make sure they see how remorseful you are.'

'I am remorseful.'

'Yeah, I know.' She drops her apple core onto the tray. 'But don't expect too much. She might wind you up.'

'There are two facilitators – one for each of us – and they make sure nothing gets out of hand.'

Angie gives Hannah a look that says – that's what you think.

Hannah's first impressions of Violet are of someone who spends a lot of money and time on herself. Her hair has TV advert shine; it falls in loose waves onto her shoulders. She's wearing a black pencil skirt, a crisp white blouse with ruffles down the centre and stiletto heels. The facilitators are both men, and after they've introduced themselves they all sit down – two and two, facing each other. Hannah has already decided she'll let Violet take control and it's clear that Violet has too so Hannah is very quickly on the back foot.

'The love of my life was murdered,' Violet begins. 'In an Edinburgh close where he was left to bleed to death. He was gasping for breath, clutching at his side where the knife was plunged in. He was taken from me before we had a chance to marry, before he had the chance to meet his children.' She pauses. 'My beautiful children will never meet their father.' She talks like this for five minutes or more, using phrases like 'unbelievably cruel', 'heartless', 'despicable' until Hannah's facilitator reminds her to talk primarily about the repercussions of Hannah's actions, not Hannah herself.

When it's Hannah's moment to respond, she says very little. 'I'm truly sorry for leaving your children without a father and for leaving you without your fiancé.' She looks at Violet as she says this. 'I really am sorry.'

'So why did you do it?' Violet asks, her expression stony.

'It was a moment of instinct … I thought I was saving my mother,' Hannah says slowly.

'Grant was never violent. He would never have lifted his hand to a woman.' She lays her own hand on her heart. 'I would stake my life on that.' She takes a deep breath, her eyes closed, and shakes her head as if to drive out Hannah's words; her hair lifts and settles in a swirl of rich brown waves. 'Like mother, like daughter.' She opens her eyes and leans forward to say, 'You are a lying little cu—'

'Violet, please!' It's her facilitator who speaks but both are on their feet, and Violet does not resist when they ask for the meeting to be suspended and for Violet to leave the room.

Hannah sits quietly until her facilitator returns. 'Did that go well, or …?'

'You did well, Hannah,' he says. 'That's all that matters.'

That's not all that matters to Hannah; she is disappointed by the outcome, but not for long. A few weeks later one of the prison officers drops a magazine in her lap. 'You can stop feeling guilty about that one,' she says.

On the front cover is a photo of a TV celebrity in a bikini – Diet with Debbie – and written to one side, attention-grabbing headlines: WHAT'S YOUR MAN DOING WRONG IN THE BEDROOM? TAKE CHARGE OF YOUR LIFE

BEFORE IT TAKES CHARGE OF YOU and HOW I FORGAVE MY FIANCÉ'S KILLER.

Hannah opens the magazine and finds an article about Violet, her twins and her new man: 'Brad has brought such love into our lives. He is respectful. He doesn't try to take their father's place but I know he loves them as much as I do.' She describes meeting 'the girl who murdered my beloved Grant'. And goes on to say, 'This act will not define us.' She talks about the effects of restorative justice, how she has forgiven Hannah Stewart – a poor, drug-addicted girl who had no future. 'It's important for myself and the twins not to carry the burden of anger.' The four of them are pictured on a pearl-pink sofa, the two adults holding one twin each. The perfect nuclear family.

Hannah's final impressions of Violet are of a woman who has left her grief far behind her.

The third life-changing event happens when she's been in prison for nine hundred and four days: her mother is diagnosed with breast cancer. Hannah has barely heard the news, and is nowhere close to coming to terms with it, when Morag deteriorates suddenly, dying from the effects of the chemotherapy rather than the cancer. 'It weakened her heart,' her dad tells her, his face grey with grief and tears.

Hannah is allowed out for her funeral. The weather is changeable; clouds obscure the sunshine, and as Morag's body is laid to rest in the ground, a rainbow arcs over the horizon. 'Her disease was brought on by stress,' her Aunt Dee hisses into her ear. 'I bloody well hope you're ashamed of yourself.'

She's not allowed to stay for the wake. The prison officer takes her back immediately and she spends the evening in her room staring up at the ceiling, too sad, too sick with grief to even cry.

It's not until after her mother's death that her cousin Alex first comes to visit. 'I wasn't expecting you …' She trails off.

'I didn't have a chance to speak to you at your mum's funeral,' he says. 'I'm sorry she died, Hannah. Really sorry.'

'Me too,' Hannah says quietly.

Alex fills her in on the Linlithgow gossip, such as it is, and makes her smile with stories of the people he mixes with at work. The hour flies by and when the buzzer sounds for the visitors to leave, her face falls. 'That went really quickly,' she says.

'I know. And we haven't talked about you yet.' He stands up. 'I'll come back again, if you like?'

'Yeah, I would like.'

As he leaves the room he turns around to check her eyes are still on him.

Five years, two months and six days.

One thousand, eight hundred and ninety-two days.

Forty-five thousand, four hundred and eight hours.

Enough minutes to travel the earth on foot and find yourself back where you began.

Enough seconds to pick a fight, start a war, bring peace to the world.

The day of her release is an emotional one. She is desperate to leave the confines of prison but afraid she won't be strong enough to rebuild her life outside. 'One step at a time,' Angie says. And Hannah hugs her friend, knowing it's unlikely they'll ever meet again.

Ruby and her dad have told her they'll be on the other side of the prison gate. They have a friendship of sorts.

For Hannah's sake, George is willing to see past Ruby's involvement in his daughter's downfall and Ruby is grateful for that. She has taken enough punishment. Soon after Hannah was found guilty, she became depressed and could barely leave her bedroom. After six months of Celia and Sinead doing their best, it was Lennie who stepped up. The whole family moved in to Ruby's house and filled every space with noise and company. Trish hadn't taken much persuading: they could rent out their own place, help the girls through university, and there would be room for even more dogs. Teenage girls, a boisterous toddler and baskets of puppies – Ruby had no option but to be swept up in the rush of it all.

Lennie didn't get past the first heat in *Mastermind* but two years later he made it to the semi-finals of *MasterChef* and Ruby used some of her inheritance to invest in a café in Stockbridge for him to run to his heart's content. They were business partners. He kept a corner table free for her and she went there most days for lunch. He fed her, kept her sane, proved himself the best friend she could ever hope for.

When Hannah steps outside, the day is bright and breezy, and she squints against the light, feels the sun's warmth on her cheeks before the wind blows her face cold again.

Three people stand in the car park ahead of her. Her cousin Alex has come too, leaning up against the car, pretending to look casual. 'Good to see you, Hannah,' he says.

'What brought you here, then?'

'Collecting a cousin from prison? It was on my bucket list.'

She smiles and then they both laugh. It's enough to

cut through the awkwardness. George and Ruby move forward to hug her. Hannah doesn't look them in their eyes; the weight of her own emotion has her close enough to tears as it is.

They climb into the car, Hannah and Alex in the back. 'Where to first, Hannah?' her dad says, as he turns the key to start the engine.

'Could we just drive around?' she says, a tremor in her voice. 'I'd like to see Edinburgh again.'

'Sure, we can do that.'

As the car moves off, Hannah stares through the window behind her and watches the prison grow smaller and smaller, until it disappears altogether.

Acknowledgements

A special thank you to two people who generously provided me with career specific knowledge: Sergeant Rose Hanson for insights into police procedure and Brian Porter, CCTV Operator, with whom I spent an informative, eye-opening morning learning about his work.

My writing friends, Mel, George and Neil who read my early chapters and helped me to understand what worked and what didn't.

Cicely Aspinall, Jenni Leech, Morag Lyall and Euan Thorneycroft for all their careful reading, advice, support and encouragement.

I always thank my three sons – why? – they don't read my books! – but they have always championed my writing, and they continue to enrich my life in the best possible way.

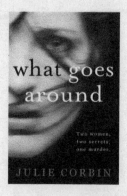

NOW THAT YOU'RE GONE

Isla's brother, an ex-Marine and private investigator, has just been found drowned in the River Clyde. But Isla is convinced he was murdered.

The coroner declares it an accidental death. The police are happy to close the case. Determined to find out what really happened the night Dougie died, and what he was doing in Glasgow, she starts looking into his unsolved cases.

What she finds will put her in grave danger and force her to question everything she thought she knew about those closest to her . . .

Out now in paperback and ebook.

MULHOLLAND
BOOKS
HODDER

WHERE THE TRUTH LIES

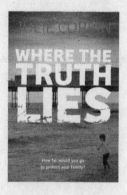

How far would you go to protect your family?

Claire's husband has been keeping secrets. About the whereabouts of the witness to the murder trial he's prosecuting. And about the letters he's been getting, threatening to kill their four-year-old, unless he tells the blackmailer where the witness is hiding.

With their daughter's life at stake, it is left to Claire to untangle the web of lies and half-truths and find out just who might be responsible. And to stop them. Before it's too late.

Out now in paperback and ebook.

HODDER

TELL ME NO SECRETS

You can bury the past but it never dies.

Grace lives in a quiet, Scottish fishing village – the perfect place for bringing up her twin girls with her loving husband Paul. Life is good.

Until a phone call from her old best-friend, a woman Grace hasn't seen since her teens – and for good reason – threatens to destroy everything. Caught up in a manipulative and spiteful game that turns into an obsession, Grace is about to realise that some secrets can't stay buried forever.

For if Orla reveals what happened on that camping trip twenty-four years ago, she will take away all that Grace holds dear . . .

Out now in paperback and ebook.

HODDER

DO ME NO HARM

When her teenage son Robbie's drink is spiked, Olivia
Somers is devastated. She has spent her adult life
trying to protect people and keep them safe – not
only as a mother, but also in her chosen profession as
a doctor. So she tries to put it down to a horrible
accident.

But someone from the past is after revenge.
Someone closer to her family than she could possibly
realise. Someone who will stop at nothing until they
get the vengeance they crave.

And, as she and her family come under increasing
threat, the oath that Olivia took when she first became
a doctor – to do no harm to others – will be tested to
its very limits.

Out now in paperback and ebook.

HODDER